About

In 2002 **Janice Maynard** [...] to pursue writing full-ti[...] sexy, character-driven, c[...] written for Kensington a[...] be part of the Mills & Boon family – a lifelong dream. Janice and her husband live in the shadow of the Great Smoky Mountains. They love to hike and travel. Visit her at JaniceMaynard.com

Cathy Williams is a great believer in the power of perseverance as she had never written anything before her writing career, and from the starting point of zero has now fulfilled her ambition to pursue this most enjoyable of careers. She would encourage any would-be writer to have faith and go for it! She derives inspiration from the tropical island of Trinidad and from the peaceful countryside of middle England. Cathy lives in Warwickshire her family.

Maisey Yates is a *New York Times* bestselling author of over one hundred romance novels. Whether she's writing strong, hardworking cowboys, dissolute princes or multigenerational family stories, she loves getting lost in fictional worlds. An avid knitter with a dangerous yarn addiction and an aversion to housework, Maisey lives with her husband and three kids in rural Oregon. Check out her website, maiseyyates.com or find her on Facebook.

Bachelor Bosses

April 2022
Calling the Shots

July 2022
The Boss' Baby

May 2022
The Ex Appeal

August 2022
Boardroom Antics

June 2022
The Deal

September 2022
Up Close and Personal

Bachelor Bosses:
Up Close and Personal

JANICE MAYNARD

CATHY WILLIAMS

MAISEY YATES

MILLS & BOON

First Published in Great Britain 2022
By Mills & Boon, an imprint of HarperCollins*Publishers,* Ltd
1 London Bridge Street, London, SE1 9GF

www.harpercollins.co.uk

HarperCollins*Publishers*
1st Floor, Watermarque Building,
Ringsend Road, Dublin 4, Ireland

ISBN: 978-0-263-30577-7

HOW TO SLEEP WITH THE BOSS

JANICE MAYNARD

For Caroline and Anna: beautiful daughters,
dear friends, exceptional women…

One

"I want you to push me to my limits. So I can prove to you that I can handle it."

Patrick stared across his paper-cluttered desk at the woman seated opposite him. Libby Parkhurst was not someone you would pick out of a crowd. Mousy brown hair, ordinary features and clothes at least one size too big for her slender frame added up to an unfortunate adjective. *Forgettable*.

Except for those eyes. Green. Moss, maybe. Not emerald. Emerald was too brilliant, too sharp. Libby's green eyes were the quiet, soothing shade of a summer forest.

Patrick cleared his throat, absolutely sure his companion hadn't intended her remark to sound provocative. Why would she? Patrick was nothing more to her than a family friend and a prospective employer. After all, Libby's mother had been his mother's best friend for decades.

"I appreciate your willingness to step outside your comfort zone, Libby," he said. "But I think we both know this

job is not for you. You don't understand what it involves."
Patrick's second in command, Charlise, was about to com-
mence six months of maternity leave. Patrick needed a replacement ASAP. Because he had dawdled in filling the
spot, his mother, Maeve Kavanagh, had rushed in to supply an interviewee.

Libby sat up straighter, her hands clenched in her lap,
her expression earnest and maybe a tad desperate. "I do,"
she said firmly. "Maeve described the position in detail.
All I'm asking is that you run me through the paces before
I have to welcome the first group."

Patrick's business, Silver Reflections, provided a quiet,
soothing setting for professionals experiencing burnout,
but also offered team-building activities for high-level
management executives. Ropes courses, hiking, overnight
survival treks. The experience was sometimes grueling
and always demanding.

The fill-in assistant would be involved in every aspect
of running Silver Reflections. While Patrick applauded
Libby's determination, he had serious doubts about her
ability to handle the physical aspects of the job.

"Libby…" He sighed, caught between his instincts about
filling the position and his obligation to play nice.

His unwanted guest leaned forward, gripping the edge
of his desk with both hands, her knuckles white. "I need
this job, Patrick. You know I do."

Libby had him there. He'd witnessed in painful detail
what the past year had been like for her—as had most of
the country, thanks to the tabloids. First, Libby's father had
been sent to prison for tax fraud to the tune of several million. Then eight weeks ago, after months of being hounded
by the press and forced to adopt a lifestyle far below her
usual standards, Libby's emotionally fragile mother had
committed suicide.

Quite simply, in the blink of an eye, Libby Parkhurst

had gone from being a sheltered heiress to a woman with virtually no resources. Her debutante education had qualified her to host her father's dinner parties when her mother was unable or unwilling to do so. But twenty-three-year-old Libby had no practical experience, no résumé and no money.

"You won't like it." He was running out of socially acceptable ways to say he didn't want her for the job.

Libby's chin lifted. She sat back in her chair, her spine straight. The disappointment in her gaze told him she anticipated his rejection. "I know your mother made you interview me," she said.

"I'm far past the age where my mother calls the shots in my life." It was only partly a lie. Maeve Kavanagh wielded maternal guilt like a sharp-edged sword.

"I don't have anything left to lose," Libby said quietly. "No home. No family. No trust fund. It's all gone. For the first time in my life, I'm going to have to stand on my own two feet. I'm willing and able to do that. But I need someone to give me a chance."

Damn it. Her dignified bravery tugged at heartstrings he hadn't tuned in ages. Why was Libby Parkhurst his problem? What was his mother thinking?

Outside his window, the late-January trees were barren and gray. Winter still had a firm hold on this corner of western North Carolina. It would be at least eight weeks before the first high-adventure group arrived. In the meantime, Libby would surely be able to handle the hotel aspects of the job. Taking reservations. Checking in guests. Making sure that all reasonable requests were accommodated.

But even if he split Charlise's job and gave Libby the less onerous part, he'd still be stuck looking for someone who could handle the outdoor stuff. Where was he going to find a candidate with the right qualifications willing to work temporarily and part-time?

If this had been an emotional standoff, Libby would have won. She never blinked as she looked at him with all the entreaty of a puppy begging to be fed. He decided to try a different tack. "Our clients are high-end," he said. "I need someone who can dress the part."

Though her cheeks flushed, Libby stood her ground. "I've planned and overseen social events in a penthouse apartment overlooking Central Park. I think I can handle the fashion requirements."

He eyed her frumpy clothing and lifted a brow…not saying a word.

For the first time, Libby lowered her gaze. "I suppose I hadn't realized how much I've come to rely on the disguise," she muttered. "I've dodged reporters for so long, my bag-lady routine has become second nature."

Now he was the one who fidgeted. His unspoken criticism had wounded her. He felt the taste of shame. And an urgent need to make her smile. "A trial period only," he said, conceding defeat. "I make no promises."

Libby's jaw dropped. "You'll hire me?"

The joy in her damp green eyes was his undoing. "Temporarily," he emphasized. "Charlise will be leaving in two weeks. In the meantime, she can show you how we run things here at the retreat center. When the weather gets a bit warmer, you and I will do a dry run with some of the outdoor activities. By the end of February, we'll see how things are going."

He had known "of" Libby for most of his life, though their paths seldom crossed. Patrick was thirty…Libby seven years younger. The last time he remembered seeing her was when Maeve had taken Patrick and his brothers to New York to see a hockey game. They had stopped by the Parkhurst home to say hello.

Libby had been a shy redheaded girl with braces and a ponytail. Patrick had been too cool at the time to do more than nod in her direction.

And now here they were.

Libby smiled at him, her radiance taking him by surprise. "You won't be sorry, I swear."

How had he thought she was plain? To conceal his surprise, he bent his head and scratched a series of numbers on a slip of paper. Sliding it across the desk, he made his tone flat…professional. "Here's the salary. You can start Monday."

When she saw the amount, Libby's chin wobbled.

He frowned. "It's not a lot, but I think it's fair."

She bit her lip. "Of course it's fair. I was just thinking about how much money my family used to spend."

"Is it hard?" he asked quietly. "Having to scrimp after a lifetime of luxury?"

"Yes." She tucked the paper in her pocket. "But not in the way you think. The difficult part has been finding out how little I knew about the real world. My parents sheltered me…spoiled me. I barely knew how to cook or how much a gallon of milk cost. I guess you could say I was basically useless."

Feeling his neck get hot, he reached for her hand, squeezing her fingers before releasing her. Something about Libby brought out his protective instincts. "No one is useless, Libby. You've had a hell of a year. I'm very sorry about your mother."

She grimaced, her expression stark. "Thank you. I suppose I should tell you it wasn't entirely a surprise. I'd been taking her back and forth to therapy sessions for weeks. She tried the suicide thing twice after my father's trial. I don't know if it was being without him that tormented her or the fact that she was no longer welcome in her social set, but either way, her pain was stronger than her need to be with me."

"Suicide never makes sense. I'm sure your mother loved you."

"Thank you for the vote of support."

Patrick was impressed. Libby had every right to feel sorry for herself. Many women in her situation would latch onto the first available meal ticket…anything to maintain appearances and hang on to the lifestyle of a wealthy, pampered young socialite.

Libby, though, was doing her best to be independent.

"My mother thinks the world of you, Libby. I think she always wanted a daughter."

"I don't know what I would have done without her."

Silence fell suddenly. Both of them knew that the only reason Patrick had agreed to interview Libby was because Maeve Kavanagh had insisted. Still, Patrick wasn't going to go back on his word. Not now.

It wouldn't take long for Libby to realize that she wasn't cut out for the rigorous physical challenges that awaited her at Silver Reflections. Where Charlise had been an athlete and outdoorswoman for most of her life, Libby was a pale, fragile flower, guaranteed to wilt under pressure.

Over the next two weeks, Patrick had cause to doubt his initial assessment. Libby dived into learning her new responsibilities with gusto. She and Charlise bonded almost immediately, despite the fact that they had little in common, or so it seemed.

Charlise raved about Libby's natural gifts for hospitality. And the fact that Libby was smart and focused and had little trouble learning the computer system and a host of other things Charlise considered vital to running Silver Reflections.

On the second Friday morning Libby was on his payroll,

Patrick cornered Charlise in her office and shut the door. "Well," he said, leaning against the wall. "Is she going to be able to handle it?"

Charlise reclined in her swivel chair, her amply rounded belly a match for her almost palpable aura of contentment. "The girl's a natural. We've already had four clients who have rebooked for future dates based on their interactions with Libby. I can honestly say that I'm going to be able to walk away from here without a single qualm."

"And the outdoor component?"

Charlise's glow dimmed. "Well, maybe a tiny qualm."

"It's one thing to run this place like a hotel. But you and I both know we work like dogs when we take a group out in the woods."

"True. But Libby has enthusiasm. That goes a long way."

"Up until a year ago I imagine she was enjoying pedicures at pricey Park Avenue salons. Hobnobbing with Fortune 500 executives who worked with her dad. It's a good bet she never had anyone steal her lunch money."

Charlise gave him a loaded look. "You're a Kavanagh, Patrick. Born with a silver spoon and everything that goes with it. Silver Reflections is your baby, but you could walk away from it tomorrow and never have to work another day in your life."

"Fair enough." He scratched his chin. "There's one other problem. I told Libby that she would have to dress the part if she planned to work here. But she's still wearing her deliberately frumpy skirts and sweaters. Is that some kind of declaration of independence? Did I make a faux pas in bringing up her clothing?"

"Oh, you poor, deluded man."

"Why does no one around here treat me with respect?"

Charlise ignored his question. "Your mother offered to buy Libby a suitable wardrobe, but your newest employee is independent to say the least. She's waiting to go shopping until this afternoon when she gets her first paycheck."

"Oh, hell."

"Exactly."

"Wait a minute," he said. "Why can't she wear the clothes she had when her dad went to prison? I'll bet she owned an entire couture wardrobe."

"She did," Charlise said, her expression sober. "And she sold all those designer items to pay for her mom's treatments. Apparently the sum total of what she owns can now fit into two suitcases."

Patrick seldom felt guilty about his life choices. He did his best to live by a code of honor Maeve had instilled in all her boys. Do the right thing. Be kind. Never let ambition trump human relationships.

He had hired Libby. Now it was time to let her know she had his support.

Libby was in heaven. After months of wallowing in uncertainty and despair, now having a concrete reason to get up every morning brought her something she hadn't found in a long time…confidence and peace.

For whatever reason, Patrick Kavanagh had made himself scarce during Libby's first two weeks. He'd left the training and orientation entirely up to Charlise. Which meant Libby didn't constantly have to be looking over her shoulder. With Charlise, Libby felt relaxed and comfortable.

They had hit it off immediately. So much so that Libby experienced a pang of regret to know Charlise wouldn't be coming back after today. Just before five, Libby went to Charlise's office holding a small package wrapped in blue paper printed with tiny airplanes. Charlise and her accountant husband were looking forward to welcoming a fat and healthy baby boy.

Libby knocked at the open door. "I wanted to give you this before you go."

Charlise looked up from her chore of packing personal items. Her eyes were shiny with tears. "You didn't have to do that."

"I wanted to. You've been so patient with me, and I appreciate it. Are you okay? Is anything wrong?"

Charlise reached for a tissue and blew her nose. "No. I don't know why I'm so emotional. I'm very excited about the baby, and I want to stay at home with him, but I love Silver Reflections. It's hard to imagine not coming here every day."

"I'll do my best to keep things running smoothly while you're gone."

"No doubts on that score. You're a smart cookie, Libby. I feel completely confident about leaving things in your hands."

"I hope you'll bring the baby to see us when the weather is nice."

"You can count on it." She opened the gift slowly, taking care not to rip the paper. "Oh, Libby, this is beautiful. But it must have been way too expensive."

Libby grimaced. She had been very honest with Charlise about her current financial situation. "It's an antique of sorts. A family friend gave it to my parents when I was born, engraved with the initial *L*. When I heard you say were going to name the baby Lander, after your father, I knew I wanted you to have it."

"But you've kept it all this time. Despite everything that's happened. It must have special meaning."

When Libby looked at the silver baby cup and bowl and spoon, her heart squeezed. "It does. It did. I think I held on to the set as a reminder of happier times. But the truth is, I don't need it anymore. I'm looking toward the future. It will make me feel good to know your little boy is using it."

Charlise hugged Libby tightly. "I'll treasure it."

Libby glanced at her watch. "I need to let you get out of here, but may I ask you one more thing before you go?"

"Of course."

"How did you get this job working with Patrick?"

"My husband and Patrick's brother Aidan are good friends. When Patrick put out the word that he was starting Silver Reflections, Aidan hooked us up."

"And the high-adventure stuff?"

Charlise shrugged. "I've always been a tomboy. Climbing trees. Racing go-karts. Broke both arms and legs before I made it to college. At different times, thank goodness."

"Good grief." Libby thought about her own cocoon-like adolescence. "Do you really think I can handle the team building and physical challenges in the outdoors?"

The other woman paused, her hand hovering over a potted begonia. "Let me put it this way…" She picked up the plant and put it in a box. "I think you'll be fine as long as you believe in yourself."

"What does that mean?"

"I've heard you talk about Patrick. He intimidates you."

"Well, I—" Libby stopped short, unable to come up with a believable lie. "Yes."

"Don't let him. He may come across as tough and intense at times, but underneath it all, he's a pussycat."

A broad-shouldered masculine frame filled the doorway. "I think I've just been insulted."

Two

Libby was mortified to be caught discussing her new boss. Charlise only laughed.

Patrick went to the pregnant woman and kissed her cheek, placing his hand lightly on her belly. "Tell that husband of yours to call me the minute you go to the hospital. And let me know if either of you needs anything… anything at all."

Charlise got all misty-eyed again. "Thanks, boss."

"It won't be the same without you," he said.

"Stop that or you'll make me cry again. Libby knows everything I know. She's exactly who you need… I swear."

Patrick smiled. "I believe you." He turned to Libby. "How about dinner tonight? I've tried to stay out of the way while Charlise showed you the ropes, but I think it would be good for the two of us to get to know each other better. What do you say?"

Libby felt herself flush from her toes to the top of her head. Not that this was a date. It wasn't. Not even close.

But Patrick Kavanagh was an imposing specimen. Despite his comfortably elegant appearance at the hotel, she had the distinct sense that beneath the dark suits and crisp ties lurked someone who was very much a man's man.

The kind of guy who made a woman's toes curl with just one look from his intense blue-gray eyes. He was tall and lean and had a headful of unruly black hair. The glossy, dark strands needed a comb. Or maybe the attention of a lover's fingers.

Her heart thumped hard, even as her stomach tumbled in a free fall. "That would be nice," she said. *Great*. Now she sounded like a child going to a tea party at her grandma's house.

Charlise picked up her purse and a small box. Patrick hefted the larger carton and followed her out of the room, leaving Libby to trail behind. Outside, the air was crisp and cold. She shivered and pulled her sweater more tightly across her chest.

Patrick stowed Charlise's things and hugged her. The affection between the two was palpable. Libby wondered what Charlise's husband was like. Obviously, he must be quite a guy if he let his wife work day after day with the darkly handsome Patrick Kavanagh.

Charlise eased behind the wheel, closed the car door and motioned for Libby to come closer. Patrick's phone had rung, and he was deep in conversation with whoever was on the other end.

Libby rested a hand in the open window and leaned down. "You're going to freeze," she said.

The pregnant woman lowered her voice. "Don't let him ride roughshod over you. You're almost too nice sometimes. Stand up to him if the occasion warrants it."

"Why would I do that? He's the boss."

Charlise grinned and started the engine. "Because he's too damned arrogant for his own good. All the Kavanagh men are. They're outrageously sexy, too, but we women have to draw a line in the sand. Trust me, Libby. Alpha males are like dangerous animals. They can smell fear. You need to project confidence even when you don't feel it."

"Now you're scaring me," Libby said, only half joking.

"I've known Patrick a long time. He admires grit and determination. You'll win his respect. I have no doubt. And don't worry about the survival training. What's the worst that could happen?"

Libby watched the car drive away, burdened with an inescapable feeling that her only friend in the world was leaving her behind in the scary forest. When she turned around, the lights from the main lodge of Silver Reflections cast a warm glow against the gathering darkness.

Since Patrick was still tied up on the phone, she went back to Charlise's office—now Libby's—and printed out the staff directory. She planned to study it this weekend. Facts and figures about everyone from the housekeeping staff to the guy who kept the internet up and running. Even at an executive retreat center famed for creating an atmosphere of solitude and introspection, no one at the level of these guests was going to be happy without a connection to the outside world.

Patrick found her twenty minutes later. "You ready to go? I guess it makes sense to take two cars."

Silver Reflections was tucked away in the mountains ten miles outside of town. In the complete opposite direction stood the magnificent Silver Beeches Lodge. Perched on a mountaintop overlooking Silver Glen, it was owned and operated by Maeve Kavanagh and her eldest son, Liam. Libby hesitated before answering, having second thoughts. "I'm sure you must have better things to do with your weekend. I'm not really dressed for dinner out."

Patrick's eyes darkened with a hint of displeasure. "If it

will make you feel better, I'll include these hours in your paycheck. And dinner doesn't have to be fancy. We can go to the Silver Dollar."

Patrick's brother, Dylan, owned a popular watering hole in town. The saloon was definitely low-key. Certainly Libby's clothing would not make her stand out there. "All right," she said, realizing for the first time that Patrick's invitation was more like an order. "I'll meet you there."

During the twenty-minute drive, she had time to calm her nerves. She already had the job. Patrick wasn't going to fire her yet. All she had to do was stick it out until they did some of the outdoor stuff, and she could prove to him that she was adaptable and confident in the face of challenges.

That pep talk carried her all the way into the parking lot of the Silver Dollar. The requisite pickup trucks were definitely in evidence, but they were interspersed with Lexus and Mercedes and the occasional fancy sports car.

Libby had visited this corner of North Carolina a time or two over the years with her mother. Silver Glen was a high-end tourist town with a nod to alpine flavor and an unspoken guarantee that the paparazzi were not allowed. It wasn't unusual to see movie stars and famous musicians wandering the streets in jeans and baseball caps.

Most of them eventually showed up at the Silver Dollar, where the beer was cold, the Angus burgers prime and the crowd comfortably raucous. Libby hovered on the porch, waiting for Patrick to arrive. The noise and color and atmosphere were worlds away from her native habitat in Manhattan, but she loved it here.

At Maeve's urging, Libby had given up the New York apartment she could scarcely afford and had come to North Carolina for a new start. Truth be told, her native habitat was feeling more and more distant every day.

Patrick strolled into view, jingling his car keys. "Let's

grab a table," he said. "I called Dylan and told him we were on our way."

In no time, they were seated. Libby ordered a Coke… Patrick, an imported ale. Dylan stopped by to say hello. The smiling, very handsome bar owner was the second oldest in the seven-boy Kavanagh lineup. Patrick was the second youngest.

Patrick waved a hand at Libby. "Do you remember Libby Parkhurst? She's going to fill in for part of Charlise's maternity leave."

Dylan shook Libby's hand. "I do remember you." He sobered. "I was sorry to hear about your mother. We have an apartment upstairs here at the Silver Dollar. I'd be happy to give it to you rent-free until you've had a chance to get back on your feet."

Libby narrowed her gaze. "Did your mother guilt you into making me an offer?"

Dylan's neck turned red. "Why would you say that? Can't a man do something nice without getting an inquisition?"

Libby stared from one brother to the other. Apparently, down-on-her-luck Libby had become the family *project*. "If you're positive it won't be an imposition," she said slowly. "I'm taking up a very nice guest room at Maeve's fancy hotel, so I'm sure she'd rather have me here."

Dylan shook his head. "Maeve is delighted to have you *anywhere*. Trust me. But she thought you'd like some privacy."

Patrick studied Libby's face as she pondered the implications of living above the bar. It was hardly what she was used to…but then again, he had no idea what her life had been like after the tax guys had swooped in and claimed their due.

Dylan wandered away to deal with a bar-related problem, and on impulse, Patrick asked the question on his mind. "Will you tell me about this past year? Where you've been? How things unfolded? Sometimes it helps to talk to a neutral third party."

Libby sipped her Coke, her gaze on the crowd. Friday nights were always popular at the Silver Dollar. He studied her profile. She had a stubborn chin, but everything else about her was soft and feminine. He would bet money that after one night in the woods, Libby was going to admit she was in over her head.

When she looked at him, those beautiful eyes gave him a jolt—awareness laced with the tiniest bit of sexual interest. He shut down that idea quickly. Maeve would have his head on a platter if he messed with her protégé. And besides, Libby wasn't his type. Not at all.

Libby's lips curved in a rueful half smile. "It was frightening and traumatic and definitely educational. Fortunately, my mother had a few stocks and bonds that were in her name only. We managed to find an apartment we could afford, but it was pretty dismal. I wanted to go out and look for work, but she insisted she needed me close. I think losing the buffer of wealth and privilege made her feel painfully vulnerable."

"What about your father?"

"We had some minimal contact with him. But Mama and I both felt betrayed, so we didn't go out of our way to visit. I suppose that makes me sound hard and selfish."

Patrick shook his head. "Not at all. A man's duty is to care for his family. Your father deceived you, broke your trust and failed to provide for you. It's understandable that you have issues."

She stared at him. "You speak from experience, don't you? My mother told me about what happened years ago."

Patrick hadn't expected her to be so quick on the uptake. Now he was rather sorry he'd raised the subject. His own father, Reggie Kavanagh, had been determined to find the lost silver mine that had made the first Kavanaghs in North Carolina extremely wealthy. Reggie had spent months, years…looking, always looking.

His obsession cost him his family.

"I was just a little kid," Patrick said. "My brother Liam has the worst memories. But yeah…I understand. My mother had every right to be bitter and angry, but somehow she pulled herself together and kept tabs on seven boys."

Libby paled, her eyes haunted. "I wish I could say the same. But not all of us are as strong as Maeve."

He cursed inwardly. He hadn't meant to sound critical of Libby's mother. "My mother wasn't left destitute."

"True. But she's made of tough stock. Mama was never really a strong person, even in the best of times."

"I'm sorry, Libby."

Her lips twisted, her eyes bleak. "We can't choose our families."

In an instant he saw that this job idea was laden with emotional peril for Libby Parkhurst. When it became glaringly obvious that she couldn't handle the physically demanding nature of Charlise's role as his assistant, Libby would be crushed. Surely it would be better to find that out sooner than later. Then she could move on and look for employment more suited to her skill set. Libby was smart and organized and intuitive.

There was a place for her out there somewhere. Just not at Silver Reflections.

He drummed his fingers on the table. "I looked at the weather forecast. We're due to have a warm spell in a couple of days."

"I saw that, too. Maeve says you almost always get an early taste of spring here in the mountains, even if it doesn't last long."

"She's right. And in light of that, why don't you and

I go ahead and take an overnight trip, so I can show you what's involved."

Libby went from wistful to deer in the headlights. "You mean now?"

"Yes. We could head out Monday morning and be back Tuesday afternoon." Part of him felt guilty for pushing her, but they had to get past this hurdle so she could see the truth.

He saw her throat move as she swallowed. "I don't have any outdoor gear."

"Mom can cover you there. And my sisters-in-law can loan you some stuff, too. No sense in buying anything now."

"Because you think I'll fail."

She stared him down, but he wasn't going to sugarcoat it. "I think there is a good chance you'll discover that working for me isn't what you really want."

"You've made up your mind already, haven't you?" He was surprised to see that she had a temper.

"No." Was he being entirely honest? "I promised you a trial run. I've merely moved up the timetable, thanks to the weather."

Libby's gaze skewered him. "Do I need a list from you, or will your mother know everything I need?"

"I'll email you the list, but Mom has a pretty good idea."

Libby stood up abruptly. "I don't think I'm that hungry, after all. Thank you for the Coke, *Mr. Kavanagh*. If you'll excuse me, it sounds like I have a lot to do this weekend."

And with that, she turned her back on him and walked out of the room.

Dylan commandeered the chair Libby had vacated, his broad smirk designed to be irritating. "I haven't seen you crash and burn in a long time, baby brother. What did you say to make her so mad?"

"It wasn't a date," Patrick said, his voice curt. "Mind your own damned business."

"She could do better than you, no doubt. Great body, I'm guessing, even though her clothes are a tad on the eccentric side. Excellent bone structure. Upper-crust accent. And those eyes... Hell, if I weren't a married man, I'd try my luck."

Patrick reined in his temper, well aware that Dylan was yanking his chain. "That's not funny."

"Seriously. What did you say to run her off?"

"It's complicated."

"I've got all night."

Patrick stared at him. "If you must know, Mom shoved her down my throat as a replacement for Charlise. Libby can handle the retreat center details, but there is no way in hell she's going to be able to do all the outdoor, back-country stuff. When I hired her, she asked me to give her a chance to prove herself. I merely pointed out that the weather's going to be warm the first of the week, so we might as well go for it."

"And that made her mad?"

"Well, she might possibly have assumed that I expect her to fail."

"Smart lady."

"How am I the bad guy here? I run a multilayered business. I can't afford to babysit Mom's misfits."

Dylan's expression went from amused to horrified in the space of an instant.

Libby's soft, well-modulated voice broke the deadly silence. "I left my sweater. Sorry to interrupt."

And then she was gone. Again.

Patrick swallowed hard. "Did she hear what I said?"

Dylan winced. "Yeah. Sorry. I didn't have time to warn you. I didn't see her coming."

"Well, that's just peachy."

The waitress appeared, notepad in hand, to take Patrick's order. "What'll you have?" she asked.

Dylan shook his head in regret. "Bring us a couple of burgers, all the way. My baby brother needs some cheering up. It's gonna be a long night."

Three

Not since the wretched aftermath of her father's arrest had Libby felt so small and so humiliated. She'd thought Patrick liked her…that he was pleased with her work to date. But in truth, Libby had been foisted on him, and he resented her intrusion.

Her chest hurt, almost as if someone had actually sucker punched her. When she made it back to her room on the third floor of Maeve's luxurious hotel, Libby threw herself on the bed and cried. Then she cussed awhile and cried some more. Part of her never wanted to see Patrick Kavanagh again. The other part wanted to make him ashamed for having doubted her. She wanted to be the best damn outdoorswoman he had ever seen.

But since that was highly unlikely to be the actual scenario come Monday, perhaps the best course was to explain to Maeve that the job hadn't worked out.

There would be questions, of course, lots of them. And although there might be other jobs in Silver Glen, perhaps as a shop assistant making minimum wage, it would be difficult to find a place to live on that kind of paycheck. She owed Maeve a huge debt of gratitude. Not for anything in the world did she want to seem ungrateful.

Which left Libby neatly boxed into an untenable situation.

Saturday morning she awoke with puffy eyes and a headache. It was only after her third cup of coffee that she even began to feel normal. Breakfast was out of the question. She felt too raw, too bruised. There was no reason to think Patrick would be anywhere near the Silver Beeches Lodge, but she wasn't taking any chances.

After showering and dressing in jeans and a baggy sweater, Libby sent a text to Maeve, asking her to drop by when she had a minute. In the meantime, Libby studied her paycheck. She had planned to buy the first pieces of her professional wardrobe this weekend. But if she was going to be fired Tuesday night, it made no sense to pay for clothes she might not need.

One step at a time.

When Maeve knocked on the door around eleven, Libby took a deep breath and let her in.

Maeve hugged her immediately. "I want to hear all about the job," she said, beaming. "I saw Charlise in town Wednesday, and she said you were amazing."

Libby managed a weak chuckle. "Charlise is being kind."

The two of them sat down in armchairs beside the gas log fireplace. Although now Libby could barely afford the soap in the bathroom, the upscale accommodations were familiar in their amenities. Growing up, she had traveled widely with her parents.

Maeve smoothed a nonexistent wrinkle from her neatly pressed black slacks. Wearing a matching blazer and a fuchsia silk blouse, she looked far younger than her age, certainly too young to have seven adult sons. "So tell me," she said. "How do you like working for Patrick?"

"Well…" Libby hesitated. She'd never been a good liar, so she had to tiptoe through this minefield. "I've spent most of my time with Charlise. But everyone on the staff speaks very highly of your son."

"But what do *you* think? He's a good-looking boy, isn't he?"

At last Libby's smile felt genuine. "Yes, ma'am. Patrick is a hottie."

"I know I'm prejudiced, but I think all my sons turned out extremely well."

"I know you're proud, and rightfully so."

"Five of them already married off to wonderful women. I think I'm doing pretty well."

Uh-oh. "Maeve, surely you're not thinking about playing matchmaker. That would be extremely uncomfortable for me."

Maeve's face fell. "What do you mean?"

"I'm starting my life from scratch," Libby said. "I have to know I can be an independent person. Although I was too naive to realize it at the time, my parents sheltered me and coddled me. I want to learn how to negotiate the world on my own. Romance is way down the list. And besides, even I know it's not a good idea to mix business with pleasure."

If a mature, extremely sophisticated woman could sulk, that's what Maeve did. "I thought you'd appreciate my help."

"I *do*," Libby said, leaning forward and speaking earnestly. "You looked out for me at the lowest point in my life. You helped me through Mama's death and took me in. I'll never be able to thank you enough. But at some point, you have to let me make my own choices, my own mistakes. Otherwise, I'll never be sure I can survive on my own."

"I suppose you're right. Is that why you wanted to see me this morning? To tell me to butt out?"

Libby grinned, relieved that Maeve had not taken offense. "No. Actually, I need your help in rounding up some hiking gear. Patrick wants to take advantage of the warm weather coming up to teach me what I'll need to know for the team-building, outdoor-adventure expeditions."

"So soon? Those usually don't begin until early April."

"I think he wants to be sure I can handle the physical part of the job." Libby spoke calmly, but inwardly she cringed, Patrick's words still ringing in her ears. *I can't afford to babysit Mom's misfits.*

Maeve stared at her intently. Almost as if she could tell something else was going on. "Write down all your sizes," she said. "I'll gather everything you need and meet you here tomorrow around one."

"I really appreciate it."

Maeve stood. "I have a lunch appointment, so I need to run. You'll get through this, Libby. I know how strong you are."

"Mentally or physically?"

"They go hand in hand. You may surprise yourself this week, my dear. And you may surprise Patrick, as well."

Patrick's mood hovered somewhere between injured grizzly and teething toddler. He was ashamed of himself for letting his aggravation make him say something stupid. But damn it, he'd been talking to his brother…letting off steam. He didn't go around kicking puppies and plucking the heads off flowers.

He was a nice guy.

Unfortunately for him, he could think of at least one person who didn't think so.

During the weekend, he gathered the equipment he would need to put Libby through her paces. Normally, he and Charlise shared the load: supervising the employees who organized the meals, interacting with the executives, teaching skills, coaching the group through difficult activities.

But Charlise was not only accustomed to being outdoors, she also had a great deal of experience in living off the land.

Libby didn't. It was as simple as that.

Patrick tried to juggle things in his mind, ways for him to take over some of Charlise's duties so that Libby could handle a lighter load. But that would only postpone the inevitable. This first experience had to play out as closely as possible to the real thing, so Libby would understand fully what was involved and what she could expect.

By Monday morning, his mood hadn't improved. He'd gone through his checklist on autopilot, but of course, he'd had to cover Charlise's prep, as well. He arrived at Silver Reflections several minutes before eight so he would have some time to mentally gear up for the day's events.

Libby's car was already parked in the small wooded lot adjacent to the building. It was an old-model Mercedes with a badly dented fender. Suddenly Patrick remembered where he had seen the car before. Liam's wife had driven it a couple of years ago until a teenage kid backed into her at the gas station.

Liam had decided it wasn't worth fixing and bought Zoe a brand-new mommy van. The damaged car had been in Liam's garage the last time Patrick saw it. Apparently, Maeve wasn't opposed to getting the whole family in the act when it came to her "rescue Libby" plan.

Patrick headed inside, greeted the receptionist with an absent wave and holed up in his office. Taking a deep breath, he leaned a hip against his desk, pulled his phone out and sent a text.

We'll leave at nine if that works for you...

 Libby's response was immediate: I'll be ready.

Meet me out front.

 He wondered if Libby was nervous. Surely so. But he knew her well enough already to be damned sure she wouldn't let the nerves show.

 At 8:55 he hefted all their gear and headed outside, only to get his first shock of the day. Libby leaned against a tree, head back, eyes closed. On the ground at her feet lay a waterproof jacket. From head to toe, she was outfitted appropriately. Sturdy boots, lightweight quick-dry pants, a white shirt made of the same fabric and an aluminum hiking pole. He came do a dead stop and swallowed hard.

 Every bit of what she was wearing was borrowed. Yet inexplicably she managed to look like a model for some weird amalgam of *Vogue* and L.L.Bean. The clothing fit her better than anything she had worn so far in his employ. Suddenly, he realized that Dylan was correct. Libby Parkhurst had a kick-ass body.

 When he shifted from one foot to the other, he dislodged a piece of gravel. Libby's eyes snapped open, her expression guarded. "Good morning," she said.

 He hated the guilt that choked him. "Libby, I—"

 She held up a hand. "I don't want to talk about it."

 They stared at each other for several long seconds. He couldn't get a read on her emotions. So he shoved aside the memory of her face in Dylan's bar and forced himself to zero in on basics.

 "Three things," he said tersely. "The moment you feel

anything on your foot begin to rub, we stop and deal with it. A major key to hiking in the mountains is taking care of your feet. Blisters can be incapacitating. Understood?"

"Yes, sir."

Her smart-ass tone was designed to annoy him, but he didn't take the bait. "Secondly, if I'm walking too fast for you, you have to say so. There's no need to play the martyr."

"Understood."

"Lastly, you have to drink water. All day. All the time. Women don't like the idea of peeing in the woods, so they tend to get dehydrated. That's also dangerous."

The look on Libby's face was priceless. "Got it," she mumbled.

"Am I being too blunt?" he asked.

She gnawed her lip. "No. I suppose I hadn't thought through all the ramifications."

"That's what this trip is about."

He slid one of two backpacks off his shoulder. "I need to make sure the straps are adjusted correctly for you." Without asking, he stepped behind her and helped settled the pack into position. With a few quick tugs, he was satisfied. Finally, he moved in front of her and fiddled with the strap at her chest.

Libby made some kind of squawk or gasp. It was only then that he realized his fingers were practically caressing her breasts. He stepped back quickly. "I'm sure you can manage the waistband," he muttered.

"Uh-huh." She kept her head down while she dealt with the plastic locking mechanism. After a moment, she stared off into the woods. "I'm good."

"Then follow me."

Libby had taken yoga classes from the time she was fourteen, although during the past year, she'd had to keep up the discipline on her own. She was limber and more than moderately fit. But Patrick's punishing pace had her gasping for breath by the third mile.

His legs were longer than hers. He knew the rhythm of walking over rough terrain. And she was pretty sure he had loaded her pack with concrete blocks. But if Charlise could do this, so could she.

Fortunately, the boots Maeve had found for Libby were extremely comfortable and already broken in. Given Patrick's warning, Libby paid close attention to her feet. So far, no sign of problems.

It helped that the view from behind was entertaining. Patrick's tight butt and long legs ate up the miles. She had long since given up estimating how far they had come or what time it was. Since her phone was turned off to save the battery, she was dependent upon Patrick's knowledge of the forest to get them where they needed to go.

At one point when her legs ached and her lungs burned, she shouted out a request. "Water, please." That was more acceptable to her pride than admitting she couldn't keep up.

Patrick had a fancy water-thingy that rested inside his pack and allowed him to suck from a thin hose that protruded. Not the kind of item a person borrows. So he had tucked plastic pouches of water for Libby in the side pockets of her pack. She opened one and took a long, satisfying gulp. It took everything she had not to ask how much farther it was to their destination.

The two of them were completely alone…miles away from the nearest human. The wind soughed through the trees. Birds tweeted. The peace and solitude were beautifully soothing. But a chasm existed between Patrick and her. At the moment, she had no desire to breach it.

As forecasted, the warming trend had arrived with a

vengeance. Temperatures must already be in the upper sixties, because Libby's skin was damp with perspiration.

Patrick hadn't said a word during their stop. He merely stood in silence, his attention focused on the scenery. The trail had ascended a small ridgeline, and through a break in the trees, they could see the town of Silver Glen in the distance.

"I'm good," she said, stashing the water container. "Lead on."

Her body hurt and her lungs hurt, but eventually, she fell into a rhythm that was almost natural. *One foot in front of the other. Zen-like state of being. Embrace the now.*

It almost worked.

When they stopped for lunch, she could have sworn it was at least seven in the evening. But the sun was still high in the sky. Patrick had a more sophisticated standard for trail food than she had anticipated. Perhaps a certain level of cuisine was de rigueur for his Fortune 500 clients. Instead of the peanut butter and jelly she had expected, they enjoyed baked-ham sandwiches on homemade bread.

When the meal was done and Patrick shoved their minimal trash into his pack, she finally asked a question. "What do you do if you have someone who can't handle the hiking?"

He zipped his pack and shouldered it. "Companies apply to come to Silver Reflections. We have a long waiting list. Most of the elite businesses institute some kind of wellness programs beforehand. They'll include weight loss, stress management, regular exercise…that kind of thing. So by the time they come to North Carolina, most of the participants are mentally and physically prepared for the adventure rather than dreading it."

"I see." But she didn't really. Patrick was already walking, so she stumbled after him. "But what about people that aren't prepared? Do they make them come anyway?"

Patrick didn't turn around, but his voice carried. "A lot of top corporations are beginning to realize the importance of physical well-being for their employees as a means to increase the bottom line. If an executive has a physical limitation, then of course he or she isn't forced to come. But if an otherwise physically capable person chooses not to attend to his or her health and fitness, then it might be a sign that a top-shelf promotion isn't in the cards."

With that, the conversation ended. Patrick was walking as quickly as ever, making it look easy. Maybe Libby had slipped into the numb stage, or maybe she was actually getting used to this, but her aches and pains had receded. Perhaps this was the "runner's high" people talked about. Endorphins at work, masking the physical discomfort.

At long last, Patrick stopped and took off his pack to stretch. Libby followed suit, looking around curiously. It was obvious they had reached their destination. Patrick stood on the edge of a large clearing. The area was mostly flat. About thirty feet away, a narrow creek slid and tumbled over rocks, the sound of the water as soothing as the prospect of wetting tired feet in the chilly brook.

Patrick shot her a look, clearly assessing her physical state. "This is base camp."

"There's not much to it," she blurted out.

"Were you expecting a five-star hotel?"

His sarcasm on top of everything else made her angry, but she didn't want him to get the best of her. So she kept her mouth shut. If he wanted her to talk, he was going to have to initiate the conversation.

Somehow, it seemed almost obscene to be at odds with another human in the midst of such surroundings. Though it would be several more weeks until the new green of spring began to make its way through the sun-kissed glades, even now the forest was beautiful.

She dropped her pack and managed not to whimper.

Though it galled her to admit it, maybe Patrick was right. Maybe this job was not for her. It was one thing to come out here alone with him. But in the midst of an "official" expedition, Libby would be expected to pull her weight. Her new boss wouldn't be free to coach her if she got in over her head.

He knelt and began pulling things from his pack. "The first thing Charlise usually does is put up our tents. I'll be teaching the group how to do theirs."

"Okay." How hard could it be? The one-man tents were small.

"First you'll want the ground cover. It's the thing that's silver on one side and red on the other. Silver side up to preserve body heat."

Libby was a fast learner. And she was determined to acquit herself well. "Got it."

Patrick pointed. "Leader tents go over there." He stood, hands on hips, while she struggled to spread the ground tarps and smooth them out.

Next came the actual tents. Claustrophobically small and vulnerably thin, they were actually not that difficult to set up. Lightweight poles snapped together in pieces and threaded through a nylon sleeve from one corner of the tent to the opposite side. Repeat once, and it was done. The only thing left was to secure the four corners to the ground with plastic stakes.

All in all, not a bad effort for her first time. Even Patrick seemed reluctantly impressed. He handed her a rolled-up bundle that was about eighteen inches wide. "Look for a valve on one corner. It's not difficult to blow up. And it won't look like much when you're done. But having this pad underneath your upper body and hips makes for a much more comfortable night."

He was right. Even when she inflated the thin *mat-*

tress, it didn't seem like much of a cushion. But she wasn't about to say so.

To give Patrick his due, he didn't go out of his way to make her feel nervous or clumsy. Still, having someone watch while she learned new skills was stressful.

At last, both tents were up, pads and sleeping bags inside. The full realization that she and Patrick were going to spend the night together hit her hard. No television. No computers. Nothing at all for a distraction. He was gorgeous and unavailable. She was lonely and susceptible.

Nevertheless, the job was what she needed. Not the man. She couldn't let him see that she was seriously attracted to him. Cool and casual was the plan.

She stood and arched her back. "What next?"

Four

Patrick hadn't expected much from a young, pampered, New York socialite. But perhaps he was going to have to eat his words. During the morning, he had set an intentionally punishing pace as they made their way through the woods. Libby stayed on his heels and never once complained.

Was it the past year that had made her resilient, or was she naturally spunky and stubborn? That would remain to be seen.

He glanced at his watch. Even with this current springlike spell, it was still February, which meant far less daylight than in two months when he traditionally scheduled his first team-building treks. Kneeling, he pulled a small camp stove from his pack. "I'll show you how to use this," he said. "The chef at the retreat center has a couple of part-time assistants who prepare our camping meals the day before."

"I assumed the execs would have to cook for themselves. Isn't that part of the outdoor experience?"

"In theory, yes. But so far, we've only done short trips... two days, one night. So our time frame is limited. Since we want them to do a lot of other activities, we preprepare the food and all they have to do is warm it up. We don't spend too much time on meals."

Once Libby had mastered the stove, she glanced up at him. "Surely you don't expect the entire group to use something this small."

"No. I have a group of local guys who come along to carry the food, extra stoves and extra water."

He stared at her, disconcerted by feelings that caught him unawares. He was *enjoying* himself. Libby was a very soothing person to be around. When she stood up, he walked away, ostensibly picking up some fallen limbs that had littered the campsite.

Grappling with an unexpected attraction, he cursed inwardly. With Charlise, he never felt like he was interacting with a woman. He treated her the same way he did his brothers. Charlise was almost part of his family. While he was delighted that she and her husband were so happy about the upcoming birth, he would be lying if he didn't admit he was feeling a little bit sorry for himself. Silver Reflections had been going so well. He had honed these outdoor events down to the finest detail. Then Charlise had to go and get pregnant. And his mother had saddled him with Libby. A remarkably appealing woman who'd already managed to get under his skin.

What was he going to do about it? Nothing. It would be a really bad idea to get involved personally with his mother's beloved Libby. Not only that, but with Charlise out of commission, he had no choice but to work twice as hard. And ignore his libido.

Surely he could be excused for being a little grumpy.

Libby called out to him. "What now?"

He turned around and caught her rolling her shoulders. She'd be sore tomorrow. Backpacking used a set of muscles most people didn't employ on a daily basis.

"I'll show you how we string our packs up in the trees," he said.

"Excuse me?"

He sighed, the look of befuddlement on her face the sign of an outdoor newbie. "Once we set up camp, we won't be hauling our backpacks everywhere. We'll use this as home base and range around the area."

"Why can't we leave the packs in our tents?"

"Bears," he said simply.

Up until that point, Libby had done an admirable job keeping her cool, but now she paled. "What do you mean, *bears*?"

"Black bears have an incredible sense of smell. And they're omnivorous. Anytime we're away from camp— and at night when we're sleeping—we'll hang our packs from a high tree limb to discourage unwanted visitors. Don't keep any food in your tent at all, not even a pack of crackers or scented lip balm or toothpaste."

"I washed my hair with apple shampoo this morning." Her expression was priceless.

"Not to worry. I should have told you. But the scent won't be strong enough by the end of the day to make a difference."

"Easy for you to say," she grumbled as she glanced over her shoulder, perhaps expecting a bear to lumber into sight any moment.

Patrick unearthed a packet of nylon rope. "There will be plenty of tall men around to do this part, but it never hurts to gain a new life skill. Watch me, and then you can try."

"If you say so."

He found a rock that was maybe four inches around

and tied it to the end of the rope. "Stand back," he said. Fortunately for his male pride, his first shot sailed over the branch. He reached for the rock again and removed it. "Now all you have to do is attach one end to your pack, send it up, and tie it off." When Libby seemed skeptical, he laughed, his good humor restored for the moment. "Never mind. I won't make you practice this right now. We have better things to do."

"Like what?"

He grabbed a couple of water pouches and a zippered nylon case, then hefted both packs toward the treetops, securing them. "I'm going to show you where I teach the groups how to rappel."

Libby's expression was dubious. "Does Charlise do the rappelling thing?"

It was the first time she had seemed at all reluctant to approach something new. "No. Not usually. So if you don't want to try it, you can watch me. But I do want you to get a feel for the whole range of activities we offer. C'mon… it's not far."

As they passed the two tents, neatly in place for the upcoming night, he felt his pulse thud. He'd never thought of camping out as sexual or even sensual. When he spent time with a woman, it was in fine restaurants or at the theater. Perhaps later on soft sheets in her bedroom. But certainly not when both parties were sweaty—and without a luxurious bathroom at hand.

He stumbled. Damn it. Libby was messing with his head.

The large rock outcropping was barely half a mile away. He strode automatically, only slowing down when he realized that Libby was lagging behind. When she caught up, he moved on without speaking.

Though she had been cooperative and pleasant all day, his inadvertent insult from Friday hung between them like a cloud. He would have to address it sooner or later, whether she liked it or not.

When they arrived at their destination, he unzipped the bag and pulled out a mass of tightly woven mesh straps. "Sometimes, if we have women along, I might ask you to help them get into their gear. If a female seems extremely modest or uneasy, it can be difficult for me or one of the guys to help with the harness...you know...too much touching."

Libby nodded. "I understand."

She stared at him intently as he prepared the equipment. Something about her steady regard made the back of his neck tingle. "I'm going to go around the side of that ridge and come out on top," he said. "That cliff is only about thirty feet high, but it looks really far off the ground when you're standing up there, particularly if you've never done anything like this before."

"I can imagine."

He tossed her a thin ground cloth to sit on. "Feel free to relax while I get up there. And you don't have to worry about ticks or other bugs. It's still too early for a lot of creepy crawlies."

Libby *hadn't* been worrying about creepy crawlies, but she was now. Ick. Her legs itched already from the power of suggestion.

If her companion had been any man other than Patrick Kavanagh, she might have assumed he was showing off. He could have explained how the rappelling worked without a demonstration. Maybe he just liked doing it. It was a sure bet he didn't have any interest in impressing her.

Without Libby to slow him down, he appeared at the top of the small cliff in no time at all. She shaded her eyes and watched as he secured himself to a nearby tree. He checked all of his connections and waved. Then, looking

like an extremely handsome and nimble spiderish super-
hero, he stepped backward off the rock shelf and danced
his way to the bottom.

His skill was striking.

Something about a man so physically powerful and at
ease with his body was very appealing. For a moment, she
thought about other, more primal things he might do exceedingly well…but no. She wouldn't go there.

Once before when she was young and immature, she'd
fallen under the spell of a magnetic, powerful man—with
disastrous results. History would not be repeating itself.
She was older now, old enough to be tempted. But sex
and romance were off the table. Keeping this job had to
be her focus.

The demonstration took some time. Once Patrick
reached the bottom, he had to go back to the top and untie
his ropes.

Finally, he reappeared, striding toward her. She handed
him his water. He dropped down beside her, barely breathing heavily, and took long gulps. Already, the sun was
sliding lower in the sky, and a chill began to linger in the
shadows.

Libby pulled her knees to her chest and linked her arms
around her legs. "That was pretty cool. Have you always
been fond of the outdoors?"

Patrick wiped the back of his arm across his forehead.
"Would you be surprised to know that I worked in adver-
tising for several years in Chicago?"

She gaped at him. "Seriously?"

His smile was self-mocking. "Yes. I loved the competi-
tive atmosphere—stealing big accounts, coming up with
the next great ad campaign. Brainstorming with smart,
focused, energetic colleagues. It was a great environment
for a young man."

She snorted. "You're still young."

"Well, you know what I mean."

"Then what changed?"

He shrugged. "I missed the mountains. I missed Silver Glen. I didn't know how deeply this place was imprinted on my DNA until I left. So one day, I turned in my notice, and I came home."

"And started Silver Reflections."

"It took a couple of years, but yeah…it's been a pretty exciting time."

"So who's the real Patrick Kavanagh? The man I just watched scramble down a cliff? Or the sophisticated guy who roams the halls of his übersuccessful, private, luxurious executive getaway?"

His quick grin startled her. "Wow, Libby…was that a compliment?" Without waiting for an answer to his teasing question, he continued. "Both, I guess. Without the time in Chicago, I doubt I would have understood the needs of the type A men and women who eat, sleep and breathe work. I was one of them…at least for a few years. But I realized my life was missing balance. For me, the balance is here. So if I can offer rest and recovery to other people, then I'm satisfied."

"And your personal life?" Oops. That popped out uncensored. "Never mind. I don't want to know."

He chuckled but kept silent.

They were sitting so close, she could smell his warm skin and the hint of whatever soap he had used that morning. Not aftershave. That would be the equivalent of inviting bears to munch on his toes. Even mentally joking about it gave her a shiver of unease.

Not long from now, it was going to get dark. Very dark. Her nemesis, Patrick Kavanagh, was the only person metaphorically standing between her and the wildness of nature.

To keep her mind off the upcoming night, she asked another question. "Do you have any regrets?"

"Yes," he said quietly. "I'm sorry I said something so stupid and unkind, and I'm sorry you heard it."

She flushed, though in the fading light, maybe he couldn't see. "I told you I don't want to talk about it. You're entitled to your opinion."

He touched her knee. Briefly. As if to establish some kind of connection. "I admire the hell out of you, Libby. I didn't mean what I said on Friday night. My mother is one of the best people I know. Her instincts are always spot-on. Her compassion and genuine love for people have influenced my brothers and me more than we'll ever know."

"You called me a misfit."

Patrick cursed beneath his breath. "Don't remind me, damn it. I'm sorry. It was a crappy thing to do."

"I think the reason it hurt me was because it's the truth."

Patrick leaped to his feet and dragged her with him, his hands on her shoulders. "Don't be ridiculous."

He looked down at her, his jaw tight. He was big and strong and absolutely confident in everything he did. With the five-inch difference in their heights, it would be easy to rest her head on his shoulder. She was tired of being strong all the time. She was tired of not knowing who she was anymore. And she really wanted the luxury of having a man like Patrick in her life. But survival trumped romance right now.

"You've been a trouper today," he said quietly.

"But I'm not Charlise."

One beat of silence passed. Then two.

"No. You're not. But that doesn't mean you aren't capable in your own way."

He wasn't dodging the truth. Where she came from they called that *damning with faint praise*.

"I can learn," she said firmly. Was she trying to convince Patrick or herself?

His small grin curled her toes in her boots. "I know that. And I'm sorry I hurt your feelings. I'm not usually such an animal. Please forgive me."

She wasn't sure who was more surprised when he bent his head and kissed her. When either or both of them should have pulled away, some spark of longing kept them together. At least it felt like longing on her part. She didn't know *what* Patrick was thinking.

His lips pressed hers firmly, his tongue teasing ever so gently, asking permission to slide inside her mouth and destroy her with the taste of him. Her arms went around his neck. Clinging. Her body leaned into his. Yearning. It had been well over a year since she had been kissed. Echoes of past mistakes set off alarms, but she ignored them.

The moment of rash insanity set her senses on fire, helping her forget that she'd walked through her own kind of purgatory. It felt so good to be held. So safe. So warm. She trembled in his embrace.

"Patrick..." She whispered his name, not wanting to stop, but knowing they were surely going to regret whatever madness had overtaken them.

He jerked as if he had been shot. Staggered backward. "Libby. Hell..."

The exclamation encompassed mortification. Shock. Regret.

It was the last one that stung, despite knowing that keeping distance between them was for the best.

She managed a smile, though it cost her. "We'd better get back to camp. I'm starving, and it's going to be dark soon."

His apology should have erased the friction, yet they faced each other almost as adversaries.

He nodded, his expression brusque. "You're right."

This time, following him through the forest came naturally. No matter the strained atmosphere between them, in this environment, she trusted him implicitly to take them wherever they needed to go.

Dinner was homemade vegetable soup warmed on the camp stove. The chef had made the entrée and added fresh Italian rolls to go with it. While Libby tended to the relatively foolproof job of preparing the meal, Patrick started a campfire and rolled a log near the flames so they would have a comfy place to sit.

With the cup from a thermos, Patrick ladled soup into paper bowls that would later be burned in the fire. He'd explained that the aluminum spoons they used were light in a pack and good for the environment.

Libby ate hungrily. It was amazing how many calories one consumed by walking in the mountains. Neither she nor Patrick spoke. What was there to say? He didn't really want her here. Not to replace Charlise. And beyond that, they were nothing to each other. Virtual strangers. Except she normally didn't go around kissing strangers. She jumped when an owl hooted nearby. Though she was wearing a long-sleeved shirt and the day had been warm, she scrambled to find her jacket. Huddling into the welcome warmth, she stared into the fire and tried not to think about the night to come.

If she had any hope of convincing Patrick that she was capable of filling Charlise's shoes, she had to act as if spending a night in the dark, scary woods was no big deal.

She stared into the mesmerizing red and gold flames, listening to the pop and crackle of the burning wood. The scent of wood smoke was pleasant…a connection, perhaps, to her ancestors who had lived closer to the land.

She and Patrick had eaten their meal in complete silence. Libby was okay with that. All she wanted to do now was get through this overnight endurance test without embarrassing herself.

She cleared her throat. "So, it's already dark. And it's awfully early to go to bed. What do people do in the woods when they camp out during the winter?"

Patrick's face was all planes and angles in the glow of the fire. He was a chameleon—dashing and elegant as a Kavanagh millionaire, but now, a ruggedly masculine man with unlimited physical power and capability. Looking at him gave her a funny feeling in the pit of her stomach.

The sensation was no secret. She was seriously in lust with her reluctant boss, despite his arrogance and his refusal to take her seriously. He could be funny and charming. He had been remarkably patient, even when saddled with his mother's charity case.

But the truth was, he didn't want her on his team. And when it came to the attraction that simmered between them? Well, that was never going to amount to anything, no matter how many hours they spent alone in the woods. She pressed her knees together, her heart beating a ragged tempo as she waited for an answer to what was one part rhetorical question and the other part a need to break the intimate quiet.

If she had a tad more experience, or if she honestly believed that Patrick felt a fraction of the sexual tension that was making her jumpy, she might make a move on him. But despite his kiss—which was really more of a hands-on apology—she didn't delude herself that he had any real interest in her.

Women like Charlise were more his type. Athletic superwomen. Not timid females afraid of the shadows.

Besides, she had to stay focused on starting her life over. She was on her own. She had to be strong.

She had almost forgotten her question when he finally answered.

Five

"Speaking for myself, I suppose it depends on who I'm with."

Patrick wasn't immune to the intimacy of the moment. He still reeled from the impact of the kiss. But all else aside, his mother would kill him if he played around with Libby. Libby was emotionally fragile and just coming out of a very rough period in her life. He couldn't take advantage of her vulnerability, even if she was already worming her way into his heart.

A part of him wanted to tell her how much fun sleeping-bag sex could be. But that would be crossing the line, and Libby Parkhurst was off-limits. He'd be exaggerating anyway. Most of the women he'd been serious about would run for the hills if he suggested anything of the sort.

It occurred to him suddenly that his love of outdoor adventure had largely been segregated from his romantic life. He hiked with his brothers. He took clients out in the woods with Charlise. But he'd never really wanted to bring a woman along in a personal, *intimate* sense.

Yet with Libby, he was tempted. Unfortunately, temptation was as far as it went. He had to keep her at a distance or this whole scenario might blow up in his face. Particularly when he had to fire her.

He picked up a tiny twig and tossed it into the fire. "You can always listen to music. Did you bring an iPod? It was on the list."

Libby nodded, her profile disarmingly feminine in the firelight. "I did. But if I have earbuds in, I won't be able to hear the wild animals when they come to rip me limb from limb."

Patrick chuckled. Despite Libby's lack of qualifications for the job as his assistant, he enjoyed her wry take on life. He also respected the fact that she acknowledged her fears without being crippled by them. As if he needed more reasons to be intrigued by her. But that didn't make her an outdoorswoman.

"I won't let anything happen to you, I swear." It was true. Libby might not be the one to cover the maternity leave, but he felt an overwhelming urge to protect her.

Eventually, Libby needed a moment of privacy in the woods. He had known it was coming. But he was pretty sure she wasn't comfortable about the dark.

When she stood up, she hedged. "I, uh…"

"You need to go to the bathroom before we call it a night."

"Yes."

He'd seen her blush before. Right now her face was probably poppy red. But he couldn't tell in the gloom. He handed her a flashlight. "Do you want me to go with you, or shall I stay here and face the fire?"

Long silence.

"Face the fire. But if I'm not back in ten minutes, send out the rescue squad."

Again, that easy humor. He sat and concentrated on the flames, feeling the heat on his face. His libido thrummed on high alert. It had never occurred to him that spending a night in the woods with Libby Parkhurst would test his self-control.

He had forgotten to glance at his watch when she left. How long had she been gone? Now she had *him* hearing all sorts of menacing sounds in the forest. "Libby," he called out. "You okay?"

He held his breath until she answered.

"I'm fine." Her voice echoed from a distance, so he stayed put.

At last she reappeared. "What time do we need to be up in the morning?" she asked.

"I'll get breakfast going...most importantly, a pot of coffee. You can pop out of your tent whenever you're ready."

"What about our packs?"

"I'll take care of it. When you get in your tent, make sure to take your boots off and put them by the exit. That way you won't get your sleeping bag muddy. The bedding I brought is warmer than the type we use in April. I hope you'll be comfortable."

"I'll be fine. Good night, Patrick."

He wished he could say the same. He was wired and horny. That was a dangerous combination.

With moves he had practiced a million times, he scattered the coals and made sure the fire was not in danger of spreading while they slept. Then he took both packs and hung them from a nearby treetop.

After crawling into his own tent and taking off his boots, he zipped the nylon flap and got settled for the night. His sleeping bag was high-tech and very comfortable. The temperature outside was perfect for snuggling into his down cocoon and sleeping.

Which didn't explain why he lay on his back and stared into the dark. The noises of the night were familiar to him. Hooting owls. Sighing wind. The *click-clack* of bare winter branches rubbing together.

Libby's tent was no more than four or five feet away from his. If he concentrated, he thought he might be able to hear her breathing.

He was almost asleep, when a female whisper roused him.

"Patrick. Are you awake?"

"I am now." He pretended to be gruff.

"What am I supposed to do if a bear tries to eat my tent?"

He grinned, even though she couldn't see. "Libby. People camp out in this part of the country all the time. We're not far from the Smoky Mountains. It's perfectly safe, I swear."

"I was kidding. Mostly. And I'm not being a wimp. I just want to be prepared for anything. But people *do* get attacked by bears. I went online and did a search."

"Are you sure you weren't reading stories about grizzlies? We don't have those in North Carolina."

"No. It was black bears. A woman died. They found her camera and she had been taking pictures."

"I remember the story you're talking about. But that was a long time ago and the woman, unfortunately, got too close to the bear."

"But what if the bear gets too close to me?"

He laughed. "Would you like to come sleep in my tent?" As soon as the words left his mouth, he regretted them. He hadn't consciously meant to flirt with her, but the feelings were there.

Long silence. "You mean with you?"

"Well, it doesn't make much sense just to swap places. If it will help you be more comfortable, I'm sure we can manage to squeeze you in here if we try."

Another, longer silence. "No, thank you. I'm fine. Really."

"Your choice." He paused. "Tell me, Libby. Did your family never vacation outdoors? National parks? Boating adventures? Anything like that?"

He heard the sound of rustling nylon as she squirmed to get comfortable.

"No. But I have a working knowledge of all the major museums in Europe, and I can order a meal at a Michelin-starred restaurant in three languages. I've summered in the Swiss Alps and wintered in Saint Lucia. Still, I've never cooked a hot dog over a campfire."

"Poor little rich girl."

"Not funny, Patrick. I happen to know the Kavanaghs are loaded. So you can't make fun of me."

"*Can't* or shouldn't?"

She laughed, the warm sound sneaking down inside him and making him feel something both arousing and uncomfortable.

"I'm going to sleep now," she said.

"See you in the morning."

Aeons later, Libby groaned. Morning light meant the dawn of a new day, but she was too warm and comfortable to care. For the past hour, she had actually been sleeping peacefully. Now, however, she had to go to the bathroom. And unlike any normal morning, she couldn't crawl back into bed afterward, because she would be completely awake.

She felt as if she had barely slept all night. Every noise was magnified in her imagination. She would doze off finally, and then minutes later some ominous sound would wake her up. It was an endless cycle.

To make matters worse, Patrick had fallen asleep almost instantly after their "bear" conversation. She knew this, because he'd snored. Not an obnoxious, chain-saw sound, but a quiet masculine rumble.

How did he do it? How did he sleep like a baby in the middle of the woods? Her hips were sore from lying on the ground, even with the pad, and she didn't know how *anyone* could manage restful slumber without some white noise.

Hiking enthusiasts talked about the peace and quiet of nature. Clearly they had never actually spent a night in the outdoors. The forest was *not* a silent place.

Though the temperatures were supposed to hit the sixties again this afternoon as the February warm spell lingered, this morning, there was a definite nip in the air. She shivered as she sat up and fumbled her way into her jacket. She could already smell the coffee Patrick had promised.

She rummaged in her pocket for the small cosmetic case she'd brought with her. A comb and a mirror and some unscented lip balm. That was it. Fortunately, the mirror was tiny, because she didn't really want to see her reflection. She had a feeling that her appearance fell somewhere between "dragged through a bush backward" and "one step away from zombie."

Putting on boots was her first challenge. Then, after struggling to tame her hair and redo her ponytail, she shook her head in defeat. She didn't need to impress Patrick with her looks. Why did it matter?

When she unzipped her tent and climbed out, she didn't glance in Patrick's direction. Instead, she headed off into the relative privacy of the forest. After taking care of her most urgent need, she returned to the campsite. Patrick looked rested, but his hair was rumpled and his jaw was shadowed with dark stubble.

Still, he looked gorgeous and sexy. Life wasn't fair at all.

He looked up from his contemplation of the fire when she sat down. "Mornin'," he said. The word was gruff.

She nodded, unable to come up with a scintillating response. The mood between them was undeniably awkward.

He poured her a cup of coffee. "Careful, it's hot."

"Thanks." Adding sugar and a packet of artificial creamer, she inhaled the steam, hoping the diffused caffeine would jump-start her sluggish brain. So far, the five-word conversation between her and her boss was taxing her will to live.

Two cups later, she began to feel slightly human. Even so, the fact that she had been wearing the same clothes for twenty-four hours made her long for a hot shower.

"What next?" she asked. The sooner Patrick taught her the drill, the sooner they could go home.

"We break down camp. With a group event, we'll have the camp stoves set up right over there. The guys that packed in the food and supplies will be your assistants. The meal is simple, homemade oatmeal with cinnamon and brown sugar for those who want it. Precooked bacon that we crisp up in a skillet. Whole oranges. And of course, coffee."

"Will I have to cook the oatmeal?"

"No. Only warm it. It's mostly a matter of being organized and making sure everyone gets served quickly. They're always eager to get started on the rest of the day, so we try not to drag out the meal process."

"I can handle that."

"You ready to head out?"

Gulp. Of course. She noticed he didn't say "head home." Clearly there was more to be learned.

She paid close attention as Patrick showed her how to

break down the tents and put out the fire. Once they reloaded their packs, the site was pristine. It went without saying that a company like Silver Reflections would respect the sanctity of the natural world.

Patrick wasn't very talkative this morning. Perhaps he was regretting their momentary lapse. Or maybe he had other issues on his mind. Losing Charlise's expertise for six months had to be frustrating for him. Maybe everyone would have been a lot happier if Patrick had simply stood up to Maeve and told her he would find his own, far more qualified, temporary employee.

Still, even given the circumstances far beyond her comfort zone, Libby realized she really wanted this job. Beneath the physical challenges she was experiencing lurked exhilaration that she was facing her fears and conquering them…or at least trying to…

This morning's hike was shorter, no more than three or four miles. And Patrick's pace was more of a stroll than a death march. With the sun shining and the birds singing, it was almost easy to dismiss her sleepless night.

When they stopped for a snack, Patrick didn't take the time to unpack any kind of seating tarp. Instead, they leaned against trees. Recent rains had left the ground damp, particularly beneath the top layer of rotting leaves. He fished salted peanuts and beef jerky from his pocket. "This will give you energy," he said.

"Do I look that bad?"

His lips quirked. "Maybe a little frayed around the edges. Nothing to worry about. But it will be several hours before we get home, so you have to keep up your strength."

She bit off a piece of jerky, grimacing at the taste. "That sounds ominous. What's next? Building a canoe from a tree? Making blow darts from poison berries? Killing and skinning a wild animal with my bare hands?"

Patrick chuckled. "You've been watching too many movies."

"Then what?"

"We're going underground."

Her stomach fell somewhere in the vicinity of her boots. "Um, no. I don't think so. I got locked in a closet for several hours when I was a little kid and I've been claustrophobic ever since. I don't do caves."

It seemed as if he were baiting her, but she couldn't be sure.

"No caves in these mountains," he said. "It's the wrong kind of geology. You might find some large rock overhangs that provide shelter…but not the places where spelunkers investigate tunnels deep into the earth."

"Then what?"

"A mine." He didn't smile. In fact, his face was carefully expressionless.

Was this the part where she was supposed to throw up her hands and say "I quit"? "What kind of mine?" she asked, thinking about every Appalachian horror story she had heard about shafts collapsing and miners being buried alive.

"Years ago, it was one of hundreds of silver mines in the area, but it's long since been tapped out."

"Then why go in?"

"The claustrophobia you mentioned is a very real fear for many people. When we bring groups out, I go down into the mine with three at a time. Usually, the participants have been prepped in advance about what to discuss. Something simple, but work-related. We sit in the dark as they try to carry on a conversation without panicking."

"And if someone *does* freak out?"

"Their colleagues talk them through it…part of the team-building aspect. You'd be surprised. Sometimes it's the tough macho guys who can't handle it. It's an eye-opener all the way around."

"Well, thanks for telling me about it," she said, her voice high-pitched and squeaky. "I'll do absolutely everything you want me to do *above*ground, no questions asked. But I think I'll take a pass on the mine thing. I hope that's not a deal breaker."

Patrick took her hands, staring into her eyes like a hypnotist. "You can trust me, Libby, I swear."

She exhaled, an audibly jerky sigh. "This might be a good time to mention that my childhood was spent learning how to be scared of everything. My mom wouldn't take me into Central Park because of muggers. No Macy's Thanksgiving Parade because of lurking kidnappers in the crowd. If a spider ever had the temerity to invade our apartment, things went to DEFCON 1 in a hurry. She didn't want me to have a boyfriend, so she told me I could get pregnant from kissing."

"You and I are in trouble, then."

She ignored his attempt at levity. "I was afraid of drowning in the bathtub and being exposed to radioactivity from the microwave. My Halloween candy had to be checked for razor blades, even though it was all a gift from our neighbors across the hall, people we had known for years. I could go on, but you get the idea."

"You know that your mother had serious issues."

"Yes." It was hard to admit it out loud.

"People don't commit suicide for no reason. Your father's fall from grace may have devastated her, but surely it was more than that."

"I know." She swallowed hard, chagrined to feel hot tears threaten her composure. "I also learned to be afraid that I might be like her."

"Bullshit."

Patrick's forceful curse shocked her.

He squeezed her hands, and released her only to pull her against his chest for a brief hug. Then he stepped back and brushed a damp strand of hair from her forehead. The compassion in his gray-blue eyes stripped her raw.

"Libby," he said quietly, "you may not be the right person for this job, but you're strong and independent and amazingly resilient. Not once have you whined about what the last year has been like for you. During terrible, tragic circumstances, you cared for your mother when she couldn't care for herself. You did everything a loving daughter could do. And even though it may seem like it wasn't enough, that's not true."

"I tried to get help for her."

"By selling all your clothes and jewelry to pay for treatment."

"How did you know that?"

He shrugged. "Charlise told me."

Of course. "It wasn't like I had a use for all that stuff," she said.

"Doesn't matter. You gave everything you had. You walked a hard road. You're nothing like her, I promise. Nothing at all. And you don't have to go down into a mine to prove it."

Six

Patrick felt out of his depth. He was neither a grief counselor nor a psychiatrist. All he could do was make sure Libby knew how much he respected and admired her. And better yet, he could resist the urge to muddy the waters with sex.

She stared at him, her expression impossible to decipher. "I've changed my mind," she said quietly. "I want to do it. Not to impress you or to convince you to let me keep the job, but to prove something to myself."

"There are other ways," he said quietly, now suddenly positive that he had made a mistake in bringing her.

"But we're here. And the time is right. Let's go."

She took off down the clearly marked trail, forcing him to follow along behind. Their destination was a little over two miles away. With Libby setting the pace, they made it to the mine's entrance in forty-five minutes. She stopped dead when he called out to her.

The mine was unmarked for obvious reasons. No reason to tempt kids and reckless adults into doing something stupid.

He caught Libby's arm. "We've had engineers reinforce the first quarter mile. Enough to withstand even a mild earthquake. We do get those around here. I wouldn't take clients in there if it was dangerous."

"I know." She bit her lip. "How do we do this?"

"We'll carry our packs in our arms. I'll go first, using a headlamp. You stay on my heels. When we get to a certain spot, I'll spread something on the ground and we'll sit. At any moment if you change your mind, all you have to do is say so."

"How long do you normally stay underground?"

"An hour."

When she paled, he backpedaled quickly. "But we can always walk in and simply turn around and walk out." He hesitated. Was his role to encourage her or to talk her out of this? "Are you sure, Libby?"

She nodded, her pupils dilated. "I'm sure. But since I'm pretty nervous, you won't mind if I disappear into the woods for a minute?"

He looked at her blankly.

"To relieve myself."

"Ah." While she was gone, he followed suit and then waited for her return.

Though the day was bright and sunny, Libby's skin was clammy when she reappeared. He touched her shoulder. "You might want to roll down your sleeves and put on your jacket. It will be cool in the mine." They had shed layers as they walked and the air grew warmer.

Libby did as he suggested and then stared at him. "What now?"

"Let's do this." He pushed aside the undergrowth that had taken over the mine's entrance since last year. Facing him was a wooden door set into the dirt. He wrestled it loose and pushed it aside. "Door stays open," he said. "No getting locked inside, I swear."

"Is that supposed to make me feel better?"

He shot her a glance over his shoulder. She was smiling, but in her eyes he saw apprehension. Even so, her jaw was set, her resolve visible.

"Follow me," he said.

Libby put one foot in front of the other, blindly trusting Patrick Kavanagh to lead her into the bowels of the earth. Months ago when she and her mother were grief stricken and displaced, trying to start a new life, Libby had been anxious and stressed and worried.

But not like this. Her skin crawled with unease. People were meant to exist in the light. Her heartbeat deafened her. "Patrick!" She called out to him, her stomach churning.

He stopped immediately, dropping his pack and turning to face her. The beam of his headlamp blinded her. They weren't far into the mine. Daylight still filtered in behind them.

"Steady," he said. Knowing his eyes were on her only amplified her embarrassment.

She held up a hand. "Don't touch me. I'm fine."

Patrick nodded slowly. "Okay."

Suddenly, she wanted to throw herself into his arms. He was strong and self-assured and utterly calm. She was a mess. No wonder he thought she couldn't handle Charlise's job.

Slowly, they advanced into the mine. A quarter of a mile sounded like nothing at all. But in reality, it felt like a marathon.

Her panic mounted. No matter how slowly she breathed and how much she told herself she could do this, her chest tightened and her stomach curled. "Wait," she said. Frustration ate at her resolve. Mind over matter wasn't working.

She dropped her pack and wrapped her arms around her waist. "Give me a couple of minutes. I can make it."

Patrick dumped his pack as well and removed his head-lamp so that the light pointed at their feet. "It speaks volumes that you even tried this, Libby."

Wiping her nose with her sleeve, she shook her head. "I hate being so stupid." Now would be a good time for him to hold her and distract her with his incredibly hot and sexy body. But apparently, that wasn't going to happen anytime soon. Or ever.

"You're not stupid. Lots of people have fears…heights, spiders, clowns."

His droll comment made her laugh. "Clowns? Seriously?"

"Coulrophobia. It's a real thing."

"You're making that up."

She heard him chuckle.

"I wouldn't lie to you."

"What are you afraid of, Patrick?"

Before he could answer, a muted rumble sounded in the distance.

"Hang on, Libby," he said.

Before she could ask what or why, a roaring crash reverberated in the tunnel. Debris rained down on them, first in a gentle fall, and then in a heavy shower that choked them and pelted their heads.

She heard Patrick curse. And then she stumbled.

Patrick fumbled in total darkness for Libby's arm. They had both gone down in the chaos. His brain looked for answers even as he searched frantically for his companion. He latched onto her shoulders and shook her. "Say something, damn it. Are you hurt?"

Dragging her into his lap he ran his hands over her head and limbs, checking for injuries. When he found none, he sighed in relief. He chafed her hands and rubbed her face until she stirred.

"Patrick?" she muttered.

"I'm here." Just then, her entire body went rigid and she cried out.

"We're okay," he said firmly. "There's no need to panic."

She was silent, telling him louder than words she thought he was crazy. After a moment she tried to sit up. "What happened?"

He kept an arm around her, feeling the shudders that racked her body. Though he would walk through hot coals before admitting it, the infinite, crushing darkness was pretty damn terrifying. "I'm not exactly sure, but I can make a guess. The mine hasn't caved in. I told you we've had it checked and reinforced."

"Then what?" Her head was tucked against his shoulder, her hands curled against his chest, her fingernails digging into his shirt, as if she wanted to climb inside his skin.

"I think it was a quick tremor…a small earthquake."

"In North Carolina?"

"I told you. It happens. And we've had so damn much rain in the last three weeks, it's possible there was a landslide that blocked the entrance."

Nothing he could say was going to make the facts any more palatable. Libby's skin, at least the exposed part, was icy cold, far colder than warranted by the temperature in the mine. He worried she might be going into shock. So they had to take action…anything to break the cycle of panic and disbelief.

"I need to walk back to the entrance and see what it looks like."

Her grip on his shirtfront tightened. "Not without me."

He smiled in the dark. "Okay. But first we have to find the headlamp."

He let go of his precious cargo with one hand and sifted through the debris.

Libby was pressed so close to his chest he could feel the runaway beat of her heart. "Is it there?"

He found the elastic strap and lifted it out of the pile of dust and twigs and small stones. But when he flicked the switch, nothing happened. Feeling carefully around the outer portion of the LED lamp, he realized that the whole lens had shattered.

"It's here," he muttered. "But it's broken."

"What about our phones?"

How exactly was he supposed to answer that? Did he need to tell her they could be stranded for days and needed to preserve the batteries? On the other hand, if they were going to be rescued, it made sense to get as close to the entrance of the mine as possible. Unless, of course, there was another landslide. Highly unlikely, but possible.

"I have a couple of backup flashlights," he said. "All I have to do is locate my pack and get them. Will you be okay for a minute if I let go of you?"

"Of course."

The right words, wrong tone. She was perilously close to the breaking point.

Cursing himself for bringing her down into this hell-hole, he set her aside and reached out his hands like a blind man. The first pack he found was Libby's. Since he had loaded it himself, he knew the exact contents. But he had put the flashlights in his pack, because they were heavy.

Moments later, he found his own equipment. When he located the item he wanted and flicked the switch, the small beam of light was as welcome as fresh water in the desert.

Libby stared at him owlishly. "Thank God," she said simply.

"You have stuff in your hair," he said. "Not insects," he

added quickly. Leaning forward, he combed his fingers through the ends of her ponytail and picked tiny debris from the rest of her head. "There," he said. "All better."

His conversation was nonsensical. He freely admitted that. But what in the hell were you supposed to say to the beautiful woman you were buried alive with—the very one you were hoping to keep at arms' length because she was vulnerable and trusting and not the woman you needed in your life either personally or professionally?

"It's not my real color," Libby said.

"Excuse me?" He was befuddled, maybe a little bit in shock himself.

"The color," she said. "I'm a redhead. Maybe you remember from when I was a kid. But after the mess with my father, I started dying my hair so I would blend into the crowd. Now I'm afraid to change it back."

"Tomorrow," he said firmly. "Tomorrow you should make an appointment with a stylist and go back to being you."

At last, she smiled. A weak smile, but a smile. "You are so full of it."

"I'm serious. Men love redheads."

"You know what I mean. I'm not an idiot. The chances of us getting out of here anytime soon are pretty slim. No one is expecting us back until dinnertime. That's several hours from now. And by the time they start to wonder where we are, it will be dark."

"So we'll wait," he said. "We have a decent amount of food and water. If we're careful, it will last."

"How long?" The question was stark.

"Long enough."

He got to his feet, ignoring the lash of pain in his left calf. "Come on, woman. Let's see what happened. We'll take our gear with us."

They hadn't really come all that far. It didn't take long

to retrace their steps. Unfortunately, his guess was spot-on. With or without a tremor as the inciting incident, a goodly portion of the hillside had come sliding down on top of the mine opening. Wet, sludgy earth filled the entrance. Trying to burrow out would only make the whole pile shift and slither, much like digging a hole at the beach.

But Libby looked at him with such naked hope he had to do something. "Stand back," he said. "Maybe it's not as bad as it looks."

"May I hold a flashlight, too?"

It wasn't a good idea. Batteries were like gold in their situation. Still, she needed the reassurance of sight. Later on they could sit in darkness.

He reached into his pocket for the spare flashlight and handed it to her. "I'm serious," he said. "Don't get too close."

For a moment, he was stymied. Using his bare hands to dig seemed ineffective at best, but even mentally cataloging the contents of his backpack, he couldn't think of a damn thing that might serve as a shovel.

In the end, he tucked the flashlight under his armpit and awkwardly began to gouge his fingers into the wet mess. Dry dirt wouldn't have been so bad, but the mud was a frustrating opponent.

After ten minutes of concerted effort, he had made no headway at all. Not only that, he was starting to feel dizzy. He stumbled backward, his filthy arms outstretched. "This isn't going to work. I'm sorry, Libby."

"You're hurt," she said, alarm in her voice. "You're bleeding below the knee."

He blinked, trying to focus his thoughts. Maybe adrenaline had masked his injury, because now his leg hurt like hell. "I don't want to touch the flashlight with all this gunk on my hands. Can you look at my leg?"

Libby squatted and touched his shin. "Whatever it was cut all the way through the cloth."

"Probably a piece of glass. We've found all kinds of broken bottles and crockery down here over the years."

He flinched when she carefully rolled up the leg of his pants.

"Oh, God, Patrick," she gasped. "You need stitches. Sit down so I can look at it."

"Wait. Find the tarp in my pack. We're going to have to make a place to get comfortable." *Comfortable* wasn't even on the map of where they were located. But they would take what they could get.

Libby moved quickly, locating the large tarp and spreading it with one side tucked up against the wall of the mine so they could lean against something. When she was done, he pointed to an outside zip pocket of his pack. "There's a small, thin towel in there. Can you wet it, just barely, so I can get the worst of this off?"

Libby did as he asked, but instead of giving him the towel, she took his hands in hers and began wiping his fingers clean. It was a difficult chore, especially given the lack of water.

He still held the flashlight under his arm. Though he couldn't see Libby's face, there was enough illumination for him to watch as she removed the muck. It was an intimate act…and an unselfish one…because the process dirtied her skin, as well.

But finally he was more or less back to normal.

"Sit down now," she urged.

He was happy to comply.

With his back against the wall of the mine, he took a deep breath. He felt like hell, and his leg had begun to throb viciously. There's a first aid kit," he said gruffly. "Big outer pocket. Antiseptic wipes."

Libby put a hand on his thigh, perhaps to get his attention. "You've lost a lot of blood, Patrick. A lot. The cut is four inches long and gaping."

"Clean it the best you can. We'll use butterfly bandages." The words were an effort. "I'll hold the flashlight."

It occurred to him that he could reach his own leg…do his own medical care. But he couldn't seem to work up the energy to try.

Libby's touch was deft but gentle. Wisely, she didn't waste time getting rid of all the blood. He watched her concentrate on the cut, making sure the edges were clean, dabbing at tiny bits of dirt that might cause infection later. When she was satisfied, she sat back on her heels. "I'll let it dry a minute," she said, "before I use the butterfly thingies."

"Can you get me a couple of painkillers?" he asked, hurting too much to act macho at this particular moment.

"Of course."

He took them with a sip of water and sighed. "Is the skin dry?"

Libby traced around the wound with a fingertip. "Yes." She tore open a small packet and gently affixed the Band-Aid, pulling the open edges of the cut together. It took two more before she was satisfied. "The bleeding has stopped."

"Good." He closed his eyes. "Sit between my legs," he said. "It will keep us both warm."

He needed the human contact, but more than that, he needed a connection to Libby specifically. She might be completely wrong for him on far too many levels, but right now, they had each other and no one else. He wanted to feel her and know she was okay.

Seven

Libby felt like she was in a dream. But when she settled between Patrick's thighs, her legs outstretched, her back against his chest, the situation got a whole lot more real.

Strong arms wrapped around her waist. Big masculine hands clasped beneath her breasts. Patrick's breath warmed the side of her neck. "Are you going to be okay?" she asked. The tenor of his breathing alarmed her. That and his silence.

"It's just a cut. Don't worry about it."

She might be inexperienced when it came to medical care, but she wasn't stupid. Patrick needed a proper hospital, an IV of fluids and red meat. Instead, he was stuck down here with her.

"What time is it?" she asked, feeling her anxiety rise again now that the immediate crisis was past.

"We have to turn off the flashlights," he said quietly, the words ruffling her hair.

She didn't know which part worried her the most—the

fact that he deliberately ignored her question, or the regression to pitch-black darkness. Without vision, the world seemed ominous.

"Do you sing?" she asked.

He groaned. "You don't want to hear that, I promise."

"I'm sorry, Patrick, but if you don't talk to me, I might go bonkers."

"Okay, okay." The words held amusement.

"Tell me about your family. My mother used to keep in touch with Maeve all the time, but I don't really know much about the Kavanagh clan. What are your brothers up to these days?"

"Liam is the oldest. He married a woman named Zoe who is sort of a free spirit. We love her, and she's a perfect match for my stick-in-the-mud brother."

"Go on."

"You saw Dylan at the pub. His wife is Mia. Dylan adopted her little girl."

"Next is Aidan?"

"That's right. He and Emma divide their time between New York and Silver Glen. Then comes Gavin. He runs a cybersecurity firm here in Silver Glen. His wife is Cassidy, and they have twin baby girls."

"What about Conor? Wasn't he the big skier in the family?"

"Still is. He ended up marrying a girl he knew way back in high school. Her name is Ellie."

"Which leaves you and James…is that his name?"

"Yep. My baby brother…who happens to be four inches taller than I am and thirty pounds heavier. We call him the gentle giant."

"You love him. I hear it in your voice."

"Well, when you're the last two in a string of seven, you end up bonding. It was either that or be terrorized by our siblings on a regular basis. With James on my side, I had a tactical advantage."

"Your mother takes credit for marrying off the first five. I suppose you and James are next in her sights."

"Not gonna happen."

The blunt, flat-toned response shocked her. "Oh?"

"Let me rephrase that. I can't speak for my brother, but I'm not interested in tying the knot. Earlier, you asked me what I was afraid of and I never got a chance to answer you. The truth is, it's marriage. I tried it once and it didn't pan out. So I plan on being happily single."

She turned toward him, which was dumb, because she couldn't see his face. "You're divorced?"

"Worse than that."

"She died?" Libby gaped in the darkness, horrified, feeling as if she had stepped in the middle of a painful past Patrick didn't want to share. But now that the door was open, she couldn't ignore the peek inside this complicated man.

Patrick sighed, his chest rising and falling. He pulled her back against him. "No. The marriage was annulled."

It was a good thing Patrick was willing to talk about his past, because the only thing keeping Libby from climbing the walls was concentrating on the sound of his voice. All around her, the dark encroached. Would they have to sleep here and wake up here and slowly starve to death?

Panic fluttered in her chest. "What happened?" she asked.

Patrick wasn't a fan of rehashing his youthful mistakes, but he and Libby had to do something to maintain a sense of normalcy. The medicine had dulled the pain in his leg, though he still felt alarmingly weak.

He rested his chin on her head, inhaling the faint scent of her skin. Her upper-class upbringing meant she'd been taught the rules of polite behavior at an early age. He was sure Libby would never ask that kind of personal question under different circumstances.

But here in the mine, such considerations were less important than the need to feel connected.

He played with the fingers of her right hand, fingers that were bare. Where were the diamonds, the pearls, the precious gems this young, wealthy woman had worn? All sold for her mother's treatment. Libby's mom had betrayed that sacrifice by killing herself.

The picture of Libby he'd had in the beginning was fading rapidly, the colors blurred by the reality of who she was. She'd been a Madison Avenue heiress…no doubt about that. But Libby Parkhurst was so much more than the sum of what she had lost.

His feelings toward her were confusing. He wanted to protect her, both physically and emotionally. And though it was disconcerting as hell, he was beginning to *want* her. In the way a man wants a woman.

Even here in this dank, dark mine shaft—and even though he had a throbbing wound in his leg—his body reacted to the feel of her in his arms. Their relationship had been thrown into fast-forward. He was bombarded with emotions—tenderness, affection and definitely admiration. For a woman who had barely been able to contemplate walking into the mine shaft and back out again, it was nothing short of remarkable that she was still able to function, considering what had happened.

He realized she was still waiting for an answer about his marriage. "My girlfriend got pregnant," he said. "One of those terrible clichés that turns out to be true. I'd been careful to protect both of us, but…"

"Accidents happen."

"Yes. My brothers and I had been brought up with a very strict code of honor. Her parents wanted us to get married, so I agreed. In hindsight, I doubt my mother was thrilled, but what could she do?"

"And the annulment?"

"When the little boy was born, he was dark-skinned… African-American. Even for a girl who was terrified to tell her parents she was involved in a mixed-race relationship and even though she was embarrassed to admit she'd been cheating on her boyfriend, it was clear that the gig was up. We didn't need to have a paternity test done. The truth stared us in the face."

"Oh, Patrick. You must have been devastated."

He winced, even now reacting to a painful, fleeting memory of what that day had done to him. "We'd been living together as husband and wife. We had both graduated from high school…rented a small house. Even though I'd been upset and angry and not at all ready to become a father, after nine months, I'd finally come around to the idea. I was so excited about that little boy."

"And then you lost him."

"Yes. I walked out of the hospital and never looked back. I went home. Slept in the bed where I'd grown up. But nothing was the same. You can't rewrite history and undo your mistakes. All you can do is move forward and not make those same mistakes again."

He wanted to know what Libby was thinking, but he kept on talking. It was cathartic to rehash what had been a chaotic, deeply painful time in his life. It was a subject never broached by the Kavanagh clan. They had swept it under the rug and moved on.

"I didn't abandon the baby," he said, remembering the infant's tiny face. "I want you to know that. His father stepped up. As soon as the annulment was final, he married the mother of his child and they made a family."

"You must have been so hurt."

It was true. He'd been crushed. But he had never let on how much it affected him.

"Adolescence is tough for everybody," he muttered.

Libby turned on her side, nestling her cheek against his chest and drawing up her knees until they threatened his manhood. "You're a good man, Patrick Kavanagh."

He stroked her hair. "I'm sorry about this," he said.

Libby sighed audibly. "It will be something to tell our children one day." She stopped dead, realizing what she had said.

"Don't worry about it, Libby. I'm a very popular uncle, and I like it that way."

"Have you told Maeve how you feel?"

"I think she guesses. She hasn't quite put the marital screws on me like she has the others."

"I'm warning you, it's only a matter of time. You'd better watch your step around her. She's wonderful, but sneaky."

After that, they dozed. Patrick dreamed restlessly, always fighting an ominous foe. Each time he awoke, his arms tightened around Libby. She was his charge, his responsibility. He would do everything in his power to make sure she got out of this mess in one piece.

At last, they couldn't ignore the rumbles of hungry stomachs. "What do you want?" he asked. "Beef jerky or peanuts?"

"I'll take the nuts, I guess."

He handed her the water. "Three sips, no more. We have to be smart about rationing."

"Can we please turn on one of the phones and find out what time it is? Do you think there's any hope of getting a signal down here? We're near the surface."

"I'll look. And no. I don't think there's a chance at all of having a signal."

"You really suck at this cheering up thing."

He checked the time, oddly comforted by the familiar glow of the phone screen. "Seven fifteen."

"So it's dark outside."

"Yes." He turned off the electronic device and stowed it. "It doesn't really matter, though, does it? Not to us?"

"I suppose not." She sighed. "Tell me something else. Do you have big plans for the weekend?"

"I'm flying up to New York Friday morning to do an orientation for one of the teams coming in April. Peabody Rushford is a world-renowned accounting firm with A-list clients. We'll sit around a big conference table, and I'll go over the checklist with all of them. They'll ask questions…"

"May I go with you?"

He paused, taken aback. Maybe Libby was simply trying to convince herself she wouldn't still be trapped underground come Friday. "I'm not sure there's any reason for you to be there," he said. "I don't want to hurt your feelings, but this job is not the one for you. I think you know that."

"Maybe so. But I was thinking of a more personal agenda."

His mind raced, already inventing sexual scenarios where he and Libby ended up naked on soft sheets. "What kind of agenda?"

"I haven't been back to my building since the day my mother and I had to leave. I thought I could go see it. I can't get inside the apartment, of course. Someone else lives there now. But I think even standing on the street would give me some closure."

"Then of course you can come with me," he said. "I wish I could fly us up there in my new toy. I bought a used Cessna recently, but it's still being overhauled. So we'll have to take the jet."

"*Now* who sounds like the poor little rich kid?" she teased.

"You've got me. But to be fair, the Kavanaghs share the jet with several others owners."

"Well, that makes it okay, of course."

"If I were you, I don't think I would alienate the only human being standing between me and solitary confinement."

"Not funny, Patrick."

"Sorry."

They sat in silence. The teasing had kept the darkness at bay for a few moments, but the truth returned. They were trapped…with no hope of rescue until morning at least, and maybe not even then.

Libby stood up, accidentally elbowing him in the ribs. "I have to stretch," she said.

"Don't go far."

"Hilarious, Kavanagh."

He might as well stand up, too. But when he moved, he cursed as pain shot up his leg, hot and vicious.

Libby crouched beside him. "Give me the flashlight."

"Why? We need to save the battery."

"I'm going to look at your leg. Don't argue with me."

She was cute when she was indignant. He surrendered the flashlight wordlessly.

In a brightly lit room, he would have been able to examine his own leg. With nothing but the thin beam of the flashlight, though, he had to rely on Libby for an up-close diagnosis. "How does it look?"

"Bad."

"Bad as in 'needs an antibiotic,' or bad as in 'heading for amputation'?"

She turned the flashlight toward his face, blinding him. "That isn't funny. If we stay in here much longer, you could be in serious trouble."

He covered his eyes. "I choose to laugh instead of cry."

"I'll bet you've never cried in your life. Alpha males don't do that."

"I cried when my father disappeared."

Eight

"Oh, Patrick." Libby's heart turned over. She would bet every dollar of her first paycheck that he hadn't meant to say something so revealing. She sat back down, feeling warm and almost secure when he enfolded her in his arms again. "I know we touched on this during my interview, and I'm sorry to open up old wounds... Did he really just go away?"

"I was a little kid, so some of my memories are fuzzy... but I've heard the story a hundred times. My father was obsessed with finding the silver mine that launched the Kavanagh fortunes generations ago. He would go out for days at a time...and then one weekend, he simply never came back."

"I'm sorry."

"It was a long time ago."

Libby had a blinding revelation, which was really pretty funny considering she was sitting in total darkness. She and Patrick had both been betrayed by their fathers. But luckily for Patrick, *his* mother was a rock.

"Did anyone have a valid theory about what happened?"

"In the beginning, there were lots of possibilities. The police posed the idea that he might have simply abandoned us, started a new life. But his passport was in the safe at home and none of his clothes or prized possessions were missing. He couldn't have left the country, and since none of the family vehicles had been taken, the final conclusion was that he had been killed somewhere in the mountains."

"You mean by wild animals?"

"It's possible. Or he could have fallen."

"But his body was never found."

"Exactly. Which meant that everyone's best educated guess was that my dad went down inside a mine—looking for remnants of a silver vein—and the mine collapsed."

"Oh."

Patrick's arms tightened around her. "This probably isn't the best conversation for us to be having at the moment."

"It does have a certain macabre theme."

"Remember, Libby…this mine we're in *didn't* collapse. It's just that the entrance has been blocked."

"A fine distinction that I'm sorry to say is not very comforting."

"You have *me*. That's something."

Actually, that was a lot. Patrick's reassuring presence was keeping most of her panic at bay…at least for stretches at a time. But their enforced intimacy had created another problem.

In the two weeks she had worked for him, she'd done her best to ignore the fact that he was a handsome, funny, intellectually stimulating man on whom she had a perfectly understandable crush. She'd kept her distance and been a model employee.

But now, with his strong arms holding her tight and his rumbly voice giving her goose bumps when his warm breath tickled her neck and cheek, she was suddenly, madly infatuated. That's all it was. An adrenaline-born rush of arousal. Part of the fight-or-flight response.

The same thing would have happened if she and Patrick had been cave people fleeing from a saber-toothed tiger. Of course later, once they were safe, they might have had wild monkey sex on a fur pelt by the roaring fire.

Her mouth went dry, and the pit of her stomach felt funny. "Patrick?" Clearly her brain cells were being starved of oxygen. Or maybe she was truly losing it, because the next words that came out of her mouth were totally inappropriate. "Will you kiss me?"

She felt his whole body stiffen. "Never mind," she said quickly. "That was just the claustrophobia talking."

"We're not going to die. I promise." His voice sounded funny…as if he had swallowed something down his windpipe.

"And by extrapolation I'm supposed to understand that imminent death is the only situation in which you could see yourself kissing me? Because I'm *one of your mother's misfits*, and a general pain in the ass?"

"You're not playing fair, Libby."

She turned in his embrace, her hands finding his face in the dark. His jaw was stubbly. She rubbed her thumbs over his strong chin. "Kiss me, Patrick," she whispered. "I know I'm taking advantage of you in your weakened state, but please. I've wondered for days what kind of woman you want. I know it's not me. Under the circumstances, though, you could bend the rules…right?"

"Libby, darlin'…"

The way he said her name was pure magic. "I'm listening."

He made a noise that sounded like choked laughter. "You were never spanked as a child, were you?"

She shrugged. "My nannies loved me. So, no. Is that an offer?"

"What about the spiders and the mud and the dungeon ambience?"

"Are you stalling?"

"I don't want you to be embarrassed when we get out of here."

"Embarrassed that I asked for a kiss, or embarrassed that I kissed my boss? I don't think that last one is a problem. You've pretty well admitted that my days are numbered when it comes to working for Silver Reflections."

His hands tangled in her hair, his lips brushing her forehead. "For the record, I haven't completely made up my mind about your status at Silver Reflections. Plus, kissing will make us want other things."

"Too late," she said, breathless…longing. "I already want those other things, but I'm willing to settle for a kiss."

"God, you're a brat."

Somehow, the way he said it turned the words into a husky compliment. "Shall I leave you alone, Patrick?"

His fingers tightened on her skull. "No. That's not what I want at all."

Before she could respond, he angled her head and found her mouth with his. The first kiss was barely perceptible… no more than a faint brush of lips to lips. Even so, she melted into him, stung by a wild burst of hunger that couldn't be satisfied by anything less than full body contact.

The kiss deepened. Patrick muttered something, but she was too lost to translate it. They had done this once before. That "sort of an apology" kiss they had shared in the woods. But she hadn't taken him seriously at the time. She'd thought he was just being nice. Charming. Offering sophisticated reparation for a thoughtless, hurtful mistake.

This was different. This was desperation. Need. Raw, unscripted masculine hunger.

Her fingers fumbled with his shirt buttons, tearing at them until she could rest her cheek against hot male skin. She nipped a flat nipple with her teeth. "I'm getting used to the dark," she whispered.

He groaned. "I'm not." He did his own version of seek-and-find, palming her breasts and squeezing them gently. "I want to see you…all of you."

There were no words to describe the feel of his hands on her bare flesh. It didn't matter that his fingers were probably still mud streaked…or that she shivered with her shirt unbuttoned. She was drowning in pleasure.

Need became a demanding beast, telling her there was a way…insisting that the less-than-perfect circumstances weren't as important as the yearning to take Patrick Kavanagh and make him hers. Her brain made a bid for common sense, reminding her that getting involved sexually with Patrick Kavanagh was a really bad idea.

But other parts of her body spoke more loudly. "How big is this tarp?" she asked, her fingers trembling as she unbuckled his belt.

Patrick found himself in uncharted territory. At any given moment he could find his way through a dense forest on a moonless night with no more than a compass and his knowledge of the mountains. Right now, however, he was a blind man struggling in quicksand.

This was insanity. Complete and utter disregard for the seriousness of their situation. He had to call a halt…

"Touch me," he begged.

When Libby's fingers closed around his erection, he sucked in a sharp breath.

"You fascinate me, Patrick," she said softly, her firm

touch on his body perfect in every way...as if they had been lovers forever and knew exactly what the other liked.

"I'm no different from any other guy," he croaked, feeling his temperature rise as sweat broke out on his brow. "We see, we want, we take."

"And what if *I* take *you*?"

His heart stopped. He tried to remember all the reasons why he was supposed to be a gentleman. The family connection. Libby's recent losses. His mother's disapproval.

Nothing worked. He wanted Libby. Badly. Enough to ignore his better judgment.

After that, it was only a matter of logistics. It could work. Not ideal, but doable. He fumbled with his pants, trying to lower them, but Libby was plastered against his chest, and he couldn't bear to shove her away, even for a moment.

"Wait," she cried. "Stop."

"Damn it, woman, this was *your* idea." He would stop if he had to, but why in the hell was she blowing hot and cold?

She put her hand over his mouth. "Listen," she said, urgency in her tone. "I heard something."

Patrick heard something, too. But it was the sound of his libido crying out in frustrated disbelief. "What are you talking about?"

"Shut up and listen."

Now she was making him mad.

And then he heard it. A scraping sound. And something else. Something human. *Holy hell.* "Button your blouse."

He struggled with his own clothing, and then cursed when he needed her help to stand up. The pain meds had worn off, and his leg was one big ache. Funny how lust was a stunningly effective narcotic. Fumbling for the flashlight, he took Libby's hand and they moved forward.

"We can't get too close," she whispered.

He squeezed her hand. "Cover your ears. I'm going to yell. *"We're down here!"* His plea echoed in their prison.

But from the other side of the mud and rock, a garbled response told him someone had heard the three simple words.

Libby's fingernails dug into his palm. "Who do you think it is?"

"Does it matter? As long as it's not the Grim Reaper, I'm a fan."

They clung to each other, barely breathing.

Suddenly, an unwelcome sensation intruded. "Libby," he said hoarsely. "My ankle is wet."

She reached inside his jacket. "Is that a flashlight in your pocket, or are you glad to see me?" Dropping to her knees, she shone the light on his leg. "Oh, hell, Patrick. The butterfly strips came loose. You're bleeding like a stuck pig. We have to sit you down. Let me find the tarp."

"No," he muttered, feeling woozy. "A little dirt won't hurt me." Leaning on Libby with a death grip, he bent his knees and stumbled onto his butt, cursing when his leg cried out in agony.

She hovered at his side, crouching and combing her fingers through his hair. "Are you okay?"

"Never better."

Without fanfare, a hole opened up in the mud. The unmistakable sounds of shoveling reverberated off the tunnel walls.

A voice, oddly disembodied, floated through the twelve-inch opening. "Patrick! You okay, man?"

Patrick swallowed. "I'm fine."

He licked his lips, shaking all over. "That's James, my brother. How did he know we were here?"

Libby put her arms around him, holding him close. "To quote a man I know, does it matter? Hang on, Patrick. It won't be much longer."

At last, the opening was large enough so they could

lean through and allow themselves to be tugged out like bears from honey pots. Patrick staggered but made it to his feet. He blinked, seeing four of his brothers staring at him. He must look worse than he thought. "Thanks for coming, guys."

And then his world went black.

Libby had her arm around Patrick's waist, but she was no match for his deadweight when he lost consciousness. They both went down hard, despite the fact that James reached for his brother.

"What's wrong with him?" James asked, alarm and consternation in his voice. Then he eased Patrick onto his back and saw the injury for himself.

Libby disentangled herself but stayed seated. "He's lost a lot of blood. The cut will need stitches."

After hasty introductions, Liam Kavanagh rescued the two backpacks from the mine. James and Dylan hoisted their injured sibling onto a portable litter and started back. Gavin gave her a weary smile. "I'm gonna piggyback you," he said. "It will be faster that way."

In the end, the trip through the forest took over two hours. The Kavanagh men had to be exhausted. It was four in the morning by the time they walked out of the woods and into the main lodge of Silver Reflections. Maeve was waiting for them, her face creased with worry.

The only brothers missing were Aidan, who, she learned, was out of town, and Conor who had gone to summon an ambulance. He'd kept his mother company during the rescue operation.

Maeve grabbed Libby into a huge hug. "Oh, my God. We've been out of our minds with worry." She bit her lip, eyeing Patrick's pale face as his brothers set the litter on a padded bench seat. "The ambulance is waiting."

Liam had radioed ahead to let Maeve know they were on the way.

In the hustle and bustle that followed, Libby found herself curled into a deep, comfy armchair by a fire someone had been kind enough to build in the middle of the night. When all the men disappeared, Maeve touched her arm. "Come on, sweetheart. I'll take you back to the hotel before I follow them to the emergency room. Are you sure you don't need medical attention?"

"No, ma'am. I'm fine."

Libby dozed in the car, waking up only as Maeve pulled up in front of Silver Beeches.

Maeve gazed at her, exhaustion on her face. "Do you need help getting upstairs?"

Libby knew her older friend was anxious to check on her son. "I'm fine, Maeve. Go see to Patrick. I'm going to bed as soon as I can get there."

Looking at her reflection in the bathroom mirror a short time later was a lesson in humility. Libby had seen corpses who had more color…and more fashion sense for that matter. Her clothes were filthy and torn, her hair was a tangled mess and, as an added indignity, her stomach rumbled loudly, making it known that sleep was going to have to wait.

The shower felt so good, she almost cried. After shampooing her hair three times and slathering it with conditioner, she used a washcloth to scrub away the grime from the rest of her body. She wove on her feet, fatigue weighting her limbs.

When she was clean and dry, she ordered room service. Six in the morning wasn't too early for bacon and eggs. She had every intention of cleaning her plate, but she managed only half of the bounty before she shoved the tray aside and fell facedown onto the soft, welcoming bed.

Nine

Patrick wolfed down half of a sausage biscuit and watched as the female doc stitched up his leg. Thanks to several shots of numbing medicine, he was feeling no pain.

James leaned against the wall, as if guarding the room from unwanted intruders. Since they were the last people in the ER, Patrick was pretty sure any danger had been left behind at the mine. He and James had finally convinced all the others to go home and get some rest.

Patrick looked at his brother over the doctor's head. "Thanks, bro. You want to explain to me how you knew where I was?"

James's grin was tired but cocky. "I came up to Reflections yesterday to grab one of your gourmet lunches and see if you wanted to hike with me. The people at the front desk said you were in the forest teaching a new recruit the ropes. I set out around the mountain to catch up with you."

"You know where the campsite is...but have you ever even *been* to the mine?"

"No…but I've heard you talk about it. So I used my Boy Scout tracker skills and followed your trail. I eventually stumbled across the landslide. The mud was thick and slimy and fresh. It was then I realized you might be in trouble."

"Me and Libby…"

"Yeah. Since when do you camp out with pretty ladies?"

"It wasn't like that."

"I saw how she looked at you."

"We'd been through a tough time. It was a bonding experience." Patrick managed to keep his expression impassive, but his body was another story. "How did you dig us out?"

James grimaced. "That was the bad part. After I discovered I had *nothing* that was going to do the job, I ran back several miles to the knoll where we can usually get a phone signal and called Conor. He alerted everyone else. We all met up and brought the proper supplies."

"I owe you one, baby brother."

"Don't worry. I'll collect sooner or later. Like maybe an introduction to your newest employee?"

"I don't think so," Patrick snapped.

James raised an eyebrow. "Feeling a little territorial, are we?"

"She's not your type."

"Mom told me her story. She sounds like an amazing woman."

"She is. But she's had a tough time, and she doesn't need strange guys sniffing around."

"I'm not a strange guy… I'm your brother."

The doctor looked up from her work and smiled. "Do I need to referee this squabble?"

Patrick looked down at the long, red, angry wound on his leg. He hadn't needed a transfusion, but it was a close call. "No, Doc," he said, shooting his brother a glare.

Fortunately, Patrick's medical care wrapped up pretty quickly. In the car, James lifted an inquiring eyebrow. "Am I taking you home?"

Patrick gazed out the window, feeling exhausted and surly. "I want to go up to the hotel and make sure Libby is okay."

"She'll be asleep by now."

"Mom would give me a key."

James drummed his fingers on the steering wheel. "I know the two of you just spent the night together in a creepy, dark tunnel, but that doesn't give you the right to act like a stalker. Think, man. You can't open her door and peek in on her. That's way over the line."

Patrick slumped into his seat. His selfish need to see her would have to wait. "I guess you're right. Take me home."

After a shower, a light meal and five hours of sleep, Patrick found himself awake and antsy. The cut was on his left leg, so he wasn't limited as far as driving. When he couldn't stand being inside his house for another minute, he drove to Silver Reflections. His employees seemed perplexed to see him after his ordeal, so he holed up in his office.

Liam had left the two backpacks inside Patrick's door. Patrick dumped them out and started putting things away. One of the staff would take care of cleaning the tarps and other items. The rest Patrick stowed in specially labeled drawers along one wall of his suite.

When all of that was done, he couldn't wait any longer. He sent a text to Libby.

Hope you're feeling okay. You don't have to go Friday if you're not up to it. And stay home tomorrow...you deserve a rest...

He didn't dare say what he was really thinking…that he needed time to figure out what to do about her.

He hit Send and spun around in his leather chair. Maybe he'd been more affected by the experience in the mine than he realized, because his concentration was shot. When someone knocked at his door, he frowned, tempted to pretend he wasn't there.

But, after all, he was the boss. "Come in. It's open."

Libby was the last person he expected to see. She smiled. "I just got your text. Thanks for the consideration, but I couldn't sleep all day. I've been in my office talking to a guest who's disgruntled because he came here to relax and it's too peaceful to sleep. Apparently he lives in a brownstone walk-up across the street from a fire station."

"Ah. Maybe he needs more help than we can give."

"Maybe."

"I'm serious, Libby. Take tomorrow off. And do you still want to go to New York?"

"If you'll have me."

He would be damned glad to have her six ways to Sunday, but that wasn't what she meant. "You're welcome to come with me. As long as you know this isn't a nod from me about the job. I'll book you a hotel room this evening."

"Are you sure you want to do that? I've been learning how to manage on a budget. One room is definitely cheaper than two."

The challenging look in her eyes sent an unmistakable message. He stood up slowly and backed her against the door. "Are you sure it wasn't the adrenaline rush of certain death that sent you into my arms?" He kissed the side of her neck to test his hypothesis. His hips nudged hers. She was soft where he was hard.

Libby sighed as their bodies aligned with satisfying perfection. Her green eyes sparkled with excitement. "Perhaps it has escaped your notice, but you're a very sexy man."

"It was the bloody leg, right? Women can't resist a wounded hero."

"To be exact, I believe James was the hero."

She was taunting him deliberately. He knew that. And still, it pissed him off. "My brother is a great guy, but I doubt the two of you would get along."

"And why is that? I found him quite charming."

"If any Kavanagh is going to end up in your bed, it's going to be me." The declaration ended only a few decibels below a shout.

"Ooh…so intense. I have goose bumps. Still," she said, drawing the single syllable out to make a point. "I'm not sure it's a good idea to sleep with the boss."

"Then we won't sleep," he said. He kissed her wildly, feeling the press of her generous breasts against his chest. How had he ever thought she was meek and mousy?

Libby leaned into him, moaning when he deepened the kiss. "Your mother feels bad about our ordeal. She's treating me to a spa day and a shopping trip tomorrow. But I'll tell her no if you want me here. I'm not going to parlay this whole 'stuck in a mine' thing into special privileges."

"I *want* you to stay away," he said, entirely truthful. "I can't concentrate when you're around."

"How nice of you to say so."

He cupped her cheeks in his hands. "Be sure about this, sweet thing. If I do anything to hurt you, my mother will string me up by my ba—"

Libby clapped a hand over his mouth. "Watch your language, Mr. Kavanagh." She rubbed her thumb over his bottom lip. The simple caress sent fire streaking to his groin. "Are you *planning* on hurting me?"

He shifted from one foot to the other. "Of course not."

"Then relax and go with the flow. If nothing else in the last year, I've learned that's the only way to live…"

* * *

Libby took Patrick at his word about staying home the next day. She'd suffered no lasting physical effects from their unfortunate incarceration, but she *had* been tormented by dark dreams Wednesday night. She *needed* employment. But she *wanted* Patrick. Climbing into bed with him was not going to be in her best interests. The conflicting desires went around and around in her head. She woke up feeling groggy and vaguely depressed.

Maeve, however, refused to let any notion of gloom overshadow their day. When she met Libby in the lobby, she clapped her hands, practically dancing around like a child. "I'm so glad you're finally going to put your hair back to rights. I know your mother disliked that boring brown."

Libby raised her eyebrows. "Has anyone ever accused you of being overly tactful?"

Maeve chuckled, heading out to the large flagstone driveway where her silver Mercedes was parked. "I consider you family, my dear. And as your honorary aunt or stepmother or whatever you want to call me, I'm only doing my duty when I tell you that you have taken a beautiful young woman and turned her into a drudge."

Libby couldn't take offense. Maeve was absolutely too gleeful about restoring Libby's original looks. For a moment, Libby felt a surge of panic. She'd hidden behind her ill-fitting clothes and her nondescript hair color for the better part of a year. What if someone in New York recognized her?

As Maeve navigated the curvy road down the mountain, Libby took several deep breaths. She had started a new life. Did it matter if people knew who she was? *Libby* hadn't committed tax fraud.

Besides, most of the friends in her immediate social circle had melted away when the Parkhurst fortunes began to shatter. It was doubtful anyone would even want to acknowledge her. And as far as reporters were concerned, Libby Parkhurst was old news.

When Maeve found a parking spot in Silver Glen, the day of pampering began. First it was private massages, then manicures and pedicures at an upscale spa. Of course, most everything in Silver Glen was upscale. The beautiful alpine-themed town catered to the rich and famous.

An hour and a half later, once her Tahitian Sunset polish had dried, Libby admired her fingers and toes. This kind of self-indulgence had been one of the first things to go when she and her mother had been put out on the street.

It was amazing that something so simple could make a woman feel like she was ready to take on the world.

Next was the hair salon. Libby pulled a photo out of her wallet, one from her college graduation, and showed the stylist her original color. The woman was horrified. "Why would you ruin such an amazing head of hair? Never mind," she said quickly. "I don't even want to know. But before you leave here, young lady, I'm going to remind you what the good Lord intended you to look like."

Libby allowed the woman to whack three inches, since it had been ages since her last cut. Not only had Libby dyed her hair as part of her plan to go incognito, she had straightened it, as well. Little by little, the real Libby returned.

The stylist kept her promise. When it was done, Libby gazed in the mirror with tears in her eyes. Her natural hair was a curly, vibrant red that complemented her pale skin, unlike the dull brown that had washed her out and made her seem tired.

Now, the bouncy chin-length do put color in her cheeks. Parted on one side and tucked behind her ear on the other, the fun, youthful style framed her face and took years off her age.

Maeve beamed. "Beautiful. Absolutely beautiful."

Next stop was a charming boutique with an array of trendily clad mannequins in the window. Libby put her foot down. "I have money, Maeve. My first paycheck went in the bank this morning."

Patrick's mother frowned. "You nearly died in the service of a Kavanagh business. If I want to buy you a few things as a thank-you for not suing us, that is my prerogative."

Libby gaped. "You know I would never sue you. That's ridiculous."

But Maeve had already crossed the store and engaged the services of a young woman about Libby's own age. The clerk assessed Libby with a smile. "What kinds of things are we looking for today?"

Maeve shushed Libby when she tried to speak. The older woman steamrollered the conversation. "A little of everything. Casual chic. Business attire…not a suit, I think, but a little black dress. And a very dressy something for dinner…perhaps in ivory or even green if that's not too obvious with her fabulous hair."

The couture makeover became a whirlwind. Libby tried on so many garments, she lost count. When the frenzy was done, Maeve plunked down a credit card. "She'll wear the jeans and stilettos home…plus the peasant blouse. We'll take all the rest in garment bags."

Libby gave up trying to protest. In the months ahead, when she was able, she would do her best to repay Maeve. In the meantime, it was exciting to know that she would be able to accompany Patrick to New York looking her best.

Maeve declared herself exhausted when they returned to the Silver Beeches Lodge. "I'm going to see if Liam needs me," she said. "And if not, I'm headed home to put my feet up."

Libby hugged her impulsively. "Thank you, dear Maeve. I love you."

This time it was Maeve who had tears in her eyes. She took Libby's hands, her expression earnest. "Your mother was a precious woman...fragile, but precious. I still remember how proud she was when you were born. You were the light of her life. When you remember her, Libby, try not to think of the woman she became at the end, but instead, the woman she was at her best...the friend I knew so well."

Libby managed a smile. "It's no wonder your sons adore you."

Maeve waved a dismissive hand. "They think I'm a meddling pain in the ass. But then again, they know I'm always right."

Libby said her goodbyes and wandered upstairs to her room. She was determined to move to the apartment over the Silver Dollar saloon very soon. How many paychecks would it take before she could afford a rent payment? She chafed at the idea of living on Kavanagh charity, even if it was extremely luxurious and comfortable charity.

She and Maeve had lunched out before their appointments, so tonight, the only thing Libby ordered from room service was a chef salad. Often she ate downstairs in the dining room, but it had been a long, though pleasant, day. Sometimes it was nice to be alone and contemplate the future.

After her modest dinner, she packed the suitcase Maeve had loaned her. At one time, Libby had owned a wide array of expensive toiletries. Now she was accustomed to nothing more than discount-store moisturizer, an inexpensive tube of mascara and a couple of lipsticks for dressing up.

Her lace-and-silk nightgown and robe were remnants of the past. As were the several sets of bras and undies she possessed. It was one thing to sell haute couture at a resale shop. No one wanted underwear.

As she crawled into bed, she checked her phone. Patrick had messaged her earlier to let her know he would be sending a taxi to pick her up at seven o'clock tomorrow morning. They would rendezvous at the brand-new airstrip on the other end of the valley.

Patrick's brief text—and her equally brief response—was the only communication Libby had shared with him since she'd walked out of his office Wednesday afternoon. She missed him. And she had gone back and forth a dozen times about whether or not she was doing the right thing.

Their flirtatious conversation had left the status quo up in the air. What was going to happen when they got to New York?

She could tell herself it was all about finding closure… a bid for saying goodbye to her old life. And maybe trying one more time to convince Patrick she could do the job at Silver Reflections.

But she had a weak spot when it came to her fascinating boss. The possibility of sharing his bed made her shiver with anticipation. Right now, that agenda was winning.

Ten

Patrick had decided to bring in one of the standby pilots the Kavanaghs sometimes used instead of flying himself. For one thing, the deep cut in his leg was still sore as hell. And for another, he liked the idea of sitting in the back of the jet with Libby. She was no stranger to luxury travel... so it wasn't that he wanted to see her reaction when he dazzled her with sophistication and pampering.

It was far simpler than that. He wanted to spend time with her.

He arrived at the airstrip thirty minutes early. The past two nights, he hadn't slept worth a damn. He kept reliving the moment the landslide happened. The instant Libby faced one of her worst fears. Because of him. Residual guilt tied his gut in a knot.

Not that she had suffered any lasting harm. Nevertheless, the experience in the mine was unpleasant to say the least. He never should have let her go down there.

He was already on the jet when the taxi pulled up. Peeking through the small window of the plane, he saw Libby get out. The day was drizzly and cold. She was wearing a black wool coat and carried a red-and-black umbrella, her face hidden. All he could see was long legs and sexy shoes.

The pilot was already in the cockpit preparing for take-off. Patrick went to the open cabin door and stood, ready to lend a hand if Libby needed help on the wet stairs. She hovered on the tarmac as the cabdriver handed a suitcase and matching carry-on to Patrick. Then she came up the steps.

Patrick moved back. "Hand me your umbrella." He'd been wrong about the coat. It wasn't wool at all, but instead, a fashionable all-weather trench-style, presumably heavily lined to deal with the cold weather in New York. A hood, edged in faux fur, framed her face.

For some reason, he couldn't look her in the eyes…not yet. "Make yourself comfortable," he said over his shoulder. After shaking the worst of the water from the umbrella, he closed it and stored it in a small closet. Then he retracted the jet's folding steps and turned the locking mechanisms on the cabin door.

"We'll be taking off in about five minutes."

At last, he turned around. Libby stood in the center of the cabin, her purse and coat on a seat beside her.

His heart punched once in his chest. Hard. His lungs forgot how to function. "Libby?" Incredulous, he stared at her. She was wearing a long-sleeve, scoop-necked black dress with a chunky silver necklace and matching earrings. The dress was completely plain. But the slubbed-knit fabric fit her body perfectly, emphasizing every sexy curve.

Even so, the dress wasn't what made the greatest impact. Nor was it the extremely fashionable but wildly impractical high heels that made her legs seem a million miles long. The dramatic jolt wasn't even a result of her darkly lashed green eyes or her soft crimson lips. It was her hair. God, her hair…

His mouth was probably hanging open, but he couldn't help it. He cleared his throat, shoving his hands in the pocket of his suit jacket to keep from grabbing her. "Whoever talked you into changing your color back to normal is a genius. It suits you perfectly." The deep red curls with gold highlights made her skin glow. The new cut framed her face and drew attention to high cheekbones and a slightly pointed chin.

Libby shrugged, seeming both pleased by and uncomfortable with his reaction. She and her mother had been harassed by reporters for months. Looking the way she did right now, it would have been impossible for her to fade into a crowd. Hence the metamorphosis from gorgeous socialite to little brown mouse.

She nodded, her eyes shadowed. "I've been hiding for a long time. But that's over, Patrick. I'm ready to move on."

He couldn't help himself. He closed the distance between them. "You're more than the sum of your looks, Libby."

"Thank you."

He winnowed his fingers through her hair. "It's so light…and fluffy…and *red*." He lowered his voice to a rough whisper. "I want to take you right here, right now. In that big overstuffed captain's chair. You make me crazy."

She looked at him, her soft green eyes roving his face, perhaps seeking assurance of his sincerity. "I want you, too, Patrick. Perhaps I shouldn't. My life is complicated enough already. But when I'm with you, I forget about all the bad stuff."

He frowned. "I'm not sure I want to be used as an amnesiac device."

"Don't think of it that way. You're like a drug. But the good kind. One that makes me feel alive in the best possible way. When I'm with you, I'm happy. It's as simple as that."

Her explanation mollified him somewhat, but he still wasn't entirely satisfied. He wanted to kiss her, but the pilot used the intercom to notify them of imminent take-off. "This discussion isn't over," he said.

They strapped into adjacent seats and prepared to be airborne. Libby turned to look out the window. Her profile was as familiar to him now as was his own. He struggled with a hodgepodge of emotions that left him feeling out of sorts.

He liked being Libby Parkhurst's savior. In the beginning he had resented his mother's interference. But once Libby was installed at Silver Reflections, it made him feel good to know he was helping make her life easier. Now that she had acquitted herself reasonably well in the woods, there was really no reason not to let her finish out Charlise's maternity leave.

But did he honestly want Libby under his nose 24/7? The situation would be perfect fodder for his mother's wedding-obsessed machinations behind the scenes. Patrick, however, was more worried about becoming a slobbering sex-starved idiot.

He had a business to run. Silver Reflections was doing very well, but any relatively new business had to keep on its toes. He couldn't afford to let his focus be drawn away by a woman, no matter how appealing.

The flight to New York was uneventful. Patrick worked on his presentation. Libby read a novel. They spoke occasionally, but it was stilted conversation. Was he the only one feeling shaken by what might happen during the night to come?

Libby felt like a girl in a fairy tale. Except this was backward. She had already been the princess with the world at her feet. Now she was an ordinary woman trying to embrace her new life.

It didn't hurt that Maeve had spoiled her with a suitcase full of new clothes. When Libby was growing up, her mother had bought Libby an entire new wardrobe every spring and fall. The castoffs were given to charity. They were always good clothes, some of them barely worn. Libby had never thought twice about it…other than the few times she had begged to keep a favorite sweater or pair of jeans.

Such excess seemed dreadful now. The clothes she'd brought with her this weekend would have to last several years. They were quality items, well made and classic in style. Perhaps Maeve was more perceptive than Libby realized, because during their wild shopping spree, Maeve had never once suggested anything that was faddish, nothing that would be dated by the next season.

On the other hand, Libby knew it wasn't the clothing that defined her new maturity. The past year had been a trial by fire. She had struggled with the emotional loss of her father, grieved the physical loss of her mother and juggled all of that alongside the almost inexplicable loss of her own identity.

And now there was Patrick. What to do about Patrick?

He disturbed her introspection. "Do you have any current plans to see your father?"

"Will you think I'm a terrible person if I say *no*?"

His smile was gentle and encompassed an understanding that threatened her composure. "Of course not. No one can make that decision for you."

She picked at the armrest. "I've sent him the occasional note. And of course, I called him after Mother, well…you know."

"Was he able to attend the funeral?"

"No. The request to the prison would have had to come from me, and I didn't think I could handle it. I was pretty much a mess. Fortunately, my parents had actually bought plots where my father grew up in Connecticut. They even prepaid for funerals. So at least I didn't have to worry about that."

"Has he written to you?"

"Only twice. I think he's ashamed. And embarrassed. But mostly angry he got caught. My father apparently subscribed to the theory that tax fraud isn't actually a crime unless someone finds out what you've done."

"He's not alone in that view."

"Doesn't make it right."

"How long does he have to serve?"

"Seven to ten. It was a lot of money. And apparently he was not exactly repentant in front of the judge."

"Time in prison can change people. Maybe it will show him what matters."

"I suppose…" But she was dubious. Her father was accustomed to throwing his weight around. His money had made it possible for him to demand *what* he wanted *when* he wanted. She had tried to find it in her heart to have sympathy for him. But she was still too shattered about the whole experience.

Patrick leaned forward and pointed out her window. "There's the skyline."

Libby took in the familiar sight and felt a stab of grief so raw and deep it caught her off guard. Patrick didn't say a word. But he used his finger to catch a tear that rolled down her cheek, and he finally offered her a pristine handkerchief to blow her nose.

"It's not my home anymore," she said, her throat so tight she could barely speak.

Patrick slid an arm around her shoulders. "It will always be your *first* home. And at some point, the trauma of what happened will become part of your past. Not so devastating that you think of it every day."

"I hope so."

"Silver Glen is a pretty good place for a fresh start. I know you came to the mountains to heal and to get back on your feet financially. My mother would be over the moon if you decided to stay forever."

"What about you, Patrick?"

The impulsive query came from her own lips, but shocked her nevertheless. It was the kind of needy leading question an insecure woman asks. "Don't answer that," she said quickly. "I don't know why I said it."

His expression was impassive, his thoughts impossible to decipher. "I have nothing to hide. I've already told you how I feel about marriage. I get the impression you're the kind of woman who will want a permanent relationship eventually. Maybe you can find that in Silver Glen. I don't know. But in the meantime, we've come very close to a line you may not want to cross when you're no longer in fear for your life."

"Don't patronize me," she said slowly. "I mentioned the one-hotel-room thing when I was safely out of the mine and standing in your office. Did you forget about that?"

"A relationship forged under duress doesn't usually stand the test of time."

She scowled, even as the plane bumped down on the runway at LaGuardia. "For a guy who's barely thirty, you pontificate like someone's grandmother."

He sighed, his jaw tight. "Are we having our first fight?"

"No," she snapped. "That happened when you called me a *misfit*."

"So many things are clear now," he muttered, his hot gaze skating from her lips to her breasts. "It's the red hair. I could have saved myself a lot of heartache if I'd known that the woman I interviewed in the beginning was not a mouse, but instead an exotic, hotheaded spitfire."

"Patronizing *and* chauvinistic."

A deep voice interrupted their quarrel. "Um, excuse me…Mr. Kavanagh? We have to deplane now."

Libby groaned inwardly, embarrassed beyond belief. How much had the pilot overheard? Grabbing her coat and shoving her arms into the sleeves, she scooped up her purse and climbed over Patrick's legs to head for the exit. He let her go, presumably lingering to deal with their luggage.

A private limo awaited them, a uniformed driver at the ready. When Patrick climbed in to the backseat with her, she ignored him pointedly, her face still hot with mortification.

How was a woman supposed to deal with a man who was both brutally honest and ridiculously appealing? Was she seriously going to settle for a temporary fling? And what was the time limit? When Charlise came back in six months, did the affair and the job end on the same day?

Patrick took her hand. "Quit sulking."

Her temper shot up several notches. She gave him a look that should have melted the door frame. "I've changed my mind. I want my own hotel room. I need a job more than I need you."

He stroked the inside of her wrist with his thumb. "Don't be mad, my beautiful girl. We're in New York. Alone. Away from my meddling family. We can do anything we want…anything at all."

His voice threatened to mesmerize her. Deep and husky with arousal, his words had the smooth cadence of a snake charmer. She shivered inwardly. "How easy do you think I am?" Her indignation dwindled rapidly in inverse proportion to the increase in her shaky breathing and the acceleration of her rushing pulse.

Patrick lifted her wrist and kissed the back of her hand. "You're not easy at all, Libby. You're damned difficult. Every time I think I have you figured out, you surprise me all over again."

She caught the chauffeur's gaze in the rearview mirror. The man lifted an eyebrow. Libby blushed again and stared out the window. "Not now, Patrick. We're almost there."

Patrick settled back in his seat, but the enigmatic smile on his face made Libby want to kiss the smirk off his face. Fortunately for her self-control, the car pulled up in front of their destination. While Patrick swiped his credit card, Libby slid out of the vehicle, shivering when a blast of cold air flipped up the tail of her coat.

"Where's our luggage?" she asked, suddenly anxious about Maeve's nice suitcases and Libby's new clothes.

"The driver is taking them on to the Carlyle. They'll hold them for us until check-in time."

He took her arm. "C'mon. We're early, but I want to make sure they're ready for us." Ushering her through sleek revolving doors, he hurried her into the building and onto the elevator. Fortunately for Libby, the small space was crowded, meaning she didn't have to talk to Patrick at all.

On the twenty-seventh floor, they exited. An eerily perfect receptionist greeted them. Behind her in platinum letters were the words *Peabody Rushford*. Libby took off her coat, using the opportunity to look around with curiosity. It was difficult to imagine anyone from this upscale environment insisting that executives participate in one of Patrick's field experiences.

Moments later, after a hushed communication via a high-tech intercom system, they were escorted to the boardroom where Patrick would do his presentation. Every chair at the glossy conference table was situated at an exact ninety-degree angle. Crystal tumblers filled with ice water sat on folded linen napkins.

Not a single item in the room was out of place. Except Libby. She felt ill at ease. Why had she agreed to accompany Patrick? Oh, wait. Tagging along had been her idea.

She was still holding out hope that she could convince him to give her the job.

The executives trickled into the room, first one or two, and then three or four, until finally, the entire team was assembled. Eight men, four women. Plus the graying boss. She guessed his *underlings* ranged in age from early thirties to late forties. Libby was easily the youngest person in the room.

Patrick greeted each participant warmly, introducing himself with the self-deprecatory charm she had come to expect from him. He was confident and humorous, and he interacted with both men and women equally well. When everyone was seated, there were three chairs remaining at one end of the table. Libby took the middle one, leaving a buffer on either side.

She was here as an interested observer. No need to get chummy. Not now at least. The future remained to be seen. If she continued to work for Patrick—and it was possible he might decide to let her stay on—then no doubt, she would be meeting these people in April.

Honestly, it was hard to imagine any of this crew getting dirty in the woods. The women wore similar quasi uniforms. Dark formfitting blazers with matching pencil skirts and white silk blouses. Their hairstyles fell into two camps…either sophisticated chignons or sharply modern pixie cuts.

The men were equally polished. Their dark suits resembled Patrick's. Though he wore a red power tie, the executives' neckwear was more conservative. Finally, the room settled, and Patrick began his spiel.

Libby knew Patrick was smart. But seeing him operate in this environment was eye-opening. He spoke to the group as an equal…a man with experience in their world as well as the master of his own domain, Silver Reflections.

As the orientation proceeded, Libby watched the faces

around the table. One of the women and several of the men were actively engaged, frequently asking questions… demonstrating enthusiasm and anticipation. Others exhibited veiled anxiety, and some were almost hostile.

Patrick had shared with Libby that the CEO was an ex-marine…a man both hard in business and in his physical demands on himself. For him to insist that his top management people participate in Patrick's program was asking a lot. Libby wondered if anyone would bail out, even if it might mean losing their jobs.

During the official Q and A time at the end, one of the quieter women who hadn't said a word so far raised her hand. When Patrick acknowledged her, she pointed at Libby. "Does she work for you? I'd like to hear what she has to say."

Patrick gave Libby a wry glance and shrugged. "Libby?"

All eyes in the room focused on her. She cleared her throat, scrambling for the right words. She would never forgive herself if she botched this for Patrick. "Well, um…"

The woman stared at her with naked apprehension. Clearly she wanted some kind of reassurance and saw Libby as a kindred spirit.

Libby smiled. "I certainly understand if anyone in this room, male or female, has reservations about spending a night or two in the woods, particularly if your personal history doesn't include campouts and bonfires. To be honest, I was the same way. But when I came to work for Patrick, it was important for me to try this *immersion* experience. I had to prove to myself that I could step outside my comfort zone."

The woman blanched. "And how did that go?"

Libby laughed softly. "I'll be honest. There were good parts and bad." No reason to go into the mine-shaft fiasco. "On the plus side, the setting is pristine and beautiful and serene. If you haven't been much of a nature lover in the past, I think you'll be one when the weekend is over."

"And the less wonderful parts?"

Though only one woman was doing the interrogation, Libby had a strong suspicion that others around the table were hanging on Libby's comments, looking for reassurance.

"Spending the night on the ground was a challenge, even with a comfy sleeping bag and a small pad. I'm a light sleeper to start with, so I found it difficult to relax enough to sleep deeply, even though I was tired."

"Anything else?"

Libby hesitated. Patrick grinned and nodded, as if not perturbed at all by anything she might have to say. "Well," she said, "there's the issue of using the bathroom in the woods. Women are always at a disadvantage there."

A titter of laughter circled the table.

Libby continued. "But all of this is minor stuff compared to the big picture. You'll learn to rely on teamwork to get simple tasks done like meals and setting up camp and taking it down. I think you'll see your coworkers in a new light. And I promise you that you'll find skills and talents you never knew you had. Patrick is not a drill sergeant. He's a facilitator. His knowledge is formidable. You can feel entirely safe with him in charge."

For a split second, the room was silent. Patrick was no longer smiling. If anything, he looked as if someone had punched him in the stomach. What was he thinking?

The woman asking the questions breathed an audible sigh of relief. "Thank you, Libby. I feel much better about this now."

The boss nodded. "I encourage my people to ask questions. It's the only way to learn."

Now some of the men seemed chagrined. Suddenly the woman in the group who had seemed like the weakest link had earned the boss's respect. Libby was pleased that her own small contribution had helped.

After the session adjourned, most of the staff returned to their offices. The boss lingered to speak with Patrick, expressing his opinion that the orientation had gone extremely well.

Then it was time to go. Patrick and Libby retraced their steps to the lobby, both of them quiet. Libby stood on the sidewalk, huddled into her coat. "Do we split up now? And meet at the hotel later?"

Patrick pulled up her hood and tucked a stray strand of hair inside. "Is it important for you to be alone when you revisit your old building?"

She searched his face. "No. Not really. But I assumed you had other things to do."

He kissed the tip of her nose. "My business is done. I'd like to take you to lunch, and then we'll face your past together."

"I might cry."

Patrick chuckled. "I think I can handle it. C'mon, I'm starving."

Eleven

Patrick hailed a cab and helped Libby in, then ran around to the other side and joined her. Heavy clouds had rolled in. The sky overhead was gray and menacing. He gave the driver an address and sat back. "If you don't mind, Libby, I thought we would try a new place Aidan recommended. It's tucked away in the theater district, off the beaten path for tourists. He says they have the best homemade soups this side of North Carolina."

Libby smoothed the hem of her coat over her knees, unwittingly drawing attention to her legs. He had plans for those legs.

She nodded. "Sounds good, but I'm surprised. I thought men needed more than soup to consider it a meal."

"I might have forgotten to mention the gyros and turkey legs." His stomach growled on cue.

Libby laughed. "Now I get it."

"You were amazing back there," he said. "I never realized how much better these weekend trips would be if all the participants have the opportunity to calm their fears beforehand. Everything you said was perfect."

"But you've always done orientations…right?" She frowned.

"I have. Yes. But the dynamics of these high-powered firms are interesting. No one wants to appear weak in front of the boss."

"Then how was today different?"

"I think your presence at the table connected with that woman. She saw you as an ally. And perceived you to be truthful and sincere. So that gave her the courage to speak out. Truthfully, I think there were others in the room who shared some of the same anxieties. So even though they didn't *ask*, they also wanted to know what you had to say."

"I'm glad I could help."

Patrick glanced at his watch. "Now, we're officially off the clock…business concluded."

"There's a lot of the day still ahead."

He leaned over, took her chin in his hand and kissed her full on the lips. "I'm sure we can find some way to fill the time."

"I'll leave the planning up to you." Her demure answer was accompanied by a teasing smile that made him wish he could ditch the rest of the day's agenda and take her back to their room right now. Unfortunately, waiting wasn't his strong suit.

The change in her appearance still threw him off his stride. The Libby with whom he had communed out in the woods and down in the mine was spunky and cute and fun. He'd been aroused by her and interested in bedding her.

This newly revamped Libby was something else again. She made him feel like an overeager adolescent caught up in a surge of hormones that were probably killing off his brain cells in droves. His libido was louder than ever. *Take Libby. Take Libby. Man want woman.*

To disguise his increasing agitation, he pulled out his phone. With a muttered "excuse me," he pretended to check important emails. Libby was neither insulted nor overly perturbed by his distraction. She stared out the window of the cab, perhaps both pleased and yet anxious about revisiting her old stomping grounds.

That was one thing he loved about her. She wasn't jaded, even though a woman from her background certainly could be. Perhaps she had always been so fresh and open to life's surprises. Or maybe the places she and her mother had lived after being kicked out of their lavish home had taught Libby to appreciate her past.

The café where they had lunch was noisy and crowded. Patrick was glad. He wasn't in the mood for intimate conversation. His need to make love to Libby drowned out every other thought in his head.

Libby, on the other hand, chatted happily, her mood upbeat despite the fact that she was facing an emotional hurdle this afternoon.

He drank his coffee slowly, absently listening as his luncheon date conversed with the waitress about what it was like to be an understudy for an off-Broadway play. At last, the server walked away and Libby smiled at Patrick. "Sorry. I love hearing people's stories."

He raised an eyebrow. "Yet I haven't heard all of yours. What did you study in college? Who did you want to be when you grew up? How many boyfriends did you have along the way?"

A shadow flitted across her face. "I was an English major."

"Did you want to teach?"

"No. Not really. My parents wouldn't have approved."

"Too plebeian?" he asked, tongue in cheek.

Libby rolled her eyes at him. "Something like that."

"Then why the English major?"

She shrugged, her expression slightly defensive. "I loved books. It was the one area of study where I could indulge my obsession with the printed word and no one would criticize the hours I spent in the library."

"Is that what your parents did?"

Her smile was bleak this time. "They told me no man would want to marry a woman who was boring. That I should learn to entertain and decorate a house and choose fine wines and converse about politics and current events."

"Sounds like a Stepford wife."

"I suppose. It became a moot point when my father decided to defraud the government. My standing in society evaporated, not that I minded. At least not on my own account. I did feel very sorry for what it did to my mother. She never signed on for coupon clipping and shopping at discount clothing stores. My father spoiled her and pampered her, right up until the day he was carted away in handcuffs."

"That's all behind you now. Nothing but good times ahead."

He heard his own words and winced inwardly. What did *he* know about the struggles Libby faced? Even several years ago when he decided to give up his career in Chicago, it wasn't a huge risk. The Kavanagh family had deep pockets. He had started Silver Reflections with his own money, but if he had run into financial difficulties, there would have been plenty of help available to him. Never in his life had he faced the challenges that had been thrust upon Libby.

She wiped her mouth with a napkin and reapplied her lipstick. Watching her smooth on the sultry red color was an exercise in sexual frustration.

When she looked up, she caught him staring. He must have put on a good show, because she didn't appear to notice how close to the edge he was. Instead, she grimaced. "Let's go see my building before I get cold feet."

The sentence would have made sense, even if the words had been literal. The temperature outside had to have dropped at least ten degrees since they had arrived in the city.

He hailed another cab and looked at Libby. "You'll have to give the address this time."

"Of course." She nodded, her expression hard to decipher. But as they whizzed through the streets of the city, he saw her anxiety level rise.

When he took one of her hands in his, it was ice-cold. "Where are your gloves?"

"I didn't have any that matched this coat, and I wanted to look nice for your business associates."

"Oh, for God's sake, Libby. Here. Take mine." The ones in the pocket of his overcoat were old and well-worn, but they were leather, lined with cashmere. At least they would keep her warm in transit.

She barely seemed to notice his offering, but she didn't protest when he slid the gloves onto her hands. Finally, the cab stopped. "We're here," she said. For a moment, she didn't move.

"Libby? Are we going to get out?"

She looked at him blankly.

"Libby?" He kissed her nose. "C'mon, darlin'. There's no bogeyman waiting for you. Nothing but bricks and mortar."

"I know that."

Even so, when they stood on the sidewalk, she huddled against him, pretending to shelter herself from the wind. But they were shielded by the building, and the biting breeze had all but disappeared.

He put his arm around her shoulder, at a loss for how to

help her. "Which floor was yours?" he asked…anything to get her to talk.

"The penthouse. Daddy liked looking down on Central Park."

Patrick stood quietly, holding her close. "I'm here, Libby. You're not alone."

At last, she moved. He thought she meant only to walk past the impressive building, but she stopped in front of the double glass doors and, after a moment's hesitation, stepped forward to open them.

Before she could do so, a barrel-chested, white-haired man in a gray uniform with burgundy piping flung them wide. "Ms. Libby. Good God Almighty. I've been worried sick about you. I'm so sorry about your mother, baby girl. Come let me hug you."

Libby launched herself into the man's embrace and wrapped her arms around his ample waist. "Oh, Clarence. I've missed you so much."

Patrick watched in bemusement as the two old friends reconnected. He entered the lobby in deference to the cold, but hung back, unwilling to interfere with Libby's moment of closure.

At last, the old man acknowledged his presence. "Come on, Libby. Tell me about this handsome young fellow."

Libby blushed, her face alight with happiness. "That's my boss, Patrick Kavanagh. Patrick, this is Clarence Turner. He's known me since I was in diapers."

Clarence beamed. "Sweetest little gal you ever saw. And she grew up as beautiful on the inside as she was on the outside. For my sixtieth birthday, she made me a banana cream cake from scratch. Nicest thing anyone had ever done for me since my wife died."

Patrick stuck out his hand. "An honor to meet you, sir."

Clarence looked at Libby, his face troubled. "I'd take you upstairs if I could, but I think it would upset you. The new owners redid the whole place. You wouldn't recognize it."

"It doesn't matter," Libby said. "Seeing you is enough. I always thought my parents and I would give you a big, awesome gift when you retired…maybe a trip to Hawaii… or a new car. Turns out you'll be lucky to get a card and a pack of gum from me now."

She smiled and laughed when she said it, but Patrick knew it troubled her not to be able to help her old friend in any substantial way. Patrick made a mental note to follow up on the situation and see what he could do in Libby's name.

Clarence shot Patrick an assessing glance. "I thought maybe the two of you were an item," he said, not so subtly. "A man could do a lot worse than to marry Libby Parkhurst."

Before Patrick could reply, Libby jumped in. "Patrick and I are just friends. Actually, I'm working for his company temporarily. Patrick's mother and mine were good friends. Maeve Kavanagh has been helping me get back on my feet." She hugged Clarence one more time. "We have to go. But I promise to write more often. You're still at the same address?"

"Yes, indeed. They'll have to take me out of there feet-first." He looked at Patrick one more time and then back at Libby. "You're going to be okay, Libby. I never saw a girl with more grit or more light in her soul."

"Thank you for that, old friend."

When Patrick saw Libby's soft green eyes fill with tears, he decided it was time to go. "Nice to meet you, sir. I hope our paths will cross again."

Though Libby glanced over her shoulder and waved one last time as they braved the cold again, she didn't protest. Patrick had a feeling that the emotional reunion had taken more out of her than she realized.

On the sidewalk, he tipped up her chin and kissed her forehead. "How 'bout we go on the hotel and check in? I think we both could use a nap. If we're going to have a night on the town, you need your beauty sleep. And now that I think about it, I probably should get some play tickets."

They climbed into a cab and Libby took his hand. "What if we skip a play and just go out to dinner? That way we'd be back to the hotel early."

He swallowed, aware that the cabbie was perhaps listening, despite the fact that he had his radio on. "I'd like that very much." He clenched his other fist. "I want to be alone with you," he muttered.

"We could skip the nap, also."

In her eyes he saw everything he wanted and more. "I booked two rooms," he said hoarsely. "I didn't want to take advantage of you."

"I'm not weak, Patrick. I can take care of myself. And I was mad when I asked for that second room. We don't need it. I don't expect anything from you except pleasure."

"Pleasure?" His mouth was dry, his sex hard as stone. His brain had for all intents and purposes turned to mush.

She leaned into him. "Pleasure," she whispered. "You're a smart man. You'll figure it out."

Fortunately for Patrick's sanity, it was a brief cab ride. He paid the fare, aware all the while that Libby watched him.

He couldn't bear to look at her. He was too close to the edge.

At the front desk, the polite employee didn't blink an eye when Patrick canceled one of the rooms. The clerk dealt with the credit card and handed over the keys. "We've been holding your luggage, Mr. Kavanagh. I'll have it sent up immediately, along with a bottle of champagne and some canapés. Is there anything else we can do for you?"

Patrick swallowed, his hand shaking as he signed the charge slip. "No. Thank you."

He turned to Libby. "You ready to go upstairs?"

Twelve

Libby linked her hand in his. "I'm ready." She was under no illusions. If she hadn't pushed the issue, Patrick might well have ignored the spark of attraction between them. He was wary of hurting Libby, and he had a healthy respect for his mother's good opinion.

Libby rested her head on his shoulder. They were alone in the elegant elevator. "No one will know about this but you and me, Patrick. You're not interested in a relationship, and I'm not, either. But that doesn't mean we can't enjoy each other's company."

His grip tightened on her hand when the elevator dinged. The bellman had come up on the service elevator, so there was a busy moment as Patrick opened the door and the luggage was situated. A second bellman came on the heels of the first, this one pushing a cart covered in white linen. The silver ice bucket chilled a bottle of bubbly. An offering of fancy cheese spreads and toast fingers resided on china dishes, along with strawberries and cream.

Once the efficient Carlyle employees disappeared, tips in hand, Patrick leaned against the door. "May I offer you a strawberry...or a glass of champagne?"

Libby nodded, her heart in her throat. "The latter please." She was accustomed to drinking fine champagne, but it had been a very long time. When Patrick handed her a crystal flute, she tipped it back and drank recklessly. The bubbly liquid was crisp and flavorful.

Patrick followed suit, although he sipped his drink slowly, eyeing her over the rim. "Have I told you how sexy you look in that dress?"

She was crestfallen. "I thought it was suitably professional."

"It *is* suitable," he said. "And professional. But the woman inside makes it something else entirely."

"Like what?" She held out her glass for a refill. Her knees were shaky. Was she going to chicken out now? She couldn't remember the last time she had experienced such genuine, shivery, sexual desire.

Patrick filled her flute a second time. But before he handed it to her, he took a sip...exactly where her lipstick had left a faint stain. "Tastes amazing," he said.

She kicked off her heels and curled her toes against the exquisite Oriental rug. Ordinarily, she hated panty hose with a passion, but the weather today had been a bit much for bare legs. There was no good way for a man to remove them...romantically speaking.

"Will you excuse me for a moment?" she asked, setting down her half-empty glass.

"Of course."

In the opulent bathroom, she covered her hot red cheeks with cold hands. She was going to have sex with Patrick Kavanagh. Casually. Temporarily.

Good girls didn't do such things. But then again, she'd

been a good girl for much of her life, and look where it had gotten her.

Rapidly, she stripped off her panty hose and stuffed them in a drawer of the vanity. She fluffed her hair and then held a damp cloth to her cheeks, trying to tame the wild color that was a dead giveaway as to her state of mind.

When she could linger no longer, she returned to the sitting room. It was lovely, with pale green and ecru walls. Antique French furnishings lent an air of romance. Patrick had even lit a candle, though it was the middle of the day.

He came to her and slid his hands beneath her hair, his smile holding the tiniest hint of male satisfaction. "Are you shy, Libby love?"

"Maybe. A little bit. I'm suddenly feeling rather unsophisticated."

"I don't want sophistication. I don't need it." His eyes had gone all dark and serious, the blue-gray irises like stormy lakes.

She curled her fingers around his wrists, not to push him away, but to hold on to something steady as her emotions cartwheeled. "What *do* you want and need, Patrick?"

He scooped her into his arms. "You, Libby. Only you."

On the way to the bedroom, he stopped to pick up the heavy pillar candle. But he couldn't manage it and Libby, too. Not without tumbling them all to the floor in a pile of hot wax. The image made her smile.

Patrick scowled. "Are you laughing at me?"

She looped an arm around his neck. "I wouldn't dare. I was merely contemplating all the ways I could use hot wax to drive you wild."

He stumbled and nearly lost his balance. His jaw dropped. Not much. But enough to let Libby know her little comment had left him gobsmacked. It felt good to have the upper hand, even if for only a moment.

The bedroom was something out of a fantasy…soft lavender sheets, fresh violets in a crystal vase…a Louis XIV chaise longue upholstered in sunshine-yellow and aubergine brocade. The ivory damask duvet had already been folded back. All Patrick had to do was gently drop Libby on the bed.

"Don't move," he said. "I'm going back for the ambience."

She barely had time to blink before he returned. He put the candle on the ornate dresser, a safe distance away. Then he closed the drapes, shutting out the gray afternoon light.

Libby propped her elbows behind her. "I thought you wanted a nap," she teased.

"Later," he said.

His jaw was tight, his cheekbones flushed. As he walked slowly toward the bed, he stripped off his tie and shirt and jacket with an economy of motion that was both intense and arousing…as if he couldn't bear to waste a single second. Libby's breath caught the first time she saw his bare chest.

"Nice show," she croaked. Her throat was dry, but the champagne was in the other room.

When he stood beside the bed, he unbuckled his belt and slid it free. Next went the shoes and socks. When he was down to his pants and nothing else, he crooked a finger. "Come here and turn around."

Trembling all over, she got up on her knees and presented her back to him. His fingertips found the top of her zipper and lowered it slowly. He cursed.

She looked over her shoulder, alarmed. "What's wrong?"

His expression was equal parts torment and lust. "You're too young. Too vulnerable. Too beautifully innocent."

"I'm not *entirely* innocent."

"I'm not talking about that kind of innocence," he said gruffly, stroking the length of her spine. He unfastened her bra, sliding his arms around her and palming her achy breasts. "It's *you*. All these things have tried to defeat you and yet you're still like a rosy-eyed child. As if nothing bad could ever happen."

She took one of his hands and raised it to her lips. "I'm only young in calendar years, Patrick. Life gave me an old soul, whether I wanted it or not. Now, quit agonizing over this and come to bed."

Patrick knew he was a lucky man. At this point in his life, he possessed most everything he'd ever wanted. But he had never wanted anything or anyone the way he wanted Libby Parkhurst. He wanted to be her knight, her protector, her one and only lover. The intensity of the desire overwhelmed him and left a hollow feeling in his chest. Because to have Libby in his life on a permanent basis would mean changes he wasn't prepared to make.

He wasn't in love with her. This was about sex. Nothing more.

He helped her out of the black dress. Underneath it, her bra and panties were pink lace. He'd never particularly been a fan of pink. But on her, it was perfect.

When she was completely naked, he sucked in a breath. "Get under the covers," he said gruffly. "Before you freeze."

He wondered if she saw through his equivocation. The room was plenty warm. But he needed a moment to collect himself. Turning away from the bed, he stripped off his pants and briefs. His erection could have hammered nails. He ached, almost bent over with the need to thrust inside her and find peace. When Libby flicked off the only remaining lamp, he turned around.

In the light from the single candle, her hair glowed like a nimbus around a naughty angel.

She curled on her side, the covers tucked to her chin. "I'm feeling nervous," she said quietly.

Did the woman have no filters? No emotional armor? "I'm feeling a bit shaky myself," he admitted.

Her eyes widened when she spotted the physical evidence of his excitement for the first time. "Really? 'Cause from over here it seems like you're good to go."

Her droll humor made him laugh. He flipped back the covers and joined her, his legs tangling with ones that were softer and more slender. "You have no concept of how much I want to make love to you."

"Why, Patrick? Why me?"

"Why not you?" He teased the nearest nipple, watching in fascination as it budded tightly.

"That's not an answer." She cried out when he bent to suckle her breast. But she must have meant for him to continue, because she clutched his head to her chest, her fingers twined in his hair.

She smelled like wildflowers and summer love affairs. In the midst of winter, she brought warmth and sunshine into this room, this bed.

He kissed her roughly. "Not everything in life can be explained, Libby."

Her arms wrapped around his neck, threatening to choke him. "Try."

"You give me something no one else ever has," he admitted quietly. "When I'm with you, everything seems right."

He saw in her eyes the recognition of his honesty. It wasn't something he planned. In fact, he felt damned naked in more ways than one. But if he couldn't give her forever, at least he could give her this.

"Make love to me, Patrick."

It was all he needed to hear and more. Later there would

be time for drawn-out foreplay and fancy moves. But at the moment, all he could think about was being inside her.

Reaching for the condoms he had dropped on the nightstand, he sheathed himself matter-of-factly, trying not to notice the way Libby's gaze followed his every motion. "Now, my Libby. Now."

He eased on top of her, careful to shield her from his entire weight. For a moment, he couldn't move. He was hard against her thigh, shuddering with the need to take and take and take.

Libby reached up and cradled his face in her hands. "I want you, too, Patrick."

"You wouldn't lie about not being a virgin...would you?"

Her eyes darkened with an emotion he didn't understand. "I don't lie about *anything*."

That was the problem. Few people in life were as transparent as Libby. If he hurt her, either physically or emotionally, he would know it. Immediately. Was he prepared for that responsibility? The first one, yes...no question. But the second?

Slowly, he eased inside her, pressing all the way until he could go no farther. Her sex was warm and tight. Yellow spots danced behind his eyelids. Every muscle in his body was tense.

Libby curled her legs around his waist, unwittingly driving him deeper still. "This is nice," she said, catching her breath.

"Nice?" He clenched his teeth. He was damned if he would come like a teenage boy—all flash and no substance.

Libby squeezed him inwardly, her mouth tipped up in a tiny smile that told him she enjoyed flexing her newfound power. "I give you high marks for the opening sequence. Very impressive delivery. Appealing package."

He choked out a laugh. "Haven't you ever heard of calling a spade a spade? You can refer to it as a co—"

She clapped a hand over his mouth with a move that was beginning to seem familiar. "No I can't."

"Where did you say you went to school?"

"Catholic everything. My parents were Protestant, but they liked the idea of surrounding their baby girl with nuns."

"Can we please not talk about nuns right now? It's throwing me off my game."

She nipped his chin with sharp teeth. "Proceed. You're doing very well so far."

When he flexed his hips, he managed to erase the smile from her face. "How about now?"

Libby tipped back her head and sighed, arching into his thrust. "Don't ever stop. What time is checkout tomorrow?"

The random conversation confounded him. As a rule, his bed partners were not so chatty. "Eleven. Twelve. Hell, I don't know. Why?"

Green eyes, hazy and unfocused, gazed up at him. "I want to calculate how many more times we can do this before we have to go home."

Libby was in deep trouble. She'd been lying to herself so well, she didn't even see the cliff ahead. And now she was about to tumble into disaster. Again.

At sixteen there had been some excuse. Not so much in her current situation.

Patrick was big and warm and solid, and that wasn't even taking into consideration the body part currently stroking her so intimately. He surrounded her, filled her, possessed her. The smell of his skin, the silky touch of his hair against her breasts. She could barely breathe from wanting him.

"Hush now, darlin'," he groaned, his Southern accent more pronounced as he ground his hips against hers. When he zeroed in on a certain spot, she cried out, her orgasm taking her by surprise.

The flash of climax was intense and prolonged, wave after wave of pleasure that left her lax and helpless in his embrace. But Patrick was lost, as well. His muffled shout against her neck was accompanied by fierce, frantic thrusts that culminated in his wild release.

When the storm passed, the room was silent but for their harsh breathing.

Coming back to New York had triggered an avalanche of feelings. And not only about her father's fall from grace. There was that other business, as well. The thing that still shamed her and made her question her judgment about men. She had never wanted to be so vulnerable again. But Patrick wouldn't hurt her, would he? At least not the way she'd been hurt before.

Thirteen

Libby was having the most wonderful dream. She was floating in the ocean, the sun beaming down in gentle benediction. The temperature was exactly right. A warm blanket cocooned her as the breeze ruffled her hair.

Some sound far in the distance brought her awake with a jerk. Every cell in her body froze in stunned disbelief. Patrick Kavanagh lay half on top of her, his regular breathing steady and deep.

Holy Hannah. What had she done? Other than make it perfectly clear to Patrick that she was ready for dalliance with no expectation of anything more lasting than a weekend fling…

She eased out from under her lover, wincing when he muttered and frowned in his sleep. Fortunately, he settled back into slumber. He wasn't kidding about the nap. On the other hand, he probably needed it. The preceding week hadn't been a walk in the park. Maybe Patrick had experienced the same disturbing nightmares she had.

Caves with endless tunnels. Suffocating darkness. Musty air. Crypts and death. That's what came from having a too-vivid imagination.

Tiptoeing around the bed, she made her way into the other room and found her carry-on with her toiletry bag. Since she was naked as a baby at the moment, it also seemed prudent to locate her gown and robe. Patrick didn't stir when she quietly opened the bathroom door.

Once she was safely on the other side, she exhaled shakily. Nothing in the course of her admittedly limited sexual experience—much of it negative—had prepared her for Patrick's lovemaking. He was thorough. And intense. And enthusiastic. And generous. Did she mention generous? She'd lost track of her own orgasms. The man was a freaking genius in the bedroom. Who knew?

She wrapped a towel around her hair to keep it dry, and took an abbreviated shower. The thought of getting caught in the act was too terrifying to contemplate. The man had seen her naked. But that didn't mean a woman didn't like her privacy.

When she was clean and dry, she put on her silky nightwear. The soft ivory gown and robe were old, but still stylish and comfy. The fact that they were very thin gave her pause, but it was better than being nude.

Her hair did well with nothing more than a good brushing. Now all she had to do was pretend to be blasé, make her way through a fancy dinner and convince Patrick to sleep on the sofa.

She needed to put some distance between them. A barricade against doing something stupid. He'd already told her that marriage wasn't in the cards for him. Which meant this relationship was going nowhere.

If she let herself share his bed again, all bets were off. She might end up begging, and that would be the final indignity. He'd already called her a misfit once. She was sure as heck not going to let him pity her for crushing on him like a teenage girl.

She sat on the edge of the bathtub for ten minutes, trying to decide how to stage her return to the bedroom. In the end, Patrick took the matter out of her hands. He jerked open the door without ceremony and sighed—apparently in relief—when he saw her.

"I didn't know where you were," he complained.

The man was stark naked, his body a work of art. His *penis*—she could whisper that word in the privacy of her own head—hovered at half-mast, but was rapidly rising to attention. And apparently, the man had no modesty at all, because he stood there in the doorway, hands on hips, and glared at her. Not seeming at all concerned with his nudity. His spectacular, mouthwatering nudity.

"Where would I go?" she asked, trying not to look below his waist.

He ignored the question and strode toward her, dwarfing the generous dimensions of the bathroom. "I fail to see why you're wearing clothes. Aren't you the one who was doing mathematical calculations about potential episodes of sexual activity per hour?"

"That wasn't me," she lied, leaning back as his *stuff* practically whacked her in the nose.

His good humor returned. Without warning, he scooped her into his arms. "For future reference, no pj's unless I say so. And now that I think about it, no pj's at all."

Her cheek rested over the reassuring *thump-thump* of his heart. "These aren't pajamas. It's a peignoir set."

"I don't care if it's Queen Elizabeth's royal dressing gown. Ditch it, my love. Now."

He set her on her feet and, without further ado, lifted the two filmy layers over her head, ignoring her sputtering protests. "Patrick!"

He tossed the offending garments aside and ran his

hands from her neck to her shoulders, to her breasts, and all the way down to her bottom. "God, you're beautiful," he muttered.

"Oh, Patrick."

"Oh, Patrick." He mocked her gently. "Is that 'Oh, Patrick, I want to have sex with you again' or 'Oh, Patrick, you're the best lover I've ever had'?"

She caught her bottom lip with her teeth, torn between honesty and the need to keep his ego in check. "Well, both. But to be fair, you're only number two, so there's still room for comparison down the road."

His gaze sharpened. "Only number two?"

"I'm barely twenty-three."

"Yes, but a lot of girls are sexually active at sixteen."

"Not in my family. You do remember the nuns, right?"

"There you go again. Mentioning nuns at inappropriate moments. For the record, I knew one or two good little Catholic girls who taught me a lot about life. And sex."

Her eyes rounded. "Well, not me."

He thumbed her nipples, sending heat streaking all the way down to the damp juncture between her thighs. "You were amazing, Libby. Who taught you that thing you did there at the end?"

She shrugged demurely. "I read books."

"I see."

"You don't believe me?"

"You're awfully talented for a relative beginner."

The compliment was unexpected. "That's sweet of you to say."

"You want to tell me about number one?" Patrick seemed troubled, though she couldn't understand why.

She didn't. Not at all. The memory made her wince. "Maybe another time."

"Fair enough." He tipped his head and nibbled the side of her neck. "This will be slower, I promise."

She shuddered, her hands fisting at her sides. "I had no complaints."

Again, he scooped her into his arms, though this time he sat on the edge of the bed and turned her across his knees. "Do you have any spanking fantasies?"

She looked at him over her shoulder. "I can't say that I do, but feel free to test the hypothesis."

The sharp smack on her butt shocked her, even as the heat from his hand radiated throughout her pelvis. "That hurt, Patrick."

He chuckled. "Isn't that the point?"

The truth was, there was more to the sharp-edged play than hurt, but she didn't want to give him any ideas. She wriggled off his lap and knelt on the floor, resting her elbows on his bare knees and linking her hands underneath her chin. "I'll bet you know all sorts of kinky stuff, don't you?"

He grabbed handfuls of her hair and tugged gently. "Like the scenario where the desert sheikh takes the powerless English woman captive."

"I'm not English," she pointed out.

Patrick smiled tightly, sending a frisson of feminine apprehension down her spine. "We'll improvise. For the moment, let's see how you do on the oral exam. If you don't object, how about getting a washcloth and cleaning me up?"

"You mean so I can…?" Her voice trailed off. His erection bobbed in front of her. "Um, sure." She scuttled to the bathroom, painfully aware of his gaze following her progress. When she returned, he had leaned back on both hands. He didn't say a word.

But his challenging gaze tested her mettle. The balance of power was already unequal. He saw her as naive. Susceptible to being charmed by a man of experience. Though any and all of that might be true, she was determined to knock him off his feet.

Feigning confidence she did not possess, she sat at his hip and ran the washcloth over his intimate flesh, squeezing lightly. She smiled inwardly when he gasped, even though he tried to pretend it was a cough. "Too hard?" she asked, her expression guileless.

"No." Sweat beaded his forehead.

She continued to do her job, around and around, up and down. When she was finished, his flesh had turned to stone, and his chest rose and fell with every rapid breath.

Dropping the wet cloth on the floor, she bent, placed a hand on each of his thighs and took him in her mouth.

Patrick was pretty sure he had died and gone to heaven. He'd had blow jobs before. But none like this. His skin tightened all over his body. Libby's mouth was in turns delicate and firm. He couldn't predict her next move, and the uncertainty ratcheted up his arousal exponentially. He had promised her slow this time around, but already, he was at the breaking point. "Enough," he said, the word hoarse.

She looked up at him, her wide-eyed innocence no doubt damning him eternally for the lustful thoughts that turned him inside out. Putting his hands under her arms, he dragged her up onto the bed and kissed her recklessly. "Tell me what you want, Libby."

"I've never been on top."

Sweet holy hell. He swallowed hard. "Is that a request?"

She shrugged. "If you don't mind."

He took care of protection and moved onto his back. "You're in charge," he said, wondering if it were really true. He would hold out as long as he could, but the odds were iffy.

Libby seemed pleased by his gruff words. "I don't feel

very graceful," she complained as she attempted to mount the apparatus.

"The view from this side isn't bad."

When she slid down onto him without warning, he said a word that made her frown. "That's what we're doing, but you don't have to call it that."

She leaned forward, curling her fingertips into the depressions above his collarbone. "Don't you like this position?"

No one could be that naive. He gripped her firm ass and pulled her against him more firmly. "I've got your number now, Libby. You think you can drive me insane. But that's a two-edged sword. Wait until later when I tie your wrists to the bedposts and tickle you with a feather. You won't be so smug then, now will you?"

Her mouth formed a small perfect O. Her eyes widened. "Isn't that kind of advanced? We haven't known each other all that long. I think we should take things slowly…you know, get comfortable with each other before we branch out."

"I'm pretty damn comfortable right now." He put his hands under her breasts and bounced them experimentally. "These are nice."

She flushed. "Why are men so obsessed with boobs?"

"Maybe because we don't have any. I don't know. But you have to admit, they're beautiful."

"Now you've made me all weepy." Suppressing a smile, she leaned down and rested her forehead against his. "I didn't know it would be like this with you."

"Like what?"

"So easy. But so scary."

"I scare you?" He lifted her and eased her back down, making both of them gasp.

Without warning, she went for the dismount, nearly unmanning him in the process. She bounced off the bed and stood there, arms flung wide, her expression agitated. "You're ruining me for other men. I won't be able to find a husband after this."

He frowned. "I thought you were concentrating on re-building your life. That you didn't want a husband."

"Not today. Or tomorrow. But someday." She shook her head. "Now every guy I go to bed with is going to have to measure up to *that*." She pointed at his erection, seeming aggrieved by its very existence.

"You're overreacting. My co—" He stopped short. "My male *appendage* is perfectly normal," he said. "And people have casual sex all the time. Once we leave this hotel, it won't seem like such a big deal."

She folded her arms around her waist, apparently forgetting that she was bare-ass naked. "You know this from experience?"

"I have more than you, apparently. So, yes. And PS—it's bad form to walk out in the middle of the performance."

"I'm sorry." But she stood there so long he began to be afraid that she was actually going to call a halt to their madness.

He sat up and held out a hand. "Come back to bed, Libby. Please."

Her small smile loosened the knot in his stomach. "Well, if you ask that nicely…"

When he could reach her hand, he tugged, toppling her off balance and happily onto his lap. Libby sputtered and squirmed and protested until he flipped her and reversed their positions. Staring down at her, he felt something break apart and reform…a distinct seismic shift in his consciousness. Fortunately, he was good at ignoring extraneous details in the middle of serious business.

"Tell me you want me," he demanded.

"I want you."

"That wasn't convincing."

She linked her hands at the small of his back. "Patrick Kavanagh...I'll go mad with lust if you don't take me... right now."

"That's better." He shifted his weight and slid inside her, relishing the tight fit, the warm, wet friction. This was rapidly becoming an addiction, but he couldn't find it in his heart to care. His brain wasn't in the driver's seat. "I want you, too," he said, though she hadn't asked.

Libby's expressive eyes were closed, leaving him awash in doubt. What was she thinking? In the end, it didn't matter. His gut instincts took over, hammering home the message that she was the woman he needed. At least for now.

He felt the inner flutters that signaled her release. At last, he gave himself permission to finish recklessly, selfishly. Again and again, he thrust. Scrambling for a pinnacle just out of reach. When the end came, it was bittersweet. Because he realized one mind-numbing fact.

Libby Parkhurst had burrowed her way beneath his guard. And maybe into his heart.

Fourteen

"Hurry up, woman. We have dinner reservations in forty-five minutes."

Libby laughed, feeling happier than she had in a very long time. "I'll be ready in five." She leaned toward the mirror and touched up her eyeliner, then added a dash of smoky shadow.

After asking her preferences earlier in the day, Patrick had made reservations at an exclusive French restaurant high atop a Manhattan skyscraper. The evening promised to be magical.

She resisted the urge to pirouette in front of the mirror. The dress Maeve had bought for her was sexy and sophisticated and exceedingly feminine. The fabric was black lace over a gold satin underlay. The skirt ended modestly just at the knee, but the back dipped to the base of her spine.

Patrick rested his hands on her shoulders and kissed the nape of her neck, his hot gaze meeting hers in the mirror. "We could skip dinner," he said.

He was dressed in an expensive, conservative dark suit. The look in his eyes, however, was anything but ordinary.

She put her hand over one of his. "We need to keep up our strength. And besides, it would be a shame to waste all this sartorial splendor on room service."

"I could live with the disappointment," he muttered. He lifted the hem of her dress and stroked her thigh. "You can't go bare legged. It's cold outside."

"I thought you would be a fan of easy access."

"Maybe in July. But not tonight. I care about you too much to see you turn into a Popsicle."

Despite her distaste for the hosiery, she knew he was right. With that one adjustment to her wardrobe, she was ready. At least her black coat was fairly dressy. At one time she had owned an entire collection of high-end faux furs. But those were long gone.

Their cab was waiting when they got down to the lobby. It was dark now, and the wind that funneled between the buildings took her breath away as they stepped outside. Patrick didn't have to say, "I told you so." At least her legs had a layer of protection from the elements.

On the way, he played with the inside of her knee. "We could stay another night," he said.

The words were casual, but they stopped her heart. Because she wanted so very badly to say yes, she did the opposite. Too risky. She was letting him too close. "I don't think so," she said. "Your sister-in-law Zoe offered to help me move to Dylan's apartment Sunday afternoon, maybe find a few pillows and pictures to spruce it up. You probably remember she did a stint as a vagabond for a couple of years, so she has a good eye for a bargain."

"I see. We'll go back, then."

Had she wanted him to talk her into staying? Was she hurt that he dropped the idea so easily?

She didn't want to answer those questions, not even to herself.

They made it to the restaurant with ten minutes to spare. An obsequious maître d' seated them near the floor-to-ceiling windows at a table overlooking the city. Patrick tipped the man unobtrusively and pulled out Libby's chair.

"Does this suit your fancy?"

"Perfect," she sighed. The restaurant was new. And crowded. Discreet music filtered from hidden speakers overhead. Their fellow diners—men and women alike—dazzled in stunning couture clothing. Expensive accessories. Flashy jewelry. At one time, this had been Libby's life.

Patrick touched her hand across the table. "You okay?"

She shook off the moment of melancholy. "Yes. More than okay."

Another puffed-up employee, this one their waiter, appeared at the table. "Would Monsieur like to order for the lady?"

Patrick shook his head, smiling. "I don't think so."

Libby picked up her menu, and in flawless French ordered her favorite dish of scallops and prawns in cream sauce. The man had the decency to look chagrined before he turned to Patrick. "And you, sir?"

"I won't embarrass myself in front of the lady. Please bring me a filet, medium, and the asparagus in lemon butter."

"My pleasure."

When they were alone again, Libby grinned. "You set him straight, but so very nicely."

"The owners probably taught him that spiel. It's not his fault."

Libby gazed out the window, soaking in the vista of the city she considered home. "I don't think I'll stay in Silver Glen after this summer," she said impulsively. It would be impossibly difficult to be around the man who didn't want marriage and forever.

Patrick, caught in the act of sipping his wine, went still, his glass hovering in midair. "Oh? Why not?"

The reality was too painful, so she fed him a lesser truth. "I need to be independent. If I lean on your mom or even the Kavanaghs in general, I won't know if I really have the guts to rebuild my life. Here in New York, at least everything is familiar. I know the turf...and I have contacts...maybe even friends if I can figure out which ones still care about me now that my bank account is empty."

"So you don't see yourself becoming part of a place like Silver Glen?" His expression was curiously blank.

"I think we've established that I'm not much of a country girl. The concrete jungle is more my speed. I know which deli has the best pastrami, and I can tell you the operating hours of the Met and Natural History. I memorized the subway system by the time I was fourteen. I've seen the Rockettes dance every December since I was three years old...well, except for this past one. New York is home to me."

"I see."

His gaze was odd, turbulent. Did he think she was somehow insulting his beloved hometown?

"Don't get me wrong," she said hurriedly. "North Carolina is incredibly beautiful. And I'm happy to be living there for the moment. But when I think about the future, I can't see myself in Silver Glen."

In the heavy silence that followed her pronouncement the waiter returned, bearing their meals. The food was amazing, the presentation exceptional. But the evening had fallen flat.

She was honestly mystified. Patrick should be glad she wasn't going to hang around. He was the one with the matchmaking mother. And he'd made no secret of the fact that he was not ever going to get married.

For Libby's part, it made sense to decide from the beginning that she and Patrick were nothing more than a blip on the radar. She had suffered enough trauma in her life during the past year, without adding a broken heart to the mix.

Falling in love with Patrick Kavanagh would be the easiest thing in the world. Maybe she was partway there already. But she wasn't a fool. People didn't change. Her father hadn't. Her mother hadn't. And in the end, their inability to be the people they could have been desperately hurt their only daughter more than they could have imagined.

Still, Libby was tormented by one simple question. She knew she wouldn't be satisfied until she knew the answer.

Over dessert, she took a chance. "Patrick…"

"Hmm?" Distracted, he was dealing with the credit card and the check for their meal.

"May I ask you a personal question?"

He lifted an eyebrow, his sexy smile lethal. "I think we've reached that point, don't you?"

Maybe they had, and maybe they hadn't. But she risked it even so. "I know what happened to you when you were in high school. And I get that it was deeply painful and upsetting. But why have you decided that marriage is not for you?"

For a moment, he froze. She was certain he was going to tell her to go to hell. But then his shoulders relaxed and he sat back in his chair. "It's pretty simple really."

"Okay. Tell me."

"I've already done it. And messed it up. I choose not to take it so lightly again."

"I'm confused."

He fidgeted with his bow tie, his tanned fingers dark against the pristine white of his shirt. "Five of my brothers have gotten married so far. They've each stood in front of

God and family and made a solemn vow to one particular woman. To love and to cherish…till death do us part…all that stuff…"

"And you don't want to do that?"

"I'm telling you," he said, his voice rising slightly. "I already did it. But I cheapened the meaning of marriage. I bound myself to a woman, a girl really, whom I didn't love. And I knew I didn't love her even while I was repeating the vows."

"But you weren't an adult…and you were doing what was expected of you."

"Doesn't matter. The point is, I had my chance, and I made light of a moment that's supposed to be sacred. So I'm not going to take another woman in front of the altar knowing that I've already betrayed her before we ever start."

It made a weird sort of sense.

Poor Patrick…chained by the strength of his own regrets to life as a bachelor. And poor Libby…on the brink of falling for a man who didn't want anything she had to offer in the relationship department. It might have been funny if it hadn't been so wistfully sad.

Over one last cup of coffee, they sat in silence. Her question and his answer had driven an invisible wedge between them. She played with the silver demitasse spoon, watching the blinking lights far below…the traffic that never ceased. The Empire State Building off to her left was lit up, but the colors puzzled her. "I wonder why they went for pink and white this weekend," she murmured.

Patrick leaned forward. "Seriously? Tomorrow is Valentine's Day, Libby."

"Oh. Well, this is awkward."

"Why? Because you don't know what day it is?"

She lifted her chin. "No. Because you and I are the last two people who should be having a romantic dinner."

"Humans are good at pretense." The tinge of bitterness was unlike him.

But since her Cinderella experience was winding down, she chose to ignore his mood. She reached for his hand. "I don't want to fight with you, Patrick." She rubbed her thumb across the back of his hand. "Let's go back to the hotel. Please."

Patrick was not accustomed to self-doubt. He made decisions and followed through. He was mentally, physically and emotionally strong. People respected him…admired his integrity.

Then why did he feel as if he were failing Libby on every level?

He was so rattled by his jumbled thoughts that he forgot to call a cab before they got down to the street. "Stay inside a minute," he said.

But Libby had already gone on ahead, calling out to him with excitement in her voice. "Come look, Patrick. It's snowing…"

He followed her and pulled up short when the scene slammed into him with all the force of a freight train. Libby stood in the glow of a streetlight, arms upraised, her face tipped toward the sky. She was laughing, her features radiant. The sheltered heiress who had lost everything and been forced by harsh circumstances to grow up in a hurry, still had more joie de vivre in her little finger than Patrick could muster at the moment.

She had made love to him…openly, generously. Never once holding back or trying to protect herself from his *rules* for relationships. Even knowing that he was an emotionally locked-up bastard, she gave him everything. Her sweetness…her enthusiasm…her amazing body.

He should be kneeling at her feet and begging her forgiveness. Instead, he was going to commit the unforgivable sin. He was going to let her go.

As the snowfall grew heavier and the wind stilled, the whole world became hushed. Although he was miles from home, this particular gift of winter was the same everywhere. People stopped. Time stopped. Quiet descended. The swirl of white was an experience linked to childhood. Simple joy. Breathtaking wonder.

When he finally managed to hail a cab, he and Libby were coated in white. Strands of damp hair clung to her forehead, and her cheeks were pink. She laughed at him when he tried to brush the melting flakes from her shoulders. "Leave it," she said. "We'll be home soon."

He knew it was a slip of the tongue. A hotel, however lovely, was not home. But he was almost certain that Libby possessed a talent he lacked…the ability to make a real home with nothing more than her presence and her giving heart.

The trip from the cab to their suite seemed inordinately long. He shook, not from the cold, but from an amalgam of fear and desperation. This was it, most likely. His last chance to be with her intimately. His last opportunity to memorize the curve of her breasts, the softness of her bottom pressed to his pelvis as they curled together in sleep.

Libby's mood had segued from delight to quiet introspection. Perhaps she had picked up on the chaos inside him. But no matter the reason, she gave him space. Made no requests. He almost wanted her to demand something from him. To beg him to change. To plead with him to make an exception for her.

Libby, however, treated him like a grown man. She respected his choices, even as she made plans to go her own way. It was the most painful "letting go" he could have imagined.

As he fumbled with the key to their door, Libby slipped

her arm through his and leaned her head on his shoulder. "I think that last glass of wine was one too many," she murmured.

The door opened, and he scooted her through, backing her against it when it closed. His hands clenched her shoulders. His forehead rested against hers. "I need you." He meant to say more than that, but she understood.

She smiled at him as she unbuttoned her coat. "I know, Patrick. And it's okay, I promise. I won't ask for more than you're willing to give." She tossed the coat aside. "But we have tonight."

Fifteen

He undressed her reverently, as if she were a long-awaited Christmas gift. Either Libby was very tired, or she understood his need to be gentle in this moment, because there was no mad stripping of clothes, no sex-crazed fumbling to get naked. With her head bowed, she submitted to his hands, even when those hands trembled and even when he cursed a stuck zipper.

At last, she was nude. He lifted her in his arms and carried her a few steps to the settee. Depositing her carefully, he stepped back and removed his own clothing. She watched him drowsily, her green eyes glowing with pleasure.

Her gaze was almost tactile on his bare skin. At last, it was done. He held out a hand. "Come with me."

That she obeyed instantly messed with his head. Was she trying to win him over? Or was she humoring a slightly deranged man who temporarily held her captive?

Did it matter?

As soon as she stood up, he recognized the possibilities in the elegant piece of furniture. "How do you feel about playacting the emperor and the concubine?"

"On someone else's furniture?" She was scandalized. "Not without something to protect it."

"Don't move." He raced to the bedroom and grabbed the blanket off the foot of the bed, along with a strip of condoms. When he returned, Libby had taken him at his word.

She stood, arms at her sides, and stared from him to the settee and back again. "I never took gymnastics classes. So don't get any kinky ideas."

"Kinky ideas are the best," he said. Teasing her was almost as much fun as making love to her. She sputtered and blushed and scowled adorably. Giving her a moment to get used to the idea, he flipped the thick duvet out and over the settee and sat down, palms flat on his thighs. "I'm ready."

Libby tilted her head to one side and pursed her lips. "Clearly."

"Well, come on."

"And do what?"

"Sit on my lap."

He watched as she assessed every possible permutation of that suggestion.

"Umm…"

"Don't be a chicken. You're a fearless woman who survived a night in the mine. Surely you're not afraid of a little role-playing."

"I'm not afraid of anything," she said firmly.

"I know it. And now you know it, too."

The look on her face was priceless. Libby had changed. She had grown. She was no longer the same woman who had professed timidity during her job interview.

"I don't know what to say. Thank you, Patrick."

He tucked his hands behind his head. "Don't thank me. You're the woman who has been slaying dragons."

She inhaled, making her breasts rise and fall in a way that would turn any man's brain to mush. "Okay, then…"

"Wait. Stop." He'd forgotten the protection. But, within seconds, he was sheathed and ready to go. "Come and get me."

"Isn't that supposed to be my line?"

He tickled the insides of her thighs as she gingerly straddled his lap. "I think an emperor would expect more bodily contact." He grabbed her butt and kneaded her warm, resilient flesh. "We should have a mirror," he complained, wishing he had been more prepared.

Libby cupped his neck with her hands and leaned in to kiss him. "Focus, Kavanagh. You have a naked woman on your lap."

"That's my problem," he complained, thoroughly aggrieved. "I forget my name when I touch you. It makes decision-making dicey at best."

"I'll help," she promised. "Give me something to decide."

"Well," he drawled. "It would be nice if you could get a little closer."

Fortunately, Libby was a smart woman. "Like this, you mean?" She lifted up and lowered, joining their bodies perfectly.

He buried his face in her scented breasts. "Exactly like that."

This particular position might have been a miscalculation. The visual stimulation combined with a somewhat passive role on his part made his body burn. He had barely entered her, and already he wanted to come.

Damn it.

But as much as he wanted to move, the urge was strong to simply hold her there. And pretend she was his to keep.

She tapped him on the head. "Hello in there. The last emperor who wanted me was a bit more…um…*active*."

"You want active, little concubine?" he muttered. "How about this?" He surged upward, burying himself so deeply inside her, he wasn't sure he could find his way out.

"Patrick!" Libby cried out, stopping his heart.

"Did I hurt you?" he asked, pulling back to examine her face.

"You didn't hurt me." She bit her lip. "But it was definitely…"

"What? Definitely what?"

One shoulder lifted and fell. "Wicked. Memorable. Deep."

He swallowed hard. "I see. Would you consider those positive adjectives?"

She wiggled her butt, making him squeeze his eyes shut as he counted to ten and tried to hold on.

"Oh, yes, my emperor," she whispered. "Very positive indeed."

Libby might have lied a little bit. That last move on Patrick's part left her hovering on a line between pleasure and pain. She had never felt more desired, nor more completely possessed.

He trembled against her…or maybe that was her own body shaking. Was good sex always this momentous? Her basis for comparison was woefully inadequate. She'd had one terrible experience and now this one.

She raked her teeth along the shell of his ear. "Make love to me, Patrick. I want it all. Don't hold back."

Her request tore through his last thread of restraint. He lunged into her once…twice…then a third time, before he tumbled them both onto the floor and lifted one of her legs over his shoulder.

Suddenly, she felt exposed…vulnerable. Their bodies were no longer joined. Patrick was talented, but even he couldn't manage that trick while airborne. He stroked a fingertip in her damp sex, making her squirm as he stared at her intimately.

"Do you trust me, Libby?"

"Of course, I do."

"Close your eyes."

"But I…"

"Close them."

She obeyed the command, quivering in his grasp. "What are you going to do?"

"Hush, Libby."

She sensed him moving, and then she arched her back in instinctive protest when she felt his hands spread her legs apart. Moments later, his warm breath gave her the first warning of what he was about to do seconds before she felt the rough pass of his tongue on her sex.

A groan ripped from her gut, shocked pleasure swamping her inhibitions. She tried to escape, even so. But he locked her legs to the rug and continued his lazy torture.

She came more than once…loudly. And in the end, she barely had the breath to whisper his name when he moved inside her and drove them both insane…

It was still dark when Libby awoke. She was sore and satiated but oddly uncertain. Some sound had dragged her from a deep sleep. Patrick breathed quietly at her back, his arms wrapped around her waist, his face buried in her hair.

"Patrick," she said, turning to face him. "I think your phone is vibrating." It had to be bad. No good news ever came at…what was it? Four in the morning?

Her companion grumbled, but reached for his phone on the bedside table. "What?"

Patrick sat straight up in bed. "How bad is it?"

The tone in his voice alarmed her. "What's wrong?"

He ignored her until he finished the call. "It's Mia…

Dylan's wife. She's in the hospital with a ruptured appendix. And there are complications."

"Oh, no…"

"There's nothing we can do to help."

"Are you trying to convince me or you? Come on, Patrick. You know we need to go back. At least we can be there to lend moral support. People die from a ruptured appendix sometimes. Dylan must be out of his mind."

"Thank you for understanding," he said quietly.

They barely spoke as they gathered up their things and dressed. Patrick hardly acknowledged Libby's presence. She forgave him his silence, though, because she knew what it was like to be sick with fear.

A car waited for them when they exited the hotel. Apparently nothing ruffled the overnight desk clerk, even guests rushing out with their hair askew and wearing rumpled clothing from the night before.

At the airport, the pilot was ready. The flight back to Silver Glen seemed endless. Patrick stared out the window. Libby dozed. By eight in the morning, they were touching down on the new airstrip.

James was waiting for them, the car warm and toasty, despite the frigid early-morning air. As James stowed their bags into the trunk, Patrick helped Libby into the backseat and then joined James up front.

"How is she?" Patrick asked. "And tell me what happened. I didn't wait for details earlier when Liam contacted us."

James grimaced. "Apparently, she started having severe pain sometime after midnight, but she didn't wake up Dylan, because she didn't want to have to get Cora out of bed. By three thirty, it was so bad she had no choice. Dylan didn't take her. She went by ambulance. She's in surgery right now."

"Damn it, women are stubborn."

"Yeah."

Libby stayed silent in the backseat, hearing the concern in the siblings' voices…and the faintest hint of panic. These were big strong men. But they loved their sisters-in-law and treated them as blood relations, integral parts of this large, tight-knit family.

At the hospital, Libby staked out a seat in the waiting room and tried to become invisible. Through the glass walls adjacent to the corridor she had seen Maeve, the brothers and most of their wives from time to time, pacing the halls. Still wearing her coat to cover her inappropriate clothing, Libby closed her eyes and leaned her head against the wall. This setting brought back too many painful memories of her mother's early suicide attempts.

When Patrick finally sought her out, almost two hours had elapsed. He plopped down in a chair across from her and rested his elbows on his knees, head in his hands. Wearing his tux pants and wrinkled white shirt, he looked exhausted.

"Patrick?" Alarm coursed through her veins. "Did something go wrong? Is Mia okay?"

He sat up slowly, his expression taut with stress. "She's going to be. At least I hope so. The surgery went well, but infection is a concern. She was in recovery for forty-five minutes. They've brought her up to a room now. We've been taking turns going in to see her."

"How is she?"

"Cranky at the moment. She hates being out of control."

"I'm sure it's scary for her."

"Yeah." He pushed his hair from his forehead, his eyes weary, but laden with something else, as well. "Dylan is an absolute wreck."

At that moment, Maeve walked into the waiting room. Normally, Patrick's mother was the epitome of vigor and elegance, never a hair out of place. This morning, however, she looked every bit her age.

Patrick jumped up. "Here. Take my seat, Mom. I'm going to find some coffee."

Maeve managed a smile, but her hands trembled as she sat down and looked at Libby. "It's a hard thing to watch your children suffer. My poor Dylan is stoic, but I was afraid he was going to have a heart attack. He loves Mia deeply. And I do, too, of course. A man's love for his wife, though, is a sacred thing."

"I'm so glad it looks like Mia is going to be okay."

"Would you mind driving me home, dear? I told Patrick I was going to ask you. He's already had your things sent up to the lodge."

"Are you okay, Maeve?" The older woman was definitely pale.

Maeve nodded. "I'm fine. Just a little shaky, because I never ate breakfast. My car is in the parking lot."

They made their way downstairs, pausing to speak to various members of the family. But Patrick had not returned. As they exited the hospital, Libby's stomach growled. "Would you like to stop at the diner for a meal?"

"Actually, that sounds wonderful. Thank you, dear."

The little restaurant wasn't crowded. Maybe because it wasn't a weekday. Libby and Maeve grabbed a booth and ordered bacon and eggs with a side of heart-shaped pancakes in honor of the holiday. Coffee and orange juice came out ahead of the food. Libby drained her cup in short order, hoping the jolt of caffeine would kick in soon. Maeve did the same, but she eyed Libby over the rim.

"I'm glad you suggested breakfast, Libby. I wanted to ask how the New York weekend went. I see you're still wearing that lovely dress."

Libby drew the collar of her coat closer together, thankful that the temperatures justified her attire. "We left in such a hurry this morning, we both just grabbed our clothes from last night."

Maeve's smile was knowing. "I wasn't making a judgment call…merely commenting. So tell me…did things go well?"

"The orientation at Peabody Rushford was fascinating. Although it wasn't for *my* benefit, I learned a lot."

Maeve shook her head, her dark eyes sharp with interest. "I'm not really asking about Patrick's business dealings. My son is an astute entrepreneur. I would expect no less. Mine was a more personal question."

Most people wouldn't have the guts to pry. But Maeve was not most people. Libby could do nothing about the flood of heat that washed from her throat to her hairline. "I'm not sure what you mean."

The server delivered the food. Libby scooped a forkful of eggs, hoping the distraction would derail Maeve's interrogation.

But Patrick's mother was like a dog with a bone… a very tasty bone. "I don't expect a blow-by-blow description, but I would like to know if the two of you connected on an intimate level." She locked her steady gaze with Libby's flustered one.

Blow-by-blow? Good grief. Libby managed to swallow the eggs that had solidified into a lump in her throat. "Um…yes, ma'am. We did."

"But?"

"But what?"

"You hardly seem the picture of a young woman who has been swept off her feet by romance."

"I haven't had much sleep, Maeve. It's a long way from New York."

"Give Patrick a chance," Maeve begged. "I know he doesn't go in for big gestures and declarations of undying passion, but he's a deep man. You can unpeel the layers if only you'll be patient."

Libby reached across the table and took Maeve's hand, squeezing it for a moment. Then she sat back in the booth and sighed. The delicious breakfast had lost its appeal. "Patrick is an *amazing* man. But he's been very honest with me from the beginning, and I have to honor that. For you to interfere or for me to weave daydreams based on nothing at all, would be wrong."

Maeve's face fell. "But you care about him?"

"Of course I do. He's a lovely man. But that doesn't make us soul mates, Maeve."

"I don't want my son to spend his life alone."

Tears glistened in Maeve's eyes. Given Patrick's mother's talents for benign manipulation, Libby had to wonder if the tears were genuine. But then again, Maeve was capable of deep feeling. Everything she did came from a place of abundant love.

"Some people like being alone, Maeve. I know tons of single people who are very happy and content with their lives. Patrick has a rewarding career and a circle of intimate friends. You can't box him into a *relationship* corner he doesn't want or need."

"You sound awfully wise for a young woman of your age."

"Life is a tough teacher."

"So what you're telling me is that you won't even consider letting yourself fall in love with my son because he's told you he doesn't want to get married."

"That's about the sum of it. I may stay for the duration of Charlise's leave…as long as things don't get awkward. But I've already told Patrick that I'm thinking of going back to New York permanently. This weekend's trip told me I can handle it. I wasn't sure, to be honest. I didn't want to think about my mother's death and my father's crime every second of every day. But I think it's going to be okay."

"Well…" Maeve scowled at a strip of bacon. "It sounds like you know your own mind."

"Yes, ma'am. And don't worry about Patrick. He knows what he wants and what he doesn't want."

Maeve leaned forward. "So what *does* he want?"

"He wants to build his life here…among family. He wants to be close to you and his brothers, and their wives and children, both physically and emotionally. He wants to grow Silver Reflections and know that he's making a difference in people's lives. He wants to spend time in the mountains and to draw strength from this place you all call home."

"For a woman who hasn't found her soul mate, you surely sound as if you know a great deal about my son."

"Stop it, Maeve. I'm serious. This last year has taught me that I can't always bend the world to my will. I have to accept reality and deal with it as best I can. And even under those circumstances—sometimes difficult, sometimes tragic—I can be happy. Or at least content."

Maeve held up her hands. "You've convinced me. I'm officially done with playing Cupid…though it's awfully hard to say that on his special day."

Libby laughed, finishing her meal with a lighter heart. "Maybe *we* should be worrying about *you*, Maeve. You're still very youthful and attractive. I'm sure there are tons of eligible men out there who would like to find a woman like you."

Maeve blanched. "If that's blackmail, I stand forewarned. I like my life the way it is. I had one husband. That was enough."

"If you say so. Now please pass the syrup, let's finish breakfast so I can go back to the lodge and get out of these clothes."

Sixteen

Patrick kicked a log, not even flinching when pain shot from his toe up his leg. He liked the pain. It helped distract him from the turmoil in the rest of his body. It had been over twenty-four hours since he had seen Libby. Longer than that since they'd had sex. He was like a junkie jonesing for the next hit.

But therein lay his problem. He had to stay away from her.

The conviction had been born in an intimate New York hotel room and solidified in the antiseptic corridors of a hospital. He couldn't afford to fall in love with Libby Parkhurst. It was too dangerous.

Little memories of Friday slipped into his thoughts when his guard was down. The smell of her hair on his pillow. The humorous, self-deprecating way she spoke to his clients about sleeping in the great outdoors. Her delighted laughter as she tipped her face toward the sky while snowflakes fell on her soft cheeks.

Even the way she hugged an old man in a uniform and let him know that he was important in her life.

Libby made everything brighter, more special. If he'd been inclined to find a lover and hang on to her, that woman might be Libby. But he couldn't. He wouldn't.

Without realizing it, he'd been on his way to changing his life plan. Having Libby in his bed, turning him inside out, had begun to convince him that he might be smarter about marriage a second time. After all, he wasn't a kid anymore.

But then yesterday happened. Mia's emergency surgery. Patrick knew his brother Dylan as a laid-back, comfortable-with-the-world, confident man. But in Dylan's eyes yesterday, Patrick had seen raw terror. With the woman Dylan loved in danger, Patrick's older brother had been helpless... scared sick that he was going to lose his whole world.

Patrick didn't want that kind of responsibility or that kind of grief. He remembered well the bitter taste of failure and loss when his youthful marriage ended, and that was for a girl he hadn't even loved.

How much worse would it be if he let himself get addicted to Libby and then he lost her? Death. Divorce. Infidelity. There were any number of forces waiting to tear couples apart.

Why would he subject himself to such vulnerability?

The hours he'd spent with Libby in the Carlyle hotel had literally changed him. Her sweet, sultry beauty. Her gentleness. Her shy, eager passion. He could have wallowed in their lovemaking for days on end and never had enough.

But when he broached the subject of extending their stay, Libby hadn't jumped at the idea. Worse still, she'd spoken of returning to New York permanently. Of leaving Silver Glen. Of leaving him.

It wasn't too late to correct his mistakes. He hadn't

gone all the way into obsession. He could end this thing and walk away unscathed.

But to do so meant suffering through one very unpleasant conversation. Today was Sunday. Thank God, Valentine's Day had come and gone. There was no reason not to intercept Libby's plans before she returned to Silver Reflections Monday morning.

When he contemplated what he was about to do, the bottom fell out of his stomach. Much like the first time he'd stood atop the high dive as a ten-year-old and wondered if he had the guts to make the jump.

He took out his cell phone and started to punch in a number. Libby carried a cheap pay-as-you-go phone. But at the last minute he remembered that Zoe was helping Libby get set up in the apartment over Dylan's bar.

The two of them had vowed to hit up thrift stores and outfit Libby's new digs. Should he stop Libby before she spent any of her hard-earned cash on things she might not need?

Damn it. He'd never had to deal with any of this with Charlise at his side.

At last, he decided he had to make the call.

Libby answered on the first ring. "Hello?"

Her voice reached inside his chest and squeezed his heart. "Are you and Zoe still occupied with your move?"

"She had to cancel. But I may go over to the Silver Dollar later to get the lay of the land. What's up, Patrick?"

"We need to talk," he said gruffly. "What if I pick up some sandwiches, and you and I go for a drive?"

"It's not really picnic weather," she said, laughter in her voice.

The day was infinitely dreary, sheets of rain drenching the mountains, temperatures hovering at a raw 38 degrees.

"I know that," he said. "But I've eaten in my car before. It won't kill me."

"If you say so."

"Can you be ready in an hour?"

"Of course."

"See you shortly." Now that he had made up his mind, he wanted to get this thing done...

Libby had a good idea what was coming. Patrick was going to tell her that an intimate relationship was not a good idea since she was going to be working for him. The thing was, she sort of agreed.

At this point in her life, she needed a good job more than she needed a love interest. Maybe in time this physical attraction between the two of them might blossom into something stronger...something lasting. She was a patient person. And if that were never going to happen, then she would be a big girl and face the truth.

Despite her brave talk, the prospect of seeing Patrick again made her insides go wobbly. They had gone from sleeping in each other's arms, to panic, to rushed travel to the hospital, to nothing. Patrick had left to get coffee, and that was the last she had seen of him.

This afternoon, with one guarded phone call, he was evidently prepared to set her straight. A fling in New York was one thing. Now it would be back to business as usual.

Since they weren't going anywhere fancy, she dressed warmly in jeans, boots and a thick, forest green sweater. The pleasant weather when Patrick had taken her out in the woods was nothing but a memory. Winter had returned... with no sign of relenting.

She was waiting on the front steps of the hotel when Patrick pulled up in his sporty sedan. It didn't seem like a good idea to meet him inside where his mother might happen to see them and get the wrong idea.

Ever the gentleman, he got out and opened her door, despite the fact that a uniformed parking attendant stood nearby, ready to lend a hand. She wanted to smile at Patrick and say something light and innocuous, but the words dried up in her throat.

This man had seen her naked. He had done wonderfully wicked things to her and with her. They had slept like exhausted children, wrapped in each other's arms.

Looking at Patrick's stoic face right now, no one would ever guess any of that.

Once they were seated practically hip to hip in the interior of the car, things got worse. The windows fogged up and the tension increased exponentially. She literally said nothing.

Patrick followed her lead.

She wanted to ask where they were going. But Patrick's grim profile in the waning afternoon light didn't invite questions. Chastened, she huddled in her seat and watched as the world flew by her window.

He drove like a man possessed, spiraling down the mountain road at least ten miles above the speed limit, and then racing on past town and out into the countryside. If he had a destination, she couldn't guess what it was. Her gut said he was driving at random.

When thirty minutes had passed from the moment he fetched her at the lodge, he finally slowed the car and rolled to a stop. The scene spread out in front of them was the definition of *middle of nowhere.* If she hadn't known better, she might have been worried he was going to dump her out and drive away, leaving her to find her way back home.

Their meal was in the backseat, but she wasn't hungry. And since she'd never been one to put off unpleasant tasks, she decided to cut to the chase. "I've been expecting this conversation," she said quietly. "You're going to say that we can either be lovers or coworkers, but not both."

Patrick's hands were white-knuckled on the steering

wheel. "The rain has stopped. I need to get out of this car. Do you mind?"

His question was clearly rhetorical, because before she could respond, he had already climbed out. She joined him on the side of the road, her arms wrapped around her waist. Even with a coat over her sweater, she was cold. The graveled edges of the pavement were waterlogged and muddy. The tops of the surrounding mountains were invisible, shrouded in low clouds, though the sun was trying to peek through.

Patrick stood a few feet away, physically and emotionally aloof, with aviator sunglasses obscuring part of his face. His khakis were crisply creased. He wore a white shirt underneath a brown bomber jacket. The leather was soft and scarred, clearly the real deal. Who had given it to him? Maybe it had been a gift when he first earned his pilot's license.

A light breeze ruffled his hair. Though she couldn't see his eyes, she guessed they were more gray than blue in this light. "Are you asking *me* to decide? New York was incredible, Patrick. I want to pick sex with you and say to hell with everything else. But we don't know each other all that well, and I was serious about learning to stand on my own two feet."

"You've misunderstood me," he said, hands shoved in his pocket.

"Does that mean *you* get to choose? I have no say in the matter?"

His expression was grim, his jaw so tight he would surely have a headache soon if he didn't already. It wasn't the face of a man who was going to choose physical pleasure over their work relationship.

He held up a hand. "Stop, Libby." His voice was hoarse. "You're making this harder."

Disappointment set up residence in her stomach.

Clearly the sex that had seemed so incredibly intimate and warm and fun to her had meant nothing to him. Well, she wouldn't be an object of pity. If he thought she was going to pine away for him, he was wrong. As far as she was concerned, they could work together and pretend the past weekend never happened.

She mimed zipping her lip. "Say what you have to say."

He took off his sunglasses and tucked them in his pocket. In the battle between the clouds and the sun, the clouds had won. "I'm not asking you to choose, Libby. I think you were right. You should go back to New York."

Trembling began deep in her core and worked its way to her extremities. "I don't understand."

In his face, she saw no remnant of the tender, funny man who had made love to her so passionately and so well. He stared at her impassively. "You gave it your best shot, Libby. I admired your resolve in the woods and in the mine, but you're not who I need while Charlise is gone."

You're not who I need. The blunt statement took her breath away.

"And our physical relationship?" Now her entire body shook. She tightened her arms around herself, trying not to splinter into a million tiny pieces of disbelief and wounded embarrassment.

"One night does not make a relationship. We were great in bed, but I've already told you how I feel about marriage. If you stay in Silver Glen, and you and I *continue* to end up in bed, things will get messy.

"Messy..." She parroted the word, her thought processes in shambles.

"You have to go home, Libby. Your instincts were good about that. Silver Glen is not the place for you, and I'm not the man you want. It's better to put an end to this now with no harm done."

Somewhere, she found the strength to smile evenly,

even as jagged, breathless pain raced through her veins and threatened to cripple her. It was a hell of a time to realize she was in love with him. She inhaled and exhaled, calling upon all of her acting skills. "I can't say I'm surprised by your decision. I never really thought you were going to give me the job anyway."

He must have seen through her layer of calm. For the first time, something in him cracked...visibly. For a split second, she could swear she saw agony in his eyes. "Libby..." He took an impulsive step in her direction and reached for her arm.

She jerked away, backing up so quickly she nearly lost her footing in the loose gravel. "No. Just no. Please take me back to the hotel. I have plans to make."

The return drive seemed endless. In front of the Silver Beeches Lodge, Patrick rolled to a halt and locked all the car doors with one click. His chest heaved. "Libby..." he said her name again.

But his time she had no escape route. He leaned across the console and tangled his hands in her hair, pulling her to him for a hard, desperate kiss. It took guts and fortitude, but she didn't respond. At all.

When he finally released her and sat back, she slapped him hard across the face. In seconds, his cheek bore the dark red mark of her fingers. "You're a selfish, heartless jackass, Patrick Kavanagh...and an emotionally stunted shell of a man. I don't ever want to see you again...not even if your face is on a Wanted poster. Go to hell."

Seventeen

Patrick had known it was going to be bad…but not that it would hurt so damned much. He unlocked the doors and watched Libby exit his car and his life in one fell swoop. His throat tight, he lowered the window and called her name urgently. "Libby!"

She never hesitated…never turned around.

Patrick struggled through the next several days as if the hours were quicksand threatening to pull him under. Though he found a replacement for Charlise—a male grad student in desperate need of extra cash who was willing to work for five months and then go back to chipping away at the course work for his degree—Patrick felt no sense of relief.

He went through the motions of preparing for his first outdoor adventure group, but the tasks that normally energized and excited him felt burdensome.

Even worse, he was forced to hide out from his family.

He knew his mother well. She had surely put two and two together by now. As Libby's champion, she would have his hide for hurting her.

Even a scheduled trip to LA, a city he normally enjoyed, was torture. All he could see in his mind's eye was Libby sitting at the conference table in her stylish black dress, handing out advice to skittish executives.

Far worse were the two nights he spent in a California hotel, flipping channels when he couldn't sleep. Libby was everywhere. In the big king-size bed, the marble tiled shower, the love seat that was a close twin to a certain settee in New York.

As much as he wanted to avoid facing the music in Silver Glen, he quickly wrapped up his assignment and headed home. His mother's birthday was in two days. Zoe and Cassidy were coordinating a huge bash in the ballroom of Silver Beeches. Though Liam and Maeve had run the lodge together for years, Maeve had finally decided to step down and devote herself to her rapidly expanding crop of grandchildren.

There was no possible way for Patrick to miss such an event. Nor did he want to. But it went without saying that Libby would be in attendance, as well. Even thinking about the possibility of seeing her again made him hard. He hadn't slept worth a damn since she ran from his car.

He relived that moment time after time. In every way he spun the conversation, the truth was, Libby was probably right. But even if he had it all to do over again, he didn't think he could change. The prospect of loving her was too scary.

What if he let himself love her and something happened to her? He had watched Dylan come apart at the seams. Fortunately, Mia was on her way to a complete recovery, but even so, Dylan was probably hovering over her, making sure she obeyed doctor's orders.

Patrick was following the only possible path. He had to keep his distance. He wouldn't let love destroy him.

At last, he came up with what he decided was a rational, well-thought-out plan. He would go to the Silver Dollar—surely Libby had finished moving in by now. And she wouldn't have left town yet—not without taking a few weeks to make some plans about her future and to look for a place to live in New York. He would track Libby down in her upstairs apartment over the saloon and discuss how they would comport themselves during Maeve's celebration.

His heart beat faster at the thought of seeing her again. She wouldn't be able to call him out on the validity of his visit. Neither one of them wanted to hurt or embarrass Maeve.

To mitigate his nervousness and postpone the inevitable, he stopped downstairs in the bar first. It was midafternoon on a Friday. Only a handful of customers lingered after what would have been a predictable lunch-hour rush.

Dylan was behind the bar doing something with the cash drawer. He looked up when Patrick approached. "Howdy, stranger. I thought you'd left town. Nobody's seen or heard from you all week."

"Been busy." He sat down on a leather-topped stool.

Dylan poured him a beer. "You want to go in with Mia and me for Mom's birthday gift? We were thinking about getting her a three-day visit to that new spa over in Asheville…with the works. It's not something she would buy for herself."

"Sounds good. Just tell me how much I owe you." He drained half of his beer and felt his chest tighten. "Do you happen to know if Libby is upstairs at the moment?"

Dylan frowned. "What do you mean?"

"Well, she lives here now, doesn't she? I thought you might keep track of her comings and goings."

Dylan wiped his hands on a clean bar towel, his expression troubled. "She's not living upstairs, man."

"But she was planning to move her stuff here from the hotel. She told me."

"Libby stayed for one night. Then she went back to New York."

Patrick made some excuse to his brother and departed, scraped raw by the look of sympathy on Dylan's face. Patrick felt hollow inside. Life had kicked the heart out of him, and it was his own fault. He hadn't really thought Libby would leave. Granted, he'd told her to go back to New York, but he'd assumed Maeve had helped her get a more suitable job here in Silver Glen while Libby decided if a return to the big city was the right thing to do.

Why would she go back to New York and the friends who had shunned her after her father's arrest?

His stomach curled as he imagined innocent, open-hearted Libby living in some roach-infested apartment in a bad part of town. Possibly in actual physical danger.

God, what had he done?

He raced home and packed a bag. Then he lay awake almost all night to make absolutely sure he knew what he had to do. This was his mess. He was going to make it right. Fortunately, the jet was not in use the next day.

In a moment of absolute clarity, he saw the arrogant blunder he'd made. He'd been so entrenched in the notion that he had no business marrying anyone, he hadn't seen how much he was hurting the one woman who meant the world to him. He loved her. Right or wrong. And he couldn't let her go.

He filed his flight plan and was airborne before 8:00 a.m.

LaGuardia was busy. He had to execute a holding pattern until he was given permission to land. By the time he made it into the city, it was almost noon. He took care of several errands, then checked into the Carlyle and left on foot to walk to Libby's old building.

His idea was far-fetched, but it was the only hope he had of finding her. Fortunately, the doorman was the same old guy Libby had hugged with such fierce affection.

The man recognized Patrick right away. Patrick's plan called for bold-faced confidence.

Patrick smiled. "Hello, there. I'm hoping you can help me. I've come to see Libby and surprise her at her new place, but somehow I lost the address she gave me. Do you perhaps remember what it is? I know the two of you are close."

The elderly gentleman stared at Patrick for the longest time, leaving no doubt that he saw through Patrick's lie. But at last, he relented. He reached in his pocket and took out a scrap of paper. "Don't make me regret this."

Patrick jotted down the information in the note app on his phone and sighed in relief. At least he knew where to start. "Thank you," he said. "I appreciate your help." He pulled a folder from his pocket and handed it to Clarence. "This is an open-ended reservation at my family's hotel. For a two-week stay. You've meant a lot to Libby, and she wanted you to have this."

Hopefully, the tiny white lie would buy him goodwill in both directions.

Clarence smiled broadly. "Tell Miss Libby thank you. And I'll talk to her soon. This is mighty nice. Mighty nice."

Unfortunately, the new apartment was not in walking distance. Patrick was forced to grab a cab and slowly make his way downtown in rush-hour traffic. Contrary to his worst fears, the address pointed him toward TriBeCa... and a trendy collection of redesigned lofts.

This was far beyond anything Libby could afford right now. Had she found a man...an old friend willing to take her in? His gut cramped at the possibility. He took the elevator and rang the bell for 2B. Moments later, he heard footsteps. But nothing happened. There was a security peephole in the door.

Taking a chance, he stared straight at it. "Open up, Libby. I know you're in there, and I'm prepared to stand out here all night."

Libby leaned her forehead against the door and fought back tears. To peek outside and see Patrick in the flesh decimated her hard-won composure. She'd thought she had herself under control.

Turned out, she was wrong.

She cracked the door open, but left the chain on. "Why are you here?" she asked, her tone carefully dispassionate. Obviously it wasn't to declare his undying love for her.

"Maeve's birthday party is tomorrow night. Are you planning to be there?"

The hand behind the door, the one he couldn't see, clenched in a fist. "No. It's too expensive to fly and I don't have a car."

"You're willing to disappoint your mother's good friend…the woman who has done so much for you?"

She was getting tired of trying to read his mood through the crack. But she knew him well enough not to let him in. "Maeve will understand. She knows my financial situation."

"I brought the jet to pick you up, so money is not really an issue."

"I said I'm not going. Goodbye, Patrick."

He stuck his large leather shoe in the opening, foiling her attempt to shut him out. "Now who's being selfish and emotionally stunted?"

Had her words actually wounded him? Why else would he remember them almost verbatim? What would it take to make him leave her alone? And more importantly, what would it take to convince herself she hadn't fallen in love with him?

"What do you want?" she asked. Her heart was in shreds, and she didn't have the will to fight. The past few days had almost done her in. She wanted the man on the other side of the door with every fiber of her being. But she wasn't going to beg. Her dignity was all she had left.

"Please let me in, Libby."

She glanced behind her at the clock on the wall. Spencer would be home soon. This awkward confrontation couldn't last too long. "Fine," she said. "But only for a moment. I have things to do."

After disengaging the chain, she stepped back and let him come in. The dimensions of the loft were generous, but Patrick's size and personality made an impact, even so.

"Have you eaten?" he asked.

"Yes, sorry." But she wasn't sorry at all. And she wasn't going to offer to cook for him.

"This is quite some place."

"Yes. It's very nice."

"I thought all your friends dropped you when your dad went to prison."

"Spencer was doing an eighteen-month stint with the Peace Corps in Bangladesh. Manhattan society news travels slowly over there."

"And now Spencer is back and took you in?"

"Yes."

"And your future employment?"

"Zoe loaned me some money. I interviewed today for a position as a personal shopper at Bergdorf Goodman. Turns out I have skills in that area. As soon as I'm able, I'll be paying her back…"

"And Spencer, too?"

"Of course."

Patrick's expression was moody, as if he resented the fact that she had landed on her feet. What was it to him? He hadn't been willing to give her a job or a place to live... or even a tiny piece of his heart.

"Shall I tell Maeve that I flew up here to get you, but you were too busy to come to her birthday party?" He leaned against the wall in the foyer, his hands shoved in his pockets.

"Why would you do that?"

"To get my way."

Wow. There it was. Not even dressed up.

At that moment, the door opened without ceremony and a large, handsome blond man entered. He stopped short when he saw Patrick. Then he lifted an eyebrow. "Libby?"

"Patrick was just leaving," she said hurriedly. She took the newcomer by the arm and dragged him toward the kitchen, but he refused to go very far. Instead, she had to whisper in his ear.

He straightened after a moment and eyed Patrick with distrust. "I see."

She squeezed his arm. "I'm going back to Silver Glen for a couple of nights. But don't worry about me. I'll be fine."

"You'd better be."

Ten feet away, Patrick practically vibrated with incensed testosterone overload. She had to get him out of the apartment. "You win, Patrick," she said. "But I need some time. I'll meet you at the airport in two hours. Take it or leave it."

He nodded once, scowled at her and walked out.

The blond man chuckled. "Poor bastard. He's madly in love with you and you let him think you're living with me."

"Well, I am living with you," Libby said, giving him a big hug.

"Yeah, but with me *and* Spencer, who happens to be my beautiful, sexy wife."

Libby winced. "I might possibly have led him to believe that Spencer is male...and that *you* are Spencer."

"That's stone-cold, love. But he probably deserved it."

Libby threw some things in a bag, her heart racing with adrenaline. She didn't have a gift for Maeve, but Maeve would understand. Coat, keys, phone, small suitcase. In forty-five minutes, she was running downstairs and out to the street.

Then she stopped dead, because leaning against a lamppost was Patrick Kavanagh. "I said I would meet you at the airport," she protested.

He shrugged. "I didn't trust you not to run."

There was accusation in his voice...and something else. Fatigue? Sadness? What did he want from her?

"Well, I'm here."

They faced each other silently. Being this close to him ripped apart the web of lies she had told herself to keep going every day. The truth punched her with a ferocity that took her breath. She was madly, deeply, unfortunately in love with Patrick Kavanagh.

He raked a hand through his hair, for the first time revealing a trace of vulnerability. "The airport is shut down for fog. We can't leave until tomorrow morning."

She swallowed. "Okay. Call me and let me know what time." She turned to go back inside the building.

Patrick caught her in two steps, his hands warm on her shoulders. "We need to talk, Libby. Come back to the hotel with me. We'll have dinner there. Casual. Nothing fancy. I'll get you a room if you want it. Or—" He stopped short as if he hadn't meant to say that.

"Or what?"

"Nothing," he muttered. "Never mind. Come have dinner with me. Please."

He was the last person on earth she wanted to have dinner with. And the only person. He didn't deserve to be given the time of day. But she let herself be persuaded. And not because she was weak, and he smelled wonderful. She would hear him out, for Maeve.

After that, Patrick was a complete gentleman. He kept his distance in the cab. At the hotel, he handed her bag to a bellman and steered Libby toward the dining room. The restaurant was conservatively old-school, reminding her of birthday dinners with her parents.

She ordered the lobster bisque. Her appetite lately had been almost nonexistent, but the rich, warm soup was perfect. Patrick chose the duck. Because the captain and servers were attentive, it was easy to let conversation touch on innocuous topics.

But at last, over cappuccino and crème brûlée, Patrick made an overture she hadn't expected. "We need some privacy, Libby. Will you come upstairs with me?"

What did he mean, *privacy*?

Well, hell. She wasn't going to be a coward about this. "For talking? Or something else?"

His throat flushed dark red and his eyes flashed with some strong emotion. "I'll let you make that call."

When he stared at her with storms in his blue-gray irises, she was helpless to resist. Or maybe that was the lie she told herself, because she didn't *want* to resist.

She folded her napkin and set it on the table. "Fine. We'll go upstairs."

The tension in the elevator would have been unbearable except for the older couple who joined them during the brief ride to an upper floor.

At Patrick's door, Libby waited nervously for him to fish the key from his pocket. It was a different room, of course. But the furnishings were similar enough to remind her of every last thing she and Patrick had shared just days earlier in this same city...this same hotel.

Libby took a seat. Patrick stood and paced.

"If you're feeling guilty, I absolve you," she said, the words flat. "You were right. The job at Silver Reflections wasn't suited for me. But you needn't worry. I've landed on my feet, and things are going very well. I should thank you for firing me."

"I didn't exactly *fire* you," he protested, the muscles in his neck corded and tight.

"What would *you* call it?"

He exhaled. "A mistake. A bad mistake. I acted like a complete ass, and I hope you will find it in your heart to forgive me."

"I make no promises. What about the sex?" she asked recklessly, fighting for her happiness, unwilling to let a blindly stubborn man ruin what they had.

"I can't deny it was incredible. But my life was rocking along pretty damn well until you came along." His voice faltered.

"Well, mine wasn't. A thousand apologies, emperor." She made her tone as snide and nasty as she could manage. And she leaped to her feet, no longer content to sit and let him scowl at her.

He grabbed her wrist to reel her in, his chest heaving. "I will not fail at marriage again, Libby."

Eighteen

Her heart dropped to her feet until she looked deeply into his eyes and saw the secret he was trying so hard to keep. Her jaw dropped. "You love me…"

"No I don't." His denial was automatic but totally unconvincing.

She cupped his face in her hands. "I love you, too, Patrick. But we don't have to get married," she said softly, "if that's what scares you. We can live in sin. You'll be the black sheep of the family."

At last the line between his eyebrows disappeared. "It's the twenty-first century. You'll have to do more than that to get me ostracized."

"I'll try my best. But it will have to be something really awful, won't it? Like maybe you and I making a baby without a ring on my finger? Your mom would hate that."

She saw the muscles in his throat work. "I'd hate it, too," he muttered. "This isn't how things should be, Libby. I've already stood before a priest and repeated marriage vows.

You deserve a man who can come to you with a clean past, a blank slate."

Going against all her instincts, she released him and put the width of the room between them. Still, she couldn't sit down. Too much adrenaline pumped through her veins. She busied herself at the minibar. "Would you like something to drink?"

"No. Look at me, Libby. You know I'm right. You're young and sweet and you deserve all the traditional trappings of an extraordinary wedding. You deserve to be the perfect bride."

She set down the small unopened bottle of liquor. "Here's the truth, Patrick…the last year has taught me that life is seldom perfect. I won't have my father to walk me down the aisle, because he's in prison. My mother won't be at my side helping me pick out a dress, because she took a bottle of pills."

"I'm sorry about all those things."

There was one more secret she knew she should disclose. Something that might make him understand. "Patrick?" She forced herself to perch on the sofa. The gas logs in the fireplace burned cheerfully. "Please sit with me. I want to tell you a story."

His expression guarded, and with reluctance in every line of his body, he nodded. But instead of joining her, he took a chair opposite, putting a low antique table between them as a barrier. "I'm listening."

This was harder than she had thought it would be. But if she didn't tell Patrick, perhaps she would never be free. "You keep calling me innocent, but you had to realize that I wasn't a virgin when you and I made love."

"I knew that. But neither was I. I've never approved of the double standard for women. I don't care about the men in your past, Libby. It's not important."

She leaned forward, her hot face in her hands. Shame flooded her stomach. "Well, it sort of is," she muttered.

Patrick made some kind of motion. "I don't want to hear your confession."

She sat up and stared at him before looking away and shaking her head. "I'm not giving you a choice. I was a very rebellious teenager, Patrick. I'd been spoiled and pampered, and I thought the world was my oyster. I'd barely dated at all, because my parents were so strict."

Patrick inhaled sharply. "Libby…"

"Don't interrupt. Please. The thing is, my father's best friend was newly divorced that year. He began flirting with me every time he came over to the apartment. I didn't really think of it as flirting. But I was smug about the fact that an older, sophisticated man was interested in my thoughts and opinions. It made me feel very grown-up."

Beneath his breath, Patrick said a word that was succinct and vehement. She had to ignore him to get through this.

"I turned sixteen in February. That fall was the beginning of my senior year. Most of my classmates had boyfriends, but I didn't. So I started telling everyone about *Mitch*."

"Was that his real name?"

She shrugged. "His middle name. I wasn't entirely stupid. I didn't want to get him or me in trouble. But as time passed and no one ever saw my 'boyfriend' at parties or other social occasions, they began to accuse me of making him up. The more teasing I took at school, the closer I grew to my father's friend. The attention of this handsome, very masculine man soothed my adolescent feelings of inadequacy."

"A man old enough to be your father."

"It didn't seem that way. To me, he was close to perfect."

"So what happened?"

Apparently, in spite of himself, Patrick wanted to know.

"In October, my father had to go to a financial seminar in Chicago. He wanted my mother and me to accompany him. But the trip sounded beyond boring to a teenage girl, even though my mom promised me shopping. I insisted that I was almost an adult and that they could certainly trust me. I begged them to let me stay home for the two nights they would be away."

"Oh, Libby…"

"It wasn't really a big deal. I planned to watch *inappropriate* movies on cable and paint my toenails and text with my friends. Maybe even sneak into my parents' liquor cabinet and have a single glass of sherry. I felt very daring and independent."

"And then Mitch came over."

"How did you know that?"

"It's not that hard to figure out. He knew you were going to be alone."

Libby grimaced. "I was an easy mark. He pretended he dropped by to see Daddy, and then feigned surprise that my father wasn't home. Later on, of course, I understood that Mitch knew exactly where my parents were and that I hadn't gone with them to Chicago. But at the time, it seemed like a happy accident. I asked him to come in."

Patrick had gone white beneath his tan. "He raped you."

Even now, the memory of that night made her shudder. "I wish it were that simple. I didn't understand all that much about men. I certainly didn't know that when they started drinking they were more dangerous. But I was having so much fun and he was complimenting me on my looks and my intelligence…anyway, when he kissed me the first time, I thought it was okay. For a minute."

"And afterward?"

"Something inside me said I should go to my bedroom

and lock my door. But I didn't want him to think of me as a child. So I ignored that little voice. And I paid the price."

"God, Libby…"

Tears stung her eyes, though she didn't let them fall. "It was a long time ago. And I'm fine…really I am. I just wanted you to know that I wouldn't come to marriage unscathed, either. Not that you've asked me, but you know…"

Patrick staggered to his feet, his heart and his composure shattering into pieces like brittle glass. He went to the sofa and sat down, scooping her into his lap. For a long time, they just sat there…not speaking, her head tucked against his shoulder.

He stroked her fiery hair, wanting desperately to find the son of a bitch with the middle name Mitch and avenge Libby's honor.

At last, he drew a deep breath and let go of the past that had held him with invisible chains. "I adore you, Libby Parkhurst. How could I not? You're beautiful and brave and you have the most extraordinary outlook on life." He tipped her backward over his arm and kissed her, shuddering with relief as she kissed him in return.

When they separated and sat side by side, her green eyes were damp, but then his were, too, so they were even. "Don't move," he said.

Her face expressed first puzzlement and then astonishment when he slid off the sofa and onto one knee, pushing the table aside. Reaching into his pocket, he pulled out a turquoise leather box and flipped it open. "Marry me, Libby," he pleaded, the words hoarse, his throat raw.

She stared at the multicarat single stone as if it were a snake. "You have a ring?"

Her bewilderment made him feel lower than low. "Of course, I do," he said. "I'll change this for a diamond if you want, but I've always thought redheads should wear emeralds." Libby didn't protest when he slid the simple platinum band with the exotic jewel onto her finger.

She held her hand up, her eyes wide. "It's extraordinary."

"I have no doubts about us, Libby, not anymore. And it's not because of your confession. You've opened my eyes to how stupid I've been to deliberately throw away something so amazingly good. I'm sorry I insulted you and fired you and tried to break your heart. I was an idiot. I bought the ring this afternoon, but then I got cold feet." He rested his forehead against her knee. He'd said his piece. The outcome was up to her now.

Her silence lasted too damn long. When he felt her fingers in his hair, he braced for a refusal.

But Libby took him by surprise. She slid down beside him, her legs curled to one side. "This is a very beautiful rug," she said. "I suppose we shouldn't do anything to ruin it."

He scowled at her. "Damn it, Libby. Don't toy with me. I've had a hell of a day."

"And whose fault is that?"

"I know I said I didn't care about other men in your life, and I really don't, but tell me one thing. Is Spencer expecting to share your bed? He's a big guy, and I want to know if I'm going to have to fight for your hand."

Libby's eyes widened, and she laughed, staring down at her fingers as if mesmerized by the brilliant green stone Patrick had spent several hours choosing. "Spencer is my dear friend. She and I were best buddies in school. The man you met at the loft is her husband, Derek."

Patrick exhaled, torn between frustration at Libby's deliberate deception and relief that no one else had a claim on his fiancée. "You're going to lead me in a merry dance, aren't you? I'll never be able to turn my back. And when you gang up with my sisters-in-law, Lord help us all."

He stretched out his legs and banged his shin on the table leg. "Wait a minute," he said, aggrieved. "You haven't said you'll marry me."

"I didn't?" Guileless green eyes looked up at him.

He started to sweat. "Say it, Libby. Right now."

She sighed, leaning forward to unbutton his shirt. "Yes, Patrick Kavanagh. I will marry you. Now, are you satisfied?"

He kissed her hard, moving over her and pressing her into the sofa. But it was a damned uncomfortable position. "I'm not satisfied at all," he stuttered. "Bedroom. Now." He dragged her to her feet, trying to undress her and walk at the same time. They made it as far as the still-closed door, but his patience frayed.

He lifted her hands over her head, trapping her against the polished wood with the weight of his body. Her breasts, mostly exposed in a sexy bra, heaved.

Libby's gaze was dreamy. "Let's come here for our honeymoon," she said.

"But during the summer. When you don't have to wear so many clothes." He gave up on the wrist-holding thing and unzipped her pants. "Help me, woman."

Finally, aeons later, they were both nude. He held her tightly, his face buried in her hair. "This is forever. I hope you know that."

Libby sighed deeply. "I'm counting on it, my love."

Twenty-four hours later, Libby stood in one of the private salons at the Silver Beeches Lodge and hid a yawn behind her hand. The emerald ring hung on a chain tucked inside her dress. All around her, the Kavanagh family, along with an intimate circle of friends, laughed and danced and partied. Maeve, the guest of honor, beamed continuously, delighted to have all her loved ones under one roof.

By prior agreement, Patrick and Libby had arrived at the festivities separately. For the past two hours they had stayed on opposite sides of the room. Either Dylan or Zoe must have warned everyone not to make a big deal about Libby's presence after a weeklong absence, because no one said a word out of place. All the attention was centered on Maeve—as it should be.

Still, it was a good bet that all the Kavanaghs knew Libby was no longer working for Patrick, and that things had ended badly.

After a sumptuous dinner, Maeve opened gifts. Her family and friends showered her with offerings of love and affection. For a brief moment, Libby allowed herself to grieve the fact that her own children would have only one grandmother. But then the moment passed.

She was luckier than most.

At last, when the babies were asleep and even the grown-ups were starting to fade, it was clear the party was over. Patrick stepped to the center of the room and gave his mother a hug. "I have one last gift for you, Mom."

Maeve seemed confused. "But I thought the spa thing had your name on it, too."

Little by little, the room fell silent. All eyes were on Patrick. "This is something more personal," he said.

Unobtrusively, Libby removed the emerald from its resting place and slipped it onto her left finger. It had pained her not to wear it, even for this one brief evening.

Patrick stood—tall and strong—with an almost palpable air of contentment and joy surrounding him.

Maeve stared at her boy, her brow creased. "Well, don't keep me in suspense. Where is it?"

Patrick grinned broadly, crooking a finger. "It's not an *it*. It's a *who*."

Libby threaded her way through the crowd, smiling as

the swell of exclamations followed her progress. When she joined Patrick, he put an arm around her.

"Mom," he said. "I'd like to present my fiancée, Libby Parkhurst, soon to be the daughter of your heart."

Maeve burst into tears, and the entire room fairly exploded with excitement. Libby lost track of the hugs and kisses and well wishes.

When some of the furor finally died down, Maeve held her close and whispered in her ear. "Thank you, Libby. Look at him. He's beaming."

And indeed he was. Libby's heart turned over. If she had harbored any last doubts, seeing Patrick like this in the bosom of his family and so obviously exultant and happy made her own heart swell with emotion.

Patrick finally reclaimed his fiancée and dragged her out to the car. He leaned her against the hood and kissed her long and slow. "Come home with me, my love."

Libby wrapped her arms around his neck, feeling the beat of his heart against hers. "I thought you'd never ask…"

* * * * *

THE SECRETARY'S SCANDALOUS SECRET

CATHY WILLIAMS

CHAPTER ONE

'I CALLED. Five minutes ago. You failed to pick up.' Luc Laughton flicked back the cuff of his shirt to look pointedly at his watch. 'I don't appreciate clock-watching in my employees. People who work for me are well paid for a reason.'

Cool green eyes swept over the small blonde huddled in a thick coat of indeterminate colour that looked as though it had been rescued from the local charity shop. There was, he was forced to concede, a pretty good chance that it had been, knowing her as he did.

Bright patches of colour had appeared on Agatha's cheeks. Of course she had heard the telephone ring. Of course she had known that she really *should* have picked it up—but she had been in a rush, and it wasn't as though she didn't put in her fair share of overtime when it was necessary. In fact, it was already five-forty-five, so it was hardly as though she had raced to join the five o'clock Friday-evening exodus!

'Because you're here as a favour to my mother,' Luc continued with that implacable edge of steel in his voice that made him so feared in the cut-throat world of high finance, 'doesn't mean that you can slope off on the dot of five whenever it suits you.'

'It's after five-thirty, and I wasn't sloping off.' Agatha stared down at the ground with ferocious concentration because it was a lot less traumatic than actually having to look at Luc Laughton. Looking at Luc Laughton always resulted in a thumping heart, a racing pulse and an inconvenient, prickly feeling all over her body. It had been that way since she had been a kid of thirteen and he had been eighteen—on the verge of manhood, fabulously good-looking and with the sort of dangerous, dark looks that made women stop and stare and then do a double-take every time he walked by.

How could she have failed to have a crush? All the girls in the village had had a crush on him, not that he had ever paid any of them a blind bit of notice. He was the rich kid who lived in the mansion on the hill. He had attended a top boarding school which had honed his razor-sharp intellect and invested him with the kind of cool self-assurance that Agatha had found both scary and weirdly compelling.

'If it's important, I guess I could stay on a bit longer...' she mumbled to the carpet.

Luc gave an elaborate sigh and leaned against the door frame. He had known from the very beginning that this was where the favour to his mother would end up, but what choice had he been given?

Six years ago his father had died unexpectedly, leaving behind him a financial train-wreck brought about by gross mismanagement of his company by the person he had most trusted. While Luc had been living it up at university, on the verge of leaving for Harvard to begin a Masters in economics and history, the wealth that had supported a lifestyle way beyond most people's wildest dreams had been unravelling faster than the speed of light. His charming father had played golf and entertained clients, and his unscrupulous finance director had played with the books and embezzled vast sums of money.

Luc had been summoned home to face a grief-stricken

mother and a house about to go under the hammer to pay off the creditors who had been baying like wolves at the door.

Distraught at having nowhere to live, Danielle had been taken in by the vicar and his wife. They had looked after her and seen her through some tough times for the better part of a year, until the misery of her non-existent finances had been sorted. Sufficient money had been scraped together to rent a small cottage outside the village, which had provided her with a roof over her head while Luc had abandoned his postgrad plans and begun the process of savagely, ruthlessly and single-mindedly reclaiming what had been lost.

So when, eight months ago, his mother had told him that little Agatha Havers had been made redundant a few months ago and needed a job he had had no option but to provide one. Her parents had been an invaluable rock to his mother when she had most needed one, and thanks to them he had had the freedom to instigate the meteoric rise which, less than four years later, would see his mother restored to the house that was rightfully hers.

In the high-tech glass building with its high-achieving staff, however, Agatha stood out like a sore thumb. The daughter of the local vicar of a small parish in a small village in the middle of nowhere, trained in the vital skills of gardening and potting plants, was perilously out of step in his world of mergers, acquisitions and making money.

'Has Helen gone?' Helen was Luc's personal assistant. Agatha felt sorry for her. *She* might get bits and pieces of his eagle-eyed attention, but Helen received the full brunt of it, because Luc was nothing if not an exacting task-master. Agatha could only shudder at the thought of having to be under Luc's radar all day, only to return home to all the peace and quiet of four children and a husband.

'She has. Not that that's relevant. I need you to collate the information on the Garsi deal and then make sure that all the legal documents are in order. The schedule is tight on this one, so it's all hands to the deck.'

'Wouldn't you be better off…um…getting someone a little more experienced to deal with something like that?' Agatha ventured hesitantly.

Unable to continue staring at the carpet any longer, she reluctantly looked up at him and instantly she felt as though the oxygen levels had plummeted as she feverishly absorbed the refined, beautiful angles of his face. He had inherited the olive skin and black hair from his French mother, and the green eyes of his very English, very aristocratic father, and they worked together to give him drop-dead, killer looks.

'I'm not asking you to seal the deal, Agatha.'

'I realise that, but I'm not as fast on the computer as, well…'

'Most people in the building?' Luc inserted helpfully, fighting to keep the sarcasm out of his voice. 'You've had nearly eight months to get to grips with the work and you apparently did a one-month crash course in IT.'

Agatha tried not to shudder at the memory of that particular course. Having been made redundant from the garden centre, she had spent three months at home with her mother and, sweet-natured though her mother was, she knew that her patience had been tried to the limit.

'You can't spend the rest of your days drifting through the house and tinkering in the garden, darling,' she had said gently. 'I love having you here, especially since your dad passed on two years ago, but you need a job. If you don't think that there are any jobs around here, well, why don't you perhaps think of working further afield? Maybe even London? I've had a little word with Danielle, Luc's mother, and she suggested that Luc might be able to find a spot for you in his company. He's very successful, you know—does something important in the City. All you'd need to do would be a short little computer course...'

Agatha privately thought that most ten-year-old kids had more computer savvy than her, but then computers had not been much in evidence in the vicarage. By the time she'd emerged into a world reliant on them, she had found herself wildly at sea and woefully ignorant. Computers, for her, were not friends to be played with. They were potential enemies out to get the better of her the second she pressed a wrong key.

'Yes, I did,' she said glumly. 'But I really wasn't brilliant at it.'

'You'll never get anywhere in life if you droop around convinced that failure lies just around the corner. I'm giving you a golden opportunity to take a step up from filing.'

'I don't mind filing,' Agatha said quickly. 'I mean, I know it's dull, but I never expected to...'

'To find working here exciting?' Luc held on to his patience with difficulty. Agatha, as timid as a mouse, and as background as canned elevator-music, irritated him. He could remember her as a teenager, skulking in corners, too tongue-tied to hold even the most basic of conversations with him. Apparently she was absolutely fine with everyone else, or so his mother had assured him. He had his doubts. Right now, she was trying hard to disappear into the folds of her oversized coat.

'Well?' he demanded impatiently.

'I don't think I'm really cut out for office work,' honesty compelled her to admit. 'Not that I'm not incredibly grateful for the opportunity to work here...' Or at least, she thought realistically, the opportunity to occupy a broom cupboard on the third floor from where she typed the occasional letter and received orders to file the occasional file. Mostly she was at his beck and call to do such things as sort out his dry cleaning, ensure his fridge was well stocked for those fleeting occasions when he was going to be in his apartment in Belgravia and see off his discarded women with appropriate tokens of fond farewell, ranging from lots of flowers to diamonds—a job delegated to her by Helen. In the space of eight months, five exotic supermodels had been given the red card.

'I realise you probably didn't have much of a choice.'

'None at all,' Luc agreed deflatingly. Nervous though she was, it would have been terrific if he had contradicted her statement, perhaps told her that she was, in her own way, a valued member of staff.

'Yes, Danielle and Mum can be quite forceful when they put their minds to it.'

'Agatha, why don't you sit down for a few minutes? I should have had a little chat with you sooner, but time's in scarce supply for me.'

'I know.' She hovered indecisively for a few seconds, then reluctantly shuffled back to her desk and sat down, watching as Luc perched on the edge and subjected her to one of those blistering looks that promised unwelcome revelations—probably to do with her lack of computer skills, or at the very least at her lack of enthusiasm for developing what precious few computer skills she did have.

Distracted, Luc frowned. 'What do you mean, *you know*?'

'I mean your mum always goes on about how hard you work and how you're never at home.'

Luc could scarcely credit what he was hearing. 'You're telling me that you sit around like the three witches in Macbeth, yakking about me?'

'No! Of course not.'

'Don't you have any kind of life back there? Anything better to do with your time?'

'Of course I have a life!' Or at least she had until she'd been made redundant from the garden centre. Or was he talking about her social life? 'I have lots of friends. You know, not everyone thinks that it's a top priority to head down to London at the first chance and make a fortune.'

'It's just as well I did, though, isn't it?' he inserted silkily. 'In case you'd forgotten, my mother was languishing in a two-bedroom cottage with peeling wallpaper and threadbare carpets. I think you'll agree that someone had to take charge and restore the family finances.'

'Yes.' She stared down at her fingers and then sneaked a look at him, and for a few heart-stopping seconds their eyes clashed, clear blue against deep, mossy green. That crush, which she had done her utmost to kill off, fluttered just below the surface, reminding her that, however hard she looked, Luc Laughton remained in a league of his own. Even when, like now, he was looking at her with the sort of rampant impatience that was even more insulting than open antagonism.

Her ready capitulation made him scowl. 'This…' he spread an expressive hand to encompass the office and beyond '…is real life, and thanks to it my mother can enjoy the lifestyle to which she has always been accustomed. My father made a lot of mistakes when it came to money, and fortunately I have learnt from all of them. Lesson number one is that nothing is achieved without putting in the hours.' He stood up and prowled through the tiny office, which was tucked away from the rest of the offices—and just as well, because he figured that she would have been even more lost had she been positioned in the middle of one of the several buzzing, high-energy floors occupied by his various staff.

'If you're not enjoying your job as much as you'd like, then you only have yourself to blame. Try looking at it as more than just biding time until some other gardening job comes available.'

'I'm not on the look out for another gardening job.' There were none to be had in London. She had looked.

'Take one step towards really integrating in this environment, Agatha. I don't want you to be offended by what I'm about to say…'

'Then don't say it!' She looked at him with big, blue pleading eyes. She knew that he was one of the 'cruel to be kind' breed of person with almost zero tolerance for anyone who didn't take the bull by the horns and wrestle life into subservience like him.

'He can be a little scary,' Danielle had confessed just before Agatha had moved to London. Just how scary, Agatha hadn't realised until she had started working for him. There was little direct contact, because most of her work came via Helen, who always wore a smile and pointed to any inaccuracies in her typing with a kindly shrug. On those occasions when he had descended from his ivory tower and cornered her himself, he had been a lot less forgiving.

'You can't be an ostrich, Agatha.' He paused in his restless, unnerving prowling to stand directly in front of her and waited until he had one-hundred percent of her attention. 'If you had taken your head out of the sand, you would have predicted your redundancy from that garden centre. They'd been losing money for at least two years; the credit crunch was the final straw. You could have been looking for a replacement job instead of waiting until the axe fell and finding yourself on the scrap heap.'

A rare spark of mutiny swept through her and she tightened her lips.

'But, no matter. You're here, and you are being paid a handsome wage, which you earn by taking absolutely no interest in anything at all.'

'I'll try harder,' she muttered, wondering how she could find someone so intensely attractive and yet loathe him at the same time. Were her feelings born out of habit—was that it? A silly, teenaged crush that had developed into some kind of low-lying, semi-permanent virus?

'Yes, you will, and you can start with your choice of clothes.'

'I beg your pardon?'

'I'm telling you this for your own good,' he imparted in the kind of voice that warned her that, whatever he had to say, it definitely wouldn't feel as though it was being delivered for her own good. 'Your choice of clothing doesn't really strike the right note for someone working in these offices. Look around you—do you see anyone one else who dresses in long gypsy skirts and baggy cardigans?'

Agatha was engulfed in a wave of anger and shame. He might be beautiful, but then roses were beautiful until you got to the thorns. How could she have nursed an inappropriate crush on this guy for all these years? she asked herself, not for the first time. From afar, when she'd been a kid, he had appeared all-powerful and so breathtakingly gorgeous. Even when Danielle had moved in with her parents, and she had had a chance to see the three-dimensional Luc when he had visited and stayed, she had still not been put off by the way he had always managed to eliminate her even when she had been right there in his line of vision.

She wasn't a stunning blonde with legs up to her armpits and big hair; it was as simple as that. She was invisible to him, a nondescript nobody who hovered in the periphery, helping prepare suppers and losing herself in the garden.

But he had always been scrupulously polite, even if he had barely registered her growing from a girl to a woman.

This, however, was beyond the pale.

'I'm comfortable in these clothes,' she told him in a

shaking voice. 'And I know you're doing me a huge favour by employing me, when I obviously have no talent for office work, but I don't see why I can't wear what I want. No one important sees me. I don't attend any meetings. And, if you don't mind, I really would like to go now. I have a very important date, as it happens, so if you'll excuse me…?' She stood up.

'A date? You have a *date*?' Luc was startled enough to find himself temporarily sidetracked.

'There's no need to sound so surprised.' Agatha walked towards the door, conscious of his eyes boring into her back.

'I'm surprised because you've been in London all of five minutes. Does Edith know about this?'

'Mum doesn't have to know every single thing I do here!' But she flushed guiltily. Her mother was a firm believer in the gentle art of courtship. She would have had a seizure had she known that her little girl was about to go out for dinner with a guy she had met casually in a bar whilst out with some of her girlfriends. She wouldn't understand that that was just how it happened in London, and she definitely wouldn't understand how important this date was for Agatha. At long last, she had decided to throw herself into the dating scene. Dreamy, fictitious relationships were all well and good for a kid of fifteen; at twenty-two, they were insane. She needed a real relationship with a real man who made real plans for a real future.

'Wait, wait, wait—not so fast, Agatha.' He reached out, captured her arm in a vice-like grip and swivelled her to face him.

'Okay, I'll come in really early tomorrow morning—even though it's Saturday—and sort out that stuff…' Just feeling his long fingers pressing into her coat was bringing her out in nervous perspiration and suddenly, more than ever, she wanted this date. She was sick to death with the way her body reacted to him. 'But I really, really need to get back to my flat or else I'm going to be late for Stewart.'

'Stewart? That the name of the man?' He released her, but his curiosity was piqued by this sudden insight into her private life. He really hadn't thought that she had one. In actual fact, he hadn't thought about her at all, despite his mother's pressing questions whenever he had called, asking him whether she was all right. He had given her a job, made sure that she was paid very well indeed, given her lack of experience, and frankly considered his duty done.

'Yes,' Agatha conceded reluctantly.

'And how long has this situation been going on?'

'I don't see that that's any of your business,' she mumbled with considerable daring. Was she supposed to hang around? Did he still want her to carry on working?

She decided to brave an exit, but she was sickeningly aware of him following her out of her office towards the lift. It was Friday and most of the employees on her floor had already left. She knew that the rest of his dedicated, richly rewarded staff further up the hierarchy would be beavering away, making things happen.

'None of my business? Did I just hear right?'

'Yes, you did.' Frustrated, Agatha swung round to look at him, her hands clenched into tight fists in the spacious pockets of her coat. 'Of course, it's your business what I do here between the hours of nine and whatever time I leave, but whatever I do outside working hours isn't your concern.'

'I wish I could concur but, like it or not, I have a responsibility towards you.'

'Because of a favour my parents did for Danielle a hundred years ago? That's crazy! Dad is—*was*—a vicar. Looking after the parishioners was what he did, and he enjoyed doing it. So did my mother. Not to mention that your mum was already a friend and had helped out countless times at the church fetes.' She punched the lift button and stared at it, ignoring the man at her side.

'Baking a few cakes now and again is a bit different from housing someone for a year.'

'Not for my parents. And Mum would be appalled if she thought that I was in London being a nuisance.' She had to cross her fingers behind her back when she said that. Her mother worried daily about her. Her phone calls were punctuated with anxious questions about her diet, rapidly followed up by not-too-subtle reminders that London was a very dangerous place. Sometimes, to back this up, Edith would quote from newspaper clippings, overblown, dramatic stories about knifings, murders or muggings that had occurred somewhere in London. She was unfailingly sceptical about any reassurances that Agatha was well and fine and didn't live anywhere remotely close to where said knifings or murders or muggings had occurred. Her mother would have loved nothing better than to think that Luc was taking Agatha's welfare on board.

The lift had finally decided to arrive and she looked at Luc in alarm as he stepped inside it with her.

'What…What are you doing?'

'I'm taking the lift down with you.'

'But you can't!'

'How do you work that one out?'

'You've just told me that you have this deal to complete—remember? All hands on deck?' She was about to press the 'ground' button, but Luc got there before her, and she spun round to face him in angry disbelief,

'Why are we going down to the basement?'

'Because my car is there, and I'm giving you a lift to your house.'

'Are you mad?'

'Look, do you want the truth?'

Agatha, in receipt of various home truths from him already, was heartily against hearing any more, but her mouth refused to work.

'I had my mother on the telephone yesterday,' Luc imparted bluntly. 'It would seem that I haven't shown sufficient interest in what you've been up to since you've come here.'

This was turning out to be a favour that carried a very high price. Normally indifferent to the opinions of other people, Luc dearly loved his mother, and so had gritted his teeth and listened in silence as she'd gently quizzed him about Agatha. She'd registered concern when told that he hadn't the faintest idea how she was doing. Nor had she bought in to the logic that he had fulfilled his part of the bargain and so what was the problem if he washed his hands of the problem?

Agatha gaped at him, mortified, barely noticing when the lift doors pinged open and he guided her out of the lift towards a gleaming, silver Aston Martin.

'I don't believe you,' she said in a tight, breathless voice.

'Well, you'd better start. Edith is worried. You don't sound happy; you're vague when she asks you about the job. You tell her that it's all right, by which she takes it to mean that it's making you miserable. The last time she saw you, you seemed to be losing weight.' As far as Luc could make out, under the shapeless coat she looked perfectly healthy to him.

Agatha groaned and buried her head in her hands.

'Strap up and tell me where you live.'

While he fiddled with his sat nav, giving it instructions to go to the address she could barely impart through gritted teeth, Agatha had time to conduct a quick mental review of the last hour, starting with his sudden interest in producing more challenging work for her to do.

'This is awful.' She placed cool hands on her burning cheeks.

'You're telling me.'

'Is that why you hunted me down to give me all that stuff to do?'

'Try getting one-hundred percent involved and you might have less time to spend crying down the line to your mother and complaining that you're bored and unhappy. I have no idea how I managed to get roped into a caretaker role, but roped in I've been.'

'But I don't *want* you taking an interest in me!' she all but wailed. Luc, in passing, thought that was interesting because women usually wanted just the opposite out of him.

'I'm not taking an interest in you,' he disputed flatly. 'I'm broadening your work parameters: more interesting projects. Less back-room stuff. So you can start thinking about the wardrobe issue. Front-of-house demands a more stringent dress code than sacks and old shoes.'

'Okay, I will.' Just to bring the horrifying conversation to an end.

'And call me a mug, but I'm giving you a lift back to your house because I want to find out about this date of yours, satisfy myself that you're not about to put your life at risk with some low-life drifter. The last thing I need is my mother showing up at my office like an avenging angel because you've managed to get yourself into trouble.'

If she could have burrowed a hole in the soft, cream leather of the car seat and escaped to another county, Agatha would have done so. Never had she felt so humiliated in her life before. In all the scenarios that had played in her head over the years, not one had involved Luc taking an interest in her because he had no option. Nor had she ever envisaged being told that she looked like a bag lady, which was what he had implied.

She should never have accepted this job. No good ever came of accepting hand outs, although she knew that if she voiced that opinion he would have the perfect come back. Hadn't his own mother accepted a hand out of sorts when she had moved in with her parents in their rambling vicarage? That, to her way of thinking, was different, as was the dispenser of the hand out. Luc Laughton was hardly a kindly, middle-aged man charmed at the thought of doing a favour for a neighbour in need. He was a predatory shark who would have no qualms about eating the recipient of his charity if he felt like it.

'I can take care of myself,' she opined, staring straight ahead. 'I'm not going to get myself into any trouble.'

'You obviously haven't breathed a word of this so-called date to your mother,' Luc guessed shrewdly. 'Which leads me to think that you might be ashamed of him. Am I right?'

'I haven't said anything to Mum because I've only just *met* him!'

He noticed that she hadn't tackled the issue of whether she was ashamed of the man. Was he married? If he were to guess the kind of guy she would go for, it wouldn't be a married man. Her life had been nothing if not sheltered. His distant memory was of a girl with almost no sense of style, certainly not the sort of style favoured by her peer group: short, tight skirts, skinny, tight jeans, dangly jewellery. No, if he had to take a stab in the dark, he would bet his last few bucks on a fellow garden-lover, someone who got worked up about eco issues and saving the planet.

But if that were the case wouldn't she have been on the phone in a heartbeat to tell all to Edith? Even if, as she said, he had only recently landed on the scene.

'Is he married? You can tell me, although don't expect

me to give you my blessing, because I strongly disapprove of anyone getting entangled with someone who's married.'

Agatha's head jerked round at the cool contempt in his voice. Who did he think he was, she wondered? A shining example of morality? Normally reduced to quaking jelly in his presence, she took a deep breath and said very quickly in a very high, tremulous voice, 'I don't think you have a right to disapprove of anything.'

For a few seconds she actually wondered if he had heard her because he didn't say a word. She found that she was holding her breath, which she expelled slowly when he finally answered, his voice icy cold. 'Come again?'

'I've been given the job of buying all your discards their parting presents,' Agatha admitted tightly. 'Flowers, jewellery, expensive holidays—what's so great about having a string of pointless relationships? How can you preach about married men when you think it's all right to string some poor woman along knowing that you have no intention of getting involved with her?

Luc cursed fluently under his breath, outraged that she dared bring her opinions to bear on his private life. Not that he was about to justify his behaviour.

'Since when is pleasure pointless?' was all he said, clamping down on the rising tide of his temper because for Agatha fun without commitment would be anathema. When he had launched himself into the City, climbing that first rung of the ladder which he knew would lead him to the top, he had had the misfortune to fancy himself in love with a woman who had turned from a softly spoken angel to a harpy the second the demands of work had begun to interfere with her daily need to be stroked. She had complained solidly and noisily about meetings that over ran, had dug her heels in and lashed out at trips abroad and had eventually started looking elsewhere for someone who could give her undivided attention.

It had been a salutary lesson. So leading women up a garden path was definitely not a route he was interested in taking. From the very start, they knew that commitment wasn't going to be on the agenda. He was honest to a fault which, he personally thought, was a virtue to be praised, for it was in short supply in most men.

Which brought him back to the issue of this mysterious guy about whom she was being so secretive.

'But perhaps you don't agree with me,' he drawled, flicking a sidelong glance in her direction. 'Or maybe I'm wrong. Maybe you've been bitten by the big-city bug and come to the conclusion that there's nothing pointless in having fun. Is that it? I notice you still haven't mentioned Stewart's marital status.'

'Of course he's not married! He happens to be a very nice person. In fact, he's taking me out to a very expensive restaurant in Knightsbridge—San Giovanni. Stewart says that it's famous. In fact, you've probably heard of it.'

At which point, Luc's ears pricked up. This was definitely *not* the kind of man he'd pictured and, yes, he certainly had heard of the restaurant in question. It was the frequent haunt of the rich and famous.

So what did Agatha have that would attract someone who could afford to take her there? He shot her a sidelong glance and frowned; it struck him that she did have something about her, a certain innocence that a wide-boy Londoner might find suitably challenging. He didn't like to entertain the notion but sweet, prim Agatha might just be seen as ripe for corruption.

Not an eco-warrior, not a married man…so just someone out to use her? Or was he reading the situation all wrong?

Curiosity, lamentably in short supply in his life, shifted

somewhere inside him. He had acted on the spur of the moment in offering her a lift home, and really he should be heading back to his office to put the finishing touches to reports that needed emailing sooner than yesterday. But, hell, work could wait for a little while. Hadn't he been entrusted with a mission, in a manner of speaking?

In the space of seconds, plans for the remainder of his evening were put on hold.

'I'll drive you to Knightsbridge. And before you say anything...' his sensuous mouth curved into a half smile '... there's no need to thank me.'

CHAPTER TWO

Luc settled down with a cup of coffee for the long haul. Never mind about running late; it was his experience with women that their ability to get changed in under an hour was practically zero. Agatha might not follow the normal pattern of the women he knew, but she was of the female species. Enough said.

He glanced around the poky room with an expression of distaste. He had nothing against bedsits, per se, but it was evident that, whoever the landlord was, he specialised in the art of ripping off the young and inexperienced. The walls showed promising signs of damp and the single radiator looked like something rescued from the ark. The large, old-fashioned sash window overlooking the busy pavements was reasonably attractive but the wood was peeling, and he knew that if he stood too close to it he would be in danger of frostbite from the cold air blowing through the gaps in the frame. He wondered whether he should get more details about the guy. It would take next to no effort to put the fear of God into him.

He was restlessly pacing the room, stopping to scowl with displeasure at the hundred and one little deficiencies in her living accommodation to which Agatha had grown accustomed over the months, when she emerged from her bedroom.

'I got ready as quickly as I could. You didn't have to wait here for me. I could easily have got the tube back into London.'

Luc spun round at the sound of her voice behind him, and for a few seconds he stood very still, his stunning eyes unreadable—which was a disappointment. Although she hated the situation she was in, and hated the fact that he now considered her a burden with which he had to deal, he *did* still happen to be in her bedsit and she *was* quite dressed up. For her.

'How do you think I look?' she asked nervously, stretching out her arms and trying in to suck in her stomach.

An only child adored by her parents who had given up on ever having children until she'd come along, Agatha was still keenly aware that her figure didn't fit the trend, despite all the reassurances she had had growing up. She wasn't tall enough or skinny enough or flat-chested enough ever to look fashionable. Nor was her blond hair poker-straight.

But, having been insulted about her clothes, she had made a special attempt to look as smart as she could for her date—and incidentally to prove to Luc that she wasn't the complete fashion disaster that he seemed to think she was.

'You've done something to your hair,' he commented neutrally. She had a figure. Hell, how had he managed to miss that? It was weirdly shocking to see her in figure-hugging clothes that made the most of what he now registered, with a stunned attention to detail, as a tiny waist and the sort of lush breasts that made teenage boys and grown men stop in their tracks. When had she grown up? When had she stopped being a gauche, awkward teenager who hovered in the background and become…? He had to look away because his body had been galvanised into a response that stunned him.

'Well, I left it loose. It's so curly and unmanageable that I tie it up for work.'

'And it's heart warming to see that you possess something other than a flowing skirt and baggy jumper. It bodes well for your new approach to dressing for the office, although you might want to have a serious re-think about the length of the skirt.' Slender legs encased in sheer, black tights staged an all-out battle with his self-control. He was in the grip of utter, stupefied surprise—unfamiliar territory for him.

'What's wrong with it?' She bent slightly to inspect the hem of her dress with a frown. 'It's no shorter than some of the skirts the other girls wear.' She sighed, knowing what he meant without him having to spell it out. Short and tight was only acceptable on stick insects. 'Anyway,' she added defensively, 'I wouldn't dream of wearing anything like this to work. In fact, it's the only dress I have. Well, the only—'

He was reaching for her coat, clamping down on a reaction that he deemed inappropriate, inexplicable and ridiculous, and she winced at her propensity for rambling. Her mother had always called her a chatterbox and they had all been convinced at the garden centre that her success with the difficult plants lay in her ability to talk to them about anything and everything. But Luc wasn't interested in anything she had to say. She shut her mouth abruptly, and stiffly allowed herself to be helped into her coat.

'The only *what*?'

'It doesn't matter. It wasn't very interesting, anyway. I was just going to say that I don't have an awful lot of dresses. There was never much need to wear them when I worked at the garden centre.'

'I do recall some green overalls,' he drawled.

'I've never seen you at the garden centre.' Embarrassed colour was spreading to her hairline, and she was really relieved that he was following her so that he couldn't see her face.

'You would have remembered seeing me? That garden centre was pretty big.'

'Of course I would have remembered seeing you—because…because you would have been so out of *place* there. I guess you might have been with Danielle. You might have a fleet of gardeners at the big house, but she always gets involved choosing the flowers, and the herbs, of course, for that little herb garden at the back of the kitchen.'

'No idea what you're talking about. I noticed you walking back to your house one evening in some green overalls and workman boots.'

Agatha flushed and had a vivid picture of how she must have looked to him, hurrying home still in her overalls, her boots dirty, her hair a tangled mess. And then in his office—no longer in overalls or dungarees but still dressed down in her comfortable, baggy clothes, while every other woman wafted around in high-heeled pumps and dapper little black or grey suits with their hair neatly combed back, obeying orders not to wriggle out of their pins and clips by mid-morning.

'I don't suppose you know a lot of women who would wear overalls and boots,' she said weakly, stepping into his car and slamming the door behind her.

'Not one.' He turned to her as he switched on the engine and the low, powerful car roared into life. 'In fact, the women I know wouldn't be seen dead in anything like that.'

'I know.'

'Really?'

'Well, I've seen the kind of women you've gone out with over the years. Not that I've taken any real interest, you understand, but when Danielle lived with us you often came to visit with one of your girlfriends; they all looked the same, so I'm guessing you like them with lots of make-up and designer clothes.'

'Is there a sting in the tail with that remark?' Luc looked at her wonderingly before easing his car out of its parking space to head back towards the centre.

'I don't know what you mean.'

'No,' he said shortly, still unnerved by the underhand trick his body had played on him back there. 'I don't suppose you do.'

'What do you mean, then?'

'I mean that honesty is all well and good, but in London it might pay to be a bit more streetwise.' No wonder Edith worried about her. 'For one thing, you're being ripped off by your landlord. How much are you paying for that dump?'

'It's not a dump!' But she told him, and her heart sank when he gave a bark of cynical laughter.

'The man must have seen you coming a mile off. Green round the ears, no clue as to what sort of questions to ask, waving a stash of money. So what does he do? Overcharge for a disgusting hole with erratic heating and not enough space to swing a cat. Fifteen minutes in that place and I could spot enough signs of damp and rot to get the whole house condemned.'

'It's more comfortable when the weather's warm.'

'I bet it is.' Luc's lips curled with derision. 'You don't have to spend your nights praying that the place will be warm when you wake up in the morning! It's a disgrace.'

'I suppose,' Agatha admitted on a sigh. 'But when I looked around, Mr Travis promised that he would put right loads of things. I keep asking him, but his mother's been taken into hospital and the poor man's hardly been around.'

At this Luc burst out laughing before glancing across at her with rampant disbelief at her gullibility. 'So Poor Mr Travis has a sick mother in hospital which means that he just can't find the time to make sure that the damp problem in the bedsit gets seen to—or the rotting window frames get fixed, or the rancid carpet gets taken up? I wonder how poor Mr Travis would feel if a letter from my lawyer landed on his desk tomorrow morning.'

'You wouldn't!'

'Oh, I would, believe me. The man's a crook who's decided to take advantage of you. I'm not a superstitious guy, but I'm beginning to think that my mother's phone call was the hand of fate, because another month in that place in the middle of January and *you* would have been the one occupying the hospital bed—with pneumonia! No wonder you wear ten layers of clothing when you come to work. You've probably become accustomed to that!'

'I don't wear ten layers of clothes when I come to work.' The words 'charity case' were swimming in her head, making her feel nauseous.

'You weren't equipped for life in London.' Luc steamrollered over her interruption. 'You grew up in a vicarage and spent your short working life in a garden centre watering plants. I can't say that I enjoy being anybody's caretaker, but I'm beginning to see why my mother wanted me to get involved.'

'That's the most horrible thing you could ever say to me.'

'Why?'

'Because…' Because, a little voice said nastily, she didn't want Luc Laughton to think of her as a hapless country bumpkin who needed looking after. She wanted him to think of her as a sexy young woman—or even just as a *woman.* Fat chance! He hadn't even noticed her outfit. At least in any way that could be interpreted as complimentary.

'Well? I'm not in the habit of doing good deeds, but

I'm willing to change my life rules for you. You should be flattered.'

'No one's ever flattered to think that they're too stupid to take care of themselves,' Agatha told him stiffly. Her eyes stung but she wasn't going to feel sorry for herself. She was going to remember that she was about to have dinner with a dishy, eligible man who would never have asked her out if he had thought that she was as pathetic as Luc made her out to be.

'I've always found that it pays to be realistic,' Luc responded bracingly. 'When my father died and I came home to that financial mess, I realised very quickly that I could do one of two things: I could sit around, get depressed and become bitter or I could just go out and begin to rebuild everything that was lost.'

'I find it hard to think of you getting depressed or feeling bitter.'

'I don't allow those negative feelings to influence what I do in life.'

'I wish I could be as strong minded as you,' Agatha was forced to concede, thinking of all the doubts she had nurtured over the years despite her very happy background.

When her friends had all started experimenting with make-up and going on diets so that they could look like the models in magazines, she had taken a back seat, knowing that inner beauty was all that mattered, and that wanting to look like someone else or aspire to someone else's life was a waste of time. Of course, in London, the whole inner-beauty conviction had taken a bit of a knocking. She had largely felt like a fish out of water when she had gone out with her girlfriends from work, who had developed amazing skills of transformation, morphing from office workers to vamps with a change of clothes and bold make-up. Her stretchy black dress which made her feel horrendously exposed because it was fairly short with a fairly revealing neckline was still conservative compared to the stuff some of her friends wore, and she was so unaccustomed to wearing jewellery that she had to stop herself from twiddling with the strands of chunky copper round her neck.

'I mean,' she continued, musing, 'You're so sure of yourself. You set your goals and you just go after them. Like a bloodhound.'

'Nice comparison,' Luc muttered under his breath.

'Don't you ever sit back and wonder if you're doing the right thing?'

'Never.' With more than half the journey completed, Luc thought that it was time he got down to the business of quizzing her about her date. More and more, he got the feeling that she was a loose cannon, an innocent released to the mercy of any passing opportunist. 'So this Stewart character…?' he prompted.

Brought back down to earth with a bump, Agatha blinked. Her mind had been wandering. She had almost forgotten about Stewart.

'Yes…?'

'How did you meet him?'

'Oh, usual way,' she said with a casual, studied shrug; this was the perfect opportunity to prove to him that she wasn't as abnormal as he seemed to think she was. 'At a bar. You know…'

'At a bar? You go *bar hopping*?'

'When you say "bar hopping"…'

'Moving from *bar* to *bar*,' Luc intoned very slowly, emphasising each word. 'Getting more and more drunk before finally landing up somewhere, barely able to stand.'

Agatha bid a fond farewell to nurturing that misconception for him. The whole idea sounded pretty disgusting. She had heard ample stories of girls who had got themselves in trouble by doing just that sort of thing. Her father had counselled at least three that she could remember.

'When you told me that you were worried about me getting into trouble, that's not what you were talking about, was it? You didn't really think that I might end up pregnant by some guy whose name I never found out because I had gone out and had too much to drink, did you?'

'Calm down. I don't think you're the kind of girl.'

Insult or compliment? she wondered. Compliment, she decided. 'I met him at a wine bar. Near the office, actually. I went there with a couple of girls from work. We were having a drink and the bar tender brought over a bottle of champagne and told us that Stewart had sent it for me. When I looked over, he waved and then he came across to join us, and he and I ended talking for quite a while.'

'What about?'

'Lots of things,' Agatha told him irritably. 'He's very interesting. And very smart. Also good-looking.'

'I'm beginning to get the picture.'

'He wanted to know all about what I did, which was great, because most guys just like talking about themselves.'

'I didn't realise that you were that experienced.'

'I'm not experienced…with men in London. Naturally I've been out with quite a few boys at home, and generally speaking they just want to talk about football or cars. Very stereotypical.' She slid her eyes across to Luc, and as usual her mouth suddenly went dry, and she felt hot and flustered for no apparent reason. This was the first real conversation she had ever had with him, and she was enjoying herself, much as she loathed to admit it. 'What do you talk about when you go out with a woman?' she found herself asking curiously.

'Strangely enough, I find that it's the women who tend to do all the talking.' He had little interest in holding hands over the dinner table and sharing his thoughts with someone he planned on bedding.

'Perhaps you make a good listener,' Agatha suggested doubtfully. 'Although I'm not really sure that you do. You didn't listen to me when I told you that I could take care of myself.'

'And evidence of your living conditions proves that I was right on that score.'

'Maybe I should have been a little more insistent with Mr Travis,' she conceded, giving a little ground on this one thing—because he had yet to discover, in addition to all the other problems he had listed, the temperamental fridge and its even more temperamental close relative, the oven. 'But I'm a big girl when it comes to dealing with everything else.'

'That's true enough on the surface,' Luc murmured. 'You might look the part but I have a feeling that it only runs skin deep.'

'Look the part?' Was he telling her that she was fat? She might not be a stick insect, but she wasn't fat—plump, maybe, but not fat. And, if that was what he had meant, why was she stupidly asking for confirmation? Did her capacity for masochism never end?

'You're a big girl, Agatha. Funny, I hadn't really noticed until now.' Again he tried to equate the teenager with the woman next to him, and again that weird kick that shot through his body as if he had been suddenly hot-wired.

'You mean the dress?' she suggested in a taut voice. The very same dress she had exhibited for him, hands outstretched, vainly hoping that he might compliment her. They had reached the restaurant, but she wasn't quite ready to drop the conversation, so when he parked and turned towards her she garnered her very small supply of courage and stayed put, arms folded, her full mouth flattened into a thin line. 'I'm not ready to go in just yet.'

'Pre-dinner nerves? Don't worry. If he's that good-looking, that charming and that interested in every word you have to say, I'm sure you're in for a scintillating evening.'

'It's not pre-dinner nerves. It's…it's *you!*'

'I have no idea what you're talking about.'

'You haven't said one nice thing to me all evening. I know you would never have employed me to work for your company. I know you've been forced to help me out because you think you owe my family a favour—which you don't, but you could at least *try* and be nice. You've told me that I'm no good at what I do…'

She tabulated all her points by sticking up her fingers one by one. 'You've told me that the clothes I wear to work are horrendous because I don't wear that uniform of tight suits and high heels, even though I'm hidden away most of the time. I need to invest in a new wardrobe just in case someone important sees me and falls into a dead faint, I suppose. You've told me that I wouldn't have a clue how to look after myself in a place like London, you've told me how awful my bedsit is, and now? Now you sit there telling me that I look *fat!*'

Listing all those slights out loud hadn't been a good idea. Taken one at a time, she could reason them away, but faced with all of them in their entirety was just too much. A wave of forlorn self-pity rushed over her; her eyes began to leak and it wasn't long before the leak became a flood. When she found a handkerchief pressed into her hands, she accepted it gratefully and dabbed her eyes as her silly crying jag was reduced to the odd hiccup.

Embarrassment replaced self-pity. She blew her nose and stuffed the hankie into her bag.

'Sorry. Sorry, sorry, sorry. I must be nervous; you're right.'

'I should be the one apologising.' Luc had no time for weeping, wailing women, but for some reason the sight of Agatha in floods of tears had struck right to the heart of him. Hearing her neat little summary of everything he had said to her over the course of the evening had not been one of his proudest moments.

'It's okay,' she whispered, desperate to remove herself from his presence where seconds before she had wanted to stay and speak her mind. She tilted her face to him. 'Do I look a mess? I bet my make-up's everywhere. What's he going to think?' She gave a wobbly laugh.

'That you've got amazing eyes and that you're anything but fat,' he said roughly.

And just like that the atmosphere altered with sudden, sizzling electricity. It was as if the world had suddenly shrunk to the small space between them. She thought she could actually hear the rush of blood through her veins but then she realised that she was just imagining it. Thinking straight, this was the man who hadn't had a good word to say to her.

'You don't have to say that.'

'No. I don't.' But his voice had changed imperceptibly. 'But, just for the record, you do have amazing eyes, and when I said that you're a big girl now I didn't mean it in the literal sense.'

'You didn't?'

'I meant you've grown up. That dress makes you look sexy.'

'Sexy? Me?'

'You. Why do you sound so shocked?'

Because you're saying it, she thought, while her face burnt and her pulses raced and her heart sang. 'Let's hope

Stewart agrees!' Just in case those laser-sharp eyes of his could bore a hole in her head and pluck out that inappropriate thought.

'Stewart. The hot date. Yes.' His voice was clipped and he reached to open his car door. 'I'll come in with you. Hang on...' He leaned across and carefully rubbed his finger under her eye, and then he laughed softly when she jerked back in surprise.

'Relax. Just a bit of smudged mascara. Anyone would think you'd never been touched before, Agatha.'

'I...I have my hankie. Well, *your* hankie. I can do that! Could you switch on the light? I need to have a look at my face. Make sure my eyes aren't too puffy.' She laughed shrilly, and then chattered and tutted and avoided eye contact as she inspected her face in her little hand mirror, so that by the time she had finished dabbing and rubbing she could present him with a bright, tinny smile.

'Right, all ready! Can't wait!'

Three and a half hours later, a driving, bitter rain greeted her outside.

'So, when can I see you again?'

Agatha looked at Stewart who was pressed a bit closer to her than she would have liked—unavoidable because they were both sheltering under his umbrella. She had made sure that the buttons on her coat were done up to the neck. Whilst it had been flattering to be the object of his compliments, she had felt uncomfortable under his roving eye, even though she knew that this was what she should have expected. Several times she had caught him addressing her cleavage.

Also, her mind had been all over the place, analyzing and re-analysing everything Luc had said to her, then picking apart what she remembered of their conversation so that she could begin the process all over again. She had had to ask Stewart to repeat himself several times, had failed to notice the quality of the wine, which he had brushed aside—although she knew that he had been offended from the mottled colour of his neck—and had left most of her main course because she had accidentally ordered the wrong thing from the menu, which was in Italian.

She had no idea why he wanted to see her for a second date, and it felt almost churlish to have to think about it when he had been so good to overlook her little lapses and show so much interest in everything she had to say about every aspect of her life and job, however insignificant the detail.

'Tomorrow's Saturday,' he murmured. 'I know a great little club in Chelsea. Anybody who's anybody is a member. You wouldn't believe the famous faces I've spotted there; you'd love it.'

'Maybe we can do something next week.'

Stewart pouted with disappointment but picked himself up with remarkable ease, and as he reached out to hail a cab he pulled her close to him and, before she could wriggle away, planted a hot, laughing kiss full on her mouth.

'Sure I can't tempt you back to my place? I make a pretty good Irish coffee, if I say so myself.'

Agatha laughed and declined, and was guiltily relieved when he slid into the taxi, taking his umbrella with him, cheerily insouciant to the fact that she was now in the process of being drenched. And would therefore have to hail a cab, even though a taxi ride back to North London would be a ridiculous waste of money.

And, now that she did require one, there were none to be spotted. Although…

A familiar silver car pulled up to the kerb and she found the passenger door pushed open, waiting for her to oblige.

'Get in, Agatha. Or risk pneumonia.'

'Wow. How did you do that—show up just when I was

about to start walking to the underground? Anyway...' she straightened '...I can't have you messing up your Friday night to give me a lift home because you feel sorry for me.' She dug her hands into her pockets and began walking towards the underground while the car trailed her, sped up and then the passenger door was flung open again and Luc was glaring out at her from the driver's seat.

'Get in or I'll have to get out, lift you up and chuck you in. Do you want that? Do you want that kind of scene in the middle of Knightsbridge?'

'Have you been here the whole time waiting for me?' she asked as soon as she was inside the car, luxuriating in the warmth and dryness.

'Don't be crazy, but I had to come back here for you.'

'Why on earth would you have to do that? I know you think I'm a hopeless case, but I've been getting to and from work every day on public transport. I know how to use the buses and tubes! Course, it took a little time, but I got there in the end. Mum hates it. She keeps telling me that tubes are a breeding ground for muggers. And she's only been to London a handful of times—and never on a tube! Gosh, sorry; I'm talking too much again.' But like a bad dream all thoughts of her date had disappeared like a puff of smoke.

'I got Antonio to call me when you were about to pay the bill.'

'Who's Antonio?'

'The owner of the place. We go back a long way.'

'What if Stewart and I had decided to move on to somewhere else—a club, or a bar? Or I could just have decided to go back to his place.'

'Did he ask you to?'

'As a matter of fact, he did.'

'And you turned him down. Good girl. Wise decision.'

'Who knows what I'll say the next time he asks, though?'

She looked across at him. He had changed out of his work clothes into a pair of dark jeans and a thick, black jumper. His coat had been tossed to the back seat. She was ashamed to admit even to herself that if she had all the time in the world, she would never tire looking at him.

He opened his mouth as though on the verge of saying something, only to think better of it.

'So you've arranged another date, have you?'

'Not as such…' She teased those three little words out as long as she could. 'Who knows?'

'Who knows indeed?' Luc intoned in a peculiar voice.

'What have you done this evening?' she asked a little breathlessly.

'Work. I've been working on, eh, a very interesting project, let's just say.'

'Do you know, it's great that you enjoy your job so much,' Agatha said warmly. 'Although it's a little sad that you want to spend your Friday nights doing it.'

'Your honesty is beyond belief, Agatha. I would have entertained myself in the usual way, but there was something a little more important I had to do. After doing that, I realised that I needed to have a little chat with you. Let's just say that one thing gave rise to the other.'

'Why are you being mysterious? What do we need to chat about?' Why did the words 'little chat' inspire such feelings of dread? Was he about to sack her? Had she overstepped the line with her beyond-belief honesty?

Agatha quailed at the thought of returning to Yorkshire as a failed charity case—but London, even a bedsit in London, was impossible without a pay packet at the end of the month.

'This isn't the right place. I am going to take you to your house, you are going to ask me in for a cup of coffee and we can have our chat then.'

'Can't it wait until Monday?'

'I think it's better to get it out of the way. Now, relax; tell me about your evening. Take me through how a guy who leaves a woman standing in the pouring rain sees fit to entertain her.'

Now out of a job, Agatha didn't think she had anything to lose by being totally, one-hundred percent honest. People were never honest with Luc, with the exception of his mother. They tiptoed around him, bowing and scraping, 'yes, sir', 'no sir'. He was one of those lethally good-looking men who were just too powerful for their own good. He was unapologetic in his arrogance and in his assumption that he could play by his own unique set of rules.

'I don't want to be having this conversation with you.'

'Why not? Are you embarrassed? There's nothing to be ashamed of because it was a flop. These things happen. You just have to shrug it off and move on.' Furthermore, she would be glad of his sterling advice when he filled her in on a few missing jigsaw pieces. His Friday night had been ruined, but he was upbeat about it.

Without the hassle of traffic, it took them less than half an hour before he pulled up outside her house, and Agatha hadn't said a word for the brief drive. Her evening out had been disappointing, but there was a slow resentment building inside her at the way Luc had showed up for her, like a parent collecting a child from a birthday party. And then to hear him dismiss her date as a flop, something unfortunate that she should step over and forget with a shrug, made her even more angry.

She hadn't asked him to start interfering in her life. He had barely noticed her for the past eight months, but now that he had been forced to he had decided to give the project his full and complete attention. But he still couldn't conceal the fact that he found her annoying and a nuisance. Everything about her offended him, starting with the way she didn't seem to know how to suck up to him sufficiently, and ending with the way she looked—and Luc, being Luc, he made no bones about hiding his reaction.

And now he needed to chat to her. It could only be about her job. He had gone away, added up all the reasons why she didn't belong in his company and was going to break it to her that, however indebted he felt to her mother, having her as dead weight in his office was too steep a price to pay.

'I know what you're going to say,' she burst out as soon as he had killed the engine. 'And you can just tell me right here.' She had unclasped her seat belt, and now she swivelled round to look at him.

'You know what I'm going to say?'

'Yes. I know what you think of me, and I know exactly what you're going to say.' The words tumbled out with feverish urgency.

'I don't think you have a clue what I think of you,' Luc informed her huskily. 'And you certainly don't know what I'm going to say to you. And, no, we are not going to have this conversation in my car.'

'I just want to get it over and done with,' Agatha implored, but he was already out the car and she hurriedly followed suit, fumbling in her bag for the house key and feeling the tension escalate with every step up to her bedsit.

Stepping back into the room, she switched on the light and looked around it with new eyes, Luc's eyes. She took in the discoloured walls, which she had tried to hide by sticking up two large, colourful posters, the sagging, tired furniture, the stained carpet peeping out from behind the thin Moroccan rug she had put over it and the seeping cold. He was right; who else would put up with all that?

'I'm a failure, and you've come to terms with that, and you want to find a polite way of telling me to get lost,' she said in a rush, before she had even removed her coat. 'I'm sacked, aren't I?'

'Sacked? Why would I want to sack you?' Eyes as green as the deep ocean stared steadily at her. 'I want to tell you that I know Stewart Dexter and I know what he wants from you.'

CHAPTER THREE

'You know Stewart?' Agatha's mouth fell open and she gaped at him in complete bewilderment. 'I don't understand. You've never met him before; I didn't introduce you...'

'Take your coat off and sit down.'

'If you knew him, why didn't you come across to say hello?' While she hovered, frantically trying to unravel this unforeseen turn of events, she found herself being helped out of her coat. 'Well, I guess it's a good thing that I'm not being sacked,' she breathed shakily, clutching the one thing he had said that had made sense.

His fabulous green eyes settled on her and suddenly she felt very exposed in her tight black dress and her silly, high black shoes. It was a relief to sink into the chair facing him. When she glanced down, she was accosted by the embarrassing sight of her deep cleavage and abundant breasts straining against the soft, elastic fabric of her dress. She resolved to shelve the outfit first thing in the morning.

'But I don't understand why it was so important for you to race over to the restaurant to tell me this.'

'When you mentioned the name of the guy you were meeting, it rang a bell, but I didn't think anything of it,' Luc said carefully. 'I have a finger in a lot of pies and so I meet people from a range of industries. And Dexter is a common enough surname. But then I saw the guy at the restaurant and the alarm bells started ringing.'

'Alarm bells? I don't know what you're talking about.'

'You're not going to like what I have to say.' Never one to waste time beating about the bush, Luc now paused and considered his words carefully. Staring across the table at him, her eyes wide and perplexed, Agatha looked very, very young, and strangely enough the revealing nature of her dress only accentuated that impression.

'How old are you?' he asked roughly, finding himself momentarily sidetracked.

'Sorry?'

'Forget that. It's not important. There's no easy way to say this, but Dexter might not be the guy you think he is.'

'I really don't know what you're talking about. You mean Stewart Dexter *isn't* Stewart Dexter? Who is he, then?'

'He's someone who used to work for one my companies. When I thought I recognised him, I went back to the office and did a little research.'

'You ran a background check on my date?' Agatha trembled. 'How could you *do* that?' Her huge blue eyes, staring up at him, were full of reproach.

'I'd advise any woman to run a background check on a man they'd picked up in a bar before they went out with him on a date, Agatha. This isn't a small village in Yorkshire.'

'I'm not ashamed that I trust people, Luc. I know *you* don't, and I can understand why. Your father trusted George Satz and in return he had all his money stolen from him.'

The story had run in the local newspaper for weeks, with each new revelation of embezzlement producing a fresh torrent of speculation. With Elliot Laughton no longer around to defend himself, details went uncontested. Members of staff were interviewed and their bafflement at the scale of the financial losses only added to the scandal. At the time,

Agatha had felt deeply sorry for Luc, although that was something she would never have shared with him. He had returned from university with a protective barrier around him that repelled words of sympathy. The whole business would surely have accounted for the man he was later to become—a man who would never know how to give anyone else the benefit of the doubt.

Her meandering mind returned to the present and she cleared her throat. 'Well, almost all his money. So I can see why you're so suspicious of other people—but I'm not. It would never occur to me to do a background check on anyone! Anyway, we were meeting in a public place, and there was no way that I was going to go anywhere afterwards with him.' Her angry eyes locked with his and she leaned forward, her hands balled into fists.

'Like I told you,' Luc's voice was cool and even and controlled, 'You're not savvy about the kind of guy a girl can get mixed up with in London. Dexter was sacked from the company a year and a half ago. He was a minor cog in one of the IT companies I took over. He was caught trying to hack into confidential programs to do with software. He was kicked out the second the breach was discovered by one of my people.'

'I don't believe you.'

'You don't *want* to believe me. And I don't *want* to be sitting here telling you this. But some good Samaritan's got to fill you in on the man. Naturally, in the case of a dismissal of that nature, no references were forthcoming. He disappeared and, as far as I know, he isn't working for any of the major players in the country. Did he mention the name of his employer?'

'No.' Agatha was beginning to feel giddy. 'Are you sure about all this? I mean, it's easy to confuse people...to think you recognise someone when you don't know them really...'

'I don't make those kinds of mistakes.'

Agatha was immediately silenced.

'Everyone makes mistakes,' she muttered eventually.

Luc ignored that. 'I could find out what outfit Dexter managed to inveigle his way into and get him fired, not least because he would have had to forge his references from my company.'

'I'm not a child! If Stewart is really the person you think he is, then I can just ask him outright.'

'And I'm sure he would come up with a very convincing story.'

'And I would be so easy to convince, wouldn't I? Because I'm green round the ears.'

'How is it that you are so good at making me feel like a monster?' he murmured softly. An unnatural urge to put his arms around her was squashed before it could take form. 'I'm actually doing you a favour by telling you this.'

'It doesn't feel like a favour. Even if Stewart is who you say he is—and I'm still not certain that you haven't got it wrong; people do get things wrong, even people like you— well, what does that have to do with *me*?'

'I think Dexter sought you out.'

'Sought me out? That sounds like a bit of a conspiracy theory.' Agatha's head was in a whirl.

'Course, it all could be pure coincidence, but my gut feel is that he decided to set up in competition. Have you any idea of the value of gaming software? Which is why it's one of the most highly confidential areas of all my companies. I have computer-game designers working to create games that could outrun some of the biggest sellers. After Dexter's hacking attempts, I made sure that all entries were closed down. If he really wanted to get his hands on some of my developing ideas, he might have thought that he needed to go down a different route.'

Realisation was beginning to dawn for Agatha. Naturally, Luc could be off target with his assumptions, but would he really ever make a mistake like that? When it came to business, his acumen was legendary. Everyone in the company reverently believed that everything he touched turned to gold; only someone blessed with an ability to make sound decisions would ever have possessed that Midas touch.

'Question: has Dexter been asking you all sorts of questions about the company?'

Agatha twisted in her chair so that she could look at him. 'Of course he's been interested in what I have to say.'

'I'll bet.'

If only there had been a part of her that could really and truly believe that she hadn't been used, she would have run with it. Instead, all she could volunteer feebly, was, 'Everyone deserves a second chance. Even people who come out of prison get second chances.'

She belatedly realised how often the subject of her work had cropped up in the conversation. She had been flattered at the interest and had downplayed her role in the company. In fact, she hadn't mentioned the broom cupboard once.

'I think Dexter is manipulating you to access information,' Luc told her bluntly.

'What sort of information? This is too much. My head's beginning to spin.'

Feeling disadvantaged on the chair, Agatha stood up and weaved a wobbly path to the kitchen so that she could pour herself a glass of water. She returned to find Luc standing by the window and idly peering out. He turned when he heard her but remained where he was, six foot two of towering alpha male with the subtlety of a sledge hammer.

Suddenly she was really angry that Luc was the one who

had taken it upon himself to point her in the right direction by humiliating her and then calling it doing her a favour.

She realised how much she preferred the comfort of lusting from afar. Having her heart flutter whenever she glimpsed him at a distance had been a little inconvenient but it had never threatened her peace of mind. She could remember sitting in the snug at the vicarage, curled up with a book, half-reading it, half-pleasantly day dreaming about Luc suddenly noticing her and sweeping her off her feet. At seventeen, it had been a very nice day-dream.

A living, fire-breathing Luc with a mission to save her from herself was more than she could bear. He was just *too much*. She felt like a moth helplessly drawn to the blinding brightness of a fire, knowing that the nearer she got the more dangerous her situation became.

She didn't want him to turn his attention to her; she didn't want him to think that he had to look after her because she was incapable of looking after herself. She wanted him back at arm's length and she knew that, if she could only put him there, then she would be able to get on with her life.

Agatha blinked and snapped back to the present. 'You were saying… Um, you were going to tell me what information you think Stewart wants to drag out of me. I don't know anything about computer software. I have a laptop in my bedroom, but I hardly ever use it. When I do, it's just to email.'

Luc looked at her flushed face: her half-parted mouth, her wide, incredulous eyes and that cloud of tousled fair hair that made her resemble a naughty, slightly dishevelled angel. A very sexy angel. He found that it was a struggle not to let his eyes dip to the generous curve of her breasts.

He pushed himself away from the window, suddenly restless, but it was a very small room. From whatever angle, he seemed to be confronted with the sight of her smooth skin, the shadow of her cleavage, the slope of her shoulders and her hair tumbling over them.

'You're mistaken if you think that Stewart has hunted me down so that he could use me to pick my brain about your state secrets.'

'*You* know that you wouldn't recognise one of those state secrets if it lay down in front of you waving a white flag and begging to be discovered. And I know that. But *he* doesn't, does he?'

'Oh, this is hopeless.' She had been so optimistic that life as a single girl in the dating game would begin with Stewart. But the date had failed to live up to its promise, and now this.

'The man is using you, and you have to get rid of him. Never mind the personal angle. From my point of view, you become a liability the minute your trustworthiness is in question.' He had tough lines on company security. There were no loops through which anyone could wriggle.

Agatha gaped at him. 'Even though you *know* that I would never do anything? Even though I've just told you how hopeless I am when it comes to understanding all that computer jargon? Are you saying that you don't *trust* me?'

Luc shrugged and lowered his eyes. 'Sex and pillow talk can work the strangest magic. Who's to say that he wouldn't talk you into a little hanky panky at the office when everyone else has left for the evening? He knows the layout of the building. There's virtually no chance that he could hack into anything important but I'm not willing to risk a situation that could cost me millions.'

Agatha wasn't even sure that she would have continued seeing Stewart. She had felt no real connection there. But this was about principles.

'I'll...I'll think about what you said.'

'You'll have to do a bit more than that, I'm afraid.'

'Or else I'm out of a job?'

'Regrettably.'

Agatha didn't think that he looked like a man wracked with remorse at the situation—but then dispatching a charity case wouldn't exactly bring him out in a bout of cold sweat and panic, would it? She was utterly disposable. Always one to see the silver lining in the cloud, she slumped into the chair, battered and dismayed.

Luc steeled himself and let the silence stretch between them, then he left quietly, shutting the door with a click that resonated in the room like a time bomb.

Having dug deep and uncovered Dexter for the manipulative and possibly dangerous charmer that he was, Luc had expected a positive response from Agatha. If, for instance, someone had offered him concrete proof that a woman he was dating was in it solely for the money, he knew that he would be only too quick to shed the offending gold-digger. But, then again, he was a realist through and through. Agatha was not; he had to face it.

Instead of falling on his neck with relief that he had spared her the misery of dating a guy who wanted to use her, she had been disbelieving, argumentative and had eventually put him in the position of having to issue her with an ultimatum.

What was it they said about no good deed going unpunished?

Famed for an ability to jettison pointless aggravation, Luc found himself spending the weekend in an unsettled frame of mind. He couldn't believe that she would choose a man she barely knew over his impeccable advice, not to mention over a job that was extravagantly well paid for what it was. And the prospect of firing her—whilst he would have no option if she didn't dump Dexter—wasn't something that filled him with enthusiasm. His mother had rarely asked anything of him; she was stoic by nature. Even when she had found herself at the mercy of the unforeseen, when the full story of the company collapse had emerged, she had not once looked to him for the solution; her only instinct had been to protect him from the cruelty of the press. So the thought of letting her down now was not a pleasant one.

By six on Sunday evening he was primed to do the unthinkable and he didn't waste time debating the pros and cons.

The conference call he had scheduled was cancelled with the minimum of excuses, and by seven Luc was parked outside Agatha's house in his Aston Martin. Looking up to her floor, he could see that it was in darkness. Having rung the doorbell twice to no avail, and telephoned her landline three times, he was confident that she wasn't in. He would wait—no big deal.

He didn't stop to analyse the wisdom of showing up at her bedsit to find out whether she had made her decision: Dexter or the job.

The foul humour that had been his constant companion over the weekend was dissipating. He almost missed her dark outline as she scurried towards the front door of the converted Victorian house, fumbling in her bag and dropping the key twice in the process.

Nor was Agatha aware of his car sandwiched innocuously along the kerb between a motorbike and a small white van. Frankly, she wasn't aware of very much as she scrabbled with shaking fingers to get the key in the door.

Her head was buzzing. She was utterly oblivious to the sound of his footsteps as he vaulted out of his car towards her, surprising her just as she had managed to turn the key and was opening the front door.

Agatha reacted with a shriek and, her nerves already in

shreds, swung her right arm at her assailant propelled by the full weight of her voluminous bag. The blow caught him a cracking direct hit on the side of his face.

'Good God, woman!'

Agatha squinted in the dark and recognised Luc as he nursed his jaw. Uncharacteristically, she was sorely tempted to hit him again, but instead she walked quickly into the dark hall and attempted to slam the door in his face.

Having waited for over an hour in his car for her to return, there was no way that Luc was having that. Indeed, having a woman slam a door in his face, whatever the reason, was not on his list of acceptable behaviour. He elbowed his way in, still nursing his jaw, so that she was forced to look at him.

'What are you doing here?'

'Right at this very moment in time? Wondering whether you've broken anything.'

'You shouldn't creep up on people and then you won't get hit.'

'I'm beginning to think that looks can be deceiving with you.' He lowered his hand, having satisfied himself that there was no need to visit the casualty department of the local hospital just yet.

'I don't want to talk to you.'

'Why not? Where have you been?'

'None of your business. Go away.'

'You know I'm not going to do that. We never reached a conclusion after our last conversation.'

He kept pace with her easily as she climbed the two flights to her bedsit, and before she could get any ideas about locking him out he insinuated himself into the front room behind her and then leaned against the door, watching her.

'I told you I don't want to talk to you,' Agatha muttered,

although she didn't know why she bothered to waste her breath because here he was, larger than life, in her room, waiting to get his wretched answer. It was no longer just a case of her being a ninny and getting involved with an undesirable guy, but a case of it affecting part of his company. She could understand his anxiety, but that didn't mean that she liked him being here again, making her feel awkward and self-conscious.

She got rid of her coat. Luc noted that the sexy outfit of the day before had been replaced by her stock-in-trade long skirt, thick tights just visible above her sensible black lace-ups and what looked like layers of cloth, culminating in a grey cardigan which she had buttoned to the neck. And then from nowhere he was knocked for six by a graphic image of her back in that dress, then stepping out of it wearing nothing underneath, naked, warm and pliant, leaning back so that he could play with her abundant breasts, splay his fingers against her thighs, lead her hand to his erection…The immediate stirring in his loins shocked him and he turned away abruptly and forced himself to think straight.

'I know.'

Agatha glared and shifted her weight from foot to foot, feeling his presence in the room like a suffocating weight.

'He's not worth it, you know,' Luc said harshly. The lights from the street filtered up, turning her hair to silver as it brushed in curls along her jawbone and down to her shoulders. He wondered how he had never noticed the delicacy of her features—wide eyes, a small, straight nose, a full mouth and a heart-shaped face. Maybe it was because she made it her duty never to look him fully in the eye if she could help it.

'How did you know that I went to see him?' she asked now, conforming to his theory of avoidance by staring down at the rug. 'Well, it doesn't matter. It's finished. So you don't have to worry about him enticing me into a compromising situation.'

'That's…a good outcome,' Luc said dismissively, eyes narrowed—and now she did look at him, her cheeks flushed with anger.

'I really *hate* you!' she burst out, tears forming in the corners of her eyes. 'You don't care about anyone's feelings, do you? The only thing you care about is your stupid company! You don't care that Stewart is…*was*…the first date I'd had since I moved to London!'

'And what a date he turned out to be. If you think your heart's breaking now, try projecting yourself down the road six months from now if you'd carried on going out with him! How do you think it would have felt when he turned around and dumped you because you couldn't give him what he wanted? Or when he found out that you didn't have access to the IT part of my company?'

'How can you be so *cold*?' The worst of it was that he was right. The minute she had lied to Stewart and said that she'd decided to hand in her notice—just a little white lie with her fingers crossed behind her back—she had felt him backing away from her faster than a speeding train. They had met at a small restaurant halfway between the city and her house, and his enthusiasm for the bill when she had started waxing lyrical about the stresses of working for a big company and her need to get back to a job close to nature would have been funny if she hadn't been so disillusioned. She would never know if he had wanted to get to those company secrets, as Luc had suggested, but she had to think that he really had used her to find a way into the company even if only to cause mischief for Luc having sacked him.

She knew that he was shallow and manipulative, and probably had a raging temper, which she had glimpsed for one frightening moment, but that still didn't do her ego much good.

And Luc, standing there and sneering, felt like the final straw.

'You don't know what it's like to…to think that something's going somewhere and it turns out that you've been completely wrong!' she yelled. 'You're like a block of ice!'

'He was a creep.'

'Yes, I *know* he was a creep! You don't have to tell me that. And I know I wouldn't have ended up having a relationship with him, but it would have been nice if I hadn't had my nose rubbed in it!' She stood up, shaking like a leaf, and walked towards him. 'It's easy for you because you don't *want* to get involved with anyone!'

'I did you an enormous favour.'

'Well, I don't feel much like thanking you for it.'

They were only inches apart now. Agatha didn't quite know how her feet had taken her towards him, and up this close she because dizzily aware of the golden flecks in his irises. All of a sudden it was as though the air had been knocked out of her body. He was staring down at her, his dark face perfectly still.

'Feel better?' he asked softly and she blinked, mesmerised by his voice. 'You needed to get angry, Agatha.'

'I…I don't get angry.' The gentleness in his voice sent her into a confusing, giddy tailspin. Her face felt hot and her heart was hammering in her chest so that she could barely manage to get her breath out.

'If you don't get angry now and again, you'll find that people will walk all over you. Say the word, and I would be more than happy to get angry with that loser on your behalf.'

Agatha blinked. That felt like the nicest thing that had

ever been said to her, but she didn't understand why because she was so angry with him: *wasn't she?*

'I don't believe in violence.'

'Sit. I'll get you a coffee.'

'Are you being nice to me?'

His mouth softened into a ghost of a smile which made her toes curl. She sat down, trying to gather herself while she listened to the sounds of him in the kitchen, opening and shutting cupboards and clumsily trying to make her something hot to drink. She had taken a real bruising earlier on and the prospect of being on her own with just her thoughts for company made her go cold inside.

Besides, this was a side to him that she hadn't seen before, and it was the side she suspected had the women flocking to him in droves. Because, rich or poor, Luc would always have had his fan club lining up to do whatever he wanted. When he squatted at her feet, depositing the mug on the little table he pulled towards her, she felt special. It was ridiculous, and she wanted to fight the feeling, but her encounter with Stewart had weakened all her defences.

'You were right, anyway. I don't belong here in London.'

'Because you got taken in?' He sat next to her and angled his long body so that he was facing her, his hands lightly clasped on his thighs.

'Because I wasn't sharp enough or streetwise enough to spot him.' Luc was so close to her that their arms were nearly touching. When he reached out and caught her fluttering fingers in his hand, she jumped and moved to tug her hand away but then thought better of it. It was a gesture of consolation. She was miserable. It was the first time he had ever touched her in a deliberate way, and her body responded with a surge of heated awareness that made her feel faint.

'Anyway.' She struggled to get her thoughts in order.

She still couldn't bring herself to look at him for fear that the dual onslaught of those fabulous, sexy eyes and the feel of his long fingers playing with hers would make her do something really, really stupid—especially given the fragile state of mind she was in. So instead she breathed in deeply and gulped.

'It's no good me working for you; I think you'll agree with me. I know you were made to help me out, and I'm very grateful, but I'm a liability—you said so yourself. What if you hadn't recognised Stewart? What if he had…done whatever it was you thought he would do? It's not as though I would have clued up and smelled a rat.'

She gave a choked, hysterical laugh. 'I have no experience of big business, or of finance. Or of anything, for that matter.' She thought back to her high hopes when she had first arrived in London. She had counted all the positives of stepping outside her comfort zone. She had recognised that small-village life might have been fine as a kid but that there wasn't a single young woman she knew who wouldn't trade it for the experience of working in a top company in London. She had thought she would throw herself into office life and gain lots of invaluable experience. She would make dozens of new, exciting friends and into that heady mix would come lots of boyfriends.

Yes, she had made lots of friends, but her optimism about forging a career in an office had proved to be ill-founded. She'd struggled with her computer course and she had become the dumping ground for work no one else wanted to do. How one earth could she hope to compete with all those bright young things with their degrees in economics and languages?

And where were all those thrilling young men who were going to rush in to replace her hopeless crush on Luc Laughton? Few and far between.

'I feel much better now,' she said in an unnaturally high voice and she offered him a watery smile. 'I'm definitely not going to get angry again.'

'Why not? I'm tough. I can take it.'

'I'm going to be realistic,' she told him, while her heart continued to beat a steady, crazy drum roll inside her. 'I'm going to cut my losses and go back to Yorkshire. There's no point in looking for another office job in London, and I've been to Kew Gardens to ask them if there were any vacancies and there were none. I've been thinking of doing a landscaping course. I'd like that. I'm not cut out for anything else.'

'Why don't you look at me when you're talking to me? I don't bite.'

He had kept his voice low and amused, but her refusal to meet his gaze was really beginning to get on his nerves. Was she so terrified of him or was she scared witless that something might show in her eyes—resentment at being put in the unenviable position of supplicant, manoeuvred there against her will?

He hadn't been kidding when he had told her that looks could be deceptive when it came to her, and that flash of anger which he had provoked had hinted at a passionate nature lurking below the surface. Was it something that she was aware of and shied away from?

Agatha looked up into those glittering, unreadable eyes and fought for something sensible to say, but her mouth was dry and all she could see in her mind's eye was his beautiful face close to hers, and all she could hear was her racing heartbeat and the rush of blood in her ears.

'So this is what you've been hiding.' He had never suspected it. She had managed to maintain such a low profile that even his highly developed antennae had missed it.

'What?' Agatha managed to squeak in a preternaturally high voice.

The silence thrummed between them. Agatha found that she could hardly breathe as he continued to stare at her, his dark, winged eyebrows raised speculatively.

'Is it because I've caught you in a vulnerable moment?'

'I don't know what you're talking about.'

'Course you do,' he chided softly, reaching out to brush one long finger against her cheek—then finding his body charged with a savage, urgent want that descended so fast and so hard that he sucked his breath in sharply. Agatha shuddered and closed her eyes and rested against the back of the sofa, her body yearning up towards him.

With a stifled groan, he pulled her towards him with a hungry, impatient urgency. Her hair was like silk as he curled his fingers into its tousled length.

Agatha stepped from fantasy to reality and was lost. This moment had been the fodder for a thousand dreams— a *million* dreams! A rush of heady, surreal intensity raced through her body with cyclonic force and she felt a wetness between her legs that made her want to rub her thighs together restlessly. Was this really happening? His mouth on hers was explosive, and she surrendered to it with a whimper of pleasure, her hands pulling him towards her and her body moulding against his as they fell back on the sofa.

Always in control of any situation with a woman, Luc found himself in the novel place of losing all control.

'You're not in a good place at the moment,' he murmured, striving to insert some rationality.

'Don't talk. Please don't talk. I…I want it. I want you.' She exulted in the feel of his muscled body as she shamelessly weaved her hands under his shirt and ran her fingers along the hard planes of his chest. The fantasy had been gentle and dreamlike. The reality was ferocious, dramatic and mind-blowing. Her body had parted company with her brain and common sense was being dragged along in the wake of a surging need that had swelled to an irresistible force in the space of seconds.

He shifted against her and the feel of his erection pushing hard against her stomach brought a responding need pooling like honey inside her.

'Let's go to the bedroom,' she half-moaned, half-pleaded.

If there was a fractional hesitation, Agatha didn't see it. Her eyes were half-closed and her body was in meltdown. She groaned feverishly when he eased himself off the sofa, taking her with him and laughing softly under his breath when she told him that she was too heavy to be lifted.

'How weak do you think I am?' he asked hoarsely, settling her on the bed, and then standing to appreciate the sight of her rumpled sexiness. But not for long. He couldn't shed his clothes fast enough, and he couldn't get enough of the way she was watching him, her eyes shy and greedy at the same time. It was the biggest turn-on he had ever had.

A shard of common sense prompted him to ask, 'Are you sure about this?'

Her nod was the only encouragement he needed.

CHAPTER FOUR

Luc looked appreciatively at the woman lying on the bed in front of him—warm, willing and wide-eyed. The force of his craving slammed into him with the unstoppable power of a runaway train. He seriously couldn't remember the last time a woman had provoked an urgent response like this. Was it true that variety was the spice of life? Had he become too accustomed to that Western view of beauty which dictated that it came only in a long, thin package? He didn't know and he didn't stop to analyse his body's unusual response.

His natural instinct took over and he shed the remainder of his clothes, making sure to take his time, to pace himself, enjoying her absorption in the details of his nudity.

When he sank onto the bed next to her, she trembled and released a soft, yearning sigh.

'You're beautiful,' Luc imparted in a voice that was rich, deep and unbearably erotic.

'That's not what you said before.'

'Your clothes don't do you justice.'

'I'm not thin enough,' Agatha felt compelled to point out, heady and exultant to be living a dream she had always considered out of reach, and he groaned in response as he gently began to ease her out of her top.

'I'm beginning to think that thinness is a much-overrated virtue,' he growled huskily as he feathered a finger along the inside of her bra strap, curving it along the soft fullness of her breast and watching in fascination as her nipple tightened under the lace.

Without completing the manoeuvre of taking off the bra, he instead chose to flick his tongue against her nipple as it struggled to peep out from between the swirls of lace. She writhed against him and he had to dig deep into his reserves of self-control not to take her right then, like a randy teenager having his first taste of sex.

Her breasts were big, bigger than he had always been led to assume from the nondescript, baggy clothing she had worn around the office. He liked it. A lot. In fact, it was driving him crazy.

Taking his time was all well and good in theory but practice was proving nigh-on impossible.

An expert when it came to undressing a woman, he found that he couldn't get to grips with the niggly clasp of the bra and would have happily ripped it off had she not reached behind her, with her eyes still closed, to unhook it from behind.

'I must be losing my touch...'

He was barely aware of her breathlessly telling him that his touch felt just perfect to her. He was way too absorbed in the sight of her breasts as they spilled out of their delicate restraints.

The big, pink discs of her nipples with their erect buds standing to attention pouted up at him, begging for his mouth.

Who was he to deny them both the pleasure?

He cupped them in his big hands and massaged them, rolling his thumbs over the stiffened crests before bending so that he could devote one-hundred percent of his undiluted attention to driving her crazy.

As he licked and suckled, first one, then the other, he wasn't completely sure who was being pleasured more.

When he pushed his hand below the waistband of her jeans, she literally gasped and shuddered in wild anticipation.

'Please…' Agatha curled her fingers into his hair and looked down to where his dark head was roving over her breasts, tasting them and teasing them, and drawing her nipple into his mouth so that he could savour them even more.

'Please…what?'

'I…I want you.' Her voice broke on an admission that would have been inconceivable only hours ago.

'How much?' Since when had he ever asked that question of any woman?

Agatha's eyes flickered open and she gazed at him raptly, then she gave a nervous little laugh. 'I know this is mad but I want you so much.' She ran her hand along the length of his torso, marvelling at this new-found wantonness he seemed to have brought out in her. Where had that come from? Her just uttering those words was shocking and thrilling at the same time. 'And I don't want to talk.'

'Sometimes talking can be sexy…'

Which she discovered, as he talked *and* touched, commenting on her body, as he began to unzip her jeans, telling her what he would like to do to it.

It was very, very sexy. She couldn't wait to get out of her jeans. They felt like glue against her body and as he began to tug them down she helped him, kicking them off and sending them flying to join the rest of her clothes that were heaven only knew where on the ground.

'How wet are you for me?' Luc breathed into her ear, stopping to watch her face with a crooked smile on his.

'You're embarrassing me!' She barely recognised herself.

'You're enjoying it. I like that. I never suspected…But then when you looked at me…' He circled her nipple with his fingers, zeroing in on the taut bud and playing with it till she was panting and moaning. 'Well? How much do you want this?' he pressed her softly with amusement, half at her languorous, feline movements, half at himself because he wasn't usually this vocal or, for that matter, so uncool.

'More than you know.'

The effect of those few words on him was electrifying. Discarding her underwear, he slid two fingers into her, stroking her on that most sensitive of spots so that she wriggled against his hand, pushing and arching, and dimly hoping that the walls weren't as thin as she suspected they might very well be.

'Oh no you don't,' he laughed softly; he removed his hand and began working his way down the flat planes of her stomach with his mouth.

Agatha's eyes flew open and she gave a protesting squeak.

'You can't!'

Luc interrupted his ministrations to shoot her a quizzical look from under his lashes then he gave her a devastating smile and positioned himself squarely between her legs.

Still looking at her, imagining the rosy blush invading her cheeks—because it was dark enough in the room to hide all but her most obvious reactions—he brought his mouth down to nuzzle against her damp mound.

Her instinct was to buck against him but he held her down and, lord, that questing mouth, exploring her most intimate place, sent her spiralling into a vortex of unspeakable excitement and red-hot, searing pleasure.

She had never been touched like this in her life before and

nothing could have prepared her for the primitive, surging power of her response. When she thought that it was *Luc's* mouth there, caressing her, she wanted to faint.

'I can't wait any longer,' Luc groaned. He entered her, pausing as she automatically flinched. 'You're very tense,' he murmured, looking down at her with a slight frown.

'Please don't stop.' When she opened her eyes and looked at him, she could see the naked hunger as he began to move gently and rhythmically into her.

She shifted under him and with a stifled groan Luc thrust deeper into her, no more able to keep his need for gratification under control than she was.

Having him spill into her, as she peaked with a shuddering orgasm that came in wave upon wave until it finally crested, leaving her limp, gave her the most liberating feeling she had ever experienced.

And afterwards she felt incredibly tired and incredibly peaceful. Luc had rolled onto his back and she could sense him staring up at the ceiling.

Whilst Agatha wanted to curve her body against his and rest her head on his chest so that she could feel the steady beating of his heart, his silence was sending little shards of unease through her.

She thought that this was the definition of reality, this steady drip of icy cold after the hot, euphoric rush.

'That was a mistake,' she whispered. 'You don't have to tell me.' Better to strike first. She forced herself to laugh even though the tingle of awareness that raced through her as he turned to lie on his side, looking at her, gave the lie to any chance of her feeling cool, calm and collected. In fact, now that the memory of what had taken place had its opportunity to cruelly replay itself in her head, she was dimly beginning to recall a certain reluctance on his part to make love to her. Had she thrown herself at him? Had she? She had been feeling miserable and humiliated after the fiasco with Stewart, and there Luc had been, her seemingly never-ending dream-guy, lending her a shoulder to cry on.

Maybe she had even begun to see him as more than just a fantasy when she had started working for him. True, she wasn't on his floor, and most of the time not even within his range of vision, but those snatched occasions when he called her to his office had all done their damage by feeding into her feelings for him. She had interacted with him on a level she had never dreamed possible but, instead of that interaction putting everything into perspective, it had dragged her deeper into her silly infatuation.

And now...

Agatha couldn't bring herself to actually look at him, which was ridiculous, considering her state of complete undress under the duvet.

What must he be thinking? He had been there to comfort her and she had flung herself at him with reckless abandon: what red-blooded male would resist? She could hardly blame him for responding to the invitation. No, she just had to accept that all the blame was squarely on her shoulders.

It seemed very important to salvage some of her pride, at least from the situation.

She clutched the duvet to her chest, suddenly acutely conscious of the body that had thrilled to his touch only moments previously.

'You should go,' she said feverishly.

'We need to talk about what just happened.'

'No, we don't. We really, really don't.' She reluctantly turned to look at him. He had propped himself up on one elbow and the duvet had ridden down to his waist. Her eyes were compulsively drawn to the glorious sight of his exposed chest which in turn triggered off a series of hot little recollections of how that chest had felt under her feverishly exploring hands.

'You were a virgin. Why didn't you tell me?'

'I told you I wasn't experienced. Does it make a difference?' It did; she could read it in his eyes. Her parents had never preached to her, but still she had been raised with high moral values. She had never made a decision to save herself for after marriage, but she had always known that she would save herself for someone she truly cared about. It was just her bad luck that she had picked a man who didn't truly care about her. Her virginity was an embarrassment for him.

'Of course it makes a difference!'

Because what experienced man wants to make love to a woman who hasn't a clue what she's doing?

'Are you going to talk to me? Damn it, Agatha, we at least need to discuss the fact that I didn't use any contraception.'

Agatha blanched in receipt of complications she hadn't even considered. She had been so blown away with passion that the most basic issue of consequences hadn't even begun to surface in her scrambled brain.

'Don't worry.' *Don't worry? Of course he would be worried—sick!* He had slept with her, caught up in the moment just as she had been, but smart enough now that they had exhausted their passion to ask the most fundamental of questions.

'Normally I take responsibility for contraception but this was an event that I didn't foresee.'

'There's no risk of me being pregnant.' She did some quick maths in her head and worked out that she was probably telling the truth. 'So you don't have to add that further worry to the pile. I...I'd like you to go now.'

She would have taken the first step and set an example by getting dressed, but her clothes were on the ground, and covering the short distance with nothing on was too much to bear thinking about.

'Funny, but I'm not believing you. Why did you decide to give your virginity to me?'

'I didn't *decide* anything!' The words were wrenched out of her in her last-ditch attempt to cling on to her dignity. 'It just *happened*. I was really upset over all that business with Stewart and I just wasn't thinking straight. I wasn't thinking at all,' she battled on wretchedly. Nothing in her sheltered life had prepared her for dealing with a situation like this, and it fought against everything in her that compelled her to be honest, but the instinct for survival was stronger. 'I just... fell into bed with you because you were here and I needed comfort.'

'You're telling me that I was *handy*?'

Given a way out, Agatha still shied away from using it. 'I...maybe I don't know.'

'You used me, in other words.'

'Of course I didn't use you.' She was horrified at the picture of herself that those three words conjured up. 'But people just don't think straight when they're upset. And I *was* upset.'

'You barely knew the man!' After an extraordinary high from their love-making, Luc was plummeting back down to earth faster than the speed of light. Since when had he ever been the equivalent of a bottle with which someone could drown their sorrows? If she clutched that damned duvet any tighter around her, she would be in danger of imminent strangulation.

'That's true,' Agatha was forced to concede in a shaky voice. 'But that still doesn't make this right. I'm not, you know, the kind of girl who jumps in the sack with a guy.'

'But you were so overcome with misery after a botched relationship with some loser you knew for all of three minutes that you decided to go for it? Well, on the bright side, at least there won't be any lasting consequences.'

'Sorry?' Her heart skipped a couple of beats as he pushed himself off the bed and began hunting down his clothes. She watched as he walked about the room, drinking in the sight of his magnificent naked body, and trying hard to shut the door on the pernicious shoots of bitter regret trying to eat away at all her good intentions.

She strenuously reminded herself of just how important it was for her not to sink deeper still into her crazy infatuation. Crazy infatuations led to dark, dangerous places. Whilst he was the worst possible candidate for a crush, it would be a disaster were she to fall in love with him. Which she wouldn't, because they were so ill-suited, and because he was just the kind of man mothers warned their daughters about. Except, of course, for *her* mother, who thought the world of him after she had witnessed first-hand his devotion to Danielle and the driven way he had rebuilt her shattered life. He hadn't just restored their family fortunes and beyond he had restored Danielle's pride.

'Hello? Calling Planet Earth?' Luc strode across to the bed and towered above her, wearing just his boxers. He leaned down, imprisoning her by planting both hands firmly on the bed on either side of her. This was not how the situation should have ended. He was in a filthy mood, and no amused by the way she continued to lie there, taking the blame whilst perversely managing to emerge the wounded party.

He also didn't care for the way his body was hammering at him, telling him that what he really wanted to do wa climb back into bed with her and lose himself in her lush feminine curves. What was going on here?

'I'm sorry.' Agatha reddened, caught out in the act o staring.

'Spare me the apologies. We were talking about consequences—at least there won't be any.' His eyes drifted to her full lips, and then lower, to the soft swell of her breast which she hadn't quite managed to conceal under the duvet. With his self-control threatening to break its leash, Luc dragged his eyes away from the captivating sight. Angry colour scored his fabulous cheekbones. 'The last thing I need is a one-night stand getting pregnant.'

'That's a horrible thing to say.' Agatha felt tears spring at the back of her eyes.

'Why?'

'Because...because it makes me sound cheap.'

'I would lose the moral high-ground, if I were you, considering you've just told me that you used me as a panacea for being in the *dumps*!'

'I'm sorry if you felt insulted. I never meant to hurt you.'

'Hurt me? Since when do you think you're capable of doing that?'

Luc flushed darkly then pushed himself away from the bed to stride over to the window. Even though his good sense was telling him that it was time to go, he was unnerved to find that walking out didn't seem to be that easy.

'And I wasn't using you as a panacea. I'm not that kind of person. Anyway, I don't understand why it would bother you what my reasons were. It's not as though you have lots of morals when it comes to sleeping with women.'

Outraged, Luc looked at her with eyes like black ice. 'I don't believe I'm hearing this.'

Agatha sat up with the duvet still covering her completely and pulled her knees up under it to her chest. She wrapped her arms around her knees and stared at her fingers in mute silence.

'Well? Are you going to explain that remark?'

She started, realising he was now back by the bed, his posture indicative of a man demanding answers. Except she didn't want to answer him. In fact, she wasn't even sure she wanted to speak. She just wanted to dwell on the awful truth that he saw her as a one-night stand, and thankful she was not a one-night stand that would have any lasting repercussions in the form of a pregnancy.

'I get to order all those flowers you send to women you no longer have use for,' she threw at him, suddenly mutinous. 'You don't seem to have a problem with women being handy for *you*.'

'There's an understanding that exists with every woman I have ever slept with.'

'Okay, okay.' The peacemaker in her surfaced.

'I don't encourage longevity,' he rasped harshly. 'That is something that's understood from the starting post.'

Agatha stared at him in stubborn silence and then couldn't stop herself from bursting out, 'I don't understand how you can do that!'

'Not every woman launches into a relationship thinking of marriage and playing happy families,' he said through gritted teeth. His lack of control over proceedings infuriated him.

'No,' she agreed in a tight voice, although she wanted to tell him that he was wrong. There couldn't be a single woman who was overjoyed at the prospect of a pointless fling. Or a one-night stand. Which brought her right back to her own situation and the fact that she had become the one thing she had always thought she wouldn't.

'You are the most frustrating woman I have ever met in my entire life.' Luc swore under his breath.

'You're not accustomed to women having opinions.' She had forgotten about wanting him to leave. The air between them crackled with tension. Every nerve in her body was alive and it was a powerful feeling that sabotaged every scrap of common sense.

'Of course I am. That's the biggest load of rubbish I've ever heard! I meet women in positions of power on a daily basis. We no longer live in the Dark Ages, Agatha. Women have opinions and speak their minds.'

'But not the ones you date!' she flung back, her shimmering turquoise eyes wide and clear as she looked at him.

Was it his imagination or could he see traces of pity there? Was she feeling sorry for him? Shouldn't *he* be the one in that position?

'I don't understand it,' she whispered, forgetting her own misery for a second. 'You've got everything. I mean, you're successful, you're eligible…I know there was all that business with your dad's company, and I know it must have been horribly upsetting for you, knowing that everyone in the town was talking about you, but you came out of it and showed them all. You've done what you wanted to do, you've made pots of money, and Danielle's back in the family home—so how is it that you've never wanted to take the next step and settle down? I know your mum worries about you.'

The sound of her crashing through his personal barriers left him momentarily speechless. Of course, she didn't have a clue that she had done anything wrong. The woman was from another planet. In the space of an hour, she had not only dipped her dainty toe in water no one else had dared tread before, she had dived in headfirst and splashed around!

Rage tried to push through incredulity but failed.

'The ball and chain doesn't quite have enough appeal for me at the moment.' He gathered his self-control with tremendous difficulty. 'So you might as well send that message back to the home front.'

He didn't lose his temper. He never lost his temper. Women never had that effect on him. Occasionally they might irritate, but that was about as far as it ever got. 'And I think this is an appropriate time for me to leave. You're right; mistake made, time to move on.' He began getting dressed.

'I know this probably isn't the right time to bring this up...' Her voice behind him was hesitant. 'But I won't be coming in to work tomorrow. In view of everything that's happened, I'll definitely be resigning. I can post the letter to you, if you want.'

Fear at the thought of not seeing him again tore into her with teeth like razors, but where lay her choice? The possibilities lurking in the aftermath filled her head like a swarm of angry bees. The possibility that her beautiful experience would be his regrettable one, that her role in his life would be reduced to a shaming one-night stand, that she would be forced to retreat to the sidelines and watch as he continued with his life of work and revolving women, that he would not be able to look at her without pity and contempt... Each seemed worse than the one before, and doubly worse when she thought about carrying on in her job, viewing it all first-hand and on a daily basis.

'We've covered the resignation issue,' Luc informed her flatly.

Hassle in his private life was not something he tolerated. Yes, he went out with arm candy, and sure he could understand why his mother might find that a little alarming, but arm candy didn't stress him out. *This* stressed him out. Of course she wanted to scarper. She had leapt into bed with him, and she needn't have told him that it probably would have amounted to the biggest mistake of her life as far as she was concerned. She wasn't a one-night stand kind of girl. Referring to her in that manner had been a low blow, he admitted to himself, but he wasn't going to apologise.

Nor was he going to give her the easy way out and allow her to walk away without due procedure.

'Yes, well, that was before we…'

'Rules are rules. You have to give notice. What happened in this bedroom has nothing to do with work. I don't play by those rules.'

'But—'

'I also doubt the Employment Tribunal would take a lenient view if I sacked employees at the drop of a hat. Instant dismissal is only relevant in certain circumstances. Yours doesn't fall into that category.'

'But it's going to be awkward.' She could feel herself perspiring under the duvet, and the treacherous pull of her body towards him as though she was being tugged by an invisible line, yanked in a direction she wanted to run from.

'Is it? I thought what happened was just a simple mistake that we were going to put behind us.'

'Yes,' Agatha confirmed hurriedly. 'Yes, of course.' Already he had moved on and was tackling the situation like the experienced man of the world that he was. While she clutched a quilt, got knots in her tummy thinking about her 'one-night stand' label and tried to downplay the horror of still being in his company—thinking about him while he carried on with life as though nothing had happened, following her instructions, which would be easy for him, but hellish for her. Who knew? In two weeks' time, she might even be out buying some high-wattage trinket for another of his women.

'So what's the problem?'

'No problem.'

'And,' he continued coolly, 'don't get it into your head that I'm going to have to answer for you leaving my company. I won't. When you leave, you'll explain to your mother that you left because you couldn't hack it. You'll be back to square one, jobless in Yorkshire, which isn't my problem. I won't take the blame for that situation.'

'No. Of course not,' Agatha said faintly. Her mother would be bitterly disappointed. There were no jobs to be had locally. For Agatha not even to have stuck it out for a year would seem like ingratitude, to someone who had elevated Luc to the status of a saint following the way he had taken care of his mother. He had uttered nothing to the press but to promise that the finance director would be buried for what he had done, and he had silenced wagging tongues with the sheer force of his personality. He had made sure to be a presence in the village and had let it be known, by virtue of the odd throwaway remark, that he would be merciless towards anyone who failed to support his mother.

There had been no need to adopt that approach; Danielle had always been a popular member of the community, contributing to the church fairs, helping out at fundraisers and opening the house and grounds once a year so that everyone could enjoy a summer party at their expense.

Both Agatha and her mother had been deeply impressed by the commanding way he had taken care of the situation.

Agatha now thought that she could probably find another word to describe his approach. Maybe 'high-handed'. Maybe 'arrogant'. But Edith would never believe that. She would be left with the impression that her daughter had packed in a golden opportunity because she couldn't be bothered to try hard enough.

'I could always keep looking for another job in London,' she whispered.

'Doing what? You've hardly proved yourself working for me, and what would you expect me to do about your reference?'

'My reference?'

'Well, what have you proved to me? That you have no self-motivation, no enthusiasm to try for the career ladder, open boredom with everything to do with office work.' Luc scarcely recognised his intractability. Shouldn't *he* be the one shedding the problem as fast as he could? Confusion at his own inexplicable reactions conspired to fill him with burning rage at himself.

'In other words, you'd make sure that I was unemployable in London just because we fell into bed for all the wrong reasons, and because I'm not one of those women who think it's okay to carry on falling into bed just for a bit of fun.'

'Do you really think that I'm petty enough to resort to those kinds of tactics because you've decided to play the distraught, outraged maiden?' Luc's lip curled and her eyes fluttered away from his.

If you can't take the heat, she thought, *then get out of the kitchen.* A man like Luc, a predator who ruthlessly took what he wanted out of life, wasn't going to tiptoe around her, making room for her insecurities and doubts. Lord only knew how many women he had slept with, and he had no scruples when those women outstayed their welcome.

How could she have thought that she could dump her sheltered upbringing, her morals and principles and sleep with him when she had had first-hand experience of how he treated women? How could she have been stupid enough to imagine that dreams could turn into ongoing reality?

She had built a lot of idealised fairy-tale castles in her head and she had no one else to blame because they had been exposed for what they were.

He strolled towards her and every slow step threatened her already shattered peace of mind.

'You need to start asking yourself a few questions,' he said, his voice deadly soft. 'You might waffle on until the day you die about climbing into bed with me because you were suffering some terrible bout of temporary insanity, but when you looked at me I was seeing a very different story. You *wanted* me. So why don't you be honest with yourself and cut to the chase? We didn't have sex because you weren't thinking straight. We had sex because you *wanted* it.' He felt driven to hear her admit it.

Agatha stared at him in mute silence. She could feel anger roiling just below his cold exterior and she wondered if he thought that she was playing games with him.

'No woman comes on to a man the way you did because she's a little upset and needs a bit of company.'

'I didn't come on to you.'

Luc gave a shout of mirthless laughter. 'You might make a big song and dance about the way I treat women, Agatha, but at the very least I don't have a problem with honesty. If all you wanted was a pat on the back and a shoulder to cry on you would have run screaming the second you knew I was going to kiss you. You didn't. In fact, I seem to recall...'

'No!'

Luc looked at her for a long while, then he offered an indifferent shrug. 'Don't you like thinking that you might have physical needs like any other woman?' His expression was veiled but there was nothing veiled about what he was doing to her, forcing her to confront her sexuality, throwing all her moans and whimpers of encouragement back in her face.

How tedious he must have found it, when he would be used to women who knew what they were doing in bed.

'I know I have physical needs,' Agatha whispered. At least, she did now, and the power and urgency of them terrified her.

'Now we're getting somewhere,' Luc's voice was laced with thick sarcasm.

'And it's wonderful!' she said with a bright, defensive

smile. 'And you're right, it's silly to hide behind excuses. I made love to you because I wanted to.'

Luc had lost count of the number of women who had been eager to tell him how much they wanted him. When Agatha had said it, in the heat of the moment, with the roar of passion in her ears, he had liked it. It had turned him on. He liked this even more, hearing her say it again but in the cool aftermath of sex.

There was just something so incredibly sexy about her tousled innocence and the knowledge that she had lost her virginity to him. He could hardly believe how much he wanted to savour the thought of that. It was like she had managed to dig deep inside him and pull out a primal instinct he was hardly aware of possessing.

Let her confront her own mixed-up responses, he thought. He might just wait for her to say what he knew she would—that there had never been any question of her throwing herself at him because he had just happened to be there, right time, right place.

He wasn't given to waiting for women. But, yes, he might make an exception in this case, because when he thought of those big, rosy nipples and the voluptuous, silky-smooth curves of her body, his body went into overdrive.

'See?' he drawled lazily, watching her through shuttered eyes. 'How hard was that? Ten out of ten for facing up to reality.'

Agatha fought a tide of burning resentment.

'If I can feel this way with you,' she told him fiercely, 'then how much more wonderful will it be when I make love to a man who means something to me? So you've won. I'm not sorry we made love and I'm not ashamed either. I know my virginity would have been a turn-off for you. Men like you want experienced women who don't go into meltdown after they've made love. But there's a man out there for me and I feel so much more confident now that I'll find him.'

CHAPTER FIVE

AGATHA had not been foolish enough to put any faith in the remainder of the evening to somehow miraculously put things into perspective and to fill her with a bracing optimism to face the next day, back at work after the shattering events of Sunday.

However, she was dismayed to find that no amount of stern lecturing of herself or level-headed reasoning could take away the sickening knot in her stomach as she stood in front of the gleaming lift doors, waiting for it to carry her up to her cubby hole.

She had given an awful lot of house room to the idea of hibernating in her room until her notice was up, but then that would have allowed the one-off episode with Luc to dictate her behaviour, and she didn't want that. She had spent way too long with a bunch of silly, girlhood fantasies for company and, now that those fantasies had become a very unlikely reality, she wasn't about to let them take over the role of running her emotional life.

She also wasn't going to dress like a refugee from a charity shop. She had reluctantly admitted to herself that one very good thing seemed to have come of her recklessness with Luc: she no longer felt self-conscious of her body. She had seen genuine, hot appreciation in his eyes when he had looked at her, and for the first time in her life her curves had not been a source of embarrassment. She had wantonly revelled in the attention they had provoked, and miraculously the feeling had stayed with her.

So instead of her grey, woollen skirt and blouse, and the all-encompassing cardigan which was as unflattering as it was comfortable, she pulled out the few items of clothing she possessed that were relatively fitted and suitable for work: a slim-fitting black skirt and a plain but figure-hugging cream, long-sleeved jumper. The paisley-patterned scarf, given to her by her mother as a 'you're starting work in a proper job in an office' gift, was pulled out of hibernation from a box at the bottom of her wardrobe and added vibrant colour to the outfit.

As she walked to her little office, she knew that she was getting quite a bit of attention. In fact, with a spontaneity she didn't know she possessed, she actually grinned and turned around to blow her colleague Adrian an air kiss when he wolf whistled as she passed his desk.

More than anything, she wished that she was working in the central hub of the office, where the buzz of telephones and light-hearted banter between phone calls and computer work might have distracted her from her thoughts.

Her own desk, tucked away along the corridor, could be seen as either a haven of solitude or a miserable and isolated cage. She wondered whether Personnel had stuck her out of the way because, with her limited experience, she would have been a disadvantage to all the bright young things with their degrees and top-notch computer skills. At the time, she had been told that, because she would be working more or less directly with Luc, she might occasionally be passed something of a reasonably confidential nature and so a private space would be more acceptable. Belatedly she realised that indeed she did handle some confidential stuff, if you could call dealing with his girlfriends confidential.

She pushed open the door to her little office, turned automatically to the coat hook hanging on the wall by the side of the door and was only aware of the presence of someone else in the room when she was ready to head towards her desk. Only to find Luc perched on it, his hands lightly clasped on his lap.

Agatha couldn't have received a bigger shock if she had discovered an alien at her computer terminal. Of course, she had expected to bump into him at some point in time, but not just yet. Not when she had barely had time to recover her lost equilibrium.

She stood in awkward, gaping silence for a few seconds, then stammered, 'Wh-what are you doing here?' It was an uphill struggle to remember that she was turning over a new leaf, valiantly jettisoning all the shackles that had held her down.

'I own the company. Remember? I have a right to be anywhere I want to be.'

'Yes, but…'

'But life would have been more comfortable for you if I'd been polite enough to keep out of sight until your notice was up and you could slink away unobserved?'

Agatha didn't say anything, because he had hit the nail on the head, although the prickly, heightened feeling running riot inside her now made her wonder whether her addiction to him wouldn't find her seeking him out on some pretext or other. Bad habits were difficult to stamp out.

Luc looked at her with a shuttered expression but his sharp eyes were taking everything in. He had had the rest of the evening to think about her parting shot, and the sexy little outfit she was wearing now proclaimed a sexually awakened woman on the move. A woman *he* had wakened. On the move for another man.

He wasn't ready for that yet. He also wasn't prepared to let his work suffer because his mind kept straying to one night of white-hot passion, but suffer it had. Yesterday evening, he had done the unthinkable and jeopardised a deal, albeit a small one, because he hadn't been able to focus on the finer details of the company accounts on his computer. He had only been able to salvage the mess by the skin of his teeth.

Agatha was unfinished business and that was a situation that wasn't going to work.

Every situation had its solution. In this case, the solution lay in getting her back to bed—warm, willing and of her own volition. Whether she knew it or not, it would work for both of them because, if she was his unfinished business, then he was hers. Until this was sorted, she would interrupt his work and he would interrupt her head. And, yes, it went against everything inside him to pursue this situation but the need to pursue was overpowering. He was going to throw the rule book through the window. He could only think that it was because he still wanted her and getting what he wanted was too ingrained in him to be ignored.

'Unfortunately for you, I've done a bit of thinking,' he continued, standing up and strolling to the single window that overlooked the busy pavements below. He turned back around to look at her. 'You might just get it into your head that you can slack off because you intend to leave.'

'I wouldn't do that!' Agatha protested vehemently.

'Really? Then explain the outfit. Not what I would call suitable, would you?'

'I'm only wearing what every other female under forty in this building wears!' Agatha defended herself stoutly, while making small movements to tug down the skirt which was a hefty couple of inches above the knee. 'And you told me to change my wardrobe,' she carried on, emboldened.

Privately, Luc had to concede that she had a point, but

for some reason it annoyed the hell out of him to see her flaunting herself in clothes that would bring most men to a grinding halt. Did she really expect to go unnoticed every time she left her office to run some errand that would take her past the boys working in the outer offices? Of course not. But then that was probably the intention.

'The fact is that I find myself in an unusual position,' he informed her, walking towards her, then circling like a shark sizing up edible prey. 'Having made it a rule never to sleep with an employee, I now discover that breaking the rule carries consequences. I've opened a door that you could enter to do any number of things if you decided to take revenge for being a one-night stand. Even if you *were* the one to instigate the situation.' He scowled, grimly disappointed with himself for breaking his own iron-clad code of conduct.

'I'm not into revenge! Why do you always suspect the worst of people?'

'Call it dealing with the daily reality of being wealthy. I've had more than one threat of a kiss-and-tell story. Personally, I'm indifferent to that, but my mother gets upset.'

'Do you really think that I'm the sort of girl who would do that?'

'I don't know.' He gave an elegant shrug. 'I never thought that you were the sort of girl to jump in the sack for a session of hot sex and then decide to use it as a springboard.'

Agatha flushed to the roots of her hair. She bitterly regretted those last words. They had made her sound cheap and shallow and she couldn't blame him now for thinking the worst of her.

'Because I've decided to wear normal clothes to work, doesn't mean that I'm going to put my feet up on the desk and slack off.'

He noticed that she had said nothing to defend herself

against his accusation. A lethal fury swept through him, unlike anything he had ever felt before, but none of that was reflected in his face.

'Other things come into play here,' he informed her in a grim undertone while she looked up at him in utter bemusement.

'What other things?'

'I don't care for the thought of you shooting your mouth off and discussing what took place between us.'

'You can trust me when I tell you that that's the last thing I would ever think of doing and, just in case you don't believe me, I'll happily make a deal with you. I don't say a word to anyone, and you don't.' Thoughts of her mother's disappointed face made her shudder.

'I don't do deals.' That little shudder of hers hadn't escaped his notice. 'On the other hand, I *can* make sure that I keep an eye on you.'

'Keep an eye on me?' Agatha parroted, trying to make some kind of connection in her head that would give her some insight into what he was trying to tell her.

'Your time in this little box is at an end. For the remainder of your employment here, you'll be on my floor, sitting outside my office, where I'll have ample opportunity to make sure that you're not putting your feet up. I'll also be able to make sure that you're not whiling away your time gossiping.'

Agatha's mouth dropped open and her brain braked and then slowed to a standstill before cranking back into gear. Very slowly.

'You can't be serious.'

'Never been more serious in my life. I have a reputation to protect and I intend to make sure that you don't damage it.'

'It's not as though everyone doesn't know that...'

'I don't care who knows that I play the field.' Luc helped her out, his tone dismissive. 'I do, however, care that they don't know I've been crazy enough to play the field right in my own back yard.' Only he was capable of recognising the subtle but important distinction, which was that for the first time he was willing to play the field in his own back yard.

Agatha's mind latched on to that single word 'crazy'. She wanted to tell him that she had been the crazy one ever to have allowed herself the folly of falling into his arms as if her entire life had been building up to that very moment. Instead, she resolved there and then to do everything within her power to wipe him out of her head.

She took a few shaky steps away from him towards her desk and then turned to him with a sullen shrug.

'You already have a secretary.'

'Helen's daughter has just had her second child. She would welcome a break of a few weeks. I had planned on asking my agency to send a temp over, but in all events this is a far more satisfactory solution.' And one that had occurred to him on the spur of the moment. He could only sardonically admire his talent for creativity when it came to breaking his own rules so that he could invent a couple of new ones.

'I'm not really qualified to do Helen's job.' With ever-vanishing hope, Agatha clung to that observation with the tenacity of a drowning swimmer clinging to a life belt, but in her heart she knew that it was a pretty futile hope. He was a deeply suspicious man in a situation over which he fancied he lacked total control. How wrong he was!

'She'll spend the next couple of days filling you in and I'll handle anything sensitive.'

'Will that include buying presents for your lovers?' She pressed her hand to her mouth as if she could somehow stuff the words back in and swallow them down.

Luc looked at her narrowly, eyes gleaming. When he took

one step towards her, Agatha instinctively fell back. 'Would that bother you? Would you be jealous?'

'No!'

A slow smile curved his sexy mouth and he dropped his eyes, which actually didn't do very much to release her from her semi-frozen, trance-like state. 'Well,' he drawled. 'You'll be thrilled to hear that I won't be calling on you to do that.'

Did that mean that he would recommence his high-octane love life, just omitting her from the responsibility of buying gifts, reserving restaurants and seats at operas? she wondered feverishly, and then was ashamed of letting her thoughts go down that pointless road.

'And look on the bright side. There's another reason why you should applaud my decision to bring you to the director's floor. If you decide to go into another office job after this, you'll want a good reference. Work for me and come up to scratch, and you'll be in demand the second you leave this building. All told, you can see that I'm doing you a favour.'

'Your favours never feel like favours,' Agatha breathed on a rebellious sigh.

Mutual attraction, the brief game of pursuit and capture then gratification. That was the course of events he had always followed with women, and after the gratification came the gratitude. He was cynical enough to know that he was a catch, maybe one of the biggest in the sea.

Agatha had turned that normal course of events on its head. Was that why he was driven to get her back in his bed at all costs and even at the expense of his fabled self-control?

At any rate, he sucked in his breath sharply and said with curt self-restraint, 'Come up to the director's floor when you've cleared your desk. I'll be out for the remainder of the day, but Helen will show you the ropes.'

Which, Agatha supposed as she trudged with her possessions up the lift to the plush glass-house occupied by the high and mighty at the top of the building, was something.

And at least she would be doing some real work; there was always a positive spin to be put on everything, she told herself. Also, Luc had been right: he would be able to dispatch her with reasonable references if she left with more experience, and that would mean something to him. It would reduce any residue of guilt that the job he had been forced to provide for her hadn't worked out.

As she might have expected, he had taken a pragmatic view of what had happened. Whilst she had spent the weekend unable to function, he had worked out how to make sure she was dispatched in a way that would protect his privacy and preserve his conscience.

Helen's office was private and luxurious, glass and chrome, with an adjoining door to Luc's bigger, even more luxurious office. In between being shown the systems, she played with the thought that maybe seeing Luc on a daily basis would go somewhere to getting him out of her system. Didn't familiarity breed contempt? There was never a person who longed for that as much as she did.

For the next week and a half, it really seemed to be working—in a manner of speaking. Because Luc, in full throttle, had to be seen to be believed. However early she made it to the office, he was always there before her. She brought him in a cup of coffee, and then life immediately went into the fast lane.

Even with his feet up on his desk, his tie askew, his mind was still working at such a rapid speed that she was barely able to take time out to breathe, never mind pander to the temptation to sit back and just look at him.

'Got that?'

With an efficiency Agatha would never have believed possible after the computer course she just scraped through months ago, she nodded and stood up, smoothing down her skirt in the process. When her eyes flicked to him, it was to find him staring at her with that speculative intensity that made the hairs on the back of her neck stand on end. Over the past week and a half, he had treated her with the scrupulous detachment of the boss towards his secretary. Now, as the clock ticked towards lunch time, he was finally looking at her, and all the nervousness that had been resting happily on the back burner bubbled up to the surface with ferocious speed.

'You've certainly been hiding your light under a bushel,' he drawled, pushing back his chair and then folding his hands behind his head. 'For someone in love with the outdoor life, who hated anything to do with the office, you seem to be keeping up.'

Agatha could feel his cool, inscrutable eyes resting on her, and her heart did that hammering thing that always seemed to turn her brain to mush. Had she really kidded herself that she was somehow over him because she had been able to handle working alongside him without falling apart from nerves?

The prospect of being back at square one hit her like a punch in the stomach. Despite all her good intentions, she had done nothing to move on with her love life. She could see the possibility of becoming ensconced in this new, temporary position, which was doing nothing to promote the contempt she had been waiting for—the opposite, in fact— and then feeling the separation when she finally did leave even more than she would have bargained for.

The small shoots of a plan began to form in her head and she glumly gave it room while the man who still spiked her dreams continued to look at her with that mild, dispassionate interest.

'I don't have much choice, do I?' She held his stare and tried not to fiddle with her fingers. 'Anyway, I am kind of enjoying the work,' she admitted truthfully. 'It's much more interesting than the stuff I was doing downstairs.'

'Not my fault. You came to me without much going for you by way of experience in even the most lowly of office skills, and you never showed any interest in furthering your knowledge. How was I to know that you were such a quick study?'

Agatha flushed with pleasure at the compliment.

'I've had a number of temps over the years,' Luc said, musing. 'And none of them have matched you for efficiency. In fact, a number of them fell to pieces the minute the going got a little tough.'

Agatha had no trouble believing that. She, at least, had known the nature of the beast and had adapted accordingly. Luc was brilliant, relentless, impatient with mistakes and never expected to explain anything more than once. Glimpses of his character over the years had stood her in good stead.

'Poor things,' she said sympathetically, visualising a procession of weeping, broken young girls.

'Poor things?' Luc laughed, folded his hands behind his head. 'I am the most considerate employer anyone could wish for.'

'Really?'

'Yes. Really. You seem to have managed perfectly.' He paused significantly. 'Do you think that might have something to do with our special relationship?' He trained his sharp, green eyes on her, enjoying the sight: pink cheeks, that full mouth and curly blond hair half-escaping the loose bun at the nape of her neck. Working with her was a constant challenge to suppress his rampant libido. Moreover, and to his surprise, he had quickly discovered that he had acquired a top-rate worker who was much brighter and cleverer than she gave herself credit for. He considered her wasted talking to plants in some tin-pot garden centre, but he would approach his offer to keep her on in a brand-new position later.

For the moment, he was frustrated by cravings over which he seemed to have little control. Even when he was safely out of her radius and in meetings, he had still found his concentration lapsing.

Playing the waiting game was not in his nature and he knew, more positively with each passing hour, that he needed to get a conclusion going.

'We don't have a special relationship,' Agatha said crisply.

'We had sex. Don't tell me you've forgotten. Some might say that qualifies us as having a special relationship.' He sat forward, resting both elbows on his highly polished desk and afforded her a penitent look. 'My apologies. Talking about sex in a working environment is inappropriate. What *is* appropriate,' he continued, 'Is I take you out to lunch. You deserve it; point taken that I may not always be the easiest person to work with.'

'That's very nice, thank you, but I've got some stuff I need to do at lunch time.'

Luc frowned. 'What sort of stuff? I'm the boss. I'm giving you full permission to ignore work for an hour and a half.'

'Actually, I wasn't going to work.'

'What exactly are you planning on doing? You have to eat.'

'I've brought some sandwiches in. I...I have some things

to do on the computer. Emails to write, if that's okay. Keeping in touch! I told mum that I would probably be handing in my notice and she's worried.'

'Right. Maybe another day.'

'Maybe...' Agatha looked away. 'So...is that all?'

Luc had never felt so instantly dispatched. For someone who gave the impression of being a pushover, she was as tough as nails, he thought with ill humour. What email could be so pressing that she would give up lunch with him?

'I won't be here this afternoon.' Frustration ratcheted through him as he walked over to the cupboard in which his jacket was hanging. 'Wall-to-wall meetings until six. I'll expect that due-diligence report to be completed by the time I return to the office. If it's not, you'll have to work overtime. The lawyers need it first thing in the morning.'

'Of course.' She sprang to her feet. 'Anything else?'

'That's a rather open-ended question. What did you have in mind?' He enjoyed the way she went bright red at that. His sharp eyes took in the way she stuck her hands behind her back, as though scared that they might somehow betray her, the way her pupils dilated and the way her breathing quickened. Under the polished veneer, she was still as much a prisoner to that one explosive night as he was.

'I'll see you tomorrow,' he drawled, leaving her with a backward wave of his hand.

Agatha breathed a sigh of heartfelt relief as the door closed behind him. What had he been playing at with those references to sex? Had he found it entertaining to confuse her?

With a burst of sudden determination, and a few surreptitious glances around her just in case the walls really did have eyes, she spent the next fifteen minutes surfing the Internet in search of online dating sites. It was not something she enjoyed doing but this, apparently, was the way things got done if you didn't have the sort of extensive social life that promoted lots of face-to-face meetings with exciting, eligible guys. And what harm could there be in it? She didn't really hold out much hope for finding the man of her dreams, but she might meet some interesting people. Having come to the decision that she would not return to rural Yorkshire, but instead stay where she was and try her best to hunt down another job, a few new faces might be just the thing.

She would not become her own worst enemy by allowing the debacle with Stewart to push her into self-defensive, wary reclusivity from which she would have all the time in the world to devote her thoughts to her one-night stand with Luc. She positively needed the distraction of another guy.

She registered at the biggest site. Then, in an upbeat mood, she went to the company restaurant for lunch, ignoring the limp sandwiches in her desk in favour of a more celebratory meal of spaghetti Bolognese, followed by fudge cake and lots of interesting chats with the friends she had left several floors below. It was funny to think that Luc was actually wary about her spilling the beans on their one-night affair. To become a prime target for gossip was probably the last thing in the world Agatha would ever have wanted.

Four hours later, she was leaving the impressive glass building when Luc stepped in front of her, blocking her path. She hadn't seen him, hadn't heard him. He was as light as a panther on his feet. And he didn't look in the best of moods.

'I did what you asked. I finished the due-diligence report. It's on your desk.'

'Fun lunch?'

'Sorry?' She stopped and looked at him cautiously.

'How are you getting back to your bedsit?'

'Tube,' Agatha said faintly. 'Then bus.'

Luc didn't answer. He stretched out one hand and miraculously a black cab appeared.

'I can't afford to take a cab to—'

'Get in the taxi, Agatha.'

'Are you all right? You don't look too good. Are you feeling all right?'

Luc didn't trust himself to say anything and that was a new experience for him. He waited until she was inside the taxi, then he lowered himself next to her, breaking his silence only to give the taxi driver directions to her house.

Agatha glanced across at his exquisite profile and stuttered into nervous speech, relaying calls he had received during his absence and progress she had made with a mid-sized publishing company in which Luc was interested. The company had fired Agatha's interest because it specialised in gardening books. Anxiously aware that her babbling seemed to be falling on deaf ears, but unwilling to spend the rest of the car drive in complete silence stewing in her own confusion and alarm, she instead chose to chatter on about ideas she had for rejuvenating the company.

'What's the matter?' she asked eventually. 'I mean, why are you coming back with me to my flat? I'm perfectly capable of getting there on my own. I don't need you to babysit me. I thought we'd talked this through.'

'I'm not sure we've talked it through enough.' Luc turned in his seat and looked at her with blazing intensity. 'Tell me how else you occupied yourself today. Feel free to skip the riveting conversations with clients.'

Agatha broke out in clammy, nervous perspiration. Not even the taxi pulling up outside her flat could save her from the necessity of answering because it quickly became apparent that he intended to escort her into her bedsit. She was like someone under house arrest.

'Well, what do you want to hear?' She turned on him the

second they were inside her little sitting area, hands on her hips, her blue eyes bright with anger. It wasn't fair that he should be here, crowding her space when all she wanted to do was recover from the effects of him.

'Okay, so I didn't have those sandwiches at my desk. I went to the canteen because I fancied a bit of company. And, before you accuse me of gossiping, I didn't say a word about…anything.'

'I returned to the office shortly after I left. I'd forgotten some reports.'

Agatha looked at him blankly.

'The reports were on your desk. You were at lunch.'

He strolled to the window, not for the first time thinking that her landlord should be shot. When he slowly turned round to look at her, it was to find that she had not moved from her hesitant position by the door, although she had removed her coat and placed it on the arm of the sofa.

'I don't see why I should feel guilty because I went to the office canteen for lunch,' Agatha muttered in a moment of rebellion. 'You can't keep an eye on me a hundred percent of the time, and if you've come here to haul me over the coals for nothing then please just go. I'm really tired.' She took a couple of steps and flopped wearily down onto the sofa, briefly closing her eyes and allowing the weight of everything to settle on her shoulders.

'You left your computer running when you went to lunch.' Luc walked towards her and remained towering over her until she opened reluctant eyes to look at him.

'Did I?'

'You should really close all tabs when you're on the Internet browsing through dating sites.'

It took a few seconds for the significance of his words to sink in, then she sat bolt-upright and clenched her fists at her sides.

'You were *snooping* around on my computer?'

Luc had the grace to flush but an apology couldn't have been further from his mind. 'I wanted to check and make sure that all the relevant documents had been downloaded before I wasted another journey. Checking them on your computer saved me the effort of going into my office. I use the word *your* with reservations—let's not forget that the computer actually belongs to the company, and by extension to me.'

Agatha sighed with a growing sense of defeat. 'Okay. Now you know and it's no big deal. It's the modern way of meeting people.'

'It's the modern way of getting into trouble.' He could have kicked himself for waiting for her to come to him. While he had been playing the waiting game, she had been scouring the Internet to find men. He should damn well have obeyed his finely tuned hunting instincts. They had always worked for him in the past.

This woman challenged every ounce of control he had ever mistakenly assumed he had, and it all came down to one thing: lust. If he had suspected her of playing games with him, he would have had no trouble in walking away. If—unlikely though it might be—she genuinely didn't fancy him, then he would likewise have shrugged his shoulders and put it down to one of life's little experiences. But, against all odds, Agatha both wanted to walk away *and* fancied him like mad. The combination was driving him crazy, but not as crazy as he had been when he had innocently come upon that website listing so-called eligible men.

Privately, Agatha agreed that Internet dating probably wasn't for her. In fact, as the afternoon had progressed, her optimistic thoughts about meeting interesting people via a dating site had begun to lose its appeal. By the time Luc had blocked her path outside the office, she had already come to the conclusion that she must have been suffering from temporary insanity to have cooked up the idea in the first place.

Not that she intended to admit that.

'I think you'll find that some dating agencies have an excellent record in successful partnerships.'

'Really? Is that what you were hoping for? A successful partnership?'

Agatha was busy reading the cynicism behind that pithy little question and wasn't liking it. Did he think that she was incapable of finding a lifelong partner, even on a dating site?

'These things *do* happen!' she snapped, red-faced and flustered. 'Although,' she admitted with wrenching honesty, 'I did think that it would be nice to meet a few new faces before I start looking around for another job.'

Some nice, new, shiny, bright young men who might make me forget you. She couldn't look at him. The silence grew and grew, and she really didn't know what to do with it, because her head was in a whirl and self-pity was beginning to gnaw away at her insides.

'I don't like the thought of you meeting new faces,' Luc intoned bluntly.

That brought Agatha's head snapping up and she stared at him in open-mouthed surprise. 'You don't like the thought of me meeting guys? Are you *jealous*?' She couldn't believe how quickly the empty feeling inside her was replaced by a soaring sensation of delight—which was short-lived, as Luc granted her a look of harsh incredulity.

'Jealous?' He gave a bark of laughter. 'I have never been jealous in my life!' But thinking of her even casting her eyes in another direction *did* subject him to a tide of blinding rage.

He had no problem accepting this fact, because he was

a possessive man, and there was nothing wrong with that. But jealous? No way.

'No, you're not.' Agatha dully corrected her over-optimistic interpretation. 'You still think that you need to look out for me, because if I could get taken in by a creep like Stewart Dexter then who knows how many other creeps lurking on the Internet can pull the wool over my eyes?'

Luc, still standing and commanding every ounce of her unwilling attention, finally lowered his stunning eyes and drawled in that low, lazy voice that could send her into reckless free fall, 'No new men, Agatha. You and I—we have unfinished business. We're not putting it behind us and pretending it never happened. It happened and it's going to happen again. Because it's what we both want.'

CHAPTER SIX

AGATHA was mesmerised by the rich, velvety conviction of his voice.

'No, you're wrong,' she protested weakly.

'But when I make love to you, I want to do it in comfort. This bedsit is not comfortable.' Luc overrode her feeble denial with ease. 'We'll go back to my place.'

'That's crazy!'

'Nice king-sized bed.' He strode towards her bedroom, literally a matter of a few steps, and began hunting around for some kind of overnight bag. 'Bathroom with every modern convenience known to man.' He flung some random clothes on the bed, while Agatha looked at him, stupefied and lulled into immobility. Vague, nebulous thoughts of her optimistic 'moving on' process tried and failed to take shape.

'The finest rugs, a kitchen with a fridge that actually works, plasma TV—although I don't plan on either of us sitting in front of it…' More clothes joined the ones piling up in disarray.

'What are you *doing*?' She leapt off the sofa and watched as he opened and closed drawers.

'I'm taking control.'

'Shut that drawer!'

He reached inside and pulled out an assortment of over-sized tee-shirts, holding them up for inspection before tossing them right back into the drawer. 'Sleepwear? Never mind. You won't be needing those.'

'We can't do this!' she screeched in an agonised voice.

'Why not?' His eyes clashed with her, vibrant and simmering. 'Are you going to tell me that you don't want me to make love to you? For hours? Touch you where I know you like to be touched? Lick you in places that make you squirm and beg for more?'

Agatha was squirming now, imagining all those things she had tried to firmly shut the door on. 'No. Maybe…I don't know!'

'That's okay because I know for the both of us. Feel free to stop agonising.' He walked towards her and cupped her upturned face in one hand, then he slowly lowered his head. He met with no resistance. Instead of listening to his pride and stepping back, maybe this was what he should have done all along—forced the issue caveman-style. Lord, but it felt good.

Agatha felt his mouth claim hers and she surrendered with a shameful lack of restraint, her arms reaching up to link behind his neck as though he might disappear in a puff of smoke if she didn't hold on hard to him.

Everything he had said was true. He was her irresistible passion. If he was only in it for the sex, then why shouldn't she at least take what was on offer and enjoy it while it lasted instead of making a martyr out of herself? Self-sacrifice might be noble and worthy but since when did it make a good bed companion?

Travelling back to his house with her overnight bag was unbearably exciting. Even the composed tenor of his conversation in the back seat of the black taxi fanned the flames, because underneath the light banter she could smell the hunger inside him, and it matched hers.

When they finally made it to his penthouse suite, she was ready to explode.

She was aware of very modern, neutral surroundings. Pale wooden floors covered an expanse that was vast by London standards and, sure enough, she glimpsed those magnificent rugs he had mentioned, and also huge statement-piece abstract paintings which he hadn't mentioned.

But then, after those initial moments of sanity, she was swept away on a tide of passion. At some point she knew that her clothes were off and she was on a huge bed, watching as he undressed and closed the curtains. She was so aroused by the sight of him that she had to lightly touch herself, and when he moved to stand naked in front of her, looking down and smiling, she whimpered and allowed him to complete what she had begun.

Entangled between sheets that felt like satin, and which ended up half off the bed, Agatha opened herself up to the joy of being touched by his hands, his fingers, his mouth. It all felt so *right*.

For the first time, she confronted her emotions with honesty and realised that her feelings for Luc weren't just lust. Yes, maybe they once were, but gradually she had fallen in love with the man as opposed to having fallen in lust with the one-dimensional cut-out.

When she curled her fingers into his springy black hair, and watched through half-opened eyes as he feasted on her breasts, she allowed herself the luxury of letting her love show, because he couldn't see it.

To let him witness how she really felt about him would be a sure-fire way of making him disappear as fast as he could over the horizon.

But still… She could dream, couldn't she?

When later, she was lying tucked against him, he told her that that was the best sex he had ever had, she smiled and filed the compliment away. When later still, after they had made love again, he turned to face her and said seriously that she should reconsider handing in her notice, she filed that away too under the optimistic heading of 'he can't bear the thought of being too far away from me.'

'The situation has changed,' Luc murmured, surprising himself, because having his lover working for him was far from ideal. In fact, it was downright awkward, but the thought of her finding a job in another company made his blood run cold. How long before some office lothario decided that she was fair game? The woman was sexy as hell, and she was bright too. There would be no back room for her in which to hide away from men with their eyes popping out of their heads.

Luc conceded to himself that he might possibly be jealous.

'I know.' Agatha trailed her fingers across his broad shoulders, then rested her hand on his arm and arched her body up so that she was looking at him. 'It's worse.'

'Don't tell me that you're going to start spouting all that nonsense about mistakes.' As her full breasts pushed against his chest, Luc felt himself harden. He settled his hand on her juicy derrière and pulled her towards him so that their bodies were now so closely joined that a piece of paper couldn't have been slotted between them.

'I can't think straight when you're doing that.' Agatha expelled a long, shaky breath and her eyes fluttered. She slowly moved against his hard arousal. She couldn't get enough of him. Very lightly she touched his impressive erection and felt a heady sense of power as his big body shuddered against her.

'Ditto, you little witch.' Luc parted her legs with his hand and felt the slick moisture between them.

'Stop! We...we're having a conversation,' she panted,

ending on a moan of pure bliss as his questing finger found her sensitive spot and began gently teasing it.

When he slid into her and began grinding with beautiful, rhythmic movements, she lost complete track of their conversation, only dimly recalling it when he said with a sexy growl, 'I was going to say that, just in case you get it into your head to put this down to another oversight on both our parts, I'm just going to prove to you what we've got here is so damned good.' He flipped her so that she was on top of him, her luscious breasts dangling within reach of his mouth. He simultaneously suckled on one engorged nipple while she moved against him, building up to a tempo that had him struggling not to let go until she had reached her own splintering orgasm.

'So...' he murmured when she had finally surfaced. 'You were saying?' He kissed the tip of her nose and brushed her curly hair away from her face. She felt as though she was glued to him by a fine film of perspiration, and he liked that.

'I thought you were afraid that I might not be able to keep this...you know...? Under wraps,' Agatha ventured.

'It's a chance I'm willing to take.' Which was the closest he planned on getting to telling her that he trusted her—on that score, at least. She wasn't a gossip. Nor was he going to let her in on the weird, sick feeling he got when he thought of her doing something perfectly innocuous, like standing by a photocopier or bending over to stick some filing in a cabinet, while lecherous and quite probably married men sneaked covert glances at her fulsome assets.

'So when Helen returns?'

'You won't be going back to that cupboard.'

'I won't?'

'Remember that little publishing outfit you're so interested in?'

'You mean the one with the gardening books?'

'It'll need a little steering in the right direction. You have some good ideas.'

'You mean you actually listened to what I was saying?'

'So it would seem. You're going to take it over. You're not leaving my company. I want you where I can see you.'

'Are you just finding something for me to do?' Agatha asked the question tentatively. A little voice of reason pointed out that accepting a position for which she wasn't qualified smacked of an exchange of favours, but she swept aside that mental objection and focused on the thrilling prospect of continuing to work for him.

Alert to every nuance in her voice, Luc gave the smallest of shrugs. Then he said, with enough self-assurance to kill off any lingering doubt in her head, 'Don't underestimate yourself. You catch on quick. I'll set you up with a team of three to work out strategies for getting that publishing firm in the black. Management's been a bit unstable, and no one's bothered to drag it into the twenty-first century. They need to get on board with the fact that they can be undercut in price from any online bookstore. Personally, I don't have the time to devote to sorting them out. But you? You'd do a good job. I have every faith in you.'

Agatha could barely credit what she was hearing. Another subconscious tick was put in that box in her head. She snuggled against him, and within five minutes she was asleep.

Luc felt her relax against him and felt too her easy, regular breathing as she drifted off to sleep.

He had no idea why he had suggested what in fact was a truly meteoric promotion for someone with woefully inadequate qualifications but, having suggested it, he found that he was content with the prospect.

The publishing company was small and of relatively little value. There was a limit to how much damage she could inflict, although he really did have faith in her abilities. She had proved herself to be hard-working and talented, even if she did inherently dislike office work.

Warmed by the thought of having her around him whenever he wanted, and only vaguely aware that for the first time he had broken with tradition in allowing a woman to spend the night with him, Luc eventually fell asleep.

Five weeks later and Agatha was still on a high, still living on that fabulous cloud nine where hopes could truly blossom and the unthinkable might just come to pass.

She had been promoted without any fanfare in a move that had been shrewdly calculated to stifle any opportunity for wagging tongues to spread gossip. Much had been made of her gardening background, which was a unique talent in a company full of thrusting university graduates, and its relevance to the post she had been given.

Her little team of three had been recruited from outside and they had all been established in a cosy section of his building on the first floor. Agatha adored it. She had fellow gardening enthusiasts working with her and, whilst she wasn't physically working with plants, it was as close as she could possibly get from within the confines of an office.

Sometimes Luc would pop down to check their progress. He never gave any indication of having any interest in her aside from the purely professional, although Agatha was thrillingly aware of the lazy slant of his eyes in her direction, and the light brush of his fingers against her arm when he leaned over to inspect something on her computer.

Once, just once, they had both worked late, and when everyone else had vacated the building he had led her into his office and locked the door and they had made love right there with the low sofa as their bed and the desk as their foreplay arena.

He had confessed that it was the first time he had ever done that with any woman.

That, along with lots of other little things, was filed away in her head as 'significant'.

So far, her 'significant' box held a promising number of things, including his firsts: his first to have a woman stay the night with him—in fact to have practically moved in—his first to make love to a woman in his office, his first when it came to experiencing the delights of the local supermarket because he was accustomed to having his food delivered from Fortnum and Mason if he wasn't eating out. In fact, she reckoned that she might very well be the first woman he had entertained with a home-cooked meal, and afterwards a romantic comedy on the plasma television he swore they would never sit in front of.

All of that meant something. Agatha was sure of it.

Tonight, though, was going to be special. Luc would be heading off to New York for a week. She was going to leave work early and prepare something for him. Three courses, candlelight, wine, maybe even some mood music. She had already bought the ingredients for an Italian meal, and at precisely five o'clock she left, taking the tube and bus to her place, which seemed so much smaller and dingier in comparison than she could ever have imagined possible.

It was important to keep things real. That much she *did* know. He would be dropping by at a little after seven to take her to a mega-expensive restaurant on the outskirts of the city but she had cancelled the booking. Instead, they would eat in which was always so much cosier. The weather was nudging into Spring but it was still cold and rainy. By six thirty, she was dressed and when he buzzed her from downstairs she practically flew to the intercom to let him in.

Watching him as he divested himself of his trench coat and took in the candlelight and the carefully set table, she said breathlessly, 'I decided that it's better to stay in on the last night before you head off for your trip.' She was wearing a tight jade-green dress of a kind she would never have worn before, and nothing at all underneath it, which would previously have been unthinkable.

A trace of unease slivered through him. He hadn't expected her to cook for him, although thinking about it it was hardly the first time. He saw her most evenings and going out every night had not been feasible. He marvelled at how quickly she had infiltrated his life. Other women had been entertained on a sporadic basis, when it suited him. With Agatha he appeared to have developed a routine and he wasn't entirely sure when this had happened.

'There was no need,' he drawled, shifting his attention away from the table and the candles and on to her, which was a far less thought-provoking sight.

'I know, but I thought it would be nice for us to eat in. Honestly, I know it looks as though I've gone to a lot of trouble, but I really haven't. It's just a quick meal.'

Agatha tried to hide her disappointment at his less than enthusiastic response. But she felt awkward as she fussed around him, pouring him a glass of wine and laughing a little too brightly when he told her that candles were a fire hazard.

'Aren't you in the least bit romantic?' She tried very hard not to sound wistful, but Luc's shrewd green eyes still narrowed on her flushed, upturned face resting dreamily in the palm of one hand.

'No,' he told her abruptly, closing his knife and fork on a meal that he knew would have taken her quite a while to prepare. 'So let's not spoil the occasion by going down that road. Believe me—it leads to a dead end.' He pushed back his chair and watched her, his handsome face impassive.

Trapped in the suddenly uncomfortable silence, Agatha launched into a nervous explanation of what she had prepared for dessert. Luc relaxed. Hell, he wasn't going to be seeing her for a week, possibly longer if his meetings overran. There were better things to do than eat chocolate fondant. He smiled, tilting his head to one side.

'Let's skip the fondant,' he murmured, patting his lap and zeroing in on the sway of her magnificent body as she walked towards him. He eliminated his sense of foreboding with one decisive strike. 'I'm hungry for something else…'

'You only ever think about sex,' Agatha half-laughed, although she could hear the thread of seriousness in her voice. But she sighed and yielded to her very passionate lover as he gently eased the stretchy dress off her shoulders, groaning with appreciation at the sight of her bare breasts.

He could do this to her, make all her thought processes come to a grinding halt just with one touch.

When he delicately lifted one heavy breast to his mouth, she wriggled on his lap and succumbed utterly to the soaring pleasure rushing through her like an unstoppable tide.

Somewhere along the line, he growled that this would be the last time he made love to her in her bedsit, because it was just too damned uncomfortable; she heard herself purr contentedly because that suited her fine.

Her bed might have been a lot smaller than his, but he still managed to touch her in all the right places, unerringly finding the pulsing heat of her womanhood and stoking it until she was whimpering to be brought to a climax.

He never tired of hearing that husky catch in her voice when she begged for him, and he never tired of the sight of her stripped bare with her fair hair in tousled curls around her face and her creamy, smooth, voluptuous body writhing on the bed, caught up in the mindless pleasure only he could arouse in her.

Even though he knew that she was his, possession had not yet dimmed his craving for her. Sometimes at work he would find himself propelled down to her floor on the pretext of asking her something for no better reason than he wanted the pleasure of the accidental touch.

Knowing that he would not be with her for a while, he wanted to make their love-making last. Time and again he teased her, stroking her with his fingers, his mouth, his tongue, until she was lost. When he did finally thrust into her, she was wet and hot for him and it was an earth-shattering experience.

Still tender from their extended love-making, Agatha curled against him and half-closed her eyes when he ran his fingers through her hair.

'Are you going to miss me?' She eventually sighed, and Luc stilled, because there was an undercurrent to that question that was as loud to him as the clanging of church bells.

Which seemed an unfortunate allusion.

'I'm going to be as busy as hell.' He refused to be pinned down and he felt her shift against him, propping herself up and looking at him evenly.

'What does that mean?'

'It means I probably won't have time to think about any-thing apart from making sure that we get this deal done.'

A chill breeze seemed to feather its way along her spine. She knew that she should just steer away from the topic, but perversely she couldn't.

'Will you call me?'

'What's going on here? What's this all about?'

Two things were becoming blindingly clear to Agatha.

The first was that he couldn't commit to calling her, and the second was that he couldn't commit to calling her because he wasn't even going to notice her absence. Maybe the absence of sex with her, but not *her*.

She had dressed up what they had in lots of frills and bows and called it a relationship that was really going somewhere, but the truth was that it was all about the sex for Luc. Good heavens, he couldn't even enjoy the dessert she had spent an hour and a half making the afternoon before, because he had wanted to get into bed with her.

Shame and anger curdled into a heady mix. She pulled away from him and sat up, arms folded, staring blindly ahead of her.

'You tell me,' Agatha said quietly. 'I don't know how it happened, but we're lovers.'

'You *don't know how it happened*? It happened because we can't resist one another.' He pulled her against him but she resisted and Luc, sitting up now as well, threw his hands up in a gesture that was both elegant and telling.

'Okay. What do you want me to say? That I'll call you? I'll call you.' He was infuriated that she had contrived to spoil their last evening together for what might well run into two weeks by demanding answers from him that he wasn't prepared to provide. He wasn't a man who enjoyed being penned into a corner. Frankly, any such manoeuvre from a woman was charged with risk. But he would make the concession. Why not? He wanted her more than he had wanted any woman for a very long time. She did wonders for his jaded palate, and for that reason he would relinquish his natural urge to slam his instinctive barriers into place.

'Now can we move on?' he asked, trailing his finger along the tiny ridges of her spine and then smiling as he watched the tiny responsive flex of her body. Her mouth might be saying one thing but her body was singing a completely different song, and the body could be very persuasive indeed. 'I'll phone you every day if you want,' he volunteered magnanimously.

'I don't want you to phone me!' Her eyes felt blurry now and she shrugged off his hand. She was rigid with tension. Like a high-wire walker who had taken the first step over the abyss, she now felt committed to carry on, no turning back. 'I don't want you to phone me because I've kicked up a fuss,' she told him, her face half-inclined in his direction. 'How desperate do you think I am?'

'I never said anything about you being desperate,' Luc groaned and muttered an oath of sheer frustration under his breath.

'But it's what you're thinking. And I don't blame you. I fell into bed with you and I've accommodated you every inch of the way!'

'You're getting hysterical.'

'I am not getting hysterical!' But she took a few deep breaths. 'I just...I just want to know where this is going.'

'Why is it important? We're having fun, aren't we?'

'There's more to life than having fun.'

Luc drew in a long, even breath. 'I don't want to get involved in this conversation. What we have is good. Why question it?'

'Because I need to know if I'm wasting my time with you.'

Luc's experience with women had not braced him for such a direct line of questioning. In the past, women had tried to infiltrate themselves into his life. They had never pinned him to the spot and demanded to know what his intentions were. They had nurtured implausible expectations which had manifested themselves in a sudden interest in the decor of his apartment, or a pressing need to prove what good cooks they were. Inevitably, that had signalled the end. Never had any of them come right out and asked him if they were wasting their time. What kind of a question was that?

For a few seconds, he was literally speechless.

'I'm going to have a shower,' he hedged, getting out of bed. Agatha scrambled behind him, grabbing one of her oversized tee-shirts en route.

'That's not an answer!' She screeched to a halt as he turned on the shower and stepped under it. He dwarfed the miniscule shower cubicle. Within seconds the bathroom was all steamed up. She took a few seconds to think about what she was going to say while she watched him with that compulsive fascination that she had always known to be a sign of weakness. She loved this man. She had let herself fall deeper and deeper in love with him while he had steadfastly stuck to the programme and enjoyed her for sex. In no way could she say that he had ever led her up a garden path.

'I thought I could do this,' Agatha managed to get out when the shower had been switched off and she wasn't having to shout above the sound of running water. 'I thought I could be a thoroughly modern person and have an affair with you because I'm attracted to you, but I can't.' She looked down at her fingers because it felt safer than to stare at him.

For a while, Luc didn't say anything. He began putting on his clothes. He didn't know why he should feel as if a rocket had exploded underneath him. Hadn't he known all along that she was the old-fashioned sort of girl who engaged in relationships in the hope that they were going somewhere? He wondered how he could have ignored that simple, central truth and allowed his actions to be ruled by the driving power of lust. But he had, and he was repelled by his own weakness.

'I'm sorry to hear that.' He addressed her downbent head, steeling himself against the insidious pull of sexual attraction which had been his downfall in the first place. 'And I wish I could let you buy into the fantasy that this will end in a walk up an aisle somewhere, but I can't.' He raked his fingers through his still-damp hair and frowned. 'Look at me when I'm talking to you. Please.'

Agatha reluctantly looked at him, although she strongly wanted to cover her ears and not hear what he was going to say.

'I don't know where this is going to end, or when, but marriage is never going to be on the cards.'

'You can't stay a bachelor all your life.' There. It was out in the open.

'When and if I ever do decide to get married,' Luc delivered grimly, 'It will be to a woman who understands my priorities. I've never told anyone this, but I'm going to tell you now because you deserve honesty: I was involved with a woman when my father died and I was summoned home.' His mouth twisted in distaste at the memory. 'I was faced with a mess that needed clearing up, and the only way I could clear it up was to jump in at the deep end. I worked twenty-four-hour days, seven days a week. Needless to say,' he said with biting sarcasm, 'The love of my life didn't understand having to take a back seat to work commitments that were unavoidable. So, Agatha, I don't do the romantic dramas. Not now, not ever.'

What he didn't add was that he would eventually settle down with someone whose drive and ambition matched his own, or who was content to allow him the freedom to continue with life exactly as he wanted. He didn't want the shrew in the background nagging away at him, telling him that he needed to work less, rolling her eyes to the ceiling every time he had to go abroad, trying to turn him into a domesticated, obedient man about the house. It was a well-rehearsed piece of wisdom he had lived by for as long as he could remember. He wondered why it now sounded like a tired cliché.

'I know you haven't got a clue what I'm talking about, but believe me you'll thank me for being honest with you one day. I'm not the sort of guy you need.'

'No, you're not,' Agatha said bitterly.

'You're looking for someone who wants to join you with his head in the clouds and that person is never going to be me.'

'Did you ever care about me at all?' The question was torn out of her. She set her mouth in a stubborn line and looked at him.

'Of course I cared about you.' But his voice was rife with discomfort.

'You mean you cared about sleeping with me. Maybe I was a complete idiot to think that we could be a significant part of each other's lives. I just can't believe that I've spent all this time, *wasted* all this time, falling in love with you!' Agatha blinked rapidly to clear her vision, which was going a little misty.

'I never asked you to,' Luc told her, a dark flush accentuating the dramatic contours of his face. He squashed the treacherous streak of satisfaction her admission generated in him under the ruthless onward march of pure, cool logic.

A woman in love was a responsibility. However great the sex was, he could not and would not encourage her to nurture pointless dreams.

Agatha hung her head.

'I could pretend that this was what you want, but I won't, because I'm not that bloody minded.' Her continuing silence, rather than hastening his departure, seemed to root him to the spot. 'When…when did you realise that you were in love with me?' On cue, his body reacted and he turned away abruptly.

'I don't want to talk about it.'

'No. Understandable.'

'I didn't want to. I *knew* that you weren't the kind of guy who did commitment. But I started hoping…'

Luc was mesmerised by the lone tear that trickled down her cheek and plopped onto her fingers. He extracted a wad of tissues from the box on the chest of drawers and shoved them into her hand.

'I should have done that Internet thing. It might have led somewhere.'

Luc didn't want to get into a conversation about the dangers of Internet dating. Even knowing that she was already slipping into history, he still didn't want to think of her sleeping with anyone else.

Agatha heard everything his silence was telling her. Yes, she should have done the Internet thing. They had had their fun, but she had a nesting instinct he was incapable of fulfilling. She cringed when she thought of how uncomfortable he must be, standing there while she wept and poured her heart out. It was just the sort of emotional weakness guaranteed to get on his nerves, but she wasn't able to help herself.

'It's regrettable that things have turned out this way.' Luc dragged his attention away from her and focused on bringing things back down to a level he could understand. 'But I think it's important that we get one thing straight: in no way will this impact on your job, so I don't want you handing in your resignation.'

Her fair hair tumbled over her shoulders and he could just about make out the cartoon logo on the front of the tee-shirt she had dragged on. He cleared his throat and shoved his hands into his pockets. 'You and your team are autonomous and I will ensure that Jefferies take over immediate supervision. I fully appreciate that, feeling the way you do, it might be difficult having to report directly to me.'

Agatha nodded. She felt she could hear the gentle pity in his voice, but how could she possibly get angry when she had provided him with just cause to feel like that? She took a deep, shaky breath and finally looked up at him.

'Thank you,' she said stiffly. 'I appreciate that. I'm really enjoying this project and I think I can make a real go of it.' She tore the tissue paper into little strips and then continued playing with it, giving her hands something to do and her eyes something to focus on.

'I don't know how it happened, but I let things go too far.' He couldn't free himself from the savage urge to explain himself to her.

'I'm not Miranda.'

'How do you know her name?'

'I just do. I know she must have hurt you dreadfully, but...' *But what?* She hated herself for continuing to cling.

'She taught me a valuable lesson.'

'She taught you how to become an island.'

Okay, so there was some truth in that statement, Luc recognized. But what was wrong with being an island? It was a damned sight safer to be self-reliant. But something deep inside jarred painfully, like shards of glass scraping through his flesh, and it was too heroic an effort to squash the feeling and to grope his way back to common sense.

Common sense prevailed. He was off-balance because, not only had Agatha laid her cards on the table with a forthrightness that would have had any man struggling to regroup, but in addition she looked strained, and that was all the more noticeable because he had only seen her laughing and relaxed around him for the past few weeks.

He had become accustomed to her. Of course there would be some guilt involved in causing her suffering. That was what had him feeling so sick to the stomach.

'It's because I care about you that I'm walking away, and

you would be smart to trust my experience here. I can't give you the love you want.' Every word tasted of poison. Had he felt this way with Miranda when the end had finally come? He couldn't remember. It had been a turning point in his life so *why* couldn't he remember? 'I'm going to go now. Is there anyone you could call up to stay with you?'

Agatha glared at him with undisguised hostility. That, she thought, was really taking the whole pity angle too far!

'I'm breaking off our relationship, Luc—or whatever you want to call it—because I know you don't *do* relationships. It's not the end of the world. These things happen and I'll be a stronger person for it. So, no, I don't *need* to call up anyone to stay with me. I may have been a complete fool but I'm actually not as pathetic as you think I am.' She was determined to cling to whatever shreds of dignity she had left. She didn't blame him for how things had turned out, she blamed herself, and she would pick herself up bit by bit if it killed her in the process.

'And, yes, I *would* appreciate it if you didn't pop down to where I happen to be working if you can help it—although, if you have to, it won't be the end of the world and I won't need someone close by to prop me up in case I get a fit of the vapours.' It had taken everything she possessed to say those words but at least he wasn't looking at her with that horrible, patronising sympathy she had spotted earlier. She had given him the excuse he needed to drop the condolences on her stupidity, and the accompanying pep talk on how to survive him, and there was a guarded expression on his face now.

She drew in a deep breath. Recovery had to start somewhere, and she could deal with 'guarded' a lot better than she could deal with pity.

CHAPTER SEVEN

LUC looked across the table to the striking redhead who had smiled coquettishly at him for the duration of the meal, undeterred by his unimpressive range of responses to her forays into conversation. He knew that he could sit there and display all the communication skills of a brick and she would still continue smiling and flirting; free, single and unattached, he was the most eligible guy in town.

Right now, they were winding up an eye-wateringly expensive meal at one of the top restaurants in London. It was game on to return to his apartment, where she would let him have all the assets that had been so conspicuously on display for the course of the very long and very tedious evening.

It wasn't going to happen. For the past three weeks his libido had been alarmingly unobliging. In fact, it had been non-existent. This was the first time he had actually felt driven to make an effort and he should have been enjoying the well-rehearsed game that would inevitably lead to the bedroom.

Instead, he had looked at his watch five times and was politely now waiting for her to finish her coffee so that he could get the bill and head back to his place. Alone. He had planned his excuse five minutes into their date.

The whole situation was enough to set his teeth on edge, from his lack of interest in the opposite sex to his continuing preoccupation with a woman who should have been halfwa to being forgotten. She had known from the very start tha he just wasn't the kind of guy who hurtled towards commi ment like a kamikaze pilot hell-bent on self-destruction. H had his rules and she had chosen not to play by them at th end of the day.

He should have been breathing a sigh of profound relief his narrow escape. He was not interested or, for that matte ready for commitment to anyone. When that time did arrive it wouldn't be with someone like Agatha who would expec a fairy tale, with bows and ribbons and a cherry on top.

Instead, she had been playing on his mind with the ag gravating persistence of some distant song he just couldn quite seem to get out of his head.

Not even the failsafe solution of work had come to th rescue. He had been putting in all the hours God made indeed, he had been out of the country more often than h had been in it. But he had not been able to avoid infuriatin lapses of concentration during which he would catch himse' frowning off into the distance while the rest of the worl disappeared into temporary oblivion.

And now this. Five foot eleven inches of obliging, drop dead gorgeousness and he couldn't care less. He could hav spent the last three hours sitting opposite a troll.

'Are you listening to me?' Annabel leant forward so tha he could all but see the nipples peeping above the low-cu neckline of her dress. Poker-straight hair framed a face tha could stop traffic.

'No, not really.' He signalled for the bill and felt a twing of pity for the faltering smile that greeted this slice of un adorned truth. Agatha would disapprove of this level c brutal honesty. 'I've got a heck of a lot on my mind at th moment with work.' He shrugged and raised both hands in gesture of eloquent regret. 'Bad time to be asking a woma out.' He was vaguely surprised to be going into so much lengthy detail. 'You're a very attractive woman, Annabel, but I'm not in the running for any kind of relationship at the moment.'

'Work?' That was her way out of an embarrassing situation, and the single word hovered in the air between them until he nodded.

'My feet are hardly going to touch ground for the next few months and a girl like you deserves a guy who can do her justice.' He settled the bill, barely registering the outrageous amount.

'You don't know what you're missing.' Annabel stood up, rescuing her turquoise, bejewelled clutch-bag from the table. 'But thank you for being honest with me from the beginning. It probably wouldn't have worked anyway,' she added, slipping a shawl around her shoulders. 'I like my men to be a little less stodgy.'

Stodgy? As Eddy drove him back to his apartment, Luc couldn't help but think that that description might very well have been the highlight of the evening. It was the only time he had felt the inclination to laugh out loud, at any rate.

His road was quiet by the time they pulled into a parking space and the building that housed his penthouse apartment even more so. He let himself in, took the stairs instead of the lift, silently let himself into the apartment and was heading towards the kitchen for a whisky nightcap when the sound of her voice stopped him dead in his tracks.

For a few seconds, Luc had the weirdest feeling that he had become the victim of his own inconvenient imagination. He turned round very slowly and noticed her perched at the end of the sofa, staring up at him with those enormous blue eyes. He should have seen her the minute he entered, because she had switched on the light by the sofa and was making no effort to conceal herself, but his mind had been a million miles away.

'I'm…I'm sorry. I let myself in. I was going to wait out side. In fact, I did wait outside, but it started getting chill and it's so quiet around here. I got a little spooked. I, um used the spare key you gave me. I forgot to give it bac to you when we, um…' Agatha ran out of words and jus looked at him. True to his word, he hadn't stepped foot i her office since they had broken up. All her dealings ha been with one of his henchmen. In fact, he hadn't been i the country at all, or at least not much. She had found ou that much from asking around, even though she had know how silly it was to maintain even that slim thread of interes in his movements.

Now, starved of the sight of him for three weeks, sh guiltily drank him in like an addict caving in to just on more hit.

'What are you doing here? Why the hell didn't you retur the key to me when you found out that you still had it?'

Tension ratcheted up in Luc, but alongside that ther lurked a perverse feeling of satisfaction, because there coul be only one reason she would have dumped all her loft principles and returned to his apartment. She might hav wafted lyrical about love and marriage and the 'happy eve after', but three weeks on and she couldn't do without hir or the passion she had been so quick to dismiss. She ha underestimated the power of lust and that came as no sur prise to him. Nor did the fact that she hadn't returned th key to his front door. Psychologically, she would have hel on to it as a telling reminder of what she needed whethe she wanted to admit it or not.

'I forgot, I guess.'

'In that case, you can hand it over now.' He looked at hi watch and then stared down at her with a cool, shuttere expression. 'You've effectively broken into my apartment. Now that you're here, I can't throw you out onto the streets, but in case you hadn't noticed you and I are old news. In fact, you should consider yourself lucky that I have work to do tonight, otherwise I wouldn't have returned alone.'

Agatha's face turned a shade of mortified pink. Out of the loop, she hadn't heard a word about Luc's extra-curricular activities, nor had she glimpsed any headlines in the gossip columns which she had devoured with shameful enthusiasm. Her mind began to stray and she firmly clamped it back into place because this was not the time.

Nerves were tearing through her, sharp teeth that were making a nonsense of any semblance of calm she was trying to project. It didn't help that he was standing there, looking at her as though she was something noxious that had crawled out from under a bush.

Luc had moved on big time. Was she surprised? No. Like commitment, standing still was something he didn't do. He wasn't someone given to pining or even reflection when it came to the women he left behind.

Was she hurt? Desperately. But she took a deep breath and tried not to focus on that.

It had taken a lot to come here.

'Oh. Yes. Right.' She wondered whether he had reverted to his leggy blondes. Had she been the exception to the rule? 'I wanted to tell you this face to face.'

'I really can't believe that you have anything to say to me of a personal nature, and anything else can be discussed in my office.' He turned his back to her and strolled into the open-plan kitchen for the glass of whisky he had promised himself. More than ever, he figured he needed one, although it had to be said that the evening had acquired a certain *patina* that had snapped him out of his edgy, discontented mood.

Agatha sighed and half-rose from the chair, only to fall back into it. He couldn't have made it any clearer that he wanted her out of his apartment. Did he think that if she got too close she might stage a surprise attack and fling a ball and chain around his neck before he could escape?

The enormity of what she was doing there hit her like a brick and she swallowed painfully, watching him as he poured himself a drink. It *would* be whisky. It was the only nightcap he allowed himself, and then only occasionally. He might need more than one tonight.

'So…?' Luc turned around, every muscle in his body totally relaxed as he propped himself up against the granite counter that partially separated the kitchen from the open living-area. 'Say your piece.' He swirled the ice round in his glass and took a deep mouthful as he continued to watch her intently above the rim of the glass. She looked as nervous as a kitten. Nervous and vulnerable.

The silence lengthened between them until he finally clicked his tongue impatiently and strode towards where she was huddled on the sofa. She couldn't have been more different from his date earlier on, who had been the epitome of cool, impeccably groomed, self-assured elegance.

Not the kind of woman who would cling to fantasies of picket fences, rosy-cheeked children and a domesticated husband who couldn't wait to race back to hearth and home. He hung onto this thought because, even looking like a lost waif and stray, Agatha was still managing to exert a crazy sexual pull that he could do without.

'Is it about money?' he demanded, which brought her head up in surprise. 'Because, if it is, then you've got it.'

'What are you going on about?'

'You've come here out of the blue,' Luc informed her caustically. 'And I doubt it's because you suddenly decided on paying me a social visit to discuss old times.' He felt his eyes drift over her and on cue he imagined her naked underneath the cover-all jacket and baggy clothes. The re-belliousness of his mind made him grit his teeth in rage and frustration.

'But I wasn't born yesterday and my knowledge of women is extensive.' He poured the remainder of his drink down his throat and flung himself on the chrome-and-leather sofa, facing her. 'We went out—maybe you got to thinking that you really exited the situation before you could retrieve any material benefits.'

Luc shrugged as though his conclusions, cynical though they might be, were to be expected. 'I don't have to remind you that you happen to be in an incredibly well-paid job which was tailor-made for you, but I suppose you *have* seen first-hand how my women are treated when I'm finished with them. Maybe you've decided that you deserve your own golden handshake? After all, you *did* enjoy privileges beyond the norm.' He glanced around him. Keys to his apartment, for one thing. And then a level of normalcy that, thinking about it now, was really fairly astounding. He chose not to dwell on that.

Agatha, leaning forward with her hands clasped on her knees, couldn't believe what she was hearing. Her mouth had dropped open.

'I have no problem with that,' Luc informed her mag-nanimously. 'Fair's fair, after all, and you *do* need to move out of that dump.'

'I *have* moved out!' Agatha dealt with that particular misconception straightaway.

'When?' Evidence of an independence he didn't know she had made him flush darkly. Okay, he didn't like it.

'It doesn't matter. A week and a half ago. I found some-where a bit closer to work in a nicer area.'

'Another bedsit with a crazy landlord who thinks that

mould on the walls constitutes the equivalent of patterned wallpaper?'

'No. I can afford a proper flat.' Which brought her mind swinging back to his accusations of wanting his money. 'Thanks to my generous salary. And I'm not here to try and talk you into giving me money. How could you think that I would be the sort of person to do that?'

'Most women are motivated by money.'

'I'm not *most women*, and I'm really hurt that you can sling me into that category as if…as if you don't know me at all.'

Luc scowled, on the back foot now as she looked at him with huge, hurt, accusing eyes.

'Okay.' He held both hands up in a gesture of defeat. 'So you haven't come here on a begging mission. Why, then?'

'I won't beat about the bush here, Luc. I know you're a great believer in getting straight to the point: I'm pregnant.'

For a few seconds, Luc had the strange sensation that time had slowed to a standstill and his brain was trying to function in a pool of treacle. He wondered if he had heard correctly. 'That's impossible,' he said at last, but he couldn't keep still. He stood up and began prowling through the room, raking his fingers through his hair, finally halting in front of her with narrowed eyes. 'You told me you were on the pill. I trusted you. Were you lying?' Then, as if those questions were already giving too much credence to the unthinkable, he repeated, forcefully, 'You can't be.'

'I did four tests, Luc.' She reached into her bag with a wildly beating heart and extracted a small plastic bag in which a little piece of cream plastic with two bright blue lines glared back at him triumphantly.

'This can't be happening.' He sat down heavily and regarded her with such disbelieving intensity that every syllable of the speech she had rehearsed flew out of her head with the speed of an army of rats deserting a sinking ship.

'I know it's a shock; it was a shock to me too.' She had been getting backache and had eventually gone to see her local doctor. She had expected to emerge from the surgery with a prescription for some strong painkillers and maybe some advice to get a massage. Instead, she had left on wobbly legs, having been told that she was just over two months' pregnant.

'I *was* on the pill,' she explained in a shaky undertone. 'But not that first time. That first time, we made love without any contraception. I didn't think anything would happen.'

'You *didn't think*...' Luc shook his head as reality nudged past his dazed disbelief and claimed its rightful place. Life as he knew it was about to change because she *hadn't thought*, although he had to share the responsibility for that as well. He should have taken precautions himself. He always had. But not with her. Things had happened fast and furious and he hadn't stopped to consider the consequences.

'I'm sorry.' Agatha tried to find some strength from the fact that he wasn't punching anything. She herself had had over a day to think about the situation and to try and come to terms with it. He, on the other hand, had not. How hard would it be for him now, fresh back home from a hot date, to discover that he was going to be a daddy in under seven months' time by a woman he no longer wanted in his life?

'You said there was no chance. I remember; you said it had been safe.'

His life was still in the process of crashing and burning.

'I really thought I was. I promised that I wouldn't stay long here, Luc. I wasn't sure whether I should tell you or not, but of course I knew that I had to. Look, perhaps I should go now. Leave you to try and come to terms with it.' She made a move to stand up and he ordered her to sit back down.

'And then what?' He stared at her, his normally vibrantly, bronzed skin ashen.

'I haven't come here to ask for anything. I just thought that you had to know. I don't expect you to change your life in any way.'

'Are you crazy? How can my life not change?'

'I don't need looking after, Luc. I'm more than capable and happy to be a single mother.'

'This coming from the girl who had dreams of love and marriage?'

'Let's just say that I've grown up.'

'And I'm supposed to do what, exactly? Fill me in here on this life of mine that's not going to change.'

'You carry on working, going out with women, and when the baby's born we can start talking about visiting rights. If, that is, you want to visit.'

'Are you on the same planet as me, Agatha?'

'I'm trying to make this easy for you.'

'You must fancy your chances as a magician if you think you've succeeded in doing that. What, for instance, do you intend to tell your mother? Do you think she'll fall for the stork scenario?'

'I, well, I haven't actually crossed that bridge just yet. I'm only just getting used to the idea myself, and Mum…she's old-fashioned. I can't face the thought of breaking this to her right now. I have to find some courage from somewhere first.'

'Then I suggest you do. I also suggest you don't try and stonewall by refusing to tell her who the father is. I can't take back what's happened, but I assure you that I intend to take full responsibility for any child of mine. I'm not interested in secrecy.'

'What do you mean by *full responsibility*?'

'You will be looked after financially. So will the child.' His eyes flitted to her stomach. *His child!* Not in a million years could he have ever foreseen his life becoming so spectacularly derailed, but he had to concede that there was something very sexy about the fact that she was carrying his baby in her stomach. 'Where have you moved?' He reluctantly dragged glittering eyes away from her stomach. 'Your idea of appropriate accommodation doesn't coincide with mine.'

'You can't just *take over*!'

'I'm the other half of this equation. I have as much say where you live when you're pregnant with my baby. Which brings us to the fundamental question of our relationship.'

'We don't *have* a relationship.' Suddenly everything seemed to be moving at breakneck speed.

'Like it or not, we do now, and something in me's telling me that your cherished dream might be about to come true.'

Agatha didn't have to ask for clarification on that statement. She knew exactly what he was talking about, in that wry, bitter voice. They had ended their brief affair on her outburst about wanting more than just a temporary liaison. Now, against his will, he had somehow been driven into a corner by a situation he hadn't courted and wouldn't have wanted in a million years. She had told him that his life would remain unchanged. How could she have believed that? He wasn't the sort of man who ducked responsibility, even a responsibility he didn't want.

'I won't marry you,' she whispered. 'That's not why I came here. That's not why I've told you that I'm pregnant.'

'You must know that I wouldn't be prepared to stand on the sidelines, and you must also know that no child of mine will be illegitimate. I have honour, Agatha. If you're so willing to remind me that I *must* know you, and therefore *must* know that you would never be the sort of woman to engineer a situation like this for her own benefit, then *you* must surely know *me* as well—or at least know me well enough to realise that I'm not the sort of man who would fling money at the problem and then walk away.'

'I don't care whether you're prepared to stand on the sidelines or not. I know you think that I'm a hopeless romantic who believes in stuff that you don't, but that doesn't mean that I'm a hopeless human being. A hopeless human being would…' In her head a single word reverberated like a gunshot: *problem*. Luc had been presented with a problem and he was dealing with it with the cold-blooded efficiency with which he dealt with all the problems he encountered in his life—the only difference being that this particular problem was growing inside her.

Luc jumped into the faltering silence. 'A hopeless human being would…what? Put her child before herself? Provide a stable environment? Do the right thing?'

'That's not what we're talking about,' Agatha muttered in a shaken voice.

'No? Then explain. We will be married, because it's the only possible solution to the dilemma.'

'It's not a *dilemma* and it's not a *problem*.'

'Okay. What would you like to call it? Situation? Unexpected chance event? Fateful occurrence? Choose your description. It makes little difference to the solution.'

'I'm really tired, Luc.' Agatha stood up, suddenly drained by the crazy onslaught of emotions attacking her from every angle. The ground that should have felt steady under her feet began to sway. It was like being on a boat in the middle of a choppy ocean, complete with feelings of nausea and giddiness.

'And I don't feel very well. The doctor told me that I'm

anaemic.' Her eyelids fluttered and she was dimly aware of being caught in mid-fall and swept off her feet while she struggled to contain her sickness.

In the very split second that her face had gone from its argumentative pink colour to chalk-white, Luc had been galvanized into action, catching her before she had time to collapse in a heap on the ground.

Barely had he had time to get his head around the life-changing bombshell that had been thrown at his feet like a careless hand grenade than he was racked with guilt at having dealt with the situation in a heavy-handed manner. Heavy handed, he belatedly recognised, might work for most things but it wasn't going to work here. He had reduced her to a fainting fit, and in her condition it was the very last thing she needed.

He carried her into his bedroom and gently laid her on the bed, propping her up on the soft pillows as she gradually blinked back to reality.

'Did I faint?' she whispered, reaching out and holding onto the collar of his shirt with one small hand. She felt vulnerable, fragile and scared and she just couldn't bear the thought of him leaving the room. Much as she hated it, she felt anchored by his very solid presence.

'Yes. Is it the first time it's happened?'

Agatha nodded mutely.

'You haven't been eating. Shouldn't you be bigger by now? You're as light as a feather. '

'Why are you fussing?' Agatha pursued doggedly. 'You don't care about…about this. It's just something that's come along to disrupt your life. You like to be in control of everything, and this is the one thing you can't control even if you think you can.' Her eyes filled up and she looked down hurriedly, willing them away.

'I'm calling a doctor,' Luc told her in such a gentle voice

that she had to try even harder not to cry. In full vent, Luc could be cold and intimidating and send her shooting off into realms of anger she'd hardly known she possessed. He could also be thoughtful and touchingly humane in equal measure. How had she forgotten that?

He ignored her feeble, automatic protest and half-turned away to make the call, then he spun back round to face her, sitting on the side of the bed and leaning on one hand.

'I didn't know you could get a doctor to make a visit just like that. Not that it's necessary.'

'It is necessary,' Luc informed her. 'And I have a hotline to the best doctor in London.'

'Because you're ill all the time?' She was beginning to feel sleepy and she yawned and wriggled on the bed, surprised that she could even consider nodding off when she was full of so much unresolved, pent-up emotion. She realised that she was still clutching at his shirt and she slowly released her grip.

'I'm not going to marry you,' she told him, just in case.

'I'm not going to fight with you again. You need to look after yourself and waging war with me isn't going to help.'

'I'm not waging war.'

'There you go again.'

The softness in his voice made her want to smile. She was still feeling stupidly content when the doorbell rang and a middle-aged, grey-haired man with a gentle face and shrewd, black eyes was ushered into the bedroom. While he took her pulse and examined her, he told her that he had known the family for years on a personal level, and had been Luc's doctor since Luc had moved to London to live.

'Not that I see very much of him,' he said, packing away his black bag and moving to the door where Luc had been impatiently waiting, having been dispatched there by an adamant Agatha.

'So? What's the prognosis, Roberto?' Luc frowned at Agatha who still looked incredibly wan.

'You need rest, my dear,' Roberto said, turning to face Agatha, his lined face serious. 'Your blood pressure's up, which could lead to all sorts of problems if it doesn't settle, and whilst the baby's heartbeat is strong enough I don't like those shadows under your eyes. You're obviously stressed and probably not taking in the nutrients that you should. Of course, there is no reason to eat for two, my dear, but you do need certain vital minerals so you need to eat well. I'm going to give you a prescription for folic acid, but more importantly I'm going to insist that you rest. At least for the next month until things settle. And that's an order!'

He smiled when he said that. Not that Agatha felt equipped to return the smile. How was it possible that she could have travelled such an enormous distance in such a compacted space of time? From utter confusion and panic to a complete inability to deal with the possible loss of the tiny, growing baby inside her that had generated the panic in the first place.

A range of frightening possibilities buzzed in her fraught brain as she watched Luc usher the doctor out of the room, talking to him rapidly in a low voice.

When he returned a few minutes later, his face was implacable, and Agatha felt a knot of fear twist in her stomach.

'He was lying, wasn't he?' she whispered. 'He was lying to be kind, but really it's much more serious than he told me. I know it. I can see it on your face.'

'Really? Then we need to do something about getting your eyes tested.' He resumed his place sitting on the bed next to her.

Three weeks without her had been hellishly long. Whilst he had in no way anticipated that the chain of events between them could possibly have led to this moment in time, he was fully resolved on what he needed to do.

And, first off the bat, getting her in a lather by trying to impose his will on her was out of the question.

Under no condition, he had been told by Roberto, was she to be unduly stressed. So trying to bludgeon her into marriage because it satisfied his sense of honour was going to have to go on the back burner. But look after her he would, because the idea of having a baby with her had grown on him with astonishing ease. Maybe, he had thought as Roberto had chatted to him, because the presence of the doctor had somehow turned the abstract into the real. At any rate, he would now approach his mission to protect her with all the military efficiency at his disposal, whether she liked it or not. And no one could say that he didn't have bags of it.

'I may have said things that upset you,' he began in a conciliatory voice. 'And for that accept my apologies.'

'Pardon?'

'Don't push it.' Luc smiled crookedly and was aware of her relaxing with a sense of keen satisfaction. 'I'm no good at apologies, as a rule.'

'No,' Agatha agreed distractedly, fascinated by a Luc temporarily shorn of his bold arrogance. 'I guess you don't get enough practice.'

'No need. I'm usually right.' Why understate the truth?

It was a remark so typical of him that Agatha felt her lips twitch in amusement. Lord, but she had missed him. Had missed the look of him, the sound of him, the feel of him and the glorious touch of him, and having him sitting next to her on his bed was enough to make her want to swoon.

'I won't beat about the bush. Roberto says you need rest. So as of now you are on indefinite leave from your job.' He held up his hand to silence the protest he could see rising to her lips. 'There's no argument here, Agatha. You carry on working and you jeopardise the baby. Simple as that.'

Already his mind was working and coming up with a plan of action and it was a good feeling. 'Are you prepared for that?' he asked, and nodded slightly as she shook her head. 'Didn't think so. I'm also guessing that you might not be too keen on going back to the family fold just yet.'

'You know Mum.' Agatha stared off worriedly into the distance and chewed her lip. 'I…just need a bit of time. I only just found out,' she spluttered and was brought back down to reality when he took her hand in his. The physical touch, reassuring and unthreatening, sent a flood of heated awareness rushing through her, which was silly when he was just being nice.

'Understood. And, while we're on the subject of all things family, let me just tell you that I was totally out of order when it came to dealing with this…' Luc almost fell into the trap of calling it a 'situation' once again '…unexpected occurrence. I reacted like a caveman. Sure, family honour is important, but I'm willing to concede that we no longer live in the Dark Ages. So let's forget about that proposal of mine and just focus on getting you fighting fit.'

Never had he been more placatory with a member of the opposite sex. But, then again, never had he been in a position of very nearly causing untold damage because of his own crass behaviour. He had learnt a valuable lesson and he wasn't about to disregard it. He might not have wasted a second thinking about settling down, but he was in a place without option, if only she was aware of it. Agatha, as a single mother, would set about looking for her dream guy with intent. Hadn't she already considered the Internet in her search? And there was no way that Luc was going to have his own flesh and blood brought up by another man.

But he had effectively ruled himself out of the running

by turning her down flat when she had looked at him with those big, dewy eyes and started talking about romance and fairy-tale marriages. He had hurt her and his mission now was to regain her trust.

'Fighting fit?' Agatha was beginning to feel a little dazed by his sudden *volte face*. His rapid backtracking from the crazy marriage proposal was a blessing, she told herself. But it still hurt that he had obviously had a light-bulb moment and had realised that, however high the honour stakes were, settling down with a woman for whom he felt nothing beyond maybe some affection and a keen sense of duty was just ridiculous. As he had said, his perfect woman didn't come attached to a bunch of emotional strings. She could feel herself getting breathless and worked up all over again and swallowed it back.

'You need to rest,' Luc informed her. 'And London is no place for resting. I have a house in a very quiet, rural area in Berkshire. It's close enough to London to commute but far away enough to forget what noise pollution sounds like. When I'm not around, I will ensure that there is someone around to take care of you, make sure you have nothing to worry about except putting your feet up.'

'You have a house in the country? You've never breathed a word about that. Why?'

Luc chose to ignore question number two. 'House in the country—very relaxing. And here's the thing: a magnificent garden. I think you will find it inspirational.'

He smiled complacently and wondered how long it would take to find a house to fill the spec. Not long, he reckoned. Money could work wonders when it came to things like that.

CHAPTER EIGHT

'I'M STILL not happy with this arrangement.'

Agatha had spent the past eight days at Luc's apartment, having failed to persuade him that she was more than capable of resting in her own place.

'I can't keep an eye on you if you're there,' he had told her with the finality of someone clanging shut an iron door.

Telling him that she had only just moved in, that she was wasting money on rent for a place that was uninhabited, had met with a similarly flat, negative response—although he had made a big show of tilting his head to one side and listening very carefully to every word she was saying.

'You don't need to stress about things like money,' he had assured her with a dismissive wave of his hand. 'Remember what the doctor said.'

His only concession had been to bring her work laptop home for her so that she could fill in some of the long stretches of spare time corresponding with the various customers she had set up in her new role.

Food was prepared for her by a home help which he seemed to have acquired with ridiculous speed, and he had taken to arriving back from work early every evening, although she assured him that there was no need.

Just as he gave one-hundred percent to *everything* he did,

he was giving one-hundred percent to the task of making sure that she didn't lose the baby.

Whilst that felt good, it was also disturbing to know that it was a task to which he had risen because he had had no choice. Had he not found himself thrown into the situation, she would not have laid eyes on him for dust. He had moved on with his life until she had bounced along to turn it on its head.

But what on earth could she do? She didn't want to lose this baby. Her level of attachment to it grew with each passing day. And, secretly, didn't she enjoy being fussed over, never mind that she objected at every turn? Didn't she enjoy lying on the sofa in his living room, watching television with a cup of cocoa in her hand and a stack of magazines at her side and her eyes drifting helplessly from the television to the chair, where Luc sat frowning in concentration at something on his computer? Didn't she enjoy watching him lounge on the two seater next to hers, hands clasped behind his head, making sarcastic comments at some slither of nonsense she had decided to switch on?

Take away the murky undercurrents and the dubious motives, and it was a snapshot of domestic bliss.

At least, as far as *she* was concerned. She had no idea how Luc felt because he was not to be drawn on the subject.

He had been scrupulous in his attentiveness. He had set her up in a guest bedroom and, more than anything else, that seemed to signify his thoughts on her as a responsibility to be heroically borne.

Right now, with her meagre possessions packed and the lease on her small flat cancelled before she had had time to enjoy it, they were speeding along the motorway towards whatever mysterious house in Berkshire he owned.

She had given up asking him too many questions about it and had redirected her efforts towards not succumbing to the tantalising notion that all his efforts at looking after her pointed to a man who was in it for the long haul. It was a seductive but dangerous train of thought, to be avoided at all costs. Loving him made it way too easy for her to be beguiled by mirrors and glass.

'Why not? Why aren't you happy with the arrangement?' Luc didn't glance in her direction. He had had over a week to consider this situation, to realise that the modern-day arrangement she favoured wasn't going to work for him. To work out that, whilst she seemed to appreciate the massive efforts he was making—efforts which were cutting big time into his work life—she had retreated into a shell of sorts, one from which she never ventured to discuss a future. Did she harbour some fear that she would lose the baby? Rest had improved her blood pressure but there was always an outside chance that it might rise again.

'It's like I've been thrown into a tumble drier and tossed around. First you move me into your apartment, even though I told you that I was perfectly okay to look after myself. You decide what I eat. I'm not supposed to lift a finger, and now this—it's like I'm being kidnapped.'

'Needs must. There are women who would appreciate the level of concern.'

Agatha refrained from pointing out that his level of concern had been non-existent the minute she had made the mistake of telling him what she wanted out of their relationship. His level of concern *then* had amounted to a scramble through the nearest exit-door. The wonderful level of concern he was now so eager to demonstrate was to do with the baby she was carrying inside her. She wondered, if and when her pregnancy settled, if he would be quite so assiduous in his attentions.

Which made her think of the future—that great, un-mentionable block of time hovering on the horizon. It had become increasingly clear that he was in the process of proving himself good-parent material. He wasn't a fool. He must know that he would need her on his side when it came to the business of visiting rights. Why not start right now to show her just how spectacular he could be in the father stakes when he put his mind to it?

He had clearly decided to carry on with his own life once the baby was born. She had to make a huge effort not to think of him playing happy families with their child while she watched from the sidelines as aspiring bimbos pretended to take a maternal interest. It wouldn't concern him because, in his head, he would have adequately smoothed the way.

'What am I supposed to do in a house in a village where I don't know anyone?'

'You'll know me. I intend to be around a lot.'

'I wish my life was normal again,' Agatha fretted, and he gave her a sharp, sidelong look.

'I find that wishing for the impossible is never a good idea. Life isn't going to be normal for either of us again. We just have to accept that and deal with it.'

'How can you be so...so *practical* about everything?' Agatha almost yelled at him.

'What would you want?'

'I don't know.'

'One of us has to keep a level head and I've nominated myself for the role.' He was driving away from the motorway now. He had been to the house once, but his driver had done the tedious journey while he had worked in the back. Right now, he was keeping an eagle eye on his sat nav and on the road signs, because getting lost might just alert her to the fact that he really didn't know one end of the county from the other; all these little roads down which they were driving had a tendency to look the same.

'What about *my* vote?' Agatha grumbled petulantly, but

she was finding it hard to hold on to her moral high-ground because she was riveted by the scenery. She had forgotten how enticing the countryside was, how clean the air smelled, how technicolour-bright everything seemed to be without the clutter of grey buildings, pavements and smog, and how wonderfully quiet it was, a soft silence unbroken by the sounds of cars and sirens.

'Not counting at the moment,' Luc informed her with that splendid arrogance that she had always found weirdly endearing. 'We're nearly there. Twenty minutes.'

'How often do you come here?' she asked, a question to which he seemed to give an undue amount of consideration before finally saying, 'Not often.'

'And, um, do you usually come here by yourself?' She hadn't wanted to ask the question and she was vaguely surprised that it had somehow found its way out of her mouth.

'Why?'

'No reason. I just find it hard to imagine you being this far out of London on your own and enjoying it.'

'You're the first woman to come here.'

'I wasn't asking if you brought women there.'

'No?' Luc allowed himself a slashing smile, which Agatha saw and which made her want to kick herself. Her state of health had rendered her temporarily helpless and into this uncertain vacuum Luc had muscled his way, taking charge of the reins for the sake of the baby growing inside her. She had to begin the process of stepping away from his control because how else was she going to summon up the necessary strength when she gave birth? Was his plan to keep her emotionally welded to him while he carried on with his life, adopting his role as father without the threat of any other man replacing him because she was still head over heels in love with him?

Luc didn't play by the book. If he had a game plan, then he would see nothing wrong in achieving it by whatever means it took. It was just the way he was built.

He was designed to spot weaknesses and capitalise on them if it suited his ends. It was something she couldn't allow herself to forget.

'It's beautiful here,' she said, changing the uncomfortable subject and looking away from him to stare at the flashing greenery, trees and open fields in which were nestled quaint little towns.

'Isn't it?' Never one to be bowled over by nature, Luc had to agree that there was something restful about the scenery. 'Although rumour has it that places like this are rife with intrigue and scandal.'

Agatha couldn't help herself; she laughed. 'And where did you hear that?'

'I think I gleaned it from all those ridiculous detective shows you insist on watching. Has it escaped you that most of the murders seemed to take place in quiet little backwaters?'

He was irresistible when he used that light, teasing voice. 'I'd better be careful, in that case.'

'No need to worry. I'll be more than careful for the two of us.'

There is no 'two of us'.

They had left all main roads and he glanced across at her as the car swept through some open wooden gates and up a thin, ribbon-like winding drive, bordered on both sides by a profusion of wild flowers that had been artfully planted to emphasise the majesty of the trees around which they nestled.

It was a glorious sight; the estate agent had surpassed himself. Luc had thought that the second he had glimpsed the drive up to the house, and he was reminded of it now.

Money talked, and it had spoken volumes in getting him just the right house to impress.

'Like what you see?' he murmured lazily, driving mega-slowly now so that she could delight in the abundance of flora, a dead cert to have her reeling in pleasant surprise.

When he turned his gaze to her flushed face, he was satisfied that everything was having the desired effect.

She was, quite literally, bowled over.

'Gosh.'

'I know. Stunning, isn't it?'

'I would never have associated you with a place like this in a million years,' Agatha confessed, dragging her eyes away from the marvellous, colourful landscape to briefly focus on him.

'Hidden depths.'

The house was now coming into view, slipping and slid-ing between the trees. It was not too big and not too small, with whitewashed walls and clambering roses; although there wasn't a picket fence, the low brick wall was covered in ivy and the little gate was wooden. It was a vision of exceptional prettiness that could have leapt from the pages of a story book.

'This is so different from your place in London,' Agatha breathed, her eyes wide like saucers. 'I mean, your place in London is so cold and clinical.'

'A bit like me?' Luc asked, his eyes cooling. He hadn't seen her eyes light up like that since they had been involved all those weeks ago, when she'd been still nursing dreams of permanence.

Agatha shrugged and remembered about all those de-fences she should be building around her.

'You said it. I didn't.' Then, not wanting to become em-broiled in a non-argument, she stared at the approaching house, now in full view, and gasped. 'It's…it's absolutely beautiful, Luc. What a fantastic getaway! I'm surprised you ever want to go back to London after you've been here for a weekend.'

Luc flushed. 'Too much peace can be taxing.'

'Do you have people to look after the garden and stuff?'

'Naturally.'

'Because I can have a go at looking after it for you while I'm here. It would give me something to do.'

'You're here to rest.'

'Gardening *is* restful.'

'I'll take your word on that one,' Luc said drily, drawing to a stop outside the house and moving round to open the passenger door for her. Everything they needed—including all her possessions, and enough equipment for him to work from the house at least part of the time—had been transferred in advance of their arrival. He sensed that he might just go crazy from the solitude, but the town was very close, just beyond the fields at the back, and it was deceptively close to London.

'I suppose it wouldn't do you any harm to potter in the garden. Although no heavy lifting, naturally.'

'Naturally.' She was drinking up the house now with its quirky charm, and thinking how fantastic it was that Luc should even think of owning something like this. He might be as hard as nails when it came to business, and frankly when it came to most things, but just to discover that he had purchased a house like this did indeed point to a sensitive streak in him that made her heart swell.

Inside didn't disappoint. It was beautifully furnished. The sofas were deep and comfortable and all the wood gleamed with the patina of age.

'You must have a brilliant housekeeper,' Agatha remarked, taking in the spotless surfaces and smelling the clean, pine scent of recently polished wood. 'Would you mind if I had a look around?'

Her eyes were sparkling, her cheeks flushed. She was the picture of a woman in love, in this instance with a house. Luc shrugged and nodded, then leaned indolently against the wall, watching as she poked, prodded, disappeared, re-appeared and then ventured up the staircase to where four bedrooms were interspersed higgledy piggledy with two very comfortable bathrooms. Fluffy towels were warming on the towel rails. The beds were all made up with covers of the finest Egyptian cotton. In fact, the house had had a com-prehensive face-lift since he had bought it, so underneath the olde worlde charm it bristled with the shiny sparkle of the brand new.

The cupboards in the kitchen were full to brimming. The freezer was stocked with enough food to keep them going for weeks.

Upstairs, Agatha noted that she had been put in the bed-room furthest away from his and she had to stifle a flash of disappointment. Pinning a bright smile on her face, she wan-dered back downstairs to find him fiddling in the kitchen, and for a few seconds she quietly watched from the doorway. Kitchens perplexed him. He could work every technological gadget on the face of the earth with the exception of those located in a kitchen.

'You really don't need to stay here with me, Luc,' she said from the doorway, and he turned round slowly to look at her with hooded eyes.

In her leggings and oversized shirt, her fair hair tumbling over her shoulders, she looked vulnerable and feminine.

'Tell me something I don't know.'

'You never take time off work. I don't want you feeling that you've got to stay cooped up here because I'm incapable. I'm not. I know this is your house and you must have enjoyed coming here in the past but I bet you never stayed longer than a couple of nights.'

'If I don't look after you, who will? You still haven't told your mother, so she won't be rushing here any time soon.' He knew why she still hadn't said a word to Edith. To break the news would put her in the position of revealing the father's identity. It would also compel her to find reasons to explain why she intended to remain as a single mother. For the moment, he was willing to go along with her silence, but he needed to start manoeuvring things in the direction he wanted them to take.

He abandoned his attempt to work the coffee maker and strolled lazily towards her until he was standing right in front of her.

He moved, she noted absentmindedly, with the sinewy grace of a panther, all dark, dangerous intent. Except she had no idea what he intended. Which didn't stop her heart from pounding like a frenzied drum inside her. Her nipples tightened and she broke out in a fine film of nervous perspiration. How was it that she had never felt so *alone* with him in London, even when she had been bed-bound in his apartment, which was really much smaller? The silence seemed to press against the walls, enclosing them in a little space of their own.

'The time isn't right to tell her,' Agatha mumbled uncertainly, driven to look up at him, even though it was doing dangerous things to her nervous system.

'She's going to wonder where the hell you are when that phone in the flat keeps ringing off the hook and no one answers.'

'I didn't give her the number,' Agatha confessed guiltily, sneaking a glance at him. 'She gets me on my mobile.'

Luc decided to let the matter drop. As he had discovered to his cost, that soft mouth and innocent face belied a stubborn streak that was a match for his own. Nearly.

'I won't be here all of the time, so there's no need to get in a panic. I've employed someone to be here between nine and six, so you'll have company. She'll cook, clean and do whatever else around the house that you want her to. It should give you lots of time to stretch your legs in the garden. Also, she can drive you into town whenever you want, although I won't expect you to go in more than is strictly necessary. In fact, scratch that—if you want to venture into town, I will make myself available to take you there.'

If he was intent on making himself indispensable, then he was going about it the right way, Agatha thought.

'How will you do that?' she asked carefully. 'I thought you said you'd be in London.'

'Some of the time. But it's perfectly possible to conduct business from here. You haven't been to the back of the kitchen, but there's a very passable office space there, and I've kitted it out with everything I need to keep going.'

'You'll go nuts being cooped up here in the middle of nowhere.'

'Then maybe you could distract me,' he dropped into the silence, wondering what she would do with his provocative remark. He hadn't laid a finger on her for weeks. Just at the moment, making love was out of the question, but he could do so many other erotic things with her body...

Could too many cold showers lead to some kind of health risk in a guy? If so, then he was slap bang in the firing line. After his abortive date over a week ago, he had been reluctantly forced to concede that, at least at the moment, he only desired Agatha. It was infuriating but it was undeniable. And even more infuriating was how much he missed her warm, willing body. However much he put his back out to penetrate her friendly but polite façade, he was still uneasily aware that a lot of that façade was there because she just didn't have much of a choice. She wasn't going to bite the hand to which she was temporarily indebted. It was all far from ideal.

Agatha was feverishly wondering what he had meant by it. Was he flirting with her? Trying to ensure that she didn't forget how meaningful he was to her? Laying all her cards on the table had made her vulnerable, and Luc, knowing as much as he did about women, would know precisely the extent of power he wielded over a vulnerable ex-lover. Maybe he thought that the odd word here and there, the occasional look that lingered a little too long, would keep her ensnared so that even without the bonds of marriage there would still be the bonds of emotions left intact.

No way!

'If you want distracting, then my suggestion is that you get out into that beautiful garden,' she said lightly, stepping around any contentious issues and adopting the firm, detached stand she was intent on pursuing. 'I find that always works for me.' She folded her arms and yanked her rebellious imagination back from unsteady images of her distracting him in all sorts of ways that were now one-hundred percent forbidden. 'Especially at this time of year, when it's such lovely weather to really explore what's growing out there. And I noticed an adorable wooden bench under a tree. Maybe you could take your computer out there if you happen to be around. You'll find it very relaxing. And, if it's distraction that you're looking for, then the sounds of the birds in the trees can do the job.'

Eyes narrowing, Luc abruptly turned away. 'Sounds idyllic,' he drawled, recognising the polite dismissal. 'Should I keep a watch out for Snow White and the Seven Dwarves in case they decide to pop into this slice of paradise? I have some work to catch up on. Is there anything you want to know about the house?'

Agatha shook her head, glumly fascinated at how every changing nuance of his moods had such an ability to alter her own. When he was relaxed, she relaxed, even though she knew she should always be on guard. When he was tense, she tensed. When he was attentive, she blossomed inside like a flower opening up to the first rays of the sun. And when like now he withdrew from her, with that cool, shuttered expression on his face, she just wanted to burst into tears and launch into the sort of open-ended, heart-on-sleeve speech that had sent him heading for the hills the first time.

'I'll just have a look around the garden. Then, shall I get something cooked for us to eat later?'

'No need. The freezer has a hundred and one home-cooked meals. I arranged for my chef in London to handle that. And there's ample food in the fridge as well.'

'Do you do that every time you come here?' Agatha asked, driven to hold him in conversation. 'Get your chef to prepare food for you? I guess it saves you having to go out and find somewhere to eat. What's the nearest town like?'

Since Luc had never seen it, he had to think quickly on his feet, coming up with something so stupendously vague that she was left more in the dark after his reply than she had been before it: post office. A few shops—and why would he know what ones, because he had no interest in exploring them. A pub or two. The usual. Weren't all these small, rural towns and villages much the same? he decided on the spot.

'So if you don't go into the town very often, and you really aren't into gardens, what was the appeal?'

'This is beginning to sound like the Spanish Inquisition.'

'I'm sorry. I don't mean it to. I was just curious. I mean...' She continued awkwardly as she tried to backpedal rapidly away from giving the impression that she was over-interested—or else, worse, clinging to conversation because when he wasn't around something inside her went out, like a light switch being dimmed. 'If we're going to be cooped up here together off and on, then it would be nice for us to keep the conversation light.'

Several things in that one sentence annoyed the hell out of Luc: 'cooped up', 'off and on', and 'light conversation', to be precise.

'As you may have noticed,' Luc said through gritted teeth, 'It's peaceful here. It makes a change.' He had purchased this quaint little house with a plan in sight. Now his subterfuge was beginning to cause him some disquiet. He hadn't banked on being quizzed over something as innocuous as owning a place in the country. He owned several apartments—one in New York, another in Paris and three in London which he used, occasionally, for visiting clients. What was the big deal?

'I think it's really great that you get away from work sometimes,' Agatha confided. 'Working too hard is bad for a person.'

'I think we part company on that one, Agatha.' Luc remembered just why he had been forced to break off their relationship in the first place. He reminded himself of the folly of a man like him—driven and entirely focused on his work and on the rigorous demands of having to run a multi-billion-pound empire—ever contemplating a relationship with any woman who saw the need to rein him back. Applying his intellect brought him back down to earth: he was here for a reason. She was carrying his baby, and when that baby was born he fully intended to be the sole father figure in its life. No sideline job. No visiting rights. And a ring on her finger so that there would be no temptation for her to imagine that there was a single life out there beckoning.

'Right. Yes. We do.' His coolly delivered words had the same effect as a bucket of cold water being thrown over her, and Agatha blushed and turned away. 'I'll go explore the garden,' she said in a stilted voice. Then, before he could remind her that she was a fragile piece of spun glass that needed careful handling because *his baby* depended on it, she added, irritably, 'And there's no need for you to worry. You won't have to rescue me because I've over-exerted myself by having a five-second stroll!'

But it was hardly the peaceful stroll she would have wanted. Everything around her was sumptuous, but her head was a whirlwind of tangled thoughts, and the more she picked away at them, the more tangled they became.

After half an hour, and with the temperature beginning to drop, she returned to the house, only glancing across at the kitchen on her way to the stairs. Once Luc was ensconced in front of his computer, wild horses wouldn't be able to drag him away, and she needed some time to herself.

In the corner of the room, her emptied suitcase had been tucked away under a pretty trestle table which housed an ornate, flowered jug in its matching bowl. Wandering into the adjoining bathroom, she saw the immaculate towels and an array of bath products that would have been worthy of the most expensive hotel in the world. All brand new. But, then again, why shouldn't they be? Luc hadn't said how often he visited this place, but she suspected not very, and he wouldn't want to find himself using products that had been hardened over time from lack of use.

She began running the bath, and it was only when it was run and the air was fragrant with the rose-petal smell from the bubble bath that she noticed the glaring absence of any lock on the door.

And on the bedroom door.

Old house, she thought, dismayed. Fantastically modern in all aspects except for this one.

But her room was far from his. He was currently lost in some intricacy to do with business. And she wasn't going to be long.

The weight of the anxiety she had tried to bury seeped out of her as she settled her now slightly more ungainly body into the bath, relaxing with a sigh into the foam and closing her eyes.

On the plus side it was undeniably good to be out of London, even taking into account the efforts she had made to relocate herself to somewhere a little less cramped. It was, however, the only plus that sprang to mind. Hot on its heels were a series of towering minuses; starting with the fact that she was now hopelessly dependent on a man who had only weeks previously turned his back on her, and ending with the miserable suspicion that there was more to his grand displays of attentiveness than he was letting on.

She had the trapped feeling of something very small and vulnerable slowly being circled by a much bigger, much cleverer predator.

And how was she going to deal with it? She could be entirely wrong about everything, and Luc might, just might, have turned into Mr Nice Guy, but even in her wildest dreams she found that difficult to get her head around.

Had she dozed off just for a few seconds? Had she been having a dream that involved her clutching a posy of flowers just like the ones in the rambling garden outside, watching as Luc smiled down at some other woman in front of an altar before slipping a ring on her finger?

The clarity of the dream jerked her awake. Or was it the sound of the door being pushed open?

In the first few confused seconds of disorientation, the figure of Luc by the bathroom door was like the manifestation of her dream. Except this manifestation wasn't smiling. His mouth was drawn into a tight, grim line and his eyes glittered in the subdued lighting in the bathroom.

Agatha gave a little squeak of horror when the manifestation spoke, and she struggled into a sitting position, dazed, flushed and staring wide-eyed like a rabbit suddenly caught in the headlights of a speeding car.

'Where the hell have you been?'

Agatha's mouth fell open and she heard herself stammer something about a stroll and the garden and then a bath. In spreading dismay, she realised that the bath water was now tepid and the bubbles had disappeared, leaving her exposed to Luc's raking green eyes.

With his blood pressure back to normal now that he had managed to locate her, Luc took in the scene that confronted him. And what a glorious picture it was. A now slightly more rounded Agatha was frantically trying to hide herself, but there was only so much two hands could do, and his eyes feasted on the smooth swell of her belly, the fullness of her breasts. He had dreamt of this and his body reacted as though a thousand volts of electricity had suddenly been shot through it. He almost lost his cool completely and groaned out loud. Instead, he moved swiftly towards her.

'You're shivering!' He dipped his hand into the water and grimaced. 'It's stone cold!'

'I must have nodded off.' Agatha stared at him helplessly. In the faded jeans in which he had traveled, and an equally faded rugby jumper harking back to his university days, Luc was drop-dead gorgeous. She would have given anything for him not to have had this effect on her but there was no denying the stirring she felt between her thighs and the way her nipples tightened and hardened, standing to immediate, aroused attention.

'Do you call this taking care of yourself?' Luc growled.

With no escape-route handy, she felt herself scooped out of the water and deposited gently on the ground. And because something appeared to have happened to her legs, making it impossible for them to move, she was a very naked and willing recipient of one of the large, fluffy towels that had been hanging on the heated towel-rail.

'I've been out in that bloody garden for the last thirty minutes hunting you down!' he delivered with biting reproach, as he once again swept her off her feet, kicking open the bathroom door and heading towards the king-sized bed. 'I've been worried sick!'

CHAPTER NINE

'YOU'VE been *worried*?' Agatha couldn't stop the tingle of delight that gathered in the pit of her stomach at those telling words. In fact, the feeling obscured the very fact that she was still naked, wrapped in the towel and sharing the same space as Luc: three things that should have had her running for cover.

'You should have informed me the minute you got back inside the house.'

'You were working. I didn't want to disturb you. Besides, I didn't think that I was supposed to clock in and clock out like one of the temps in your office!' Noticeably, he had dropped the 'worried sick' line of chat. Maybe he thought that an admission like that, an admission that might just possibly border on the not-entirely unemotional, would give her inappropriate ideas: ideas that he cared about her, when he patently didn't.

'It occurred to me that you might have got lost in the garden. It looks small, but there's acres of it, and quite a bit of it is woodland. With the sun going down, it would be difficult for you to find your way around.' That cool explanation was a far cry from the sudden pounding panic he had felt when he had walked round and round, calling her name with ever more urgency, imagining her merrily getting lost in the sprawling countryside like Gretel, but without the trail of breadcrumbs to find her way back home.

Rage, that she should take such little effort to look after herself, when she had been warned often and well about the necessity of doing so, was easier to deal with.

He had been flipping his phone open, ready to call the local police, when he had decided to do a check of the house.

Pushing open the bathroom door had been the last resort, for he had again called her name various times and received no response.

Little wonder when she had fallen asleep in the bath! How long had she been there? 'Are you beginning to warm up?' he asked gruffly and she nodded and pulled the towel tightly around her.

'You need to change,' he said, moving towards her. 'You'll catch some kind of chill otherwise.'

Agatha was tempted to tell him not to be foolish, but what leg did she have to stand on when she had slept in a cold bath for heaven only knew how long? Now, instead of getting her act together and putting on her adult hat, she was yawning, feeling sleepy again and not really wanting to do anything except look at him and savour the concern etched into his harsh, beautiful features.

'This is *exactly* why you can't be left on your own,' he fulminated grimly, searching through her drawers and coming up with underwear, a tee-shirt and a pair of stretchy jogging bottoms. He turned to look at her darkly. 'What if you'd been on your own and fallen asleep in the bath?'

'I expect I would have woken up eventually, a little wrinkled and a little cold.'

'The doctor said you're to take it easy. Freezing half to death in a bath because you've nodded off isn't taking it easy by anyone's standards.'

Agatha was only half-taking in what he was saying. She was fixated by the way he was moving towards the bed, her clothes in his hands and an expression of intent on his face.

'Wh…what are you doing?' she squeaked, when the mattress depressed under his weight as he sat next to her on the bed.

In truth, Luc wasn't entirely sure. He was only now coming down from his extraordinary flight of panic. He looked down at her upturned face and frowned.

He was taking charge, he thought, as the fog cleared. It was what he did. And good thing too, because she certainly seemed to be pretty poor at it. He swept aside the memory of that sickening rush that had overwhelmed him when he had gone outside to look for her. Instead, he focused on the potential hazard she posed to herself and their unborn baby.

He hooked his finger under the towel where she had pulled it tight across her breasts and felt the whoosh of her sharply indrawn breath. But, although she reached to cover his hand with hers, her eyes remained locked with his; what he read there gave the lie to her pitiful show of brushing him off.

'I…I can dress myself, Luc.' Agatha heard the breathlessness in her voice with a sense of dismay. The warmth of his finger nestling in her cleavage was scorching hot against her skin. When she shivered compulsively, she prayed that he might mistakenly jump to the conclusion that she was still cold after her silly experience in the bath.

The hot flare in his eyes told her that, whatever conclusion he had jumped to, it certainly wasn't the wrong one and she felt an answering leap in her pulses that didn't surprise her. Why should it? Even when she had been giving herself long lectures about staying away from him because he was bad for her health—even when she had told herself that he was only out to manipulate her because it suited him to have her firmly anchored under his thumb—she had still been susceptible to that ferocious charm of his and frighteningly undone by a love she hadn't been able to sweep under the carpet.

How hard had she fought to hang on to her independence once she had discovered that she was pregnant? She might not have succumbed to his marriage proposal, because not all of her pride had been squashed into the ground, but the second her health had given cause for concern she had allowed him to step into the breach and take over.

And Luc could offer degree courses on taking over. Before she had had time to think straight, she had been moved lock, stock and barrel into his apartment and then in the space of a heartbeat, here to his country house.

Her protests had been so ineffectual that it was little wonder that they had been comprehensively ignored.

A shameful sense of guilt assailed her because she *liked* having his finger touching her like a branding iron.

It took little more than a gentle tug to free her hand from its limp hold and for the towel to fall to the bed.

Agatha stared at the discarded puddle of towelling with an air of disassociation.

'You're carrying my baby.' Luc's velvety voice was a notch lower. 'I want to see how it's shaping your body.'

The sound of his voice snapped her back to reality and she made an attempt to scrabble for the towel, but he closed his hand around one slender wrist, pinning her in mid movement.

'Please, Agatha.'

'This is inappropriate,' she breathed unevenly.

'Is it? I've seen you naked before.'

'But we don't have that kind of relationship now!'

'Your breasts are bigger.' He was vaguely surprised that he could speak at all, because the sight of her was breath-taking. Literally, he felt as though the breath had been driven out of his body.

He reached out and cupped her breast, feeling the naked weight of it in his hands, and it was as though her body had been trained to react in a certain inevitable way to his touch. She fell back against the pillows, her eyelids fluttering as a wave of heat stole through her body, sending her entire system in full crash mode.

'And your nipples are bigger as well. And darker. Is that normal?'

'Luc...'

'I like it when you say my name like that,' he confessed in a ragged, unsteady voice.

There was no way that making love fully was an option but he still wanted her with every fibre of his being.

'This is so not right...'

'How can it be *not* right?' he murmured, briefly glancing at her face, but driven to look again at her even more bountiful body. 'You're pregnant with my baby. How can it not be right for me to look at you? But of course, if you want me to go, then I will...' It was a chance, but he was a gambler, and he always knew his game. The gentle quiver of her body under his raking inspection told him all that he needed to know and the curling of her fingers now in his springy hair was confirming it.

Instead of triumph, however, he just felt a bone-deep sense of peace as he traced the outline of her nipple with a wandering finger and then moved on to circle her smooth, rounded stomach. She could still get away with wearing jeans, but to his sharp eyes she had changed in a thousand little ways, from the shape and size of her breasts and nipples to the infinitesimal thickening of her waistline. Already she was beginning to put on a little weight and it suited her. It was incredibly sexy to think that all of this was due to his own flesh and blood inside her. Having never really given the question of issue a passing thought, he now wondered what the sex of the baby would be. Boy or girl? Dark hair, he imagined. Wasn't that a genetic trait that superceded the fair-haired gene?

The need to weld her to him was intense. In a little over six months she would give birth to his child, a son or a daughter; it bordered on obscene to think of another man entering her life.

That thought gave an edge to his roaming hands. When he bent to lick her big, dark nipples and he felt her squirm under him, he felt a rush of satisfaction and purpose.

'No making love,' he said ruefully, standing to remove his clothing and keeping his eyes pinned on her avid, flushed face. 'But I can still touch. Would you like that? Would you find it de-stressing?' He stepped out of his jeans, kicking them to one side, and pulled off the rugby shirt in one swift, fluid movement.

Agatha felt like someone deprived of food and sustenance for way too long suddenly confronted with a banquet. Her senses seemed to reach overload with shocking ease as she drank in the long, lean lines of his body. Assurance was in his every move as he ditched the boxer shorts and stood completely naked in front of her, proud, beautiful and clearly turned on.

She shifted when he slipped into bed with her, pushing aside the covers and looking at her with such open hunger that she wriggled under the scrutiny.

'This isn't supposed to happen,' she whispered, reaching out for sanity one last time before it disappeared altogether—then immediately contradicting her valiant words when she traced the exquisite line of his sensuous mouth with a wayward, rebellious finger.

Luc didn't answer. He gave her a slow, curling smile and then captured her finger, only to circle it with his mouth and suck gently on it while he locked his eyes on her surprised face.

He shifted a little so that she could feel what she was doing to him, heavy and urgent against her leg.

Still very gently, he moved to give the rest of her body the attention it deserved.

Agatha, caught up in a maelstrom of strong feelings and powerful sensation, could no more have fought his seductive onslaught than she could have hitched a ride to the moon. Her body responded to the lazy flick of his tongue on her nipple by heating up, yet seemingly turning to jelly. Her legs relaxed and fell open and she closed her eyes on a sigh of intense pleasure as his tongue teased and licked a burning path from one engorged nipple to the next.

Still exploring her sensitised breasts, he cupped one hand between her thighs and then slowly rubbed her, feeling her moisture like honeyed dew on his fingers until she came apart under his touch.

There was no need for him to guide her hand to him. Half-curling on her side to face him, she took him and played with him so that his hardness became as solid as steel, and he groaned and shuddered.

'I think,' he delivered unevenly, 'That I am just about to have the safest sex known to mankind.'

Far more satisfying it would have been to be able to plunge into the wet depths of her and feel her silky dampness around his sheath, but all in good time... For now, he released himself to the rhythm of her sure hand and then sank back against the pillow for a matter of a few seconds, spent, just catching his breath before giving her a wry look.

'What does it say that that was better than anything with any other woman?'

Leaving her little time to ponder that revealing reflection, he drew her gently against him.

'You can completely relax here,' he murmured soothingly into her ear. 'No need to stack up your defences. As you see, we don't have to be at war with one another. I'm a peaceful kind of guy.' He stroked her thigh and Agatha was content to gaze into those fabulous eyes and go along for the ride. 'Life,' he continued with satisfaction in his voice, 'will be infinitely more enjoyable if we can bury our differences and accept one another.'

'You mean climb into bed together?' She was beginning to review exactly what she had done and she didn't like the slow-motion picture show that was taking place in her head. But waging war with that was the seductive pull of her senses, telling her that letting him into her life like this wasn't necessarily a bad thing—was it? She had to think and she slowly eased herself away from him.

'Where are you going?'

'I need to have something to eat. I'm really hungry.'

'Now? Right this instant?'

Feet already firmly planted on the ground, Agatha nodded without looking at him. 'I'm wide awake now.'

'Wait. You don't know the layout of the place.'

'It's not that big, Luc. I think I can find my way to the kitchen and locate the fridge. If food's already been cooked, it won't test my intelligence too much to stick it on the stove.'

Luc, who had been keenly enjoying the drowsy warmth of her surrender, frowned at the subtle change of mood. Then he decided that mood swings were all part and parcel of the pregnancy process, and the fact that she had finally acknowledged what they both knew to be a fact was all that mattered. The house, which had seemed the last word in self-imposed exile—so distant from all the things he took for granted, namely the buzz of civilization—now seemed a lot more palatable. He hadn't realised how much he had missed touching her and feeling her curled against him. He also hadn't realised how much he had missed having her around him, warm, content and compliant.

'I'll join you in a while. I'm going to have a shower and I need to make a couple of calls to the office. And don't worry…' He grinned and held up his hands in mock surrender, as though she had protested. 'I'll make them here and I'll be all yours when I join you in the kitchen.'

Agatha smiled weakly back at him and climbed back into her clothes. Her body was still tingling in all the places he had touched and it maddened her that he had that effect on her. She wondered whether she had known all along that sooner or later she would end up back in bed with him. She wondered whether that tantalising prospect had formed the basis of her acquiescence to all his manipulations.

Mostly she was utterly confused at the thought of what happened next.

How could she pull back now and start preaching about being just friends? How could she get sniffy and talk about being adults, pretending that what had happened had just been a little oversight?

In a state of utter turmoil, she left him in the bedroom and wandered downstairs to the kitchen, switching on lights as she went and distracted from her train of thoughts by her real appreciation of the house. It was a house designed for someone who enjoyed exploring, because the rooms were small, quirky and quaint and all invited inspection. Rich, expensive rugs interrupted the polished parquet-flooring and there were a number of open fires in various rooms. In the depths of winter, she could imagine curling up with a book on one of the big, comfy chairs with a log fire burning, the world safely locked out.

But she realised that none of that was going to happen. She was a temporary visitor to this idyll. She didn't even know how long she would be here. A date for departure hadn't been mentioned but she was stronger now and fast approaching a time when she would be able to return to London and, to work part-time at least, if not full-time. She wouldn't need Luc around keeping his beady eye on her to make sure that she didn't do another falling-asleep-in-the-bath routine. Should she just go with the flow while she was here? Give in to the disastrous craving to be touched by him and then establish the necessary distance when she was back in London and away from his stifling presence?

She feverishly wondered whether she should have accepted his offer of a marriage of convenience when he had first made it instead of deluding herself into thinking that she was worth more than that. If she couldn't get a grip on her responses to him, if she was destined to lead a life in thrall to a man who didn't love her, then shouldn't she just have stuck the ring on her finger and legalised her foolishness?

And then there was the problem of her mother, whom she had yet to tell about the pregnancy. What was she going to say about her daughter going it alone when she had been given the option of financial stability and security from a guy who was—in her mother's eyes—perfect husband-material?

The whole chaotic mess swirled round and round in her head as she browsed through the fridge for food, finally deciding on chicken salad and some bread.

And then, more because there was no sound of Luc coming downstairs rather than nosiness, she walked through the kitchen and into the room behind it which he had told her he used as his office.

It was a honeycomb rather than a traditional office-space; yet again she was struck that he could be as at home in surroundings like that as in his own super-modern offices in London.

Everything needed for work was housed in the biggest of the spaces, a square room that overlooked the garden through a massive bay-window. Dominating the room was his desk, which was old, large and so highly polished that she could practically see her reflection on its surface when she gazed down.

A quick glance told her that there was also a sitting room, comfortably furnished with a little sofa and a couple of chairs. It was saved from having the look of a waiting room by the opulence of the Persian rug in the middle and a low sideboard that looked astronomically expensive. A bathroom completed the series of rooms. Impressed with what she saw, she was about to leave to check the food when Luc's open briefcase caught her eye; on the very top, screaming at her, was what resembled a brochure.

Agatha was not nosy by nature; she didn't pry into things that didn't concern her. But, the very second she spotted that brochure, she knew that she had to look at it because, really, what would Luc be doing with brochures? If he wanted a holiday, he had people who sorted it out for him. He only had to snap his fingers. In fact, if he wanted a cup of coffee he had only to snap his fingers. So why would he bother doing something as mundane as sourcing a travel brochure to anywhere?

Was he, maybe, going to surprise her with a trip somewhere? She squashed that treacherous thought before it could take root and guiltily took the brochure from the case.

It took a few seconds, then the dull pain of recognition washed through her.

There, on page two of the brochure, in all its glory, was

the house in which she was now standing. The estate agent was effusive about all the wonderful things that charming corner of Berkshire had to offer—and was even more effusive in its praise for the only-just-refurbished period house recently on the market which was, it would seem, a jewel. She stared down at the little snapshots of the various rooms which she had been admiring only minutes earlier.

She had had difficulty imagining Luc ever being at home in a house like this. He was a man born to live in the fast lane; a charming little place in the middle of nowhere would have been anathema to him.

Yet, even knowing this, she had still chosen to side-step the obvious and give him the benefit of the doubt, convince herself that his choice of second home showed a side of him that was calmer, more laid back and less aggressively fuelled for the cut and thrust of running an empire.

She must have been self-delusional! The house had been bought for a purpose and the purpose had been just what she had feared all along: Luc didn't want *her*, he wanted his baby, and the fastest way to ensure total control without the messiness of a marriage he had rapidly decided against was to make sure that she remained in his power. Like a complete fool, she had danced to his tune and how hard had he had to try? He knew which buttons to press when it came to her, and he had ruthlessly used that knowledge to break down her defences. Dream house, dream garden…*bingo*.

She hesitated and then, with the throb of an impending headache behind her eyes, she clasped the house details and quietly headed back up to her bedroom, turning off the stove on the way.

It was a relief to find her bedroom empty. Luc had either disappeared back to his own room to change or else to make his precious phone calls.

Having dithered about what she was going to do, how

she was going to break free of the power he had over her, Agatha was now calmly aware of what she needed to do.

She needed to leave; finding that brochure had clarified everything in her head. Luc didn't love her and he never had. Being tempted into bed with him wasn't just a sign of weakness, it was a suicide mission as far as her heart went, not to mention her chances of moving ahead with her life.

Having had him walk in on her in the middle of a bath, she was reluctant to have another, so instead she pulled her suitcase out and began stuffing her clothes inside.

She was in the middle of clearing out her meagre supply of cosmetics and cramming them into a little flowered bag when the bedroom door was pushed open and she stilled, her hand hovering above the bag, before she shoved the mascara in and slowly turned to face him.

His hair was still damp from his shower and he had changed into some black jeans and a black tee-shirt which, combined, gave him the look of a pirate. He exuded sexiness, lounging against the door frame with his arms folded and his deep-green eyes shuttered.

All over again, Agatha felt that burning, frightening response that rebelled against all her efforts to put it away. Prickles of awareness shot through her body and she stuck her hands behind her back and twined her fingers nervously together.

'What's going on?' It emerged as less of a question than a demand for information in the face of what was utterly incomprehensible.

For some reason, she had frozen him out, but Luc had convinced himself that it was a passing mood swing; he had returned to the bedroom, having first checked the kitchen, with his fine spirits fully restored. He had made his calls and had decided to put work on the back burner for the remainder of the day. He might, he had thought with a mixture of surprise and amusement, even consider taking a little break altogether. After all, the house had not come cheap, so why not take some time out to explore all the nooks and crannies of the town with which he was supposed to have at least a passing acquaintance? All in all, it was an enjoyable prospect.

'I'm leaving.'

Shock lanced through him but he was determined to keep that overblown response to himself.

'No,' he said calmly. 'You're not.'

'Don't you dare tell me what I can and can't do! I'm sick of it. I'm sick of you thinking that you can do whatever you please because you think that you're always right!'

'I know what's best for you, and getting all worked up isn't.'

On that score, Agatha grudgingly conceded to herself that he was right. She breathed in deeply and tried to gather her scattered emotions. 'No, Luc, you don't know what's best for *me*, you know what's best for *you* and you'll do anything within your power to make sure that you get what's best for you. That's just the way you've conditioned yourself to approach life. You treat human beings like pieces on a chess board that you can move around, like life is just one big game and you get to control how it's played.'

Luc flushed darkly. Instinctively, he reared up against the criticism. Not for the first time, he marvelled at the temerity of any woman who had no qualms about stampeding all over the boundaries he had in place around him. Agatha didn't care a jot about tiptoeing around his sensibilities. She spoke what was on her mind with the forceful directness of a laser-guided missile homing in on whatever target had been set.

His response to that full-on attack should have been immediate, cold withdrawal but that was an option he barely stopped to consider.

He was discomforted by the accuracy of her criticism but he wasn't going to dwell on that. Right now, his main objective was to get her to calm down, and with that in mind he took a few cautious steps towards her, treading as warily as someone on a mission to disarm a live bomb.

With the memory of that hateful brochure burning brightly in her head, Agatha stood her ground and placed her hands on her hips, leaning forward with glaring hostility.

'You need to calm down,' he said soothingly, stopping just short of putting his hands on her arms because there was a very real suspicion that any physical contact might just have the opposite effect and send her into complete meltdown.

'There's something I want to show you.' She turned away abruptly and made for her handbag into which she had stuck the brochure where it could be a constant reminder of his deception—just in case there ever came a time when she found her resolve weakening.

Luc knew exactly what he was looking at the second she held out her hand and he paled.

Watching him through narrowed eyes, Agatha detected that fleeting sign of guilt, and it felt like the death knell to all the hopes she had cherished in varying degrees over the time she had known him.

'Where did you get that?'

'It was lying at the top of your briefcase.'

'You shouldn't have been snooping around.'

'I wasn't snooping around. Your briefcase was wide open. Not that it matters anyway. Why did you lie to me? Why did you tell me that this was a second house? Do you know, I actually believed you. How dumb was I?'

She had promised herself that she would act cool and collected, that she would tell him about the house if he pressed her for a reason for her sudden, pressing need to leave. Which, of course, he would: as she had been foolish enough to hop back into bed with him, he would have been riding high on the optimistic assumption that she was once more his for the asking. When she thought about that, she just wanted to dig a hole, jump in and lie low for a thousand years.

'Okay. So I led you to believe that this was one of my other homes.'

'You didn't *lead me to believe*. You openly lied to me!'

'Does it matter?' He gave a careless shrug while Agatha watched him with jaw-dropping incredulity. He had just admitted lying to her and he still had the nerve to stand there, cool as a cucumber, and act as though it didn't matter.

'It matters to *me*!' Agatha managed to impart through tightly gritted lips.

'Why? You were in a fragile state and you needed somewhere to de-stress. I provided that place. Frankly, from my point of view, you should be thanking me.' Yes, he had been momentarily disconcerted by her attack, but now he was regrouping fast, keeping it all very controlled, speaking in a low, placating voice, trying to find the right words from a vocabulary that seemed strangely limited.

'*I* should be thanking *you*?' Agatha gazed at him in utter, helpless bewilderment.

'London was no place for you to be, not when you needed to rest. You would have been tempted to work, go out, alleviate the boredom of being cooped up. My apartment is comfortable enough, but there's no outside area. You needed a house. Somewhere peaceful. I took that on board and supplied it. What was wrong with that? What was wrong with putting your needs first?'

Agatha thought bitterly that all he needed at this point was the sound of angels and the playing of a harp. At face value, everything he said seemed to demonstrate the actions of a pious, caring guy—but what about all the things that were being left unsaid?

'You knew I didn't want to be in debt to you, Luc. You knew,' she added in a barely audible mumble, 'that I wanted to get over you...'

With that declaration out in the open, Luc at last felt that he had something to get his teeth into. 'But you haven't, have you?' he asked bluntly. 'What we did upstairs proves that, Agatha, and what's the point in running away from the obvious?'

'Did you bring me here with that at the back of your mind, Luc? Did you arrange this whole cottage thing because you knew how I felt about you? Was this perfect dream-house a cynical tool in your plans to seduce me?' Shamefully, she realised how close she had been to falling back in love with a perfect outcome. He had appealed to her most basic desires by producing a house he had known she would adore. The cruelty of the ruse was a bitter pill to swallow.

There were a thousand ways of answering that question and the most sensible choice, given her present state of mind, would have been a rapid and assured denial—but such a denial seemed suddenly impossible to voice.

'It crossed my mind that we might just end up back in bed together.'

Agatha balled her hands into fists and shot him a look of pure loathing, before staring down at her feet and counting to ten to clear some of the red mist in her head.

'I'm being honest here. I...Okay, I really missed you when you were gone. I still want you and I'm not ashamed of that.'

Agatha had an insane urge to burst out into hysterical laughter. He *missed* her! Missed her *so much*, she thought, that he had compensated by making sure not to beat a path to her door—in fact to start seeing another woman! He was all too happy to talk about still wanting her—wanting her enough, in fact, to go out and buy a house for a ridiculous sum of money. Anything to ensure that she was well and truly emotionally shackled to him, so that when she was he would then be free to release his stranglehold and pick up where he had left off with other women, knowing that she would find it impossible to replace him.

'Well, I *am* ashamed,' she said, with weariness creeping into her voice. 'And I'm mortified that I did end back up in bed with you, because you're no good for me. You're attractive, Luc, no one's going to deny that—and I'm only human, after all. But I don't feel proud of myself sleeping with you. I feel like I've let myself down.'

'Don't say that!' A sickening sense of the unreal swept over him like a tidal wave. Plans and expectations were being unpicked by the second but Luc really had no idea how to put a stop to the rapid unravelling.

'Okay. I won't. But I want to leave. Will you drive me to the station? Course, you have no idea where it is.' She gave him a tight, bitter smile. 'You may have to use your sat nav.'

CHAPTER TEN

SHE planned on going home, back to see her mother, the bearer of unexpected tidings. Of course, Luc was not going to allow her to catch a train.

'You've taken leave of your senses if you think I'm going to let you make that journey on your own on public transport,' he said determinedly, watching with a peculiar sensation of falling as she carried on flinging the remainder of her possessions into the case sprawled on the bed.

'You can't *make* me do anything, Luc.'

'I wouldn't put that to the test, if I were you.'

'Or else what?'

'I'm not above keeping you here until you calm down.'

'You wouldn't dare!'

'Don't you know that you should never say something like that to a man like me?' He shook his head and uttered a strangled, frustrated sound under his breath. 'Why don't you have a bath and then we'll talk?'

'Talk about what? Talk about the way you engineered this whole situation?' She could feel herself getting heated up all over again and she did the deep-breathing exercise thing and tried not to focus on the humiliation of having been taken for a ride, an easy conquest for a man who was out to stamp his authority over her bid for freedom.

She was also trying not to feel disappointed at the thought

of leaving the house. It was fabulous, and just exactly the sort of place she adored, even if it had been bought as a means to an end.

'I should have known that you would be the last person on the face of the earth to ever have a house like this!' she blurted out, her eyes stinging. With a sense of tired defeat, she sat on the small stool by the dressing table and watched guardedly as he took up position on the bed, pushing the open suitcase out of the way.

'Meaning?' Luc wondered whether she had any idea just how damned unpredictable she was, like a thoroughbred race-horse prone to spooking at the slightest opportunity. He was watching her very carefully now, his expression unreadable but missing nothing as the bright, feverish flush in her cheeks began to fade slightly.

He had to keep her engaged in talking to him, without the contentious issue of the house acting as a wedge and ramping up her emotions. Retrospectively he wondered whether he should have told her about the house, perhaps allowed her in on the decision-making process, shown her proof positive that he wasn't going to do a runner. Should he have done that? Unused to questioning himself, he attempted to bolster his decision to do what he had done by reminding himself that he had acted in good faith—and, really, what was wrong in employing all the means at his disposal to facilitate that event? Since when was it a crime to lever the odds in your favour?

'Since when are you the type to like small rooms, old-fashioned furniture and outdoor space? I must have been a fool to have ever bought in to your story about coming here for weekends. You don't *like* getting away from your twenty-four-hours-a-day work days! Why would you need rest and relaxation in a cottage out in the country? You don't know *how* to rest and relax! And, if you *did* want to get away for a few seconds, why would you choose to come to a place like this when you could spend a fortune and go to a hotel somewhere with Internet access and all mod cons?'

Luc gave the question some thought and then raised his eyebrows with a wry, mocking smile. 'Funnily enough, it doesn't seem as claustrophobic as I'd imagined.'

'I just don't understand how you could deceive me.'

'I'm going to run a bath for you.'

'That's not an answer!'

'I know. Come on.'

'I'm not going to have a bath with you around,' Agatha said, blushing furiously when she remembered just what had got her sitting here, mortified and angry with herself for having climbed back into bed with him again.

'I wouldn't expect you to.' Although he was pretty sure that, if she did emerge with nothing but a towel around her, neither of them would be able to help themselves. He left her sitting by the dressing table, giving her time to cool down and making sure that the bath was as fragrant and as tempting as possible. He emerged from the adjoining bathroom five minutes later to find her still on the stool, which was highly satisfactory, as a plausible alternative would have seen her trying to lug her case off the bed and transport it to the door. There was very little he would put past her.

'What are you going to do with the house when I've gone?' was the first thing she threw at him.

'Talking to you is beginning to resemble walking on broken glass,' Luc said, holding in his patience with a tight rein whilst simultaneously wondering how it was that this woman could sabotage his ability for self-control without even trying. He raked his fingers through his hair and shook his head as though trying to clear his thoughts. 'Whatever I say, you're going to interpret in the worst possible light. I've done my utmost to take care of your needs. I bought this house because I knew it was the sort of thing you liked. I could imagine you relaxing in the garden a hundred miles away from all the stress and chaos in London. And you do like the house and you do like the garden—so how is it that I've suddenly become the villain of the piece? So we made love. You wanted it as much as I did.' Frustration threatened to boil over.

'That was before I worked out that everything you did was designed to get me into bed! It's like you blackmailed me. It's like…like you took my dreams and manipulated them to get what you wanted.'

'Agatha, go and have your bath.' *Was that the best he could do?* Where was that legendary talent for persuasion when he needed it most? He turned away; she could have thrown something at that dark, lean, handsome head of his. Instead she gave an inarticulate sound of pure resentment and stood up, shaking like a leaf.

'And when I come out I want to be dropped to the station!'

'I'll do better than that. I'll drive you to your mother's house.'

'Good!' She had made her point and got her own way. So why was she feeling miserable? 'And I don't want you hanging around in here while I have a bath!'

'Fine.'

'And don't even *think* of bursting in on me! There's no lock on the wretched door.'

'The down side of some old houses. I won't burst in on you unless I suspect that you've decided to have a snooze. And just for the record, whether you like it or not, or believe me or not, I care about your welfare.'

He *cared about her welfare*. Agatha swallowed back the pressing temptation to ask how he could be so unemotional while she felt like a volcano on the verge of eruption. But why would she ever suspect that he could be otherwise? His capacity for passion was channelled into work and into sex and he had never pretended that between those two opposing poles there was anything else. He had never said a word to her, ever, about love, affection, need—not even in the heat of the moment when all barriers were down and endearments uttered only to be later sheepishly retrieved. Even when their bodies were entwined, and they were scaling heights that had left her breathless and weak, his inherent self-control was always in place.

How could she still love a man like that? How could she build up all her defences and then allow them to drop the second he laid a finger on her? Where was her pride and sense of self-worth?

Luc, keeping it calm, was angrily aware that somewhere inside there was a seething, whirling pool of turmoil that was threatening every principle by which he ruled his life. He was also aware that he didn't like it when she retreated the way she was retreating now. He liked her clingy and needy. It was a disturbing notion, and he didn't know what to do with it, so instead he chose to focus on the practicalities. He would drive her to her mother's house. It would be a long, arduous and boring trip but it would give him time to come up with a plan B now that plan A had failed so spectacularly. He had no doubt that there would be a plan B because he was nothing if not clever when it came to getting exactly what he wanted.

'If you don't mind leaving…' Agatha said haughtily and Luc shot her a frown from under his lashes, hovering for a few seconds before turning on his heels and striding out of the door. But even downstairs, sitting in the kitchen with his laptop in front of him, he couldn't concentrate on his reports, updates and emails.

He gave her exactly half an hour and then he headed up

the stairs, making sure to make sufficient noise to alert her to his arrival outside her door, which worked, because she pulled it open before he had time to knock. Her suitcase was packed and Luc eyed it with loathing.

'You said you'd drive me over to Mum's, but if you've changed your mind...'

'And what? Decided to keep you here under lock and key?'

Agatha didn't say anything. Her silence was even more unwelcome than her spirited arguing and irrational accusations: those he could deal with.

'So have you decided not to talk to me?' he ground out, heaving the suitcase off the bed as though it weighed not much more than a feather, and then half-jogging down the stairs to wait for her at the bottom. A weird, restless energy was pumping through him, making him feel as though he was uncomfortable in his own skin.

'How long will it take to get to Mum's?'

'Long enough. Several hours. I'll make stops along the way so you can stretch your legs.' He was beginning to see which way the wind was blowing and he was liking it less and less. So, personal conversation was off-limits—well, that was fine. He needed a bit of silence to think anyway.

But, after nearly three hours, the silence was as oppressive as a pair of handcuffs in a prison cell. She stared out of the window, lost in her own thoughts. On the two occasions when they had stopped at the services to stretch their legs, she had headed for the newsagent's, not bothering to look back. She had returned with an armful of magazines and some bottled water, and then settled in for the long haul with apparent fascination in the lives of the marginally rich and not-so famous, while he had glared at the road and determinedly tried to engage her in conversation, with no success.

Only when they were finally manoeuvring the familiar streets of their home town did she tear her attention away from the magazines, which she could barely make out in the darkness, and her MP3 player. She had jammed the headphones into her ears, thereby establishing that conversation was out of the question.

'What are you going to tell your mother?' It was the first time the silence had been broken in over forty-five minutes, when he had asked her how she was feeling and Agatha had shrugged and said nothing.

She was as tense as a piece of elastic stretched to breaking point and terrified of being lulled into conversation with him. He was too witty, too sexy, too engaging and far too single-minded for her. Just being in the car with him, knowing that she was being ferried to the safety of her mother's home, made her feel sick with tension. She had hardly given a moment's thought to what lay ahead. She had been too busy trying to deal with what lay right here in the present.

'I don't know,' she reluctantly conceded, her eyes skittering towards his harsh, forbidding profile and then skittering away again just as quickly. 'The truth.'

'It's always a good beginning.'

'Mum's going to be disappointed,' Agatha couldn't help saying with a catch in her voice. She rested one hand on her stomach and tried not to dwell on the disappointment angle. She and her mother had always been united against the world, since her dad had died. How was this going to sit with a woman of essentially old-fashioned values? Like a poisoned apple, she predicted.

'You underestimate people.'

'You don't know Mum.'

'I know her well enough. She's not made of glass, and she's not unaware that accidents happen.' He turned to her, pathetically relieved that she was now, at least, talking. God, he wanted her to smile. He missed that. He missed *her*, even when she was right here, sitting next to him, and it was a missing that was physical. He wondered how it was that he could ever have constructed his life around the loss of a woman who, it now turned out, had been little more than an insignificant interference in his life. Miranda had left him with a jaded palate, but her importance had been greatly exaggerated. He couldn't even remember what she looked like. Had he conclusively blown it with Agatha? He refused to entertain the notion.

They pulled into the drive to her mother's house after a very long and tedious journey and Agatha glanced at him, her hand on the door handle.

'Thanks for the ride.'

'You're not getting rid of me that quickly'

Agatha wished that he just wouldn't look at her like that, with that half-smile of his that could melt every bone in her body. Was he doing it on purpose? 'I guess you want to be a gentleman to the end and bring the bags in for me?' she returned with a tight smile and an edge of bitterness in her voice. But she didn't want to wait and hear confirmation of that, so instead she rustled in her bag for the door key which she had kept and then changed her mind at the last minute and rang the doorbell instead.

There was no chance her mother would be out and, sure enough, after only a few minutes she heard the rustling of footsteps, then a tentative face peered through the peephole in the door and registered the caller with a broad smile. Warm, welcoming arms were outstretched to embrace her the second the door was open.

'You didn't tell me that you were coming down, Aggy. What a treat! Come in, darling. If you'd said, I would have cooked you something special!' Edith was small and round, with short fair hair as flyaway as her daughter's and the same bright blue eyes. When she smiled, there were the ghosts of dimples in her cheeks.

'Mum…'

'Let me look at you!'

'Mum, I've come with, um, Luc—Danielle's son? He kindly gave me a lift here.' Propelled into the hallway, Agatha turned desperately to Luc for support, only belatedly realising how natural this instinct had become for her. He reassured her. She had handed him the power to become her backbone. She couldn't even begin to think how long it would take for her to grope her way back to some sort of independence.

'We're both here for a reason.' Luc placed his arm firmly around Agatha's shoulders and Edith's eyes rounded with surprise.

Agatha, feeling the lazy weight of his arm around her, stiffened in shock. She smiled weakly at her mother, whose eyes were darting curiously between the two of them.

'Reason?' Edith asked, bewildered.

'Ideally, my mother should be here as well, but we'll be breaking the news to her very shortly.'

'News?' Edith and Agatha parroted with varying degrees of stunned surprise.

'Darling.' He leant towards Agatha and she felt his warm breath on her skin. 'Would you like to tell your mother about our news…?'

This wasn't how Agatha had hoped to break it to her mother that she was going to be a grandma but without the ideal scenario of the perfect son-in-law. Cups of tea and a sitting position had been on the agenda but, thrown in the deep end, she managed to splutter, 'I'm, eh, going to have a baby, Mum…' She could feel the heat in her burning face and she couldn't meet her mother's eyes.

'And that's not all.' At last, the words that had eluded

him finally came to his rescue and everything settled into its rightful place. Not everything in life could be controlled; he accepted that and wouldn't have had it any other way. 'I am the very proud father and we're going to be married just as soon as the formalities are worked out...'

There might have been no fainting fit. In fact, the screech from her mother's lips had contained pure joy.

But he had put her in an impossible position and now, with her mother on the telephone tripping over her words to tell Danielle the glad tidings, Agatha finally turned to face him, white-faced and furious.

'How *could* you?' she nearly wept, walking into the sitting room on shaky legs and slumping onto the chair closest to the fireplace.

Luc took a deep breath and moved towards her, gracefully lowering himself to one bended knee and resting his elbow on the side of her chair,

'Look at me. I'm on my knees for you.'

'Stop it!'

'I can't. You do this to me. You bring me to my knees.'

'Don't joke. It's cruel,' Agatha whispered, risking a look at him.

'I wouldn't know how to joke about something like this. I know you think you were lied to over the house, and I'm sorry. And I know you think I took you there so that I could have my wicked way with you, and you're right—I did. I wanted to weld you to me and I just happened to pick the most stupid way of achieving that goal. I didn't stop to think about why it hurt so much when you weren't in my life. I didn't stop to think how it was that I couldn't get you out of my mind. I just knew that I didn't want you to have the freedom you kept harping on about.'

'I didn't want us to be together for the wrong reasons. And I didn't harp on about it.'

'You didn't have to. You said it once and it was enough to bring me out in a cold sweat.'

'But—' her voice trembled '—you don't love me.'

'My life was under control. How was I to know that falling in love would feel like the equivalent of being hit by a lorry? I always figured that love would be as controllable as every other aspect of my life. Then along you came, and half the time I no longer recognised myself. The first time you went away...' Luc's fabulous eyes glittered with emotion. 'I really made the mistake of thinking that things would revert back to normal. I would return to being the working machine I always had been, find another woman, begin the cycle all over again. How hard could it be? You were right when you said that the only lesson I learned from Miranda was how to become an island. I've only now woken up to the fact that being an island isn't what I want to be. I've also realised that I never loved her. I never knew what love was until you came along.'

Agatha found that she was holding her breath just in case this was all a wonderful dream and that blinking too much or breathing too hard would result in her having to wake up.

'Was it...hard?' she whispered, eager for the details, and he gave her a wry smile.

'You're enjoying this, aren't you?'

'No! Yes...Okay...a lot.' She stroked the side of his face and thought that she might just burst with happiness. 'I never thought you'd ever love me. When we broke up, I just decided that I had to get over you and get on with my life, and then I found out that I was pregnant...'

'And I asked you to marry me.'

'And I turned you down,' Agatha murmured ruefully,

thinking how much misery and heartbreak could have been
saved had she only known how he felt about her, then bliss-
fully thinking about how much joy and happiness lay ahead.
'I just couldn't imagine marrying you when you didn't love
me. I thought ahead to a time when you'd begin to resent
the ring on my finger and start hating me for having tied
you down with a baby you never asked for.'

'I may not have asked for a baby,' Luc growled with such
loving tenderness in his eyes that her heart sang. 'But when
you told me that you were pregnant... Put it this way, I got
used to the idea in record time, and just as quickly I knew
that I wasn't going to let you go again. When you turned
me down, I was determined not to let it get in the way of
having you. I played on the importance of the baby having
a father for all it was worth, and believe me when I tell you
that you were never going to a single mother in search of a
suitable husband. The only husband you were going to have
was *me*.'

'So you sneaked off and bought me the perfect house.'

'I figured, how could you resist a house like that? Ergo,
how would you be able to resist *me*? It may have looked
conniving to you but it was just my clumsy way of trying to
show you that I intended to stay in your life. I should have
found the words to say so, but I...didn't know how.'

'You are the most determined guy I've ever met in my
entire life, and I'm so glad you are,' Agatha breathed with
heartfelt emotion.

'I put my life on hold, pretty much,' Luc confessed, his
expressive face darkening. 'And weirdly I enjoyed it. I was
out of step with the rest of the world, but I found that, as long
as I had you in my sights, I couldn't have given a damn—and
then you found the estate agent's brochure and everything
blew up in my face.'

'Let's not dwell on that,' Agatha said anxiously. 'I just

love you so much and I just want to hear you tell me that you love me.'

'Isn't that what I've spent the past half an hour doing? Hmm? I love you. Madly. And if we didn't happen to be under your mother's roof...'

There was no need for him to continue the speculation because Agatha knew exactly what he meant and it sent a thrill of anticipation rushing through her like an injection of adrenaline.

'But we're here,' he said with a hungry, possessive look in his eyes. 'And, before your mother comes back in, tell me that you'll marry me and I haven't shot my mouth off for nothing.'

'What do you think, my dearest love?'

Luc did not let the grass grow under his feet. Within three weeks they were married in a quiet but beautiful ceremony surrounded by family and friends. The house which he had cunningly bought as a ploy to win her over became their main residence, with Luc finally admitting defeat and recognising that the only times he really felt truly alive were the times when he was with her. All those domestic values which he had previously abhorred he now embraced, with an alacrity that brought a smile to Agatha's lips and a resigned but contented shrug from him.

'We'll see how long that will last when there's a screaming baby in the house,' she teased him as she grew bigger with her pregnancy, laughing when he fussed over her, even though after the initial poor beginning she proceeded to thrive.

But when Daisy Louise was born two days shy of her due date, an apple-faced cherub with her mother's big blue eyes and her father's thatch of dark hair, Luc proved himself a force to be reckoned with. He had always given one-hundred percent to every single thing he had ever set out to do, and he poured the same unfailing enthusiasm into fatherhood.

He had been gifted a miracle, he smugly told Agatha, and their daughter was destined to achieve every superlative he could think of.

'Don't you want to try for another beautiful miracle?' he murmured lazily, looking at her in a way that could still make her bones melt.

Agatha, having forsaken her job in London in favour of opening a small landscaping concern with two of the mums she had met in the village, resisted for precisely six months. Second time round, her pregnancy was stress free and trouble free, and between Luc and her mother—who was a devoted grandmother and apt to sing the praises of her son-in-law to all and sundry—she was spoiled rotten.

But no passage of time could diminish the love they felt for one another.

She was, to Luc, the very breath of his life. And, well, for Agatha? Who ever said that fairy tales couldn't come true?

SEDUCE ME, COWBOY

MAISEY YATES

To the whole Mills & Boon team. This is the best job ever. Thank you for letting me do it.

One

Hayley Thompson was a good girl. In all the ways that phrase applied. The kind of girl every mother wished her son would bring home for Sunday dinner.

Of course, the mothers of Copper Ridge were much more enthusiastic about Hayley than their sons were, but that had never been a problem. She had never really tried dating, anyway. Dates were the least of her problems.

She was more worried about the constant feeling that she was under a microscope. That she was a trained seal, sitting behind the desk in the church office exactly as one might expect from a small-town pastor's daughter—who also happened to be the church secretary.

And what did she have to show for being so good? Absolutely nothing.

Meanwhile, her older brother had gone out into the world and done whatever he wanted. He'd broken every rule. Run away from home. Gotten married, gotten divorced. Come back home and opened a bar in the same town where his father preached sermons. All while Hayley had stayed and behaved herself. Done everything that was expected of her.

Ace was the prodigal son. He hadn't just received forgiveness for his transgressions. He'd been rewarded. He had so many things well-behaved Hayley wanted and didn't have.

He'd found love again in his wife, Sierra. They had children. The doting attention of Hayley's parents—a side effect of being the first to supply grandchildren, she felt—while Hayley had...

Well, nothing.

Nothing but a future as a very well-behaved spinster.

That was why she was here now. Clutching a newspaper in her hand until it was wrinkled tight. She hadn't even known people still put ads in the paper for job listings, but while she'd been sitting in The Grind yesterday on Copper Ridge's main street, watching people go by and feeling a strange sense of being untethered, she'd grabbed the local paper.

That had led her to the job listings. And seeing

as she was unemployed for the first time since she was sixteen years old, she'd read them.

Every single one of them had been submitted by people she knew. Businesses she'd grown up patronizing, or businesses owned by people she knew from her dad's congregation. And if she got a job somewhere like that, she might as well have stayed on at the church.

Except for one listing. Assistant to Jonathan Bear, owner of Gray Bear Construction. The job was for him personally, but would also entail clerical work for his company and some work around his home.

She didn't know anything about the company. She'd never had a house built, after all. Neither had her mother and father. And she'd never heard his name before, and was reasonably sure she'd never seen him at church.

She wanted that distance.

Familiar, nagging guilt gnawed at the edges of her heart. Her parents were good people. They loved her very much. And she loved them. But she felt like a beloved goldfish. With people watching her every move and tapping on the glass. Plus, the bowl was restricting, when she was well aware there was an entire ocean out there.

Step one in her plan for independence had been to acquire her own apartment. Cassie Caldwell, owner of The Grind, and her husband, Jake, had moved out of the space above the coffee shop a while ago.

Happily, it had been vacant and ready to rent, and Hayley had taken advantage of that. So, with the money she'd saved up, she'd moved into that place. And then, after hoarding a few months' worth of rent, she had finally worked up the courage to quit.

Her father had been... She wouldn't go so far as to say he'd been disappointed. John Thompson never had a harsh word for anyone. He was all kind eyes and deep conviction. The type of goodness Hayley could only marvel at, that made her feel as though she could never quite measure up.

But she could tell her father had been confused. And she hadn't been able to explain herself, not fully. Because she didn't want either of her parents to know that ultimately, this little journey of independence would lead straight out of Copper Ridge.

She had to get out of the fishbowl. She needed people to stop tapping on her glass.

Virtue wasn't its own reward. For years she'd believed it would be. But then...suddenly, watching Ace at the dinner table at her parents' house, with his family, she'd realized the strange knot in her stomach wasn't anger over his abandonment, over the way he'd embarrassed their parents with his behavior.

It was envy.

Envy of all he had, of his freedom. Well, this was her chance to have some of that for herself, and she couldn't do it with everyone watching.

She took a deep breath and regarded the house in

front of her. If she didn't know it was the home and office of the owner of Gray Bear Construction, she would be tempted to assume it was some kind of resort.

The expansive front porch was made entirely out of logs, stained with a glossy, honey-colored sheen that caught the light and made the place look like it was glowing. The green metal roof was designed to withstand harsh weather—which down in town by the beach wasn't much of an issue. But a few miles inland, here in the mountains, she could imagine there was snow in winter.

She wondered if she would need chains for her car. But she supposed she'd cross that bridge when she came to it. It was early spring, and she didn't even have the job yet.

Getting the job, and keeping it through winter, was only a pipe dream at this point.

She took a deep breath and started up the path, the bark-laden ground soft beneath her feet. She inhaled deeply, the sharp scent of pine filling her lungs. It was cool beneath the trees, and she wrapped her arms around herself as she walked up the steps and made her way to the front door.

She knocked before she had a chance to rethink her actions, and then she waited.

She was just about to knock again when she heard footsteps. She quickly put her hand down at her side. Then lifted it again, brushing her hair out of her face. Then she clasped her hands in front of her, then put them back at her sides again. Then she decided to hold them in front of her again.

She had just settled on that position when the door jerked open.

She had rehearsed her opening remarks. Had practiced making a natural smile in the mirror— which was easy after so many years manning the front desk of a church—but all that disappeared completely when she looked at the man standing in front of her.

He was… Well, he was nothing like she'd expected, which left her grappling for what exactly she had been expecting. Somebody older. Certainly not somebody who towered over her like a redwood.

Jonathan Bear wasn't someone you could anticipate.

His dark, glittering eyes assessed her; his mouth pressed into a thin line. His black hair was tied back, but it was impossible for her to tell just how long it was from where she stood.

"Who are you?" he asked, his tone uncompromising.

"I'm here to interview for the assistant position. Were you expecting someone else?" Her stomach twisted with anxiety. He wasn't what she had expected, and now she was wondering if she was what *he* had expected. Maybe he wanted somebody older, with more qualifications. Or somebody more… Well, sexy secretary than former church secretary.

Though, she looked very nice in this twin set and pencil skirt, if she said so herself.

"No," he said, moving away from the door. "Come in."

"Oh," she said, scampering to follow his direction.

"The office is upstairs," he said, taking great strides through the entryway and heading toward a massive curved staircase.

She found herself taking very quick steps to try and keep up with him. And it was difficult to do that when she was distracted by the beauty of the house. She was trying to take in all the details as she trailed behind him up the stairs, her low heels clicking on the hardwood.

"I'm Hayley Thompson," she said, "which I know the résumé said, but you didn't know who I was... So..."

"We're the only two people here," he said, looking back at her, lifting one dark brow. "So knowing your name isn't really that important, is it?"

She couldn't tell if he was joking. She laughed nervously, and it got her no response at all. So then she was concerned she had miscalculated.

They reached the top of the stairs, and she followed him down a long hallway, the sound of her steps dampened now by a long carpet runner the colors of the nature that surrounded them. Brown, forest green and a red that reminded her of cranberries.

The house smelled new. Which was maybe a

strange observation to make, but the scent of wood lingered in the air, and something that reminded her of paint.

"How long have you lived here?" she asked, more comfortable with polite conversation than contending with silence.

"Just moved in last month," he said. "One of our designs. You might have guessed, this is what Gray Bear does. Custom homes. That's our specialty. And since my construction company merged with Grayson Design, we're doing design as well as construction."

"How many people can buy places like this?" she asked, turning in a circle while she walked, daunted by the amount of house they had left behind them, and the amount that was still before them.

"You would be surprised. For a lot of our clients these are only vacation homes. Escapes to the coast and to the mountains. Mostly, we work on the Oregon coast, but we make exceptions for some of the higher-paying clientele."

"That's…kind of amazing. I mean, something of this scale right here in Copper Ridge. Or I guess, technically, we're outside the city limits."

"Still the same zip code," he said, lifting a shoulder.

He took hold of two sliding double doors fashioned to look like barn doors and slid them open, revealing a huge office space with floor-to-ceiling windows and a view that made her jaw drop.

The sheer immensity of the mountains spread before them was incredible on its own. But beyond that, she could make out the faint gray of the ocean, whitecapped waves and jagged rocks rising out of the surf.

"The best of everything," he said. "Sky, mountains, ocean. That kind of sums up the company. Now that you know about us, you can tell me why I should hire you."

"I want the job," she said, her tone hesitant. As soon as she said the words, she realized how ridiculous they were. Everybody who interviewed for this position would want the job. "I was working as a secretary for my father's…business," she said, feeling guilty about fudging a little bit on her résumé. But she hadn't really wanted to say she was working at her father's church, because… Well, she just wanted to come in at a slightly more neutral position.

"You were working for your family?"

"Yes," she said.

He crossed his arms, and she felt slightly intimidated. He was the largest man she'd ever seen. At least, he felt large. Something about all the height and muscles and presence combined.

"We're going to have to get one thing straight right now, Hayley. I'm not your daddy. So if you're used to a kind and gentle working environment where you get a lot of chances because firing you would make it awkward around the holidays, this might take some adjustment for you. I'm damned hard to please. And

I'm not a very nice boss. There's a lot of work to do around here. I hate paperwork, and I don't want to have to do any form twice. If you make mistakes and I have to sit at that desk longer as a result, you're fired. If I've hired you to make things easier between myself and my clients, and something you do makes it harder, you're fired. If you pass on a call to me that I shouldn't have to take, you're fired."

She nodded, wishing she had a notepad, not because she was ever going to forget what he'd said, but so she could underscore the fact that she was paying attention. "Anything else?"

"Yeah," he said, a slight smile curving his lips. "You're also fired if you fuck up my coffee."

This was a mistake. Jonathan Bear was absolutely certain of it. But he had earned millions making mistakes, so what was one more? Nobody else had responded to his ad.

Except for this pale, strange little creature who looked barely twenty and wore the outfit of an eighty-year-old woman.

She was... Well, she wasn't the kind of formidable woman who could stand up to the rigors of working with him.

His sister, Rebecca, would say—with absolutely no tact at all—that he sucked as a boss. And maybe she was right, but he didn't really care. He was busy, and right now he hated most of what he was busy with.

There was irony in that, he knew. He had worked hard all his life. While a lot of his friends had sought solace and oblivion in drugs and alcohol, Jonathan had figured it was best to sweat the poison right out.

He'd gotten a job on a construction site when he was fifteen, and learned his trade. He'd gotten to where he was faster, better than most of the men around him. By the time he was twenty, he had been doing serious custom work on the more upscale custom homes he'd built with West Construction.

But he wanted more. There was a cap on what he could make with that company, and he didn't like a ceiling. He wanted open skies and the freedom to go as high, as fast as he wanted. So he could amass so much it could never be taken from him.

So he'd risked striking out on his own. No one had believed a kid from the wrong side of the tracks could compete with West. But Jonathan had courted business across city and county lines. And created a reputation beyond Copper Ridge so that when people came looking to build retirement homes or vacation properties, his was the name they knew.

He had built everything he had, brick by brick. In a strictly literal sense in some cases.

And every brick built a stronger wall against all the things he had left behind. Poverty, uncertainty, the lack of respect paid to a man in his circumstances.

Then six months ago, Joshua Grayson had approached him. Originally from Copper Ridge, the man had been looking for a foothold back in town after years in Seattle. Faith Grayson, Joshua's sister was quickly becoming the most sought after architect in the Pacific Northwest. But the siblings had decided it was time to bring the business back home in order to be closer to their parents.

And so Joshua asked Jonathan if he would consider bringing design in-house, making Bear Construction into Gray Bear.

This gave Jonathan reach into urban areas, into Seattle. Had him managing remote crews and dealing with many projects at one time. And it had pushed him straight out of the building game in many ways. He had turned into a desk drone. And while his bank account had grown astronomically, he was quite a ways from the life he thought he'd live after reaching this point.

Except the house. The house was finally finished. Finally, he was living in one of the places he'd built.

Finally, Jonathan Bear, that poor Indian kid who wasn't worth anything to anyone, bastard son of the biggest bastard in town, had his house on the side of the mountain and more money than he would ever be able to spend.

And he was bored out of his mind.

Boredom, it turned out, worked him into a hell of a temper. He had a feeling Hayley Thompson wasn't strong enough to stand up to that. But he expected to go through a few assistants before he found one who could handle it. She might as well be number one.

"You've got the job," he said. "You can start tomorrow."

Her eyes widened, and he noticed they were a strange shade of blue. Gray in some lights, shot through with a dark, velvet navy that reminded him of the ocean before a storm. It made him wonder if there was some hidden strength there.

They would both find out.

"I got the job? Just like that?"

"Getting the job was always going to be the easy part. It's keeping the job that might be tricky. My list of reasons to hire you are short—you showed up. The list of reasons I have for why I might fire you is much longer."

"You're not very reassuring," she said, her lips tilting down in a slight frown.

He laughed. "If you want to go back and work for your daddy, do that. I'm not going to call you. But maybe you'll appreciate my ways later. Other jobs will seem easy after this one."

She just looked at him, her jaw firmly set, her petite body rigid with determination. "What time do you want me here?"

"Seven o'clock. Don't be late. Or else…"

"You'll fire me. I've got the theme."

"Excellent. Hayley Thompson, you've got yourself a job."

Two

Hayley scrubbed her face as she walked into The Grind through the private entrance from her upstairs apartment. It was early. But she wanted to make sure she wasn't late to work.

On account of all the firing talk.

"Good morning," Cassie said from behind the counter, smiling cheerfully. Hayley wondered if Cassie was really thrilled to be at work this early in the morning. Hayley knew all about presenting a cheerful face to anyone who might walk in the door.

You couldn't have a bad day when you worked at the church.

"I need coffee," Hayley said, not bothering to

force a grin. She wasn't at work yet. She paused. "Do you know Jonathan Bear?"

Cassie gave her a questioning look. "Yes, I'm friends with his sister, Rebecca. She owns the store across the street."

"Right," Hayley said, frowning. "I don't think I've ever met her. But I've seen her around town."

Hayley was a few years younger than Cassie, and probably a bit younger than Rebecca, as well, which meant they had never been in classes together at school, and had never shared groups of friends. Not that Hayley had much in the way of friends. People tended to fear the pastor's daughter would put a damper on things.

No one had tested the theory.

"So yes, I know Jonathan in passing. He's... Well, he's not very friendly." Cassie laughed. "Why?"

"He just hired me."

Cassie's expression contorted into one of horror and Hayley saw her start to backpedal. "He's probably fine. It's just that he's very protective of Rebecca because he raised her, you know, and all that. And she had her accident, and had to have a lot of medical procedures done... So my perception of him is based entirely on that. I'm sure he's a great boss."

"No," Hayley said, "you were right the first time. He's a grumpy cuss. Do you have any idea what kind of coffee he drinks?"

Cassie frowned, a small notch appearing between

her brows. "He doesn't come in that often. But when he does I think he gets a dark roast, large, black, no sugar, with a double shot of espresso."

"How do you remember that?"

"It's my job. And there are a lot of people I know by drink and not by name."

"Well, I will take one of those for him. And hope that it's still hot by the time I get up the mountain."

"Okay. And a coffee for you with room for cream?"

"Yes," Hayley said. "I don't consider my morning caffeination ritual a punishment like some people seem to."

"Hey," Cassie said, "some people just like their coffee unadulterated. But I am not one of them. I feel you."

Hayley paid for her order and made her way to the back of the store, looking around at the warm, quaint surroundings. Locals had filed in and were filling up the tables, reading their papers, opening laptops and dropping off bags and coats to secure the coveted positions in the tiny coffee shop.

Then a line began to form, and Hayley was grateful she had come as early as she had.

A moment later, her order was ready. Popping the lid off her cup at the cream and sugar station, she gave herself a generous helping of both. She walked back out the way she had come in, going to her car, which was parked behind the building in her reserved space.

She got inside, wishing she'd warmed up the vehicle before placing her order. It wasn't too cold this morning, but she could see her breath in the damp air. She positioned both cups of coffee in the cup holders of her old Civic, and then headed to the main road, which was void of traffic—and would remain that way for the entire day.

She liked the pace of Copper Ridge, she really did. Liked the fact that she knew so many people, that people waved and smiled when she walked by. Liked that there were no traffic lights, and that you rarely had to wait for more than one car at a four-way stop.

She loved the mountains, and she loved the ocean.

But she knew there were things beyond this place, too. And she wanted to see them.

Needed to see them.

She thought about all those places as she drove along the winding road to Jonathan Bear's house. She had the vague thought that if she went to London or Paris, if she looked at the Eiffel Tower or Big Ben, structures so old and lasting—structures that had been there for centuries—maybe she would learn something about herself.

Maybe she would find what she couldn't identify here. Maybe she would find the cure for the elusive ache in her chest when she saw Ace with Sierra and their kids.

Would find the freedom to be herself—whoever

that might be. To flirt and date, and maybe drink a beer. To escape the confines that so rigidly held her.

Even driving out of town this morning, instead of to the church, was strange. Usually, she felt as though she were moving through the grooves of a well-worn track. There were certain places she went in town—her parents' home, the church, the grocery store, The Grind, her brother's brewery and restaurant, but never his bar—and she rarely deviated from that routine.

She supposed this drive would become routine soon enough.

She pulled up to the front of the house, experiencing a sharp sense of déjà vu as she walked up to the front porch to knock again. Except this time her stomach twisted with an even greater sense of trepidation. Not because Jonathan Bear was an unknown, but because she knew a little bit about him now. And what she knew terrified her.

The door jerked open before she could pound against it. "Just come in next time," he said.

"Oh."

"During business hours. I was expecting you."

"Expecting me to be late?" she asked, holding out his cup of coffee.

He arched a dark brow. "Maybe." He tilted his head to the side. "What's that?"

"Probably coffee." She didn't know why she was being anything other than straightforward and sweet. He'd made it very clear that he had exacting standards. Likely, he wanted his assistant to fulfill his every whim before it even occurred to him, and to do so with a smile. Likely, he didn't want his assistant to sass him, even lightly.

Except, something niggled at her, telling her he wouldn't respect her at all if she acted like a doormat. She was good at reading people. It was a happy side effect of being quiet. Of having few friends, of being an observer. Of spending years behind the church desk, not sure who might walk through the door seeking help. That experience had taught Hayley not only kindness, but also discernment.

And that was why she chose to follow her instincts with Jonathan.

"It's probably coffee?" he asked, taking the cup from her, anyway.

"Yes," she returned. "Probably."

He turned away from her, heading toward the stairs, but she noticed that he took the lid off the cup and examined the contents. She smiled as she followed him up the stairs to the office.

The doors were already open, the computer that faced the windows fired up. There were papers everywhere. And pens sat across nearly every surface.

"Why so many pens?" she asked.

"If I have to stop and look for one I waste an awful lot of time cussing."

"Fair enough."

"I have to go outside and take care of the horses,

but I want you to go through that stack of invoices
and enter all the information into the spreadsheet
on the computer. Can you do that?"

"Spreadsheets are my specialty. You have horses?"

He nodded. "This is kind of a ranch."

"Oh," she said. "I didn't realize."

"No reason you should." Then he turned, grabbing a black cowboy hat off a hook and putting it
firmly on his head. "I'll be back in a couple of hours.
And I'm going to want more coffee. The machine
is downstairs in the kitchen. Should be pretty easy.
Probably."

Then he brushed his fingertips against the brim
of his hat, nodding slightly before walking out, leaving her alone.

When he left, something in her chest loosened,
eased. She hadn't realized just how tense she'd felt
in his presence.

She took a deep breath, sitting down at the desk
in front of the computer, eyeing the healthy stack of
papers to her left. Then she looked over the moni-
tor to the view below. This wouldn't be so bad. He
wasn't here looking over her shoulder, barking orders. And really, in terms of work space, this office
could hardly be beat.

Maybe this job wouldn't be so bad, after all.

By the time Jonathan made a run to town after
finishing up with the horses, it was past lunchtime.

So he brought food from the Crab Shanty and hoped his new assistant didn't have a horrible allergy to seafood.

He probably should have checked. He wasn't really used to considering other people. And he couldn't say he was looking forward to getting used to it. But he would rather she didn't die. At least, not while at work.

He held tightly to the white bag of food as he made his way to the office. Her back was to the door, her head bent low over a stack of papers, one hand poised on the mouse.

He set the bag down loudly on the table by the doorway, then deposited his keys there, too. He hung his hat on the hook. "Hungry?"

Her head popped up, her eyes wide. "Oh, I didn't hear you come in. You scared me. You should have announced yourself or something."

"I just did. I said, 'hungry?' I mean, I could have said I'm here, but how is that any different?"

She shook her head. "I don't have an answer to that."

"Great. I have fish."

"What kind?"

"Fried kind."

"I approve."

He sighed in mock relief. "Good. Because if you didn't, I don't know how I would live with myself. I would have had to eat both of these." He opened the bag, taking out two cartons and two cans of Coke.

He sat in the chair in front of the table he used for drawing plans, then held her portion toward her.

She made a funny face, then accepted the offered lunch. "Is one of the Cokes for me, too?"

"Sure," he said, sliding a can at her.

She blinked, then took the can.

"What?"

She shook her head. "Nothing."

"You expected me to hand everything to you, didn't you?"

She shook her head. "No. Well, maybe. But, I'm sorry. I don't work with my father anymore, as you have mentioned more than once."

"No," he said, "you don't. And this isn't a church. Though—" he took a french fry out of the box and bit it "—this is pretty close to a religious experience." He picked up one of the thoughtfully included napkins and wiped his fingers before popping the top on the Coke can.

"How did you know I worked at the church?" she asked.

"I pay attention. And I definitely looked at the address you included on your form. Also, I know your brother. Or rather, I know of him. My sister is engaged to his brother-in-law. I might not be chummy with him, but I know his dad is the pastor. And that he has a younger sister."

She looked crestfallen. "I didn't realize you knew my brother."

"Is that a problem?"

"I was trying to get a job based on my own merit. Not on family connections. And frankly, I can't find anyone who is not connected to my family in some way in this town. My father knows the saints, my brother knows the sinners."

"Are you calling me a sinner?"

She picked gingerly at a piece of fish. "All have sinned and so forth."

"That isn't what you meant."

She suddenly became very interested in her coleslaw, prodding it with her plastic fork.

"How is it you know I'm a sinner?" he asked, not intending to let her off the hook, because this was just so fun. Hell, he'd gone and hired himself a church secretary, so might as well play with her a little bit.

"I didn't mean that," she insisted, her cheeks turning pink. He couldn't remember the last time he'd seen a woman blush.

"Well, if it helps at all, I don't know your brother well. I just buy alcohol from him on the weekends. But you're right. I am a sinner, Hayley."

She looked up at him then. The shock reflected in those stormy eyes touched him down deep. Made his stomach feel tight, made his blood feel hot. All right, he needed to get a handle on himself. Because that was not the kind of fun he was going to have with the church secretary he had hired. No way.

Jonathan Bear was a ruthless bastard; that fact could not be disputed. He had learned to look out for himself at an early age, because no one else would. Not his father. Certainly not his mother, who had taken off when he was a teenager, leaving him with a younger sister to raise. And most definitely not anyone in town.

But, even he had a conscience.

In theory, anyway.

"Good to know. I mean, since we're getting to know each other, I guess."

They ate in relative silence after that. Jonathan took that opportunity to check messages on his phone. A damn smartphone. This was what he had come to. Used to be that if he wanted to spend time alone he could unplug and go out on his horse easily enough. Now, he could still do that, but his business partners— dammit all, he had business partners—knew that he should be accessible and was opting not to be.

"Why did you leave the church?" he asked after a long stretch of silence.

"I didn't. I mean, not as a member. But, I couldn't work there anymore. You know, I woke up one morning and looked in the mirror and imagined doing that exact same thing in forty years. Sitting behind that desk, in the same chair, talking to the same people, having the same conversations... I just didn't think I could do it. I thought…well, for a long time I thought if I sat in that chair life would come to me." She took a deep breath. "But it won't. I have to go get it."

What she was talking about… That kind of stability. It was completely foreign to him. Jonathan could scarcely remember a time in his life when things had stayed the same from year to year. He would say one thing for poverty, it was dynamic. It could be a grind, sure, but it kept you on your toes. He'd constantly looked for new ways to support himself and Rebecca. To prove to child services that he was a fit guardian. To keep their dwelling up to par, to make sure they could always afford it. To keep them both fed and clothed—or at least her, if not him.

He had always craved what Hayley was talking about. A place secure enough to rest for a while. But not having it was why he was here now. In this house, with all this money. Which was the only real damned security in the world. Making sure you were in control of everything around you.

Even if it did mean owning a fucking smartphone.

"So, your big move was to be my assistant?"

She frowned. "No. This is my small move. You have to make small moves before you can make a big one."

That he agreed with, more or less. His whole life had been a series of small moves with no pausing in between. One step at a time as he climbed up to the top. "I'm not sure it's the best thing to let your employer know you think he's a small step," he said, just because he wanted to see her cheeks turn pink again. He was gratified when they did.

"Sorry. This is a giant step for me. I intend to stay here forever in my elevated position as your assistant."

He set his lunch down, leaning back and holding up his hands. "Slow down, baby. I'm not looking for a commitment."

At that, her cheeks turned bright red. She took another bite of coleslaw, leaving a smear of mayonnaise on the corner of her mouth. Without thinking, he leaned in and brushed his thumb across the smudge, and along the edge of her lower lip.

He didn't realize it was a mistake until the slug of heat hit him low and fast in the gut.

He hadn't realized it would be a mistake because she was such a mousy little thing, a church secretary. Because his taste didn't run to that kind of thing. At least, that's what he would have said.

But while his brain might have a conscience, he discovered in that moment that his body certainly did not.

Three

It was like striking a match, his thumb sweeping across her skin. It left a trail of fire where he touched, and made her feel hot in places he hadn't. She was… Well, she was immobilized.

Like a deer caught in the headlights, seeing exactly what was barreling down on her, and unable to move.

Except, of course, Jonathan wasn't barreling down on her. He wasn't moving at all.

He was just looking at her, his dark eyes glittering, his expression like granite. She followed his lead, unsure of what to do. Of how she should react.

And then, suddenly, everything clicked into place. Exactly what she was feeling, exactly what she was doing…and exactly how much of an idiot she was.

She took a deep breath, gasping as though she'd been submerged beneath water. She turned her chair sideways, facing the computer again. "Well," she said, "thank you for lunch."

Fiddlesticks. And darn it. And fudging graham crackers.

She had just openly stared at her boss, probably looking like a guppy gasping on dry land because he had wiped mayonnaise off her lip. Which was— as things went—probably one of the more platonic touches a man and a woman could share.

The problem was, she couldn't remember ever being touched—even platonically—by a man who wasn't family. So she had been completely un- prepared for the reaction it created inside her. Which she had no doubt he'd noticed.

Attraction. She had felt *attracted* to him.

Backtracking, she realized the tight feeling in her stomach that had appeared the first moment she'd seen him was probably attraction.

That was bad. Very bad.

But what she was really curious about, was why this attraction felt different from what she'd felt around other men she had liked. She'd felt fluttery feelings before. Most notably for Grant Daniels, the junior high youth pastor, a couple years ago. She had really liked him, and she was pretty sure he'd liked her, too, but he hadn't seemed willing to make a move.

She had conversations with him over coffee in the Fellowship Hall, where he had brought up his feelings on dating—he didn't—and how he was waiting until he was ready to get married before getting into any kind of relationship with a woman.

For a while, she'd been convinced he'd told her that because he was close to being ready, and he might want to marry her.

Another instance of sitting, waiting and believing what she wanted would come to her through the sheer force of her good behavior.

Looking back, she realized it was kind of stupid that she had hoped he'd marry her. She didn't know him, not really. She had only ever seen him around church, and of course her feelings for him were based on that. Everybody was on their best behavior there. Including her.

Not that she actually behaved badly, which was kind of the problem. There was what she did, what she showed the world, and then there were the dark, secret things that lived inside her. Things she wanted but was afraid to pursue.

The fluttery feelings she had for Grant were like public Hayley. Smiley, shiny and giddy. Wholesome and hopeful.

The tension she felt in her stomach when she looked at Jonathan…that was all secret Hayley.

And it scared her that there was another person who seemed to have access to those feelings she examined only late at night in the darkness of her room.

She had finally gotten up the courage to buy a romance novel when she'd been at the grocery store a month or so ago. She had always been curious about those books, but since she'd lived with her parents, she had never been brave enough to buy one.

So, at the age of twenty-four, she had gotten her very first one. And it had been educational. Very, *very* educational. She had been a little afraid of it, to be honest.

Because those illicit feelings brought about late at night by hazy images and the slide of sheets against her bare skin had suddenly become focused and specific after reading that book.

And if that book had been the fantasy, Jonathan was the reality. It made her want to turn tail and run. But she couldn't. Because if she did, then he would know what no one else knew about her.

She couldn't risk him knowing.

They were practically strangers. They had nothing in common. These feelings were ridiculous. At least Grant had been the kind of person she was suited to.

Which begged the question—why didn't he make her feel this off-kilter?

Her face felt like it was on fire, and she was sure

Jonathan could easily read her reaction. That was the problem. It had taken her longer to understand what she was feeling than it had likely taken him. Because he wasn't sheltered like she was.

Sheltered even from her own desire.

The word made her shiver. Because it was one she had avoided thinking until now.

Desire.

Did she desire him? And if she did, what did that mean?

Her mouth went dry as several possibilities floated through her mind. Each more firmly rooted in fantasy than the last, since she had no practical experience with any of this.

And it was going to stay that way. At least for now.

Small steps. This job was her first small step. And it was a job, not a chance for her to get ridiculous over a man.

"Did you have anything else you wanted me to do?" she asked, not turning to face him, keeping her gaze resolutely pinned to the computer screen.

He was silent for a moment, and for some reason, the silence felt thick. "Did you finish entering the invoices?"

"Yes."

"Good," he said. "Here." He handed her his phone. "If anyone calls, say I'm not available, but you're happy to take a message. And I want you to call the county office and ask about the permits listed in the other spreadsheet I have open. Just get a status update on that. Do you cook?"

She blinked. "What?"

"Do you cook? I hired you to be my assistant. Which includes things around the house. And I eat around the house."

"I cook," she said, reeling from the change of topic.

"Great. Have something ready for me, and if I'm not back before you knock off at five, just keep it warm."

Then he turned and walked out, leaving her feeling both relieved and utterly confused. All those positive thoughts from this morning seemed to be coming back to haunt her, mock her.

The work she could handle. It was the man that scared her.

The first week of working with Hayley had been pretty good, in spite of that hiccup on the first day.

The one where he had touched her skin and felt just how soft it was. Something he never should have done.

But she was a good assistant. And every evening when he came in from dealing with ranch work his dinner was ready. That had been kind of a dick move, asking her to cook, but in truth, he hadn't put a very detailed job description in the ad. And she wasn't an employee of Gray Bear. She was his personal employee, and that meant he could expand her responsibilities.

At least, that was what he told himself as he approached the front porch Friday evening, his stomach already growling in anticipation. When he came in for the evening after the outside work was done, she was usually gone and the food was warming in the oven.

It was like having a wife. With none of the drawbacks *and* none of the perks.

But considering he could get those perks from a woman who wasn't in his house more than forty hours a week, he would take this happily.

He stomped up the front steps, kicking his boots off before he went inside. He'd been walking through sludge in one of the far pastures and he didn't want to track in mud. His housekeeper didn't come until later in the week.

The corner of his mouth lifted as he processed that thought. He had a housekeeper. He didn't have to get on his hands and knees and scrub floors anymore. Which he had done. More times than he would care to recount. Most of the time the house he and Rebecca had shared while growing up had been messy.

It was small, and their belongings—basic though they were—created a lot of clutter. Plus, teenage boys weren't the best at keeping things deep cleaned. Especially not when they also had full-time jobs and were trying to finish high school. But when he knew child services would be by, he did his best.

He didn't now. He paid somebody else to do it. For a long time, adding those kinds of expenses had made both pride and anxiety burn in his gut. Adjusting to living at a new income level was not seamless. And since things had grown exponentially and so quickly, the adjustments had come even harder. Often in a million ways he couldn't anticipate. But he was working on it. Hiring a housekeeper. Hiring Hayley.

Pretty soon, he would give in and buy himself a new pair of boots.

He drew nearer to the kitchen, smelling something good. And then he heard footsteps, the clattering of dishes.

He braced his arms on either side of the doorway. Clearly, she hadn't heard him approach. She was bending down to pull something out of the oven, her sweet ass outlined to perfection by that prim little skirt.

There was absolutely nothing provocative about it. It fell down past her knees, and when she stood straight it didn't display any curves whatsoever.

For a moment, he just admired his own commitment to being a dick. She could not be dressed more appropriately, and still his eyes were glued to her butt. And damn, his body liked what he saw.

"You're still here," he said, pushing away from

the door and walking into the room. He had to break the tension stretching tight inside him. Step one was breaking the silence and making his presence known. Step two was going to be calling up one of the women he had associations with off and on.

Because he had to do something to take the edge off. Clearly, it had been too long since he'd gotten laid.

"Sorry," she said, wiping her hands on a dishcloth and making a few frantic movements. As though she wanted to look industrious, but didn't exactly have a specific task. "The roast took longer than I thought it would. But I did a little more paperwork while I waited. And I called the county to track down that permit."

"You don't have to justify all your time. Everything has gotten done this week. Plus, inefficient meat preparation was not on my list of reasons I might fire you."

She shrugged. "I thought you reserved the right to revise that list at any time."

"I do. But not today."

"I should be out of your hair soon." She walked around the counter and he saw she was barefoot. Earlier, he had been far too distracted by her backside to notice.

"Pretty sure that's a health code violation," he said.

She turned pink all the way up to her scalp. "Sorry. My feet hurt."

He thought of those low, sensible heels she always

wore and he had to wonder what the point was to wearing shoes that ugly if they weren't even comfortable. The kind of women he usually went out with wore the kinds of shoes made for sitting. Or dancing on a pole.

But Hayley didn't look like she even knew what pole dancing was, let alone like she would jump up there and give it a try. She was... Well, she was damn near sweet.

Which was all wrong for him, in every way. He wasn't sweet.

He was successful. He was driven.

But he was temporary at best. And frankly, almost everyone in his life seemed grateful for that fact. No one stayed. Not his mother, not his father. Even his sister was off living her own life now.

So why he should spend even one moment looking at Hayley the way he'd been looking at her, he didn't know. He didn't have time for subtlety. He never had. He had always liked obvious women. Women who asked for what they wanted without any game-playing or shame.

He didn't want a wife. He didn't even want a serious girlfriend. Hell, he didn't want a casual girlfriend. When he went out it was with the express intention of hooking up. When it came to women, he didn't like a challenge.

His whole damned life was a challenge, and always had been. When he'd been raising his sister he couldn't bring anyone back to his place, which meant he needed someone with a place of their own, or someone willing to get busy in the back of a pickup truck.

Someone who understood he had only a couple free hours, and he wouldn't be sharing their bed all night.

Basically, his taste ran toward women who were all the things Hayley wasn't.

Cute ass or not.

None of those thoughts did anything to ease the tension in his stomach. No matter how succinctly they broke down just why he shouldn't find Hayley hot.

He nearly scoffed. She *wasn't* hot. She was... She would not be out of place as the wholesome face on a baking mix. Much more Little Debbie than Debbie Does Dallas.

"It's fine. I don't want you going lame on me."

She grinned. "No. Then you'd have to put me down."

"True. And if I lose more than one personal assistant that way people will start asking questions."

He could tell she wasn't sure if he was kidding or not. For a second, she looked downright concerned.

"I have not sent, nor do I intend to send, any of my employees—present or former—to the glue factory. Don't look at me like that."

She bit her lower lip, and that forced him to spend

a moment examining just how lush it was. He didn't like that. She needed to stop bending over, and to do nothing that would draw attention to her mouth. Maybe, when he revised the list of things he might fire her for, he would add drawing attention to attractive body parts to the list.

"I can never tell when you're joking."

"Me, either," he said.

That time she did laugh. "You know," she said, "you could smile."

"Takes too much energy."

The timer went off and she bustled back to the stove. "Okay," she said, "it should be ready now." She pulled a little pan out of the oven and took the lid off. It was full of roast and potatoes, carrots and onions. The kind of home-cooked meal he imagined a lot of kids grew up on.

For him, traditional fare had been more along the lines of flour tortillas with cheese or ramen noodles. Something cheap, easy and full of carbs. Just enough to keep you going.

His stomach growled in appreciation, and that was the kind of hunger associated with Hayley that he could accept.

"I should go," she said, starting to walk toward the kitchen door.

"Stay."

As soon as he made the offer Jonathan wanted to bite his tongue off. He did not need to encourage spending more time in closed off spaces with her. Although dinner might be a good chance to prove that he could easily master those weird bursts of attraction.

"No," she said, and he found himself strangely relieved. "I should go."

"Don't be an idiot," he said, surprising himself yet again. "Dinner is ready here. And it's late. Plus there's no way I can eat all this."

"Okay," she said, clearly hesitant.

"Come on now. Stop looking at me like you think I'm going to bite you. You've been reading too much *Twilight*. Indians don't really turn into wolves."

Her face turned really red then. "That's not what I was thinking. I don't… I'm not afraid of you."

She was afraid of something. And what concerned him most was that it might be the same thing he was fighting against.

"I really was teasing you," he said. "I have a little bit of a reputation in town, but I didn't earn half of it."

"Are you saying people in town are…prejudiced?"

"I wouldn't go that far. I mean, I wouldn't say it's on purpose. But whether it's because I grew up poor or it's because I'm brown, people have always given me a wide berth."

"I didn't… I mean, I've never seen people act that way."

"Well, they wouldn't. Not to you."

She blinked slightly. "I'll serve dinner now."

"Don't worry," he said, "the story has a happy ending. I have a lot of money now, and that trumps anything else. People have no issue hiring me to build these days. Though, I remember the first time my old boss put me on as the leader of the building crew, and the guy whose house we were building had a problem with it. He didn't think I should be doing anything that required too much skill. Was more comfortable with me just swinging the hammer, not telling other people where to swing it."

She took plates down from the cupboard, holding them close to her chest. "That's awful."

"People are awful."

A line creased her forehead. "They definitely can be."

"Stop hugging my dinner plate to your shirt. That really isn't sanitary. We can eat in here." He gestured to the countertop island. She set the plates down hurriedly, then started dishing food onto them.

He sighed heavily, moving to where she was and taking the big fork and knife out of her hands. "Have a seat. How much do you want?"

"Oh," she said, "I don't need much."

He ignored her, filling the plate completely, then filling his own. After that, he went to the fridge and pulled out a beer. "Want one?"

She shook her head. "I don't drink."

He frowned, then looked back into the fridge. "I don't have anything else."

"Water is fine."

He got her a glass and poured some water from the spigot in the fridge. He handed it to her, regarding her like she was some kind of alien life-form. The small conversation had really highlighted the gulf between them.

It should make him feel even more ashamed about looking at her butt.

Except shame was pretty hard for him to come by.

"Tell me what you think about people, Hayley." He took a bite of the roast and nearly gave her a raise then and there.

"No matter what things look like on the surface, you never know what someone is going through. It surprised me how often someone who had been smiling on Sunday would come into the office and break down in tears on Tuesday afternoon, saying they needed to talk to the pastor. Everyone has problems, and I do my best not to add to them."

"That's a hell of a lot nicer than most people deserve."

"Okay, what do you think about people?" she asked, clasping her hands in front of her and looking so damn interested and sincere he wasn't quite sure how to react.

"I think they're a bunch of self-interested bastards. And that's fair enough, because so am I. But whenever somebody asks for something, or offers me something, I ask myself what they will get out of it. If I can't figure out how they'll benefit, that's when I get worried."

"Not everyone is after money or power," she said. He could see she really believed what she said. He wasn't sure what to make of that.

"All right," he conceded, "maybe they aren't all after money. But they are looking to gain something. Everyone is. You can't get through life any other way. Trust me."

"I don't know. I never thought of it that way. In terms of who could get me what. At least, that's not how I've lived."

"Then you're an anomaly."

She shook her head. "My father is like that, too. He really does want to help people. He cares. Pastoring a small church in a little town doesn't net you much power or money."

"Of course it does. You hold the power of people's salvation in your hands. Pass around the plate every week. Of course you get power and money." Jonathan shook his head. "Being the leader of local spirituality is power, honey, trust me."

Her cheeks turned pink. "Okay. You might have a point. But my father doesn't claim to have the key to anyone's salvation. And the money in that basket goes right back into the community. Or into keeping the doors of the church open. My father believes in living the same way the community lives. Not higher up. So whatever baggage you might have about church, that's specific to your experience. It has nothing to do with my father or his faith."

She spoke with such raw certainty that Jonathan was tempted to believe her. But he knew too much about human nature.

Still, he liked all that conviction burning inside her. He liked that she believed what she said, even if he couldn't.

If he had been born with any ideals, he couldn't remember them now. He'd never had the luxury of having faith in humanity, as Hayley seemed to have. No, his earliest memory of his father was the old man's fist connecting with his face. Jonathan had never had the chance to believe the best of anybody.

He had been introduced to the worst far too early.

And he didn't know very many people who'd had different experiences.

The optimism she seemed to carry, the softness combined with strength, fascinated him. He wanted to draw closer to it, to her, to touch her skin, to see if she was strong enough to take the physical demands he put on a woman who shared his bed.

To see how shocked she might be when he told her what those demands were. In explicit detail.

He clenched his jaw tight, clamping his teeth down hard. He was not going to find out, for a couple reasons. The first being that she was his employee, and off-limits. The second being that all those things that fascinated him would be destroyed if he got close, if he laid even one finger on her.

Cynicism bled from his pores, and he damn well knew it. He had earned it. He wasn't one of those bored rich people overcome by ennui just because life had gone so well he wanted to create problems so he had something to battle against.

No. He had fought every step of the way, and he had been disappointed by people in every way imaginable. He had earned his feelings about people, that was for damn sure.

But he wasn't certain he wanted to pass that cynicism on to Hayley. No, she was like a pristine wilderness area. Unspoiled by humans. And his first inclination was to explore every last inch, to experience all that beauty, all that majesty. But he had to leave it alone. He had to leave it looked at, not touched.

Hayley Thompson was the same. Untouched. He had to leave her unspoiled. Exploring that beauty would only leave it ruined, and he couldn't do that. He wouldn't.

"I think it's sad," she said, her voice muted. "That you can't see the good in other people."

"I've been bitten in the ass too many times," he said, his tone harder than he'd intended it to be. "I'm glad you haven't been."

"I haven't had the chance to be. But that's kind

of the point of what I'm doing. Going out, maybe getting bitten in the ass." Her cheeks turned bright red. "I can't believe I said that."

"What?"

"That word."

That made his stomach feel like it had been hollowed out. *"Ass?"*

Her cheeks turned even redder. "Yes. I don't say things like that."

"I guess not… Being the church secretary and all."

Now he just felt… Well, she made him feel rough and uncultured, dirty and hard and unbending as steel. Everything she was not. She was small, delicate and probably far too easy to break. Just like he'd imagined earlier, she was…set apart. Unspoiled. And here he had already spoiled her a little bit. She'd said ass, right there in his kitchen.

And she'd looked shocked as hell by her own behavior.

"You don't have to say things like that if you don't want to," he said. "Not every experience is a good experience. You shouldn't try things just to try them. Hell, if I'd had the choice of staying innocent of human nature, maybe I would have taken that route instead. Don't ruin that nice vision of the world you have."

She frowned. "You know, everybody talks about going out and experiencing things…"

"Sure. But when people say that, they want control over those experiences. Believe me, having the blinders ripped off is not necessarily the best thing."

She nodded slowly. "I guess I understand that. What kinds of experiences do you think are bad?"

Immediately, he thought of about a hundred bad things he wanted to do to her. Most of them in bed, all of them naked. He sucked in a sharp breath through his teeth. "I don't think we need to get into that."

"I'm curious."

"You know what they say about curiosity and the cat, right?"

"But I'm not a cat."

"No," he said, "you are Hayley, and you should be grateful for the things you've been spared. Maybe you should even go back to the church office."

"No," she said, frowning. "I don't want to. Maybe I don't want to *experience everything*—I can see how you're probably right about that. But I can't just stay in one place, sheltered for the rest of my life. I have to figure out…who I am and what I want."

That made him laugh, because it was such a naive sentiment. He had never stood back and asked himself who the hell Jonathan Bear was, and what he wanted out of life. He hadn't given a damn how he made his money as long as he made it.

As far as he was concerned, dreams were for people with a lot of time on their hands. He had to *do*. Even as a kid, he couldn't think, couldn't wonder; he had to act.

She might as well be speaking a foreign language. "You'll have to tell me what that's like."

"What?"

"That quest to find yourself. Let me know if it's any more effective than just living your life and seeing what happens."

"Okay, now you've made me feel silly."

He took another bite of dinner. Maybe he should back down, because he didn't want her to quit. He would like to continue eating her food. And, frankly, he would like to keep looking at her.

Just because he should back down didn't mean he was going to.

"There was no safety net in my life," he said, not bothering to reassure her. "There never has been. I had to work my ass off from the moment I was old enough to get paid to do something. Hell, even before then. I would get what I could from the store, expired products, whatever, so we would have something to eat. That teaches you a lot about yourself. You don't have to go looking. In those situations, you find out whether you're a survivor or not. Turns out I am. And I've never really seen what more I needed to know."

"I don't… I don't have anything to say to that."

"Yeah," he returned. "My life story is kind of a bummer."

"Not now," she said softly. "You have all this. You have the business, you have this house."

"Yeah, I expect a man could find himself here. Well, unless he got lost because it was so big." He smiled at her, but she didn't look at all disarmed by the gesture. Instead, she looked thoughtful, and that made his stomach feel tight.

He didn't really do meaningful conversation. He especially didn't do it with women.

Yet here he was, telling this woman more about himself than he could remember telling anyone. Rebecca knew everything, of course. Well, as much as she'd observed while being a kid in that situation. They didn't need to talk about it. It was just life. But other people... Well, he didn't see the point in talking about the deficit he'd started with. He preferred people assume he'd sprung out of the ground powerful and successful. They took him more seriously.

He'd had enough disadvantages, and he wouldn't set himself up for any more.

But there was something about Hayley—her openness, her honesty—that made him want to talk. That made him feel bad for being insincere. Because she was just so...so damn real.

How would he have been if he'd had a softer existence? Maybe he wouldn't be as hard. Maybe a different life would have meant not breaking a woman like this the moment he put his hands on her.

It was moot. Because he hadn't had a different

life. And if he had, he probably wouldn't have made half as much of himself.

"You don't have to feel bad for wanting more," he said finally. "Just because other people don't have it easy, doesn't mean you don't have your own kind of hard."

"It's just difficult to decide what to do when other people's expectations feel so much bigger than your own dreams."

"I know a little something about that. Only in my case, the expectations other people had for me were that I would end up dead of a drug overdose or in prison. So, all things considered, I figured I would blow past those expectations and give people something to talk about."

"I just want to travel."

"Is that it?"

A smile played in the corner of her lips, and he found himself wondering what it might be like to taste that smile. "Okay. And see a famous landmark. Like the Eiffel Tower or Big Ben. And I want to dance."

"Have you never danced?"

"No!" She looked almost comically horrified. "Where would I have danced?"

"Well, your brother does own a bar. And there is line dancing."

"I can't even go into Ace's bar. My parents don't go. We can go to the brewery. Because they serve more food there. And it's not called a bar."

"That seems like some arbitrary shit."

Her cheeks colored, and he didn't know if it was because he'd pointed out a flaw in her parents' logic or because he had cursed. "Maybe. But I follow their lead. It's important for us to keep away from the appearance of evil."

"Now, that I don't know anything about. Because nobody cares much about my appearance."

She cleared her throat. "So," she said. "Dancing."

Suddenly, an impulse stole over him, one he couldn't quite understand or control. Before he knew it, he was pushing his chair back and standing up, extending his hand. "All right, Hayley Thompson, Paris has to wait awhile. But we can take care of the dancing right now."

"What?" Her pretty eyes flew wide, her soft lips rounded into a perfect O.

"Dance with me, Hayley."

Four

Hayley was pretty sure she was hallucinating.

Because there was no way her stern boss was standing there, his large, work-worn hand stretched toward her, his dark eyes glittering with an intensity she could only guess at the meaning of, having just asked her to dance. Except, no matter how many times she blinked, he was still standing there. And the words were still echoing in her head.

"There's no music."

He took his cell phone out of his pocket, opened an app and set the phone on the table, a slow country song filling the air. "There," he said. "Music accomplished. Now, dance with me."

"I thought men *asked* for a dance, I didn't think they demanded one."

"Some men, maybe. But not me. But remember, I don't give a damn about appearances."

"I think I might admire that about you."

"You should," he said, his tone grave.

She felt… Well, she felt breathless and fluttery, and she didn't know what to do. But if she said no, then he would know just how inexperienced she was. He would know she was making a giant internal deal about his hand touching hers, about the possibility of being held against his body. That she felt strange, unnerving sensations skittering over her skin when she looked at him. She was afraid he could see her too clearly.

Isn't this what you wanted? To reach out? To take a chance?

It was. So she did.

She took his hand. She was still acclimating to his heat, to being touched by him, skin to skin, when she found herself pressed flush against his chest, his hand enveloping hers. He wrapped his arm around her waist, his palm hot on her lower back.

She shivered. She didn't know why. Because she wasn't cold. No. She was hot. And so was he. Hot and hard, so much harder than she had imagined another person could be.

She had never, ever been this close to a man before. Had never felt a man's skin against hers. His hand was rough, from all that hard work. What might it feel like if he touched her skin elsewhere? If he pushed his other hand beneath her shirt and slid his fingertips against her lower back?

That thought sent a sharp pang straight to her stomach, unfurling something inside her, making her blood run faster.

She stared straight at his shoulder, at an innocuous spot on his flannel shirt. Because she couldn't bring herself to raise her eyes and look at that hard, lean face, at the raw beauty she had never fully appreciated before.

He would probably be offended to be characterized as beautiful. But he was. In the same way that a mountain was beautiful. Tall, strong and unmoving.

She gingerly curled her fingers around his shoulder, while he took the lead, his hold on her firm and sure as he established a rhythm she could follow.

The grace in his steps surprised her. Caused her to meet his gaze. She both regretted it and relished it at the same time. Because it was a shame to stare at flannel when she could be looking into those dark eyes, but they also made her feel…absolutely and completely undone.

"Where did you learn to dance?" she asked, her voice sounding as breathless as she had feared it might.

But she was curious about this man who had grown up in such harsh circumstances, who had clearly devoted most of his life to hard work with no frills, who had learned to do this.

"A woman," he said, a small smile tugging at the edges of his lips.

She was shocked by the sudden, sour turn in her stomach. It was deeply unpleasant, and she didn't know what to do to make it stop. Imagining what other woman he might have learned this from, how he might have held her...

It hurt. In the strangest way.

"Was she...somebody special to you? Did you love her?"

His smile widened. "No. I've never loved anybody. Not anybody besides my sister. But I sure as hell *wanted* something from that woman, and she wanted to dance."

It took Hayley a while to figure out the meaning behind those words. "Oh," she said, "she wanted to dance and you wanted..." That feeling in her stomach intensified, but along with it came a strange sort of heat. Because he was holding *her* now, dancing with her. *She* wanted to dance. Did that mean that he...?

"Don't look at me like that, Hayley. This," he said, tightening his hold on her and dipping her slightly, his face moving closer to hers, "is just a dance."

She was a tangle of unidentified feelings—knots in her stomach, an ache between her thighs—and she didn't want to figure out what any of it meant.

"Good," she said, wishing she could have infused some conviction into that word.

The music slowed, the bass got heavier. And he matched the song effortlessly, his hips moving firmly against hers with every deep pulse of the beat.

This time, she couldn't ignore the lyrics. About two people and the fire they created together. She wouldn't have fully understood what that meant even a few minutes ago, but in Jonathan's arms, with the heat that burned from his body, fire was what she felt.

Like her nerve endings had been set ablaze, like a spark had been stoked low inside her. If he moved in just the wrong way—or just the right way—the flames in him would catch hold of that spark in her and they would combust.

She let her eyes flutter closed, gave herself over to the moment, to the song, to the feel of him, the scent of him. She was dancing. And she liked it a lot more than she had anticipated and in a way she hadn't imagined she could.

She had pictured laughing, lightness, with people all around, like at the bar she had never been to before. But this was something else. A deep intimacy that grew from somewhere inside her chest and intensified as the music seemed to draw them more tightly together.

She drew in a breath, letting her eyes open and look up at him. And then she froze.

He was staring at her, the glitter in his dark eyes

almost predatory. She didn't know why that word came to mind. Didn't even know what it might mean in this context. When a man looked at you like he was a wildcat and you were a potential meal.

Then her eyes dipped down to his mouth. Her own lips tingled in response and she was suddenly aware of how dry they were. She slid her tongue over them, completely self-conscious about the action even as she did it, yet unable to stop.

She was satisfied when that predatory light in his eyes turned sharper. More intense.

She didn't know what she was doing. But she found herself moving closer to him. She didn't know why. She just knew she had to. With the same bone-deep impulse that came with the need to draw breath, she had to lean in closer to Jonathan Bear. She couldn't fight it; she didn't want to. And until her lips touched his, she didn't even know what she was moving toward.

But when their mouths met, it all became blindingly clear.

She had thought about these feelings in terms of fire, but this sensation was something bigger, something infinitely more destructive. This was an explosion. One she felt all the way down to her toes; one that hit every place in between.

She was shaking. Trembling like a leaf in the wind. Or maybe even like a tree in a storm.

He was the storm.

His hold changed. He let go of her hand, withdrew his arm from around her waist, pressed both palms against her cheeks as he took the kiss deeper, harder.

It was like drowning. Like dying. Only she didn't want to fight it. Didn't want to turn away. She couldn't have, even if she'd tried. Because his grip was like iron, his body like a rock wall. They weren't moving in time with the music anymore. No. This was a different rhythm entirely. He propelled her backward, until her shoulder blades met with the dining room wall, his hard body pressed against hers.

He was hard. Everywhere. Hard chest, hard stomach, hard thighs. And that insistent hardness pressing against her hip.

She gasped when she realized what that was. And he consumed her shocked sound, taking advantage of her parted lips to slide his tongue between them.

She released her hold on him, her hands floating up without a place to land, and she curled her fingers into fists. She surrendered herself to the kiss, to him. His hold was tight enough to keep her anchored to the earth, to keep her anchored to him.

She let him have control. Let him take the lead. She didn't know how to dance, and she didn't know how to do this. But he did.

So she let him show her. This was on her list, too, though she hadn't been brave enough to say it, even to herself. To know passion. To experience her first kiss.

She wanted it to go on and on. She never wanted it to end. If she could just be like this, those hot hands cupping her face, that insistent mouth devouring hers, she was pretty sure she could skip the Eiffel Tower.

She felt him everywhere, not just his kiss, not just his touch. Her breasts felt heavy. They ached. In any other circumstances, she might be horrified by that. But she didn't possess the capacity to be horrified, not right now. Not when everything else felt so good. She wasn't ashamed; she wasn't embarrassed—not of the heavy feeling in her breasts, not of the honeyed, slick feeling between her thighs.

This just made sense.

Right now, what she felt was the only thing that made sense. It was the only thing she wanted.

Kissing Jonathan Bear was a necessity.

He growled, flexing his hips toward hers, making it so she couldn't ignore his arousal. And the evidence of his desire carved out a hollow feeling inside her. Made her shake, made her feel like her knees had dissolved into nothing and that without his powerful hold she would crumple onto the floor.

She still wasn't touching him. Her hands were still away from his body, trembling. But she didn't want to do anything to break the moment. Didn't want to make a sound, didn't want to make the wrong move. She didn't want to turn him off or scare him away.

Didn't want to do anything to telegraph her innocence. Because it would probably freak him out.

Right, Hayley, like he totally believes you're a sex kitten who's kissed a hundred men.

She didn't know what to do with her hands, let alone her lips, her tongue. She was receiving, not giving. But she had a feeling if she did anything else she would look like an idiot.

Suddenly, he released his hold on her, moving away from her so quickly she might have thought she'd hurt him.

She was dazed, still leaning against the wall. If she hadn't been, she would have collapsed. Her hands were still in the air, clenched into fists, and her breath came in short, harsh bursts. So did his, if the sharp rise and fall of his chest was anything to go by.

"That was a mistake," he said, his voice hard. His words were everything she had feared they might be.

"No, it wasn't," she said, her lips feeling numb, and a little bit full, making it difficult for her to talk. Or maybe the real difficulty came from feeling like her head was filled with bees, buzzing all around and scrambling her thoughts.

"Yes," he said, his voice harder, "it was."

"No," she insisted. "It was a great kiss. A really, really good kiss. I didn't want it to end."

Immediately, she regretted saying that. Because it had been way too revealing. She supposed it was incredibly gauche to tell the guy you'd just kissed that you could have kissed him forever. She tried to imagine how Grant, the youth pastor, might have reacted to that. He would have told her she needed to go to an extra Bible study. Or that she needed to marry him first.

He certainly wouldn't have looked at her the way Jonathan was. Like he wanted to eat her whole, but was barely restraining himself from doing just that. "That's exactly the problem," he returned, the words like iron, "because I *did* want it to end. But in a much different way than it did."

"I don't understand." Her face was hot, and she was humiliated now. So she didn't see why she shouldn't go whole hog. Let him know she was fully outside her comfort zone and she wasn't keeping up with all his implications. She needed stated facts, not innuendo.

"I didn't want to keep kissing you forever. I wanted to pull your top off, shove your skirt up and bury myself inside of you. Is that descriptive enough for you?"

It was. And he had succeeded in shocking her. She wasn't stupid. She knew he was hard, and she knew what that meant. But even given that fact, she hadn't really imagined he wanted… Not with her.

And this was just her first kiss. She wasn't ready for more. Wasn't ready for another step away from the person she had been taught to be.

What about the person you want to be?

She looked at her boss, who was also the most beautiful man she had ever seen. That hadn't been her immediate thought when she'd met him, but she had settled into it as the truth. As certain as the fact the sky was blue and the pine trees that dotted the mountains were deep forest green.

So maybe... Even though it was shocking. Even though it would be a big step, and undoubtedly a big mistake... Maybe she did want it.

"You better go," he said, his voice rough.

"Maybe I don't—"

"You do," he said. "Trust me. And I want you to."

She was confused. Because he had just said he wanted her, and now he was saying he wanted her to go. She didn't understand men. She didn't understand this. She wanted to cry. But a lick of pride slid its way up her spine, keeping her straight, keeping her tears from falling.

Pride she hadn't known she possessed. But then, she hadn't realized she possessed the level of passion that had just exploded between them, either. So it was a day for new discoveries.

"That's fine. I just wanted to have some fun. I can go have it with someone else."

She turned on her heel and walked out of the dining room, out the front door and down the porch steps as quickly as possible. It was dark now, trees like inky bottle brushes rising around her, framing the midnight-blue sky dotted with stars. It was beautiful, but she didn't care. Not right now. She felt... hurt. Emotionally. Physically. The unsatisfied ache between her thighs intensified with the pain growing in her heart.

It was awful. All of it.

It made her want to run. Run back to her parents' house. Run back to the church office.

Being *good* had always been safe.

She had been so certain she wanted to escape safety. Only a few moments earlier she'd needed that escape, felt it might be her salvation. Except she could see now that it was ruin. Utter and complete ruin.

With shaking hands, she pushed the button that undid the locks on her car door and got inside, jamming the key into the ignition and starting it up, a tear sliding down her cheek as she started to back out of the driveway.

She refused to let this ruin her, or this job, or this step she was taking on her own.

She was finding independence, learning new things.

As she turned onto the two-lane highway that would take her back home, she clung to that truth. To the fact that, even though her first kiss had ended somewhat disastrously, it had still shown her something about herself.

It had shown her exactly why it was a good thing she hadn't gotten married to that youthful crush of hers. It would have been dishonest, and not fair to him or to her.

She drove on autopilot, eventually pulling into her driveway and stumbling inside her apartment, lying down on her bed without changing out of her work clothes.

Was she a fallen woman? To want Jonathan like she had. A man she wasn't in love with, a man she wasn't planning to marry.

Had that passion always been there? Or was it created by Jonathan? This feeling. This *need*.

She bit back a sob and forced a smile. She'd had her first kiss. And she wouldn't dwell on what it might mean. Or on the fact that he had sent her away. Or on the fact that—for a moment at least—she had been consumed with the desire for more.

She'd had her first kiss. At twenty-four. And that felt like a change deep inside her body.

Hayley Thompson had a new apartment, a new job, and she had been kissed.

So maybe it wasn't safe. But she had decided she wanted something more than safety, hadn't she?

She would focus on the victories and simply ignore the rest.

No matter that this victory made her body burn in a way that kept her up for the rest of the night.

Five

He hadn't expected her to show up Monday morning. But there she was, in the entryway of the house, hands clasped in front of her, dark hair pulled back in a neat bun. Like she was compensating for what had happened between them Friday night.

"Good morning," he said, taking a sip of his coffee. "I half expected you to take the day off."

"No," she said, her voice shot through with steel, "I can't just take days off. My boss is a tyrant. He'll fire me."

He laughed, mostly to disguise the physical response those words created in him. There was something about her. About all that softness, that innocence, combined with the determination he hadn't realized existed inside her until this moment.

She wasn't just soft, or innocent. She was a force to be reckoned with, and she was bent on showing him that now.

"If he's so bad why do you want to keep the job?"

"My job history is pathetic," she said, walking ahead of him to the stairs. "And, as he has pointed out to me many times, he is not my daddy. My previous boss was. I need something a bit more impressive on my résumé."

"Right. For when you do your traveling."

"Maybe I'll get a job in London," she shot back.

"What's the biggest city you've been to, Hayley?" he asked, following her up the stairs and down the hall toward the office.

"Portland," she said.

He laughed. "London is a little bit bigger."

"I don't care. That's what I want. I want a city where I can walk down the street and not run into anybody that I've ever seen before. All new people. All new faces. I can't imagine that. I can't imagine living a life where I do what I want and not hear a retelling of the night before coming out of my mother's mouth at breakfast the next morning."

"Have you ever done anything worthy of being recounted by your mother?"

Color infused her cheeks. "Okay, specifically, the incident I'm referring to is somebody telling my mother they were proud of me because they saw me giving a homeless woman a dollar."

He laughed. He couldn't help himself, and her cheeks turned an even more intense shade of pink that he knew meant she was furious.

She stamped. Honest to God stamped, like an old-time movie heroine. "What's so funny?"

"Even the gossip about you is good, Hayley Thompson. For the life of me, I can't figure out why you hate that so much."

"Because I can't *do* anything. Jonathan, if you had kissed me in my brother's bar... Can you even imagine? My parents' phone would have been ringing off the hook."

His body hardened at the mention of the kiss. He had been convinced she would avoid the topic.

But he should've known by now that when it came to Hayley he couldn't anticipate her next move. She was more direct, more up-front than he had thought she might be. Was it because of her innocence that she faced things so squarely? Because she hadn't experienced a whole range of consequences for much of anything yet?

"I wouldn't do that to you," he said. "Because you're right. If anybody suspected something unprofessional had happened between us, it would cause trouble for you."

"I didn't mean it that way." She looked horrified.

"I mean, the way people would react if they thought I was… It has nothing to do with you."

"It does. More than you realize. You've been sheltered. But just because you don't know my reputation, that doesn't mean other people in town don't know it. Most people who know you're a good girl know I am a bad man, Hayley. And if anyone suspected I had put my hands on you, I'm pretty sure there would be torches and pitchforks at my front door by sunset."

"Well," she said, "that isn't fair. Because *I* kissed *you*."

"I'm going out on a limb here—of the two of us, I have more experience."

She clasped her hands in front of her and shuffled her feet. "Maybe."

"Maybe nothing, honey. I'm not the kind of man you need to be seen with. So, you're right. You do need to get away. Maybe you should go to London. Hell, I don't know."

"Now you want to get rid of me?"

"Now you're just making it so I can't win."

"I don't mean to," she said, with that trademark sincerity that was no less alarming for being typical of her. "But I don't know what to do with…with this."

She bit her lip, and the motion drew his eye to that lush mouth of hers. Forced him back to the memory of kissing it. Of tasting her.

He wanted her. No question about it.

He couldn't pretend otherwise. But he could at least be honest with himself about why. He wanted her for all the wrong reasons. He wanted her because some sick, caveman part of him wanted to get all that *pretty* dirty. Part of him wanted to corrupt her. To show her everything she was missing. To make her fall from grace a lasting one.

And that was some fucked up shit.

Didn't mean he didn't feel it.

"Well, after I earn enough money, that's probably what I'll do," she said. "And since this isn't going anywhere… I should probably just get to work. And we shouldn't talk about it anymore."

"No," he said, "we shouldn't."

"It was just a kiss."

His stomach twisted. Not because it disappointed him to hear her say that, but because she had to say it for her own peace of mind. She was innocent enough that a kiss worked her up. It meant something to her. Hell, sex barely meant anything to him. Much less a kiss.

Except for hers. You remember hers far too well.

"Just a kiss," he confirmed.

"Good. So give me some spreadsheets."

The rest of the week went well. If well meant dodging moments alone with Jonathan, catching herself staring at him at odd times during the day and having difficulty dreaming of anything except him at night.

"Thank God it's Friday," she said into the emptiness of her living room.

She didn't feel like cooking. She had already made a meal for Jonathan at his house, and then hightailed it out of there as quickly as possible. She knew that if she'd made enough for herself and took food with her he wouldn't have minded, but she was doing her best to keep the lines between them firm.

She couldn't have any more blurred lines. They couldn't have any more…kissing and other weirdness. Just thinking about kissing Jonathan made her feel restless, edgy. She didn't like it. Or maybe she liked it too much.

She huffed out a growl and wandered into the kitchen, opening the cupboard and pulling out a box of chocolate cereal.

It was the kind of cereal her parents never would have bought. Because it wasn't good for you, and it was expensive. So she had bought it for herself, because she had her own job, she was an adult and she made her own decisions.

Do you?

She shut out that snotty little voice. Yes, she *did* make her own decisions. Here she was, living in her own place, working at the job she had chosen. Yes, she very much made her own decisions. She had even kissed Jonathan. Yes, that had been her idea.

Which made the fallout her fault. But she wasn't going to dwell on that.

"I'm dwelling," she muttered. "I'm a liar, and I'm dwelling." She took down a bowl and poured herself a large portion of the chocolaty cereal. Then she stared at it. She didn't want to eat cereal by herself for dinner.

She was feeling restless, reckless.

She was feeling something a whole lot like desperation.

Because of that kiss.

The kiss she had just proposed she wasn't going to think about, the kiss she couldn't let go of. The kiss that made her burn, made her ache and made her wonder about all the mysteries in life she had yet to uncover.

Yeah, *that* kiss.

She had opened a floodgate. She'd uncovered all this potential for passion inside herself, and then she had to stuff it back down deep.

Jonathan Bear was not the only man in the world. Jonathan Bear wasn't even the only man in Copper Ridge.

She could find another guy if she wanted to.

Of course, if she went out, there would be all those gossip issues she and Jonathan had discussed earlier in the week.

That was why she had to get out of this town.

It struck her then, like a horse kicking her square

in the chest, that she was running away. So she could be who she wanted to be without anybody knowing about it. So she could make mistakes and minimize the consequences.

So she could be brave and a coward all at the same time.

That's what it was. It was cowardice. And she was not very impressed with herself.

"Look at you," she scolded, "eating cold cereal on a Friday night by yourself when you would rather be out getting kissed."

Her heart started to beat faster. Where would she go?

And then it hit her. There was one place she could go on a Friday night where nobody from church would recognize her, and even if they did recognize her, they probably wouldn't tell on her because by doing so they would be telling on themselves.

Of course, going there would introduce the problem of her older brother. But Ace had struck out on his own when he was only seventeen years old. He was her inspiration in all this. So he should understand Hayley's need for independence.

And that was when she made her decision. It was Friday night, and she was going out.

She was going to one of the few places in town where she had never set foot before.

Ace's bar.

Six

"I'd like a hamburger," Hayley said, adjusting her dress and trying not to look like she was about to commit a crime.

"Hayley?" Her brother looked at her as if she had grown another head. "What are you doing in my bar?"

"I'm here to have a hamburger. And…a beer."

Ace shook his head. "You don't want beer."

Darn him for being right. She couldn't stand the smell of the stuff, and she'd honestly never even been tempted to taste it.

"No," she agreed. "I want a Coke."

"I will get you a Coke. Are Mom and Dad here?"

She sighed heavily. "No, they're not. I do go places without them. I moved out."

"I know. We talked about it last time Sierra and I went over for dinner."

Hayley's brother had never much cared about his reputation, or about what anyone thought of him. She had been jealous of that for a long time. For years, Ace had been a total hellion and a womanizer, until he'd settled down and married the town rodeo princess, Sierra West. Now the two of them had one child and another on the way, and Ace's position in the community had improved vastly.

"Right. Well, I'm just saying." She traced an imaginary pattern over the bar top with the tip of her finger. "Did I tell you I quit working at the church?"

Ace look surprised by that. "No."

"Well," she said, "I did. I'm working for Jonathan Bear. Helping out with things around the house and in the office."

Ace frowned. "Well, that probably isn't very much fun. He's kind of a grumpy sumbitch."

"I didn't know you knew him all that well."

"He's my future sister-in-law's brother," Ace said, "but no, I don't know him *well*. He's not very sociable. It's not like he comes to the West family gatherings."

"He said he knows you because he buys beer from you."

"That's how everybody knows me," Ace said.

"Except for me."

"You were *trying* to buy beer from me. I'm just not going to sell one to you."

"That's not fair."

"Sure it is," he said, smiling. "Because you don't actually want to buy beer from me. You're just trying to prove a point."

She scowled. She hated that Ace seemed to understand her so well. "Okay, maybe so. I'm kind of proving a point by being here, I guess."

"Well," he said, "it's all right by me."

"Good."

"I kind of wish you would have come on another night, though," he said, "because I have to go. I promised Sierra I would be home early, so I'm about to take off. But I'll tell Jasmine to keep an eye on you."

"I don't need anybody to keep an eye on me."

"Yes," Ace said, laughing, "you do."

Hayley frowned, and plotted how to order a beer when her brother was gone. Ultimately, she decided to stick with Coke, but when the dancing started, she knew that while she might stay away from alcohol, she didn't want to stay seated. She had danced once. And she had liked it.

She was going to do it again.

Jonathan didn't know what in blazes he was doing at Ace's. Sure, he knew what he'd told himself while getting ready, his whole body restless thanks to memories of kissing Hayley.

He had continued to push those thoughts down while pacing around the house, and then, after a while, he'd decided to go out and find someone to hook up with. He didn't do that kind of thing, not anymore. He had a couple of women he called; he didn't go trawling bars. He was too old for that.

But right now, he was too much of a hazard to his innocent assistant, and he needed to take the edge off.

And it occurred to him that if he went to Ace's bar and found somebody, the news might filter back to Hayley.

Even though she might find it upsetting, it would be beneficial in the long run. She didn't want to mess with a man like him, not really. It was only that she was too innocent realize the dangers. But she would, eventually, and she would thank him.

That decision made, he'd hauled his ass down to the bar as quickly as possible.

By the time he walked in, his mood had not improved. He had thought it might. The decision to find a willing woman should have cheered him up. But he felt far from cheered. Maybe because an anonymous body was the last thing he wanted.

He wanted *Hayley*.

Whether he should or not. But he wasn't going to have Hayley. So he would have to get the hell over it.

He moved to the bar and then looked over at the dance floor. His chest tightened up. His body hardened. There was a petite brunette in a formfitting dress dancing with no one in particular. Two men hovered nearby, clearly not minding as she turned to and away from each of them, giving them both just a little bit of attention.

She reminded him of Hayley. Out there on the dance floor acting like nothing close to Hayley.

Then she turned, her dark hair shimmering behind her in a stream, a bright smile on her face, and he could barely process his thoughts. Because it was Hayley. *His* Hayley, out there in the middle of the dance floor, wearing a dress that showed off the figure her clothes had only hinted at before. Sure, in comparison to a lot of women, there was nothing flashy about it, but for Hayley Thompson, it was damned flashy.

And he was… Well, he would be damned if he was going to let those guys put their hands on her.

Yeah, he was bad news. Yeah, he was the kind of guy she should stay well away from. But those guys weren't any better. College douche bags. Probably in their twenties, closer to her age, sure, but not the kind of men who knew how to handle a woman. Especially not one as inexperienced as Hayley.

She would need a man who could guide the experience, show her what she liked. A man who could unlock the mysteries of sex, of her body.

Dickwads that age were better off with an empty dorm room and a half bottle of lotion.

And there was no way in hell they were getting their hands on her.

Without ordering, he moved away from the bar and went out on the dance floor. "You're done here," he said to one of the guys, who looked at him as though Jonathan had just threatened his life. His tone had been soft and even, but it was nice to know the younger man had heard the implied threat loud and clear.

Hayley hadn't noticed his approach, or that the other guy had scurried off to the other end of the dance floor. She was too involved with the guy she was currently dancing with to notice. She was shaking her head, her eyes closed, her body swaying to the music. A completely different kind of dancing than the two of them had done last week.

Then her current dance partner caught Jonathan's eye and paled. He slunk off into the shadows, too.

If Jonathan hadn't already found them wanting when it came to Hayley, he would have now. If they were any kind of men, they would have stood up and declared their interest. They would have proclaimed their desire for her, marked their territory.

He still would have thrown punches, but at least he would've respected them a bit.

Not now.

"Mind if I dance with you?"

Her eyes flew open and she looked around, her

head whipping from side to side, her hair following suit. "Where are…"

"Tweedledee and Tweedledum had somewhere to be."

"Where?"

"Someplace where I wouldn't beat their asses."

"Why are you going to beat their…butts?"

"What are you doing here, Hayley?"

She looked around, a guilty expression on her face. "I was just dancing. I have to say, when I imagined getting in trouble in a bar, I figured it would be my dad dragging me outside, not my boss."

"I haven't dragged you outside. *Yet*." He added that last bit because at this point he wasn't sure how this night was going to end. "What are you doing?"

She lifted a shoulder. "Dancing."

"Getting ready to have your first threesome?"

Her mouth dropped open. "I don't even know how that would work."

He huffed out a laugh. "Look it up. On second thought, don't."

She rolled her eyes like a snotty teenager. "We were just dancing. It wasn't a big deal."

"Little girl, what you don't know about men could fill a library. Men don't *just want to dance*. And men don't *just want to kiss*. You can't play these kinds of games. You don't know the rules. You're going to get yourself into trouble."

"I'm not going to get myself into trouble. Did it

ever occur to you that maybe some men are nicer than you?"

He chuckled, a low, bitter sound. "Oh, I know that most men are a lot nicer than me. Even then, they want in your pants."

"I don't know what your problem is. You don't want me, so what do you care if they do?"

"Hayley, honey, I don't *want* to want you, but that is not the same thing as not wanting you. It is not even close. What I want is something you can't handle."

"I know," she said, looking to the right and then to the left, as though making sure no one was within earshot. Then she took a step toward him. "You said you wanted to…be inside of me."

That simple statement, that repetition of his words, had him hard as an iron bar. "You better back off."

"See, I thought you didn't want me. I thought you were trying to scare me away when you said that. Because why would you want me?"

"I'd list the reasons, but I would shock you."

She tilted her head to the side, her hair falling over her shoulder like a glossy curtain. "Maybe I want to be shocked. Maybe I want something I'm not quite ready for."

"No," he said, his tone emphatic now. "You're on this big kick to have experiences. And there are much nicer men you can have experiences with."

She bared her teeth. "I was trying! You just scared them off."

"You're not having experiences with those clowns. They wouldn't know how to handle a woman if she came with an instruction manual. And let me tell you, women do not come with an instruction manual. You just have to know what to do."

"And you know what to do?"

"Damn straight," he returned.

"So," she said, tilting her chin up, looking stubborn. "Show me."

"Not likely, babe."

He wanted to. He wanted to pick her up, throw her over his shoulder and drag her back to his cave. He wanted to bury himself inside her and screw them both senseless, breathless. He wanted to chase every man in the vicinity away from her. He wanted to make it known, loud and clear that—for a little while at least—she was his.

But it was wrong. On about a thousand levels. And the fact that she didn't seem to know it was just another bit of evidence that he needed to stay away.

"You're playing with fire," he said.

"I know. When you kissed me, that was the closest to being burned I've ever experienced in my life. I want more of that."

"We're not having this conversation in the middle of a bar." He grabbed her arm and hauled her off the dance floor, steering them both to the door.

"Hayley!"

He turned and saw one of the waitresses standing by the bar with her hands on her hips.

"Is everything all right?" she asked.

"Yes," Hayley responded. "Jasmine, it's fine. This is my boss."

Jasmine arched her brow. "Really?"

Hayley nodded. "Really. Just work stuff."

Then she broke free of him and marched out ahead of him. When they were both outside, she rounded on him, her words coming out on a frosty cloud in the night air.

"You're so concerned about my reputation, but then you wander in and make a spectacle."

"You were dancing with two men when I got there," he said. "And what's happening with that dress?"

"Oh please," she said, "I wear this dress to church. It's fine."

"You wear that to *church*?" He supposed, now that he evaluated it with more neutrality, it was pretty tame. The black stretch cotton fell past her knees and had a fairly high neckline. But he could see the curves of her breasts, the subtle slope of her waist to her hips, and her ass looked incredible.

He didn't know if hers was the sort of church that did confession, but he would sure as hell need to confess if he were seated in a row behind her during service.

"Yes," she said. "And it's fine. You're being crazy. Because...because you...*like* me. You *like me* like me."

There she went again, saying things that revealed how innocent she was. Things that made him want her even more, when they should send him running.

"I don't have relationships," he said. He would tell her the truth. He would be honest. It would be the fastest way to chase her off. "And I'm betting a nice girl like you wants a relationship. Wants romance, and flowers, and at least the possibility of commitment. You don't get any of those things with me, Hayley."

She looked up at him, her blue eyes glittering in the security light. He could hear the waves crashing on the shore just beyond the parking lot, feel the salt breeze blowing in off the water, sharp and cold.

"What would I get?" she asked.

"A good, hard fuck. A few orgasms." He knew he'd shocked her, and he was glad. She needed to be shocked. She needed to be scared away.

He couldn't see her face, not clearly, but he could tell she wasn't looking at him when she said, "That's...that's a good thing, right?"

"If you don't know the answer, then the answer is no. Not for you."

The sounds of the surf swelled around them, wind whipping through the pines across the road. She didn't speak for a long time. Didn't move.

"Kiss me again," she said, finally.

The words hit him like a sucker punch. "What? What did I just tell you about men and kissing?"

"It's not for you," she said, "it's for me. Before I give you an answer, you need to kiss me again."

She raised her head, and the light caught her face. She stared at him, all defiance and soft lips, all innocence and intensity, and he didn't have it in him to deny her.

Didn't have it in him to deny himself.

Before he could stop, he wrapped his arm around her waist, crushed her against his chest and brought his lips crashing down on hers.

Seven

She was doing this. She wasn't going to turn back. Not now. And she kept telling herself that as she followed Jonathan's pickup truck down the long, empty highway that took them out of town, toward his house.

His house. Where she was going to spend the night.

Where she was going to lose her virginity.

She swallowed hard, her throat suddenly dry and prickly like a cactus.

This wasn't what she had planned when she'd started on her grand independence journey. Yes, she had wanted a kiss, but she hadn't really thought as far ahead as having a sexual partner. For most of her life she had imagined she would be married first, and then, when she'd started wavering on that decision, she had at least imagined she would be in a serious relationship.

This was… Well, it wasn't marriage. It wasn't the beginning of a relationship, either. Of that, she was certain. Jonathan hadn't been vague. Her cheeks heated at the memory of what he'd said, and she was grateful they were driving in separate cars so she had a moment alone for a private freak-out.

She was so out of her league here.

She could turn around. She could head back to town, back to Main Street, back to her little apartment where she could curl up in bed with the bowl of cereal she'd left dry and discarded on the counter earlier.

And in the morning, she wouldn't be changed. Not for the better, not for the worse.

She seriously considered that, though she kept on driving, her eyes on the road and on Jonathan's taillights.

This decision was a big deal. She wouldn't pretend it wasn't. Wouldn't pretend she didn't put some importance on her first sexual experience, on sex in general. And she wouldn't pretend it probably wasn't a mistake.

It was just that maybe she needed to make the mistake. Maybe she needed to find out for herself if Jonathan was right, if every experience wasn't necessary.

She bit her lip and allowed herself a moment of undiluted honesty. When this was over, there would be fallout. She was certain of it.

But while it was happening, it would feel really, really good.

If the kissing was anything to go by, it would be amazing.

She would feel…wild. And new. And maybe sex with Jonathan would be just the kind of thing she needed. He was hot; touching him burned.

Maybe he could be her own personal trial by fire.

She had always imagined that meant walking through hard times. And maybe, conventionally, it did. But she was walking into the heat willingly, knowing the real pain would come after.

She might be a virgin, but she wasn't an idiot. Jonathan Bear wasn't going to fall in love with her. And anyway, she didn't want him to.

She wanted freedom. She wanted something bigger than Copper Ridge.

That meant love wasn't on her agenda, either.

They pulled up to the house and he got out of his truck, closing the door solidly behind him. And she…froze. Sitting there in the driver's seat, both hands on the steering wheel, the engine still running.

The car door opened and cool air rushed in. She looked up and saw Jonathan's large frame filling the space. "Second thoughts?"

She shook her head. "No," she said, and yet she couldn't make herself move.

"I want you," he said, his voice rough, husky, the words not at all what she had expected. "I would like to tell you that if you are having second thoughts, you should turn the car around and go back home. But I'm not going to tell you that. Because if I do, then I might miss out on my chance. And I want this. Even though I shouldn't."

She tightened her hold on the steering wheel. "Why shouldn't you?" she asked, her throat constricted now.

"Do you want the full list?"

"I've got all night."

"All right. You're a nice girl. You seem to believe the best of people, or at least, you want to, until they absolutely make it so you can't. I'm not a nice man. I don't believe the best of anyone, even when they prove I should. People like me, we tend to drag people like you down to our level. Unfortunately. And that's likely what's going to happen here. I'm going to drag you right down to my level. Because let me tell you, I like dirty. And I'm going to get you filthy. I can promise you that."

"Okay," she said, feeling breathless, not quite certain how to respond. Part of her wanted to fling herself out of the car and into his arms, while another, not insignificant part wanted to throw the car in Reverse and drive away.

"I can only promise you two things. This—you and me—won't last forever. And tonight, I will make you come. If you're okay with those promises, then get out of the car and up to my room. If you're not, it's time for you to go."

For some reason, that softly issued command was what it took to get her moving. She released her hold on the steering wheel and turned sideways in her seat. Then she looked up at him, pushing herself into a standing position. He had one hand on the car door, the other on the side mirror, blocking her in.

Her breasts nearly touched his chest, and she was tempted to lean in and press against him completely.

"Come on then," he said, releasing his hold on the car and turning away.

The movement was abrupt. It made her wonder if he was struggling with indecision, too. Which didn't really make sense, since Jonathan was the most decisive man she had ever met. He seemed certain about everything, all the time, even if he was sure it was a bad decision.

That certainty was what she wanted. Yeah, she was certain this was a bad decision, too, but she was going for it, anyway.

She had walked into this house five days a week for the past couple weeks, yet this time was different. Because this time she wasn't headed to the office. This time she was going to his bedroom. And she wasn't his employee; he wasn't her boss. Not now.

Her stomach tightened, her blood heated at the idea of following orders. His orders. Lord knew she would need instruction. Direction. She had no idea what she was doing; she was just following her gut instinct.

When they reached the long hallway, they stopped at a different door than usual. His bedroom. She had never been inside Jonathan's bedroom. It was strange to be standing there now. So very deliberate.

It might have been easier if they had started kissing here in the house, and let things come to their natural conclusion… On the floor or something. She was reasonably sure people did it on the floor sometimes.

Yeah, that would have been easier. This was so *intentional*.

She was about to say something about the strangeness of it when he reached out, cupped her chin and tilted her face upward. Then he closed the distance between them, claiming her mouth.

She felt his possession, all the way down to her toes.

He didn't wait for her to part her lips this time. Instead, he invaded her, sliding his tongue forcibly against hers, his arms wrapped tight around her like steel bands. There was nothing gentle about this kiss. It was consuming, all-encompassing. And all her thoughts about the situation feeling premeditated dissolved.

This time, she didn't stand there as a passive participant. This time, she wrapped her arms around his neck—pressing her breasts flush against his chest, forking her fingers through his hair—and devoured him right back.

She couldn't believe this was her. Couldn't believe this was her life, that this man wanted her. That he was hard for her. That he thought she might be a mistake, and he was willing to make her, anyway. God knew, she was willing to make him.

Need grew inside her, prowling around like a restless thing. She rocked her hips forward, trying to tame the nameless ache between her thighs. Trying to calm the erratic, reckless feeling rioting through her.

He growled, sliding his hands down her back, over her bottom, down to her thighs. She squeaked as he gripped her tightly, pulling both her feet off the ground and picking her up, pressing that soft, tender place between her legs against his arousal.

"Wrap your legs around me," he said against her mouth, the command harsh, and sexier because of that.

She obeyed him, locking her ankles behind his back. He reversed their positions, pressing her against the wall and deepening his kiss. She gasped as he made even firmer contact with the place that was wet and aching for him.

He ground his hips against her, and her internal

muscles pulsed. An arc of electricity lanced through her. She gripped his shoulders hard, vaguely aware that she might be digging her fingernails into his skin, not really sure that she cared. Maybe it would hurt him, but she wasn't exactly sure if he was hurting her or not. She was suspended between pleasure and pain, feelings so intense she could scarcely breathe.

And through all that, he continued to devour her mouth, the rhythm of his tongue against hers combining with the press of his firm length between her thighs, ensuring that her entire world narrowed down to him. Jonathan Bear was everything right now. He was her breath; he was sensation. He was heaven and he was hell.

She needed it to end. Needed to reach some kind of conclusion, where all this tension could be defused.

And yet she wanted it to go on forever.

Her face was hot, her limbs shaking. A strange, hollow feeling in the pit of her stomach made her want to cry. It was too much. And it was not enough. That sharp, insistent ache between her legs burrowed deeper with each passing second, letting her know this kiss simply wasn't enough at all.

She moved her hands up from his broad shoulders, sliding them as far as she could into his long, dark hair. Her fingers snagged on the band that kept his hair tied back and she internally cursed her clumsiness, hoping he wouldn't notice. She had enthusiasm guiding her through this, but that was about it. Enthusiasm and a healthy dose of adrenaline that bordered on terror. But she didn't want to stop. She couldn't stop.

Those big, rough hands gripped her hips and braced her as he rocked more firmly against her, and suddenly, stars exploded behind her eyes. She gasped, wrenching her lips away from his as something that felt like thunder rolled through her body, muscles she'd never been aware of before pulsing like waves against the shore.

She pressed her forehead against his shoulder, did her best to grit her teeth and keep herself from crying out, but a low, shaky sound escaped when the deepest wave washed over her.

Then it ended, and she felt even more connected to reality, to this moment, than she had a second ago. And she felt…so very aware that she was pressed against the wall and him, that something had just happened, that she hadn't been fully cognizant of her actions. She didn't know what she might have said.

That was when she realized she was digging her nails into his back, and she had probably punctured his skin. She started to move against him, trying to get away, and he gripped her chin again, steadying her. "Hey," he said, "you're not going anywhere."

"I need to… I have to…"

"You don't have to do anything, baby. Nothing at

all. Just relax." She could tell he was placating her. She couldn't bring herself to care particularly, because she needed placating. Her heart was racing, her hands shaking, and that restlessness that had been so all-consuming earlier was growing again. She had thought the earthquake inside her had handled that.

That was when she realized exactly what that earthquake had been.

Her cheeks flamed, horror stealing through her. She'd had... Well, she'd had an orgasm. And he hadn't even touched her. Not with his hands. Not under her clothes.

"I'm sorry," she said, putting her hands up, patting his chest, then curling her hands into fists because she had patted him and that was really stupid. "I'm just sorry."

He frowned. "What are you sorry about?"

"I'm sorry because I—I...I did that. And we didn't..."

He raised one eyebrow. "Are you apologizing for your orgasm?"

She squeezed her eyes tightly shut. "Yes."

"Why?"

She tightened her fists even more, pressing them against her own chest, keeping her eyes closed. "Because we didn't even... You didn't... We're still dressed."

"Honey," he said, taking hold of her fists and

drawing them toward him, pressing them against his chest. "You don't need to apologize to me for coming."

She opened one eye. "I...I don't?"

"No."

"But that..." She looked fully at him, too curious to be embarrassed now. "That ruins it, doesn't it? We didn't..."

"You can have as many orgasms as I can give you. That's the magical thing about women. There's no ceiling on that."

"There isn't?"

"You didn't know?"

"No."

"Hayley," he said, his tone grave, "I need to ask you a question."

Oh great. Now he was actually going to ask if she was a virgin. Granted, she thought he'd probably guessed, but apparently he needed to hear it. "Go ahead," she said, bracing herself for utter humiliation.

"Have you never had an orgasm before?"

"Yes," she said, answering the wrong question before he even got his out. "I mean... No. I mean, just a minute ago. I wasn't even sure what it was right when it was happening."

"That doesn't... Not even with yourself?"

Her face felt so hot she thought it might be on fire. She was pretty sure her heart was beating in her forehead. "No." She shook her head. "I can't talk to you about things like that."

"I just gave you your first orgasm, so you better be able to talk to me about things like that. Plus I'm aiming to give you another one before too long here."

"I bet you can't."

He chuckled, and then he bent down, sweeping her up into his arms. She squeaked, curling her fingers around his shirt. "You should know better than to issue challenges like that." He turned toward the bedroom door, kicking it open with his boot before walking inside and kicking it closed again. Then he carried her to the bed and threw her down in the center.

"Wait," she said, starting to feel panicky, her heart fluttering in her chest like a swarm of butterflies. "Just wait a second."

"I'm not going to fall on you like a ravenous beast," he said, his hands going to the top button of his shirt. "Yet." He started to undo the button slowly, revealing his tan, muscular chest.

She almost told him to stop, except he stripped the shirt off, and she got completely distracted by the play of all those muscles. The sharp hitch of his abs as he cast the flannel onto the floor, the shift and bunch of his pectoral muscles as he pushed his hand over his hair.

She had never seen a shirtless man that looked

like him. Not in person, anyway. And most definitely not this close, looking at her like he had plans.
Very, very dirty plans.

"I'm a virgin," she blurted out. "Just so you know."

His eyes glowed with black fire. For one heart-
stopping moment she was afraid he might pick up
his shirt and walk out of the room. His eyes looked
pure black; his mouth pressed into a firm line. He
stood frozen, hands on his belt buckle, every line
in his cut torso still.

Then something in his expression shifted. Nearly
imperceptible, and mostly unreadable, but she had
seen it. Then his deft fingers went to work, moving his belt through the buckle. "I know," he said.

"Oh." She felt a little crestfallen. Like she must
have made some novice mistake and given herself
away.

"You're a church secretary who confessed to having never had an orgasm. I assumed." He lowered
his voice. "If you hadn't told me outright, I could
have had plausible deniability. Which I was sort of
counting on."

She blinked. "Did you...need it?"

"My conscience is screwed, anyway. So not really."

She didn't know quite what to say, so she didn't
say anything.

"Have you ever seen a naked man before?"

She shook her head. "No."

"Pictures?"

"Does medieval art count?"

"No, it does not."

"Then no," she said, shaking her head even more vigorously.

He rubbed his hand over his forehead, and she was sure she heard him swear beneath his breath. "Okay," he said, leaving his belt hanging open, but not going any further. He pressed his knee down on the mattress, kneeling beside her. Then he took her hand and placed it against his chest. "How's that?"

She drew shaking fingers across his chest slowly, relishing his heat, the satiny feel of his skin. "Good," she said. "You're very…hot. I mean, temperature-wise. Kind of smooth."

"You don't have to narrate," he said.

"Sorry," she said, drawing her hand back sharply.

"No," he said, pressing her palm back against his skin. "Don't apologize. Don't apologize for anything that happens between us tonight, got that?"

"Okay," she said, more than happy to agree, but not entirely sure if she could keep to the agreement. Because every time she moved her hand and his breath hissed through his teeth, she wanted to say she was sorry. Every time she took her exploration further, she wanted to apologize for the impulse to do it.

She bit her lip, letting her hands glide lower, over his stomach, which was as hard and rippled as corrugated steel. Then she found her hands at the waistband of his jeans, and she pulled back.

"Do you want me to take these off?" he asked.

"In a minute," she said, losing her nerve slightly. "Just a minute." She rose up on her knees, pressed her mouth to his and lost herself in kissing him. She really liked kissing. Loved the sounds he made, loved being enveloped in his arms, and she really loved it when he laid them both down, pressing her deep into the mattress and settling between her thighs.

Her dress rode up high, and she didn't care. She felt rough denim scraping her bare skin, felt the hard press of his zipper, and his arousal behind it through the thin fabric of her panties.

She lost herself in those sensations. In the easy, sensual contact that pushed her back to the brink again. She could see already that Jonathan was going to win the orgasm challenge. And she was okay with that.

Very, very okay with that.

Then he took her hem and pulled the cotton dress over her head, casting it onto the floor. Her skin heated all over, and she was sure she was pink from head to toe.

"Don't be embarrassed," he said, touching her collarbone, featherlight, then tracing a trail down to the curve of her breast, to the edge of her bra. "You're beautiful."

She didn't know quite how to feel about that. Didn't know what to do with that husky, earnest compliment. She wasn't embarrassed because she lacked beauty, but because she had always been taught to treasure modesty. To respect her body, to save it.

He *was* respecting it, though. And right now, she felt like she had been saving it for him.

He reached behind her, undoing her bra with one hand and flicking the fabric to the side.

"You're better at that than I am," she said, laughing nervously as he bared her breasts, her nipples tightening as the cold air hit her skin.

He smiled. "You'll appreciate that in a few minutes."

"What will I appreciate?" she asked, shivering. She crossed her arms over her chest.

"My skill level." Instead of moving her hands, he bent his head and nuzzled the tender spot right next to her hand, the full part of her breast that was still exposed. She gasped, tightening her hold on herself.

He was not deterred.

He nosed her gently and shifted her hand to the side, pressing a kiss to her skin, sending electric sensations firing through her. "Don't be shy," he said, "not with me."

She waited for a reason why. He didn't give one, but she found that the more persistent he was—the more hot, open-mouthed kisses he pressed to her skin—the less able she was to deny him anything. Anything at all. She found herself shifting her hands and then letting them fall away.

As soon as she did, he closed his lips over her nipple, sucking deep. She gasped, her hips rocking up off the bed. He wrapped his arm around her, holding her against his hardness as he teased her with his lips and tongue.

Every time she wiggled, either closer to him, or in a moment of self-consciousness, away, it only brought him more in contact with that aching place between her thighs, and then she would forget why she was moving at all. Why she wasn't just letting him take the lead.

So she relaxed into him, and let herself get lost. She was in a daze when he took her hand and pushed it down his stomach, to the front of his jeans. She gasped when his hard, denim-covered length filled her palm.

"Feel that? That's how much I want you. That's what you do to me."

A strange surge of power rocketed through her. That she could cause such a raw, sexual response... Well, it was intoxicating in a way she hadn't appreciated it could be.

Especially because he was such a man. A hot man. A sexy man, and she had never thought of anyone that way in her life. But he was. He most definitely was.

"Are you ready?" he asked.

She nodded, sliding her hand experimentally over him. He moved, undoing his pants and shoving them quickly down, hardly giving her a chance to prepare. Her mouth dried when she saw him, all of him. She hadn't really… Well, she had been content to allow her fantasies to be somewhat hazy. Though reading that romance novel had made those fantasies a little sharper.

Still, she hadn't really imagined specifically how large a man might be. But suffice it to say, he was a bit larger than she had allowed for.

Her breath left her lungs in a rush. But along with the wave of nerves that washed over her came a sense of relief. "You are… I like the way you look," she said finally.

A crooked smile tipped his mouth upward. "Thank you."

"I told you, I've never seen a naked man before. I was a little afraid I wouldn't like it."

"Well, I'm glad you do. Because let me tell you, that's a lot of pressure. Being the first naked man you've ever seen." His eyes darkened and his voice got lower, huskier. "Being the first naked man you've ever touched." He took her hand again and placed it around his bare shaft, the skin there hotter and much softer than she had imagined. She slid her thumb up and down, marveling at the feel of him.

"You're the first man I've ever kissed," she said, the words slurred, because she had lost the full connection between her brain and her mouth. All her blood had flowed to her extremities.

He swore, and then crushed her to him, kissing her deeply and driving her back down to the mattress. His erection pressed into her stomach, his tongue slick against hers, his lips insistent. She barely noticed when he divested her of her underwear, until he placed his hand between her legs. The rough pads of his fingers sliding through her slick flesh, the white-hot pleasure his touch left behind, made her gasp.

"I'm going to make sure you're ready," he said.

She had no idea what that meant. But he started doing wicked, magical things with his fingers, so she didn't much care. Then he slid one finger deep inside her and she arched away, not sure whether she wanted more of that completely unfamiliar sensation, or if she needed to escape it.

"It's okay," he said, moving his thumb in a circle over a sensitive bundle of nerves as he continued to slide his finger in and out of her body.

After a few passes of his thumb, she agreed.

He shifted his position, adding a second finger, making her gasp. It burned slightly, made her feel like she was being stretched, but after a moment, she adjusted to that, too.

That lovely, spiraling tension built inside her again, and she knew she was close to the edge. But every time he took her to the brink, he would drop back again.

"Please," she whispered.

"Please what?" he asked, being dastardly, asking her to clarify, when he knew saying the words would embarrass her.

"You know," she said, placing her hand over his, like she might take control, increase the pressure, increase the pace, since he refused.

But, of course, he was too strong for her to guide him at all. "I need to hear it."

"I need… I need to have an orgasm," she said quickly.

For a moment, he stopped. He looked at her like she mystified him. Like he had never seen anything like her before. Then he withdrew his hand and slid down her body, gripping her hips roughly before drawing her quickly against his mouth.

She squeaked when his lips and tongue touched her right in her most intimate place. She reached down, grabbing hold of his hair, because she was going to pull him away, but then his tongue touched her in the most amazing spot and she found herself lacing her fingers through his hair instead.

She found herself holding him against her instead of pushing him away.

She moved her hips in time with him, gasping for air as pleasure, arousal, built to impossible heights. She had been on the edge for so long now it felt like she was poised on the brink of something else entirely. But right when she was about to break, he moved away from her, drawing himself up her body.

He grabbed a small, round packet from the bedspread that she hadn't noticed until now, and tore it open, quickly sheathing himself before moving to position the blunt head of his arousal at her entrance.

He flexed his hips, thrusting deep inside her, and her arousal broke like a mirror hit with a hammer. She gritted her teeth as pain—sharp and jagged—cut through all the hidden places within her. But along with the pain came the intense sensation of being full. Of being connected to another person like she never had been before.

She reached up, taking his heavily muscled arms and holding him, just holding him, as he moved slowly inside her.

He was *inside* her.

She marveled at that truth even as the pain eased, even as pleasure began to push its way into the foreground again.

"Move with me," he said, nuzzling her neck, kissing the tender skin there.

So she did, meeting his every thrust, clinging to him. She could see the effort it took for him to maintain control, and she could see when his control began to fray. When his thrusts became erratic, his golden skin slick with sweat, his breathing rough and ragged, matching her own.

When he thrust deep, she arched her hips, an electric shower of sparks shimmering through her each time.

His hands were braced on either side of her shoulders, his strong fingers gripping the sheets. His movements became hard, rough, but none of the earlier pain remained, and she welcomed him. Opened her thighs wider and then wrapped her legs around his lean hips so she could take him even deeper.

There was no pain. There was no shame. There was no doubt at all.

As far as she was concerned, there was only the two of them.

He leaned down, pressing his forehead against hers, his dark gaze intense as his rhythm increased. He went shallow, then deep, the change pushing her even closer to the edge.

Then he pulled out almost completely, his hips pulsing slightly. The denial of that deep, intimate contact made her feel frantic. Made her feel needy. Made her feel desperate.

"Jonathan," she said. "Jonathan, please."

"Tell me you want to come," he told her, the words a growl.

"I want to come," she said, not wasting a moment on self-consciousness.

He slammed back home, and she saw stars. This orgasm grabbed her deep, reached places she hadn't known were there. The pleasure seemed to go on and on, and when it was done, she felt like she was floating on a sea, gazing up at a sky full of infinite stars.

She felt adrift, but only for a moment. Because

when she came back to herself, she was still clutching his strong arms, Jonathan Bear rooting her to the earth.

And then she waited.

Waited for regret. Waited for guilt.

But she didn't feel any of it. Right now, she just felt a bone-deep satisfaction she hoped never went away.

"I…" He started to say something, moving away from her. Then he frowned. "You don't have a toothbrush or anything, do you?"

It was such a strange question that it threw her for a loop. "What?"

"It doesn't matter," he said. He bent down, pressing a kiss to her forehead. "We'll work something out in the morning."

She was glad he'd said there was nothing to worry about, because her head was starting to get fuzzy and her eyelids were heavy. Which sucked, because she didn't want to sleep. She wanted to bask in her newfound warm and fuzzy feelings.

But she was far too sleepy, far too sated to do anything but allow herself to be enveloped by that warmth. By him.

He drew her into his arms, and she snuggled into his chest, pressing her palm against him. She could feel his heartbeat, hard and steady, beneath her hand.

And then, for the first time in her life, Hayley Thompson fell asleep in a man's arms.

Eight

Jonathan didn't sleep. As soon as Hayley drifted off, he went into his office, busying himself with work that didn't need to be done.

Women didn't spend the night at his house. He had never even brought a woman back to this house. But when Hayley had looked up at him like that… He hadn't been able to tell her to leave. He realized that she expected to stay. Because as far as she was concerned, sex included sleeping with somebody.

He had no idea where she had formed her ideas about relationships, but they were innocent. And he was a bastard. He had already known that, but tonight just confirmed it.

Except he had let her stay.

He couldn't decide if that was a good thing or not. Couldn't decide if letting her stay had been a kindness or a cruelty. Because the one thing it hadn't been was the reality of the situation.

The reality was this wasn't a relationship. The reality was, it had been... Well, a very bad idea.

He stood up from his desk, rubbing the back of his neck. It was getting light outside, pale edges beginning to bleed from the mountaintops, encroaching on the velvet middle of the sky.

He might as well go outside and get busy on morning chores. And if some of those chores were in the name of avoiding Hayley, then so be it.

He made his way downstairs, shoved his feet into his boots and grabbed his hat, walking outside with heavy footsteps.

He paused, inhaling deeply, taking a moment to let the scent of the pines wash through him. This was his. All of it was his. He didn't think that revelation would ever get old.

He remembered well the way it had smelled on his front porch in the trailer park. Cigarette smoke and exhaust from cars as people got ready to leave for work. The noise of talking, families shouting at each other. It didn't matter if you were inside the house or outside. You lived way too close to your neighbors to avoid them.

He had fantasized about a place like this back then. Isolated. His. Where he wouldn't have to see another person unless he went out of his way to do so. He shook his head. And he had gone and invited Hayley to stay the night. He was a dumb ass.

He needed a ride to clear his head. The fact that he got to take weekends off now was one of his favorite things about his new position in life. He was a workaholic, and he had never minded that. But ranching was the kind of work he really enjoyed, and that was what he preferred to do with his free time.

He saddled his horse and mounted up, urging the bay gelding toward the biggest pasture. They started out at a slow walk, then Jonathan increased the pace until he and his horse were flying over the grass, patches of flowers blurring on either side of them, blending with the rich green.

It didn't matter what mess he had left behind at the house. Didn't matter what mistakes he had made last night. It never did, not when he was on a horse. Not when he was in his sanctuary. The house… Well, he would be lying if he said that big custom house hadn't been a goal for him. Of course it had been. It was evidence that he had made it.

But this… The trees, the mountains, the wind in his face, being able to ride his horse until his lungs burned, and not reach the end of his property… That was the real achievement. It belonged to him and no one else. In this place he didn't have to answer to anyone.

Out here it didn't matter if he was bad. You

couldn't let the sky down. You couldn't disappoint the mountains.

He leaned forward to go uphill, tightening his hold on the reins as the animal changed its gait. He pulled back, easing to a stop. He looked down the mountain, at the valley of trees spread out before him, an evergreen patchwork stitched together by rock and river. And beyond that, the ocean, brighter blue than usual on this exceptionally clear morning, the waves capped with a rosy pink handed down from the still-rising sun.

Hayley would love this.

That thought brought him up short, because he wasn't exactly sure why he thought she would. Or why he cared. Why he suddenly wanted to show her. He had never shown this view to anybody. Not even to his sister, Rebecca.

He had wanted to keep it for himself, because growing up, he'd had very little that belonged to him and him alone. In fact, up here, gazing at everything that belonged to him now, he couldn't think of a single damn thing that had truly belonged to him when he'd been younger.

It had all been for a landlord, for his sister, for the future.

This was what he had worked for his entire life.

He didn't need to show it to some woman he'd slept with last night.

He shook his head, turning the horse around and

trotting down the hill, moving to a gallop back down to the barn.

When he exited the gate that would take him out of the pasture and back to the paddock, Jonathan saw Hayley standing in the path. Wearing last night's dress, her hair disheveled, she was holding two mugs of coffee.

He was tempted to imagine he had conjured her up just by thinking of her up on the ridge. But if it were a fantasy, she would have been wearing nothing, rather than being back in that black cotton contraption.

She was here, and it disturbed him just how happy that made him.

"I thought I might find you out here," she said. "And I figured you would probably want your coffee."

He dismounted, taking the reins and walking the horse toward Hayley. "It's your day off. You don't have to make me coffee."

Her cheeks turned pink, and he marveled at the blush. And on the heels of that marveling came the sharp bite of guilt. She was a woman who blushed routinely. And he had… Well, he had started down the path of corrupting her last night.

He had taken her virginity. Before her he'd never slept with a virgin in his damn life. In high school, that hadn't been so much out of a sense of honor as it had been out of a desire not to face down an angry dad with a shotgun. Better to associate with girls who had reputations worse than his own.

All that restraint had culminated in him screwing the pastor's daughter.

At least when people came with torches and pitchforks, he would have a decent-sized fortress to hole up in.

"I just thought maybe it would be nice," she said finally, taking a step toward him and extending the coffee mug in his direction.

"It is," he said, taking the cup, knowing he didn't sound quite as grateful as he might have. "Sorry," he conceded, sipping the strong brew, which was exactly the way he liked it. "I'm not used to people being nice. I'm never quite sure what to make of it when you are."

"Just take it at face value," she said, lifting her shoulder.

"Yeah, I don't do that."

"Why not?" she asked.

"I have to take care of the horse," he said. "If you want story time, you're going to have to follow me."

He thought his gruff demeanor might scare her off, but instead, she followed him along the fence line. He tethered his horse and set his mug on the fence post, then grabbed the pick and started on the gelding's hooves.

Hayley stepped up carefully on the bottom rung of the fence, settling herself on the top rung, clutching her mug and looking at him with an intensity he could feel even with his focus on the task at hand.

"I'm ready," she said.

He looked up at her, perched there like an inquisitive owl, her lips at the edge of her cup, her blue eyes round. She was…a study in contradictions. Innocent as hell. Soft in some ways, but determined in others.

It was her innocence that allowed her to be so open—that was his conclusion. The fact that she'd never really been hurt before made it easy for her to come at people from the front.

"It's not a happy story," he warned.

It wasn't a secret one, either. Pretty much everybody knew his tragic backstory. He didn't go around talking about it, but there was no reason not to give her what she was asking for.

Except for the fact that he never talked to the women he hooked up with. There was just no point to it.

But then, the women he usually hooked up with never stumbled out of his house early in the morning with cups of coffee. So he supposed it was an unusual situation all around.

"I'm a big girl," she said, her tone comically serious. It was followed by a small slurp as she took another sip of coffee. The sound should not have been cute, but it was.

"Right." He looked up at her, started to speak and then stopped.

Would hearing about his past, about his childhood, change something in her? Just by talking to her he might ruin some of her optimism.

It was too late for worrying about that, he supposed. Since sleeping with her when she'd never even kissed anyone before had undoubtedly changed her.

There had been a lot of points in his life when he had not been his own favorite person. The feeling was intense right now. He was a damned bastard.

"I'm waiting," she said, kicking her foot slightly to signify her impatience.

"My father left when I was five," he said.

"Oh," she said, blinking, clearly shocked. "I'm sorry."

"It was the best thing that had happened to me in all five years of my life, Hayley. The very best thing. He was a violent bastard. He hit my mother. He hit me. The day he left… I was a kid, but I knew even then that life was going to be better. I was right. When I was seven, my mom had another kid. And she was the best thing. So cute. Tiny and loud as hell, but my mother wasn't all that interested in me, and my new sister was. Plus she gave me, I don't know…a feeling of importance. I had someone to look after, and that mattered. Made me feel like maybe I mattered."

"Rebecca," Hayley said.

"Yeah," he replied. "Then, when Rebecca was a teenager, she was badly injured in a car accident.

Needed a lot of surgeries, skin grafts. All of it was paid for by the family responsible for the accident, in exchange for keeping everything quiet. Of course, it's kind of an open secret now that Gage West was the one who caused the accident."

Hayley blinked. "Gage. Isn't she… Aren't they… Engaged?"

Familiar irritation surged through him. "For now. We'll see how long that lasts. I don't have a very high opinion of that family."

"Well, you know my brother is married into that family."

He shrugged. "All right, maybe I'll rephrase that. I don't have anything against Colton, or Sierra, or Maddy. But I don't trust Gage or his father one bit. I certainly don't trust him with my sister, any more now than I did then. But if things fall apart, if he ends up breaking off the engagement, or leaves her ten years into the marriage… I'll have a place for her. I've always got a place for her."

Hayley frowned. "That's a very cynical take. If Rebecca can love the man who caused her accident, there must be something pretty exceptional about him."

"More likely, my sister doesn't really know what love looks like," he said, his voice hard, the words giving voice to the thing he feared most. "I have to backtrack a little. A few months after the accident, my mom took the cash payout Nathan West gave her and took off. Left me with Rebecca. Left Rebecca without a mother, when she needed her mother the most. My mom just couldn't handle it. So I had to. And I was a piss-poor replacement for parents. An older brother with a crappy construction job and not a lot of patience." He shook his head. "Every damn person in my life who was supposed to be there for me bailed. Everyone who was supposed to be there for Rebecca."

"And now you're mad at her, too. For not doing what you thought she should."

Guilt stabbed him right in the chest. Yeah, he was angry at his sister. And he felt like he had no damn right to be angry. Shouldn't she be allowed to be happy? Hadn't that been the entire point of taking care of her for all those years? So she could get out from under the cloud of their family?

So she'd done it. In a huge, spectacular way. She'd ended up with the man she'd been bitter about for years. She had let go of the past. She had embraced it, and in a pretty damned literal way.

But Jonathan couldn't. He didn't trust in sudden changes of heart or professions of love. He didn't trust much of anything.

"I'll be mad if she gets hurt," he said finally. "But that's my default. I assume it's going to end badly because I've only ever seen these things end badly. I worked my ass off to keep the two of us off the streets. To make sure we had a roof over our heads, as much food in our stomachs as I could manage. I protected her." He shook his head. "And there's no protecting somebody if you aren't always looking out for what might go wrong. For what might hurt them."

"I guess I can't blame you for not trusting the good in people. You haven't seen it very many times."

He snorted. "Understatement of the century." He straightened, undoing the girth and taking the saddle off the bay in a fluid movement, then draping it over the fence. "But my cynicism has served me just fine. Look at where I am now. I started out in a single-wide trailer, and I spent years working just to keep that much. I didn't advance to this place by letting down my guard, by stopping for even one minute." He shook his head again. "I probably owe my father a thank-you note. My mother, too, come to that. They taught me that I couldn't trust anyone but myself. And so far that lesson's served me pretty well."

Hayley was looking at him like she was sad for him, and he wanted to tell her to stop it. Contempt, disgust and distrust were what he was used to getting from people. And he had come to revel in that reaction, to draw strength from it.

Pity had been in short supply. And if it was ever tossed in his general direction, it was mostly directed at Rebecca. He wasn't comfortable receiving it himself.

"Don't look at me like I'm a sad puppy," he said.

"I'm not," she returned.

He untied the horse and began to walk back into the barn. "You are. I didn't ask for your pity." He unhooked the lead rope and urged the gelding into his stall. "Don't go feeling things for me, Hayley. I don't deserve it. In fact, what you should have done this morning was walked out and slapped me in the face, not given me a cup of coffee."

"Why?"

"Because I took advantage of you last night. And you should be upset about that."

She frowned. "I should be?" She blinked. "I'm not. I thought about it. And I'm not."

"I don't know what you're imagining this is. I don't know what you think might happen next…"

She jumped down from the fence and set her coffee cup on the ground. Then she took one quick step forward. She hooked an arm around his neck and pushed herself onto her tiptoes, pressing her lips to his.

He was too stunned to react. But only for a moment. He wrapped an arm around her waist, pressing his forefinger beneath her chin and urging the kiss deeper.

She didn't have a lot of skill. That had been apparent the first and second times they'd kissed. And when they had come together last night. But he didn't need skill, he just needed her.

Even though it was wrong, he consumed her, sated his hunger on her mouth.

She whimpered, a sweet little sound that only fueled the driving hunger roaring in his gut. He grabbed her hair, tilting her head back farther, abandoning her mouth to scrape his teeth over her chin and down her neck, where he kissed her again, deep and hard.

He couldn't remember ever feeling like this before. Couldn't remember ever wanting a woman so much it was beyond the need for air. Sure, he liked sex. He was a man, after all. But the need had never been this specific. Had never been for one woman in particular.

But what he was feeling wasn't about sex, or about lust or desire. It was about her. About Hayley. The sweet little sounds she made when he kissed the tender skin on her neck, when he licked his way back up to her lips. The way she trembled with her need for him. The way she had felt last night, soft and slick and made only for him.

This was beyond anything he had ever experienced before. And he was a man who had experienced a hell of a lot.

That's what it was, he thought dimly as he scraped his teeth along her lower lip. And that said awful things about him, but then so did a lot of choices in his life.

He had conducted business with hard, ruthless precision, and he had kept his personal life free of any kind of connection beyond Rebecca—who he was loyal to above anyone else.

So maybe that was the problem. Now that he'd arrived at this place in life, he was collecting those things he had always denied himself. The comfortable home, the expansive mountains and a sweet woman.

Maybe this was some kind of latent urge. He had the homestead, now he wanted to put a woman in it.

He shook off that thought and all the rest. He didn't want to think right now. He just wanted to feel. Wanted to embrace the heat firing through his veins, the need stoking the flame low in his gut, which burned even more with each pass of her tongue against his.

She pulled away from him, breathing hard, her pupils dilated, her lips swollen and rounded into a perfect O. "That," she said, breathlessly, "was what I was thinking might happen next. And that we might... Take me back to bed, please."

"I can't think of a single reason to refuse," he said— a lie, as a litany of reasons cycled through his mind.

But he wasn't going to listen to them. He was going to take her, for as long as she was on offer. And when it ended, he could only hope he hadn't damaged her too much. Could only hope he hadn't broken her beyond repair.

Because there were a couple things he knew for sure. It would end; everything always did. And he would be the one who destroyed it.

He just hoped he didn't destroy her, too.

Nine

It was late in the afternoon when Hayley and Jonathan finally got back out of bed. Hayley felt... Well, she didn't know quite what she felt. Good. Satisfied. Jonathan was... Well, if she'd ever had insecurities about whether or not she might be desirable to a man, he had done away with those completely. He had also taught her things about herself—about pleasure, about her own body—that she'd never in her wildest dreams conceived of.

She didn't know what would happen next, though. She had fallen asleep after their last time together, and when she'd awoken he was gone again. This morning, she had looked for him. She wasn't sure if she should do that twice.

Still, before she could even allow herself to ponder making the decision, she got out of bed, grabbed his T-shirt from the floor and pulled it over her head. Then she padded down the hallway, hoping he didn't have any surprise visitors. That would be a nightmare. Getting caught wearing only a T-shirt in her boss's hallway. There would be a lot of questions about what they had just spent the last few hours doing, that was for sure.

She wondered if Jonathan might be outside again, but she decided to check his office first. And was rewarded when she saw him sitting at the computer, his head lowered over the keyboard, some of his dark hair falling over his face after coming loose from the braid he normally kept it in.

Her heart clenched painfully, and it disturbed her that her heart was the first part of her body to tighten. The rest of her followed shortly thereafter, but she really wished her reaction was more about her body than her feelings. She couldn't afford to have feelings for him. She wasn't staying in Copper Ridge. And even if she were, he wouldn't want her long-term, anyway.

She took a deep breath, trying to dispel the strange, constricted feeling that had overtaken her lungs. "I thought I might find you here," she said.

He looked up, his expression betraying absolutely no surprise. He sneaked up on her all the time, but of course, as always, Jonathan was unflappable. "I just had a few schematics to check over." He pushed the chair away from the desk and stood, reaching over his head to stretch.

She was held captive by the sight of him. Even fully dressed, he was a beautiful thing.

His shoulders and chest were broad and muscular, his waist trim. His face like sculpted rock, or hardened bronze, uncompromising. But she knew the secret way to make those lips soften. Only for her.

No, not only for you. He does this all the time. They are just softening for you right now.

It was good for her to remember that.

"I'm finished now," he said, treating her to a smile that made her feel like melting ice cream on a hot day.

"Good," she said, not quite sure why she said it, because it wasn't like they had made plans. She wondered when he would ask her to leave. Or maybe he wanted her to leave, but didn't want to tell her. "It's late," she said. "I could go."

"Do you need to go?"

"No," she said, a little too quickly.

"Then don't."

Relief washed over her, and she did her best not to show him just how pleased she was by that statement. "Okay," she said, "then I won't go."

"I was thinking. About your list."

She blinked. "My list?"

"Yeah, your list. You had dancing on there. Pretty

sure you had a kiss. And whether or not it was on the list…you did lose your virginity. Since I helped you with those items, I figured I might help you with some of the others."

A deep sense of pleasure and something that felt a lot like delight washed through her. "Really?"

"Yes," he said, "really. I figure we started all of this, so we might as well keep going."

"I don't have an official list."

"Well, that's ridiculous. If you're going to do this thing, you have to do it right." He grabbed a sheet of paper out of the printer and settled back down in the office chair. "Let's make a list."

He picked up a pen and started writing.

"What are you doing? I didn't tell you what I wanted yet."

"I'm writing down what we already did so you have the satisfaction of checking those off."

Her stomach turned over. "Don't write down all of it."

"Oh," he said, "I am. All of it. In detail."

"No!" She crossed the space between them and stood behind him, wrapping her arms around his broad shoulders as if she might restrain him. He kept on writing. She peered around his head, then slapped the pen out of his hand when she saw him writing a very dirty word. "Stop it. If anybody finds that list I could be…incriminated."

He laughed and swiveled the chair to the side.

He wrapped his arm around her waist and pulled her onto his lap. "Oh no. We would hate for you to be incriminated. But on the other hand, the world would know you spent the afternoon with a very firm grip on my—"

"No!"

He looked at her and defiantly put a checkmark by what he had just written. She huffed, but settled into his hold. She liked this too much. Him smiling, him holding her when they had clothes on as if he just wanted to hold her.

It was nice to have him want her in bed. Very nice. But this was something else, and it was nice, too.

"Okay, so we have dancing, kissing, sex, and all of the many achievements beneath the sex," he said, ignoring her small noises of protest. "So what else?"

"I want to go to a place where I need a passport," she said.

"We could drive to Canada."

She laughed. "I was thinking more like Europe. But… Could we really drive to Canada?"

"Well," he said, "maybe not today, since I have to be back here by Monday."

"That's fine. I was thinking more Paris than Vancouver."

"Hey, they speak French in Canada."

"Just write it down," she said, poking his shoulder.

"Fine. What next?"

"I feel like I should try alcohol," she said slowly. "Just so I know."

"Fair enough." He wrote *get hammered*.

"That is not what I said."

"Sorry. I got so excited about the idea of getting you drunk. Lowering your inhibitions."

She rolled her eyes. "I'm already more un-inhibited with you than I've ever been with anyone else." It was true, she realized, as soon as she said it. She was more herself with Jonathan than she had ever been with anyone, including her family, who had known her for her entire life.

Maybe it was the fact that, in a town full of people who were familiar with her, at least by reputation, he was someone she hadn't known at all until a couple weeks ago.

Maybe it was the fact that he had no expectations of her beyond what they'd shared. Whatever the case, around him she felt none of the pressure that she felt around other people in the community.

No need to censor herself, or hide; no need to be respectable or serene when she felt like being disreputable and wild.

"I want to kiss in the rain," she said.

"Given weather patterns," he said slowly, "we should be able to accomplish that, too."

She was ridiculously pleased he wanted to be a part of that, pleased that he hadn't said anything about her finding a guy to kiss in the rain in Paris.

She shouldn't be happy he was assuming he would be the person to help her fulfill these things. She should be annoyed. She should feel like he was inserting himself into her independence, but she didn't. Mostly because he made her independence seem…well, like *more*.

"You're very useful, aren't you?"

He looked at her, putting his hand on her cheek, his dark gaze serious as it met hers. "I'm glad I can be useful to you."

She felt him getting hard beneath her backside, and that pleased her, too. "Parts of you are very useful," she said, reaching behind her and slowly stroking his length.

The light in his eyes changed, turning much more intense. "Hayley Thompson," he said, "I would say that's shocking behavior."

"I would say you're responsible, Jonathan Bear."

He shook his head. "No, princess, you're responsible for this. For all of this. This is you. It's what you want, right? The things on your list that you don't even want to write down. It's part of you. You don't get to blame it all on me."

She felt strangely empowered by his words. By the idea that this was her, and not just him leading her somewhere.

"That's very… Well, that's very… I like it." She furthered her exploration of him, increasing the pressure of her touch. "At least, I like it with you."

"I'm not complaining."

"That's good," she said softly, continuing to stroke him through the fabric of his pants.

She looked down, watched herself touching him. It was…well, now that she had started, she didn't want to stop.

"I would be careful if I were you," he said, his tone laced with warning, "because you're about to start something, and it's very likely you need to take a break from all that."

"Do I? Why would I need a break?"

"Because you're going to get sore," he said, maddeningly pragmatic.

And, just as maddeningly, it made her blush to hear him say it. "I don't really mind," she said finally.

"You don't?" His tone was calm, but heat flared in the depths of his dark eyes.

"No," she replied, still trailing her fingertips over his hardening body. "I like feeling the difference. In me. I like being so…aware of everything we've done." For her, that was a pretty brazen proclamation, though she had a feeling it paled in comparison to the kinds of things other women had said to him in the past.

But she wasn't one of those other women. And right now he was responding to her, so she wasn't going to waste a single thought on anyone who had come before her. She held his interest now. That was enough.

"There's something else on my list," she said, fighting to keep her voice steady, fighting against the nerves firing through her.

"Is that so?"

She sucked in a sharp breath. "Yes. I want to… That is… What you did for me… A couple of times now… I want to… I want to…" She gave up trying to get the words out. She wasn't sure she had the right words for what she wanted to do, anyway, and she didn't want to humiliate herself by saying something wrong.

So, with unsteady hands, she undid the closure on his jeans and lowered the zipper. She looked up at him. If she expected to get any guidance, she was out of luck. He just stared at her, his dark eyes unfathomable, his jaw tight, a muscle in his cheek ticking.

She shifted on his lap, sliding gracefully to the floor in front of the chair. Then she went to her knees and turned to face him, flicking her hair out of her face.

He still said nothing, watching her closely, unnervingly so. But she wasn't going to turn back now. She lifted the waistband of his underwear, pulling it out in order to clear his impressive erection, then she pulled the fabric partway down his hips, as far as she could go with him sitting.

He was beautiful.

That feeling of intimidation she'd felt the first time she'd seen him had faded completely. Now she knew what he could do, and she appreciated it greatly. He had shown her so many things; he'd made her pleasure the number one priority. And she wanted to give to him in return.

Well, she also knew this would be for her, too.

She slid her hands up his thighs, then curled her fingers around his hardened length, squeezing him firmly. She was learning that he wasn't breakable there. That he liked a little bit of pressure.

"Hayley," he said, his voice rough, "I don't think you know what you're doing."

"No," she said, "I probably don't. But I know what I want. And it's been so much fun having what I want." She rose up slightly, then leaned in, pressing her lips to the head of his shaft. He jerked beneath her touch, and she took that as approval.

A couple hours ago she would have been afraid that she'd hurt him. But male pleasure, she was discovering, sometimes looked a little like pain. Heck, female pleasure was a little like pain. Sex was somewhere between. The aching need to have it all and the intense rush of satisfaction that followed.

She shivered just thinking about it.

And then she flicked her tongue out, slowly testing this new territory. She hummed, a low sound in the back of her throat, as she explored the taste of him, the texture. Jonathan Bear was her favorite indulgence, she was coming to realize. There was nothing about him she didn't like. Nothing he had done to her she didn't love. She liked the way he felt, and apparently she liked the way he tasted, too.

She parted her lips slowly, worked them over the head, then swallowed down as much of him as she could. The accompanying sound he made hollowed out her stomach, made her feel weak and powerful at the same time.

His body was such an amazing thing. So strong, like it had been carved straight from the mountain. Yet it wasn't in any way cold or unmovable; it was hot. His body had changed hers. Yes, he'd taken her virginity, but he had also taught her to feel pleasure she hadn't realized she had the capacity to feel.

Such power in his body, and yet, right now, it trembled beneath her touch. The whisper-soft touch of her lips possessed the power to rock him, to make him shake. To make him shatter.

Right now, desire was enough. She didn't need skill. She didn't need experience. And she felt completely confident in that.

She slipped her tongue over his length as she took him in deep, and he bucked his hips lightly, touching the back of her throat. Her throat contracted and he jerked back.

"Sorry," he said, his voice strained.

"No," she said, gripping him with one hand and bringing her lips back against him. "Don't apologize. I like it."

"You're inexperienced."

She nodded slowly, then traced him with the tip of her tongue. "Yes," she agreed, "I am. I've never done this for any other man. I've never even thought about it before." His hips jerked again, and she realized he liked this. That he—however much he tried to pretend he didn't—liked that her desire was all for him.

"I think you might be corrupting me," she said, keeping her eyes wide as she took him back into her mouth.

He grunted, fisting his hands in her hair, but he didn't pull her away again.

The muscles in his thighs twitched beneath her fingertips, and he seemed to grow larger, harder in her mouth. She increased the suction, increased the friction, used her hands as well as her mouth to drive him as crazy as she possibly could.

There was no plan. There was no skill. There was just the need to make him even half as mindless as he'd made her over the past couple days.

He had changed her. He had taken her from innocence…to this. She would be marked by him forever. He would always be her first. But society didn't have a term for a person's experience after virginity. So she didn't have a label for the impact she wanted to make on him.

Jonathan hadn't been a virgin for a very long time, she suspected. And she probably wasn't particularly special as a sexual partner.

So she had to try to make herself special.

She had no tricks to make this the best experience he'd ever had. She had only herself. And so she gave it to him. All of her. Everything.

"Hayley," he said, his voice rough, ragged. "You better stop."

She didn't. She ignored him. She had a feeling he was close; she recognized the signs now. She had watched him reach the point of pleasure enough times that she had a fair idea of what it looked like. Of what it felt like. His whole body tensing, his movements becoming less controlled.

She squeezed the base of him tightly, pulling him in deeper, and then he shattered. And she swallowed down every last shudder of need that racked his big body.

In the aftermath, she was dazed, her heart pounding hard, her entire body buzzing. She looked up at him from her position on the floor, and he looked down at her, his dark eyes blazing with…anger, maybe? Passion? A kind of sharp, raw need she hadn't ever seen before.

"You're going to pay for that," he said.

"Oh," she returned, "I hope so."

He swept her up, crushed her against his chest. "You have to put it on my list first," she said.

Then he brought his mouth down to hers, and whatever she'd intended to write down was forgotten until morning.

Ten

Sometime on Sunday afternoon Hayley had gone home. Because, she had insisted, she wasn't able to work in either his T-shirt or the dress she had worn to the bar on Friday.

He hadn't agreed, but he had been relieved to have the reprieve. He didn't feel comfortable sharing the bed with her while he slept. Which had meant sleeping on the couch in the office after she drifted off.

He just… He didn't sleep with women. He didn't see the point in inviting that kind of intimacy. Having her spend the night in his bed was bad enough. But he hadn't wanted to send her home, either. He didn't want to think about why. Maybe it was because she expected to stay, because of her general inexperience.

Which made him think of the moment she had taken him into her mouth, letting him know he was the first man she had ever considered doing that for. Just the thought of it made his eyes roll back in his head.

Now, it was late Monday afternoon and she had been slowly driving him crazy with the prim little outfit she had come back to work in, as though he didn't know what she looked like underneath it.

Who knew he'd like a good girl who gave head like a dream.

She had also insisted that they stay professional during work hours, and it was making it hard for him to concentrate. Of course, it was always hard for him to concentrate on office work. In general, he hated it.

Though bringing Hayley into the office certainly made it easier to bear.

Except for the part where it was torture.

He stood up from his chair and stretched slowly, trying to work the tension out of his body. But he had a feeling that until he was buried inside Hayley's body again, tension was just going to be the state of things.

"Oh," Hayley said, "Joshua Grayson just emailed and said he needs you to go by the county office and sign a form. And no, it can't be faxed."

For the first time in his life, Johathan was relieved to encounter bureaucracy. He needed to get out of this space. He needed to get his head on straight.

"Great," he said.

"Maybe I should go with you," she said. "I've never been down to the building and planning office, and you might need me to run errands in the future."

He gritted his teeth. "Yeah, probably."

"I'll drive my own car." She stood, grabbing her purse off the desk. "Because by the time we're done it will be time for me to get off."

He ground his teeth together even harder, because he couldn't ignore her double entendre even though he knew it had been accidental. And because, in addition to the double meaning, it was clear she intended to stay in town tonight and not at his place.

He should probably be grateful she wasn't being clingy. He didn't like to encourage women to get too attached to him, not at all.

"Great idea," he said.

But he didn't think it was a great idea, and he grumbled the entire way to town in the solitude of his pickup truck, not missing the irony that he had been wanting alone time, and was now getting it, and was upset about it.

The errand really did take only a few minutes, and afterward it still wasn't quite time for Hayley to clock out.

"Do you want to grab something to eat?" he asked,

though he had no earthly idea why. He should get something for himself and go home, deal with that tension he had been pondering earlier.

She looked back and forth, clearly edgy. "In town?"

"Yes," he returned, "in town."

"Oh. I don't… I guess so."

"Calm down," he said. "I'm not asking you to Beaches. Let's just stop by the Crab Shanty."

She looked visibly relieved, and again he couldn't quantify why that annoyed him.

He knew they shouldn't be seen together in town. He had a feeling she also liked the casual nature of the restaurant. It was much more likely to look like a boss and employee grabbing something to eat than it was to look like a date.

They walked from where they had parked a few streets over, and paused at the crosswalk. They waited for one car to crawl by, clearly not interested in heeding the law that said pedestrians had the right-of-way. Then Jonathan charged ahead of her across the street and up to the faded yellow building. A small line was already forming outside the order window, and he noticed that Hayley took pains to stand slightly behind him.

When it was their turn to order, he decided he wasn't having any of her missish circumspection. They shouldn't be seen together as anything more than a boss and an assistant.

But right now, hell if he cared. "Two orders of fish and chips, the halibut. Two beers and a Diet Coke."

He pulled his wallet out and paid before Hayley could protest, then he grabbed the plastic number from the window, and the two of them walked over to a picnic table positioned outside the ramshackle building. There was no indoor seating, which could be a little bracing on windy days, and there weren't very many days that didn't have wind on the Oregon coast.

Jonathan set the number on the wooden table, then sat down heavily, looking up at the blue-and-white-striped umbrella wiggling in the breeze.

"Two beers?"

"One of them is for you," he said, his words verging on a growl.

"I'm not going to drink a beer." She looked sideways. "At least not here."

"Yeah, right out here on Main Street in front of God and everybody? You're a lot braver in my bedroom."

He was goading her, but he didn't much care. He was... Well dammit, it pissed him off. To see how ashamed she was to be with him. How desperate she was to hide it. Even if he understood it, it was like a branding iron straight to the gut.

"You can't say that so loud," she hissed, leaning forward, grabbing the plastic number and pulling it to her chest. "What if people heard you?"

"I thought you were reinventing yourself, Hayley Thompson."

"Not for the benefit of...the town. It's about me."

"It's going to be about you not getting dinner if you keep hiding our number." He snatched the plastic triangle from her hands.

She let out a heavy sigh and leaned back, crossing her arms. "Well, the extra beer is for you. Put it in your pocket."

"You can put it in your own pocket. Drink it back at your place."

"No, thanks."

"Don't you want to tick that box on your list? We ticked off some pretty interesting ones last night."

Her face turned scarlet. "You're being obnoxious, Jonathan."

"I've been obnoxious from day one. You just found it easy to ignore when I had my hand in your pants."

Her mouth dropped open, then she snapped it shut again. Their conversation was cut off when their food was placed in front of them.

She dragged the white cardboard box toward her and opened it, removing the container of coleslaw and setting it to the side before grabbing a french fry and biting into it fiercely. Her annoyance was clearly telegraphed by the ferocity with which she ate each bite of food. And the determination that went into her looking at anything and everything around them except for him.

"Enjoying the view?" he asked after a moment.

"The ocean is very pretty," she snapped.

"And you don't see it every day?"

"I never tire of the majesty of nature."

His lips twitched, in spite of his irritation. "Of course not."

The wind whipped up, blowing a strand of dark hair into Hayley's face. Reflexively, he reached across the table and pushed it out of her eyes. She jerked back, her lips going slack, her expression shocked.

"You're my boss," she said, her voice low. "As far as everyone is concerned."

"Well," he said, "I'm your lover. As far as I'm concerned."

"Stop."

"I thought you wanted new experiences? I thought you were tired of hiding? And here you are, hiding."

"I don't want to…perform," she said. "My new experiences are for me. Not for everyone else's consumption. That's why I'm leaving. So I can…do things without an audience."

"You want your dirty secrets, is that it? You want me to be your dirty secret."

"It's five o'clock," she said, her tone stiff. "I'm going to go home now."

She collected her food, and left the beer, standing up in a huff and taking off down the street in the opposite direction from where they had parked.

"Where are you going?"

"Home," she said sharply.

He gathered up the rest of the food and stomped after her. "You parked the other way."

"I'll get it in the morning."

"Then you better leave your house early. Unless this is you tendering your resignation."

"I'm not quitting," she said, the color heightening in her face. "I'm just… I'm irritated with you."

She turned away from him, continuing to walk quickly down the street. He took two strides and caught up with her. "I see that." He kept pace with her, but she seemed bound and determined not to look at him. "Would you care to share why?"

"Not even a little bit."

"So you're insisting that you're my employee, and that you want to be treated like my employee in public. But that clearly excludes when you decide to run off having a temper tantrum."

She whirled around then, stopping in her tracks. "Why are you acting like this? You've been…much more careful than this up till now." She sniffed. "Out of deference to my innocence?"

"What innocence, baby? Because I took that." He smiled, knowing he was getting to her. That he was making her feel as bad as he did. "Pretty damn thoroughly."

"I can't do this with you. Not here." She paused at the street corner and looked both ways before hurrying across the two-lane road. He followed suit. She walked down the sidewalk, passed the coffeehouse, which was closing up for the day, then rounded the side of the brick building and headed toward the back.

"Is this where you live?" he asked.

"Maybe," she returned, sounding almost comically stubborn. Except he didn't feel like much was funny about this situation.

"Here in the alley?" he asked, waving his hand around the mostly vacant space.

"Yes. In the Dumpster with the mice. It's not so bad. I shredded up a bunch of newspaper and made a little bed."

"I suspect this is the real reason you've been spending the night at my place, then."

She scowled. "If you want to fight with me, come upstairs."

He didn't want to fight with her. He wanted to grab her, pull her into his arms and kiss her. He wanted to stop talking. Wanted to act logical instead of being wounded by something he knew he should want to avoid.

It didn't benefit him to have anyone in town know what he was doing with Hayley. He should want to hide it as badly as she did.

But the idea that she was enjoying his body, enjoying slumming it with him in the sheets, and was damned ashamed of him in the streets burned like hell.

But he followed her through the back door to a little hallway that contained two other doors. She unlocked one of them and held it open for him. Then she gestured to the narrow staircase. "Come on."

"Who's the boss around here?"

"I'm off the clock," she said.

He shrugged, then walked up the stairs and into an open-plan living room with exposed beams and brick. It was a much bigger space than he had expected it to be, though it was also mostly empty. As if she had only half committed to living there.

But then, he supposed, her plan *was* to travel the world.

"Nice place," he said.

"Yeah," she said. "Cassie gave me a deal."

"Nice of her."

"Some people are nice, Jonathan."

"Meaning I'm not?" he asked.

She nodded in response, her mouth firmly sealed, her chin jutting out stubbornly.

"Right. Because I bought you fish and french fries and beer. And I give you really great orgasms. I'm a monster."

"I don't know what game you're playing," she said, suddenly looking much less stubborn and a little more wobbly. And that made him feel something close to guilty. "What's the point in blurring the lines while we walk through town? We both know this isn't a relationship. It's…it's boxes being ticked on a list."

"Sure. But why does it matter if people in town know you're doing that?"

"You know why it matters. Don't play like you don't understand. You do. I know you do. You know who I am, and you know that I feel like I'm under a microscope. I shared all of that with you. Don't act surprised by it now."

"Well," he said, opting for honesty even though he knew it was a damned bad idea. "Maybe I don't like being your dirty secret."

"It's not about you. Any guy that I was… Anyone that I was…doing this with. It would be a secret. It has to be."

"Why?"

"Because!" she exploded. "Because everyone will be…disappointed."

"Honey," he said, "I don't think people spend half as much time thinking about you as you think they do."

"No," she said. "They do. You know Ace. He's the pastor's son. He ran away from home, he got married, he got divorced. Then he came back and opened a bar. My parents…they're great. They really are. But they had a lot of backlash over that. People saying that the Bible itself says if you train up a child the way he should go, he's not going to depart from it. Well, he departed from it, at least as far as a lot of the congregants were concerned. People actually left the church." She sucked in a sharp breath, then let it out slowly. "I wanted to do better than that for them. It was important. For me to be…the good one."

Caring about what people thought was a strange concept. Appearances had never mattered to Jonathan. For him, it had always been about actions. What the hell did Rebecca care if he had been good? All she cared about was being taken care of. He couldn't imagine being bound by rules like that.

For the first time, he wondered if there wasn't some kind of freedom in no one having a single good expectation of you.

"But you don't like being the good one. At least, not by these standards."

Her eyes glittered with tears now. She shook her head. "I don't know. I just… I don't know. I'm afraid. Afraid of what people will think. Afraid of what my parents will think. Afraid of them being disappointed. And hurt. They've always put a lot of stock in me being what Ace wasn't. They love Ace, don't get me wrong. It's just…"

"He made things hard for them."

Hayley nodded, looking miserable. "Yes. He did. And I don't want to do that. Only…only, I was the good one and he still ended up with the kind of life I want."

"Is that all?" Jonathan asked. "Or are you afraid

of who you might be if you don't have all those rules to follow?"

A flash of fear showed in her eyes, and he felt a little guilty about putting it there. Not guilty enough to take it back. Not guilty enough to stay away from her. Not guilty enough to keep his hands to himself. He reached out, cupping her cheek, then wrapped his arm around her waist and drew her toward him. "Does it scare you? Who you might be if no one told you what to do? I don't care about the rules, Hayley. You can be whoever you want with me. Say whatever you want. Drink whatever you want. Do whatever you want."

"I don't know," she said, wiggling against him, trying to pull away. "I don't know what I want."

"I think you do. I just think you wish you wanted something else." He brushed his thumb over her cheekbone. "I think you like having rules because it keeps you from going after what scares you."

He ignored the strange reverberation those words set off inside him. The chain reaction that seemed to burst all the way down his spine.

Recognition.

Truth.

Yeah, he ignored all that, and he dipped his head, claiming her mouth with his own.

Suddenly, it seemed imperative that he have her here. In her apartment. That he wreck this place with his desire for her. That he have her on every surface, against every wall, so that whenever she walked in, whenever she looked around, he was what she thought of. So that she couldn't escape this. So that she couldn't escape him.

"You think you know me now?" she asked, her eyes squinting with challenge. Clearly, she wasn't going to back down without a fight. And that was one of the things he liked about her. For all that she was an innocent church secretary, she had spirit. She had the kind of steel backbone that he admired, that he respected. The kind of strength that could get you through anything. But there was a softness to her as well, and that was something more foreign to him. Something he had never been exposed to, had never really been allowed to have.

"Yeah," he said, tightening his hold and drawing her against his body. "I know you. I know what you look like naked. I know every inch of your skin. How it feels, how it tastes. I know you better than anybody does, baby. You can tell yourself that's not true. You can say that this, what we have, is the crazy thing. That it's a break from your real life. That it's some detour you don't want anyone in town to know you're taking. But I know the truth. And I think somewhere deep down you know it, too. This isn't the break. All that other stuff…prim, proper church girl. That's what isn't real." He cupped her face, smoothing his thumbs over her cheeks. "You're fire, honey, and together we are an explosion."

He kissed her then, proving his point. She tasted like anger, like need, and he was of a mind to consume both. Whatever was on offer. Whatever she would give him.

He was beyond himself. He had never wanted a woman like this before. He had never wanted anything quite like this before. Not money, not security, not his damned house on the hill.

All that want, all that need, paled in comparison to what he felt for Hayley Thompson. The innocent little miss who should have bored him to tears by now, had him aching, panting and begging for more.

He was so hard he was in physical pain.

And when she finally capitulated, when she gave herself over to the kiss, soft fingertips skimming his shoulders, down his back, all the way to his ass, he groaned in appreciation.

There was something extra dirty about Hayley exploring his body. About her wanting him the way she did, because she had never wanted another man like she wanted him. By her own admission. And she had never had a man the way she'd had him, which was an admission she didn't have to make.

He gripped her hips, then slipped his hands down her thighs, grabbing them and pulling her up, urging her legs around his waist. Then he propelled them both across the living room, down onto the couch. He covered her, pressing his hardness against the soft, sweet apex of her thighs. She gasped as he rolled his hips forward.

"Not so ashamed of this now, are you?" He growled, pressing a kiss to her neck, then to her collarbone, then to the edge of her T-shirt.

"I'm not ashamed," she said, gasping for air.

"You could've fooled me, princess."

"It's not about you." She sifted her fingers through his hair. "I'm not ashamed of you."

"Not ashamed of your dirty, wrong-side-of-the-tracks boyfriend?"

Her eyes flashed with hurt and then fascination. "I've never thought of you that way. I never... *Boyfriend?*"

Something burned hot in his chest. "Lover. Whatever."

"I'm not ashamed of you," she reiterated. "Nothing about you. You're so beautiful. If anything, you ought to be ashamed of me. I'm not pretty. Not like you. And I don't even know what I'm doing. I just know what I want. I want you. And I'm afraid for anybody to know the truth. I'm so scared. The only time I'm not scared is when you're holding me."

He didn't want to talk anymore. He consumed her mouth, tasting her deeply, ramping up the arousal between them with each sweet stroke of his tongue across hers. With each deep taste of the sweet flavor that could only ever be Hayley.

He gripped the hem of her top, yanking it over

her head, making quick work of her bra. Exposing small, perfect breasts to his inspection. She was pale. All over. Ivory skin, coral-pink nipples. He loved the look of her. Loved the feel of her. Loved so many things about her that it was tempting to just go ahead and say he loved *her*.

That thought swam thick and dizzy in his head. He could barely grab hold of it, didn't want to. So he shoved it to the side. He wasn't going to claim that. Hell no.

He didn't love people. He loved *things*.

He could love her tits, and he could love her skin, could love the way it felt to slide inside her, slick and tight. But he sure as hell couldn't love *her*.

He bent his head, taking one hardened nipple into his mouth, sucking hard, relishing the horse sound of pleasure on her lips as he did so. Then he kissed his way down her stomach, to the edge of her pants, pulling them down her thighs, leaving her bare and open.

He pressed his hand between her legs, slicked his thumb over her, teased her entrance with one finger. She began to whimper, rolling her hips under him, arching them to meet him, and he watched. Watched as she took one finger inside, then another.

He damn well watched himself corrupt her, and he let himself enjoy it. Because he was sick, because he was broken, but at least it wasn't a surprise.

Everyone in his life was familiar with it.

His father had tried to beat it out of him. His mother had run from it.

Only Rebecca had ever stayed, and it was partly because she didn't know any better.

Hayley didn't know any better, either, come to that. Not really. Not when it came to men. Not when it came to sex. She was blinded by what he could make her body feel, so she had an easy enough time ignoring the rest. But that wouldn't last forever.

Fair enough, since they wouldn't last forever, anyway. They both knew it. So there was no point in worrying about it. Not really.

Instead, he would embrace this, embrace the rush. Embrace the hollowed out feeling in his gut that bordered on sickness. The tension in his body that verged on pain. The need that rendered him hard as iron and hot as fire.

"Come for me," he commanded, his voice hoarse. All other words, all other thoughts were lost to him. All he could do was watch her writhing beneath his touch, so hot, so wet for him, arching her hips and taking his fingers in deeper.

"Not yet," she gasped, emitting little broken sounds.

"Yes," he said. "You will. You're going to come for me now, Hayley, because I told you to. Your body is mine. You're mine." He slid his thumb over the delicate bundle of nerves there.

And then he felt her shatter beneath his touch. Felt her internal muscles pulse around his knuckles.

He reached into his back pocket, took out his wallet and found a condom quickly. He tore it open, then wrenched free his belt buckle and took down the zipper. He pushed his jeans partway down his hips, rolled the condom on his hard length and thrust inside her, all the way to the hilt. She was wet and ready for him, and he had to grit his teeth to keep from embarrassing himself, to keep it from being over before it had begun.

She gasped as he filled her, and then grabbed his ass when he retreated. Her fingernails dug into his skin, and he relished the pain this petite little thing could inflict on him. Of course, it was nothing compared to the pain he felt from his arousal. From the great, burning need inside him.

No, nothing compared to that. Nothing at all.

He adjusted their positions, dragging her sideways on the couch, bringing her hips to the edge of the cushion, going down on his knees to the hardwood floor.

He knelt there, gripping her hips and pulling her tightly against him, urging her to wrap her legs around him. The floor bit into his knees, but he didn't care. All he cared about was having her, taking her, claiming her. He gripped her tightly, his blunt fingertips digging into her flesh.

He wondered if he would leave a mark. He hoped he might.

Hoped that she would see for days to come where

he had held her. Even if she wouldn't hold his hand in public, she would remember when he'd held her hips in private, when he'd driven himself deep inside her, clinging to her like she might be the source of all life.

Yeah, she would remember that. She would remember this.

He watched as a deep red flush spread over her skin, covering her breasts, creeping up her neck. She was on the verge of another orgasm. He loved that. Another thing he was allowed to love.

Loved watching her lose control. Loved watching her so close to giving it up for him again, completely. Utterly. He was going to ruin her for any other man. That was his vow, there and then, on the floor of her apartment, with a ragged splinter digging into his knee through the fabric of his jeans. She was never going to fuck anyone else without thinking of him. Without wanting him. Without wishing it were him.

She would go to Paris, and some guy would do her with a view of the Eiffel tower in the background. And she would wish she were here, counting the familiar beams on her ceiling.

And when she came home for a visit and she passed him on the street, she would shiver with a longing that she would never quite get rid of.

So many people in his life had left him. As far as he'd known, they had done it without a backward glance. But Hayley would never forget him. He would make sure of it. Damn sure.

His own arousal ratcheted up to impossible proportions. He was made entirely of his need for her. Of his need for release. And he forgot what he was trying to do. Forgot that this was about her. That this was about making her tremble, making her shake. Because he was trembling. He was shaking.

He was afraid he might be the one who was indelibly marked by all this.

He was the one who wouldn't be able to forget. The one who would never be with anyone else without thinking of her. No matter how skilled the woman was who might come after her, it would never be the same as the sweet, genuine urging of Hayley's hips against his. It would never be quite like the tight, wet clasp of her body.

He had been entirely reshaped, remade, to fit inside her, and no one else would do.

That thought ignited in his stomach, overtook him completely, lit him on fire.

When he came, it was with her name on his lips, with a strange satisfaction washing through him that left him only hungrier in the end, emptier. Because this was ending, and he knew it.

She wasn't going to work for him forever. She wasn't going to stay in Copper Ridge. She might hold on to him in secret, but in public, she would never touch him.

And as time passed, she would let go of him by inches, walking off to the life of freedom she was so desperate for.

Walking off like everyone else.

Right now, she was looking up at him, a mixture of wonder and deep emotion visible in her blue eyes. She reached up, stroking his face. Some of his hair had been tugged from the leather strap, and she brushed the strands out of his eyes.

It was weird how that hit him. How it touched him. After all the overtly sexual ways she'd put her hands on him, why that sweet gesture impacted him low and deep.

"Stay with me," she said, her voice soft. "The night. In my bed."

That hit even harder.

He had never slept with her. He didn't sleep with women. But that was all about to change. He was going to sleep with her because he wanted to. Because he didn't want to release his hold on her for one moment, not while he still had her.

"Okay," he said.

Then, still buried deep inside her, he picked her up from the couch, brought them both to a standing position and started walking toward the door at the back of the room. "Bedroom is this way?"

"How did you know?"

"Important things, I know. Where the bedroom

is." He kissed her lips. "How to make you scream my name. That I know."

"Care to make me scream it a few more times?"

"The neighbors might hear."

It was a joke, but he could still see her hesitation. "That's okay," she said slowly.

And even though he was reasonably confident that was a lie, he carried her into her bedroom and lay down on the bed with her.

It didn't matter if it was a lie. Because they had all night to live in it. And that was good enough for him.

Eleven

When he woke up the next morning he was disoriented. He was lying in a bed that was too small for his large frame, and he had a woman wrapped around him. Of course, he knew immediately which woman it was. It couldn't be anyone else. Even in the fog of sleep, he wasn't confused about Hayley's identity.

She smelled like sunshine and wildflowers. Or maybe she just smelled like soap and skin and only reminded him of sunshine and wildflowers, because they were innocent things. New things. The kinds of things that could never be corrupted by the world around them.

The kinds of things not even he could wreck.

She was that kind of beautiful.

But the other reason he was certain it was Hayley was that there was no other woman he would have fallen asleep with. It was far too intimate a thing, sharing a bed with someone when you weren't angling for an orgasm. He had never seen the point of it. It was basically the same as sharing a toothbrush, and he wasn't interested in that, either.

He looked at Hayley, curled up at his side, her brown hair falling across her face, her soft lips parted, her breathing easy and deep. The feeling carved out in his chest was a strange one.

Hell, lying there in the early morning, sharing a toothbrush with Hayley didn't even seem so insane.

He sat up, shaking off the last cobwebs of sleep and extricating himself from Hayley's hold. He groaned when her fingertips brushed the lower part of his stomach, grazing his insistent morning erection. He had half a mind to wake her up the best way he knew how.

But the longer the realization of what had happened last night sat with him, the more eager he was to put some distance between them.

He could get some coffee, get his head on straight and come back fully clothed. Then maybe the two of them could prepare for the workday.

He needed to compartmentalize. He had forgotten that yesterday. He had let himself get annoyed about something that never should have bothered him. Had allowed old hurts to sink in when he shouldn't give a damn whether or not Hayley wanted to hold his hand when they walked down the street. She wasn't his girlfriend. And all the words that had passed between them in the apartment, all the anger that had been rattling around inside him, seemed strange now. Like it had all happened to somebody else. The morning had brought clarity, and it was much needed.

He hunted around the room, collecting his clothes and tugging them on quickly, then he walked over to the window, drew back the curtains and tried to get a sense of what time it was. She didn't have a clock in her room. He wondered if she just looked at her phone.

The sky was pink, so it had to be nearing six. He really needed to get home and take care of the horses. He didn't want to mess up their routine. But he would come back. Or maybe Hayley would just come to his place on time.

Then he cursed, realizing he had left his car at the other end of Main Street. He walked back to the living room, pulled on his boots and headed out the door, down the stairs. His vision was blurry, and he was in desperate need of caffeine. There were two doors in the hallway, and he reached for the one closest to him.

And nearly ran right into Cassie Caldwell as he walked into The Grind.

The morning sounds of the coffee shop filled his ears, the intense smell of the roast assaulting him in the best way.

But Cassie was staring at him, wide-eyed, as were the ten people sitting inside the dining room. One of whom happened to be Pastor John Thompson.

Jonathan froze, mumbled something about coming in through the back door, and then walked up to the counter. He was going to act like there was nothing remarkable about where he had just come from. Was going to do his very best to look like there was nothing at all strange about him coming through what he now realized was a private entrance used only by the tenant upstairs. It didn't escape his notice that the pastor was eyeballing him closely. And so was Cassie. Really, so was everybody. Damn small town.

Now, he could see why Hayley had been so vigilant yesterday.

If only he could go back and be vigilant in his door choice.

"Black coffee," he said, "two shots of espresso."

Cassie's gaze turned hard. "I know."

"I came through the wrong door," he said.

She walked over to the espresso machine, wrapped a damp cloth around the wand that steamed the milk and twisted it, a puff of steam coming out as she jerked the cloth up and down roughly, her eyes never leaving his. "Uh-huh."

"I did."

"And it's just a coincidence that my tenant happens to live upstairs. My tenant who works for you." She said that part softly, and he was sure nobody else in the room heard it.

"That's right," he said. "Just a coincidence."

Suddenly, the door to the coffee shop opened again, and Hayley appeared, wearing a T-shirt and jeans, her hair wild, like she had just rolled out of bed.

Her eyes widened when she saw her father. Then she looked over at the counter and her eyes widened even further when she saw Jonathan.

"Good morning," he said, his voice hard. "Fancy meeting you here before work."

"Yes," she said. "I'm just gonna go get ready."

She turned around and walked back out of the coffee shop, as quickly as she had come in. So much for being casual. If he hadn't already given it away, he was pretty sure Hayley's scampering had.

"You were saying?" Cassie said, her tone brittle.

"I'm sorry," he said, leaning in. "Is she your sister?"

"No."

"Best friend?"

"No."

"Is she your daughter? Because I have a feeling I'm about to catch hell from the reverend here in a few minutes, but I'm not really sure why I'm catching it from you."

"Because I know her. I know all about you. I am friends with your sister, and I know enough through her."

"Undoubtedly all about my great personal sacrifice and sparkling personality," he said.

Cassie's expression softened. "Rebecca loves you. But she's also realistic about the fact that you aren't a love-and-commitment kind of guy. Also, I do believe Ms. Hayley Thompson is younger than your sister."

"And last I checked, I wasn't committing any crimes. I will just take the coffee. You can keep the lecture."

He was not going to get chased out of the coffee shop, no matter how many people looked at him. No matter how much Cassie lectured him.

He was not the poor kid he'd once been. He was more than just a boy who had been abandoned by both parents. He was a damned boon to the town. His business brought in good money. *He* brought in good money. He wasn't going to be treated like dirt beneath anybody's shoe.

Maybe Hayley was too good for him, but she was sleeping with him. She wanted him. So it wasn't really up to anybody to say that she shouldn't.

When he turned around after Cassie gave him his coffee, the pastor stood up at his table and began to make his way over to Jonathan.

"Hello. Jonathan, right?" the older man said, his voice shot through with the same kind of steel that

Jonathan often heard in Hayley's voice. Clearly, she got her strength from her father. It was also clear to Jonathan that he was not being spoken to by a pastor at the moment. But by a fairly angry dad.

"Pastor John," Jonathan said by way of greeting.

"Why don't you join me for a cup of coffee?"

Not exactly the words Jonathan had expected, all things considered. He could sense the tension in the room, sense the tension coming off Hayley's father.

People were doing their very best to watch, without appearing to do so. Any hope Jonathan had retained that they were oblivious to what it meant that he had come down from the upstairs apartment was dashed by just how fascinated they all were. And by the steady intent on Pastor John's face.

If the old man wanted to sit him down and humiliate him in front of the town, wanted to talk about how Jonathan wasn't fit to lick the dust off Hayley's boots, Jonathan wouldn't be surprised. Hell, he welcomed it. It was true, after all.

"I think I will," Jonathan said, following the other man back to his table.

He took a seat, his hand curled tightly around his coffee cup.

"I don't think we've ever formally met," John said, leaning back in his chair.

"No," Jonathan said, "we wouldn't have. I don't recall darkening the door of the church in my lifetime. Unless it was to repair something."

Let him know just what kind of man Jonathan was. That's where this was headed, anyway. Jonathan had never met a woman's parents before. He had never been in a relationship that was serious enough to do so. And this wasn't serious, either. But because of this damn small town and Hayley's role in it, he was being forced into a position he had never wanted to be in.

"I see," the pastor said. "Hayley has been working for you for the past couple of weeks, I believe."

He was cutting right to the chase now. To Jonathan's connection to Hayley, which was undeniable. "Yes."

"I've been very protective of Hayley. Possibly overprotective. But when my son, Ace, went out on his own, he didn't find much but heartbreak. I transferred some of my fear of that happening again onto Hayley, to an unfair degree. So I kept her close. I encouraged her to keep working at the church. To live at home for as long as possible. You have a sister, don't you?"

Damn this man and his ironclad memory for detail. "I didn't think it was Christian to gossip. But I can see that you've certainly heard your share about me."

"I do know a little something about you, yes. My son is married to one of Nathan West's children, as I'm sure you know. And your sister has a connection to that family, as well."

Jonathan gritted his teeth. "Yes. My sister is with Gage. Though only God knows why. Maybe you could ask Him."

"Matters of the heart are rarely straightforward. Whether it's in the case of romantic love, or the love you feel for your children, or your sister. It's a big emotion. And it is scary at times. Not always the most rational. What you feel about Rebecca being with Gage I suppose is similar to the concerns I have about Hayley."

"That she's with a bastard who doesn't deserve her?"

The pastor didn't even flinch. "That she's involved deeply enough that she could be hurt. And if we're going to speak plainly, I suppose the question I could ask you is whether or not you would think any man was good enough for Rebecca, or if you would be concerned—no matter who it was—that he wouldn't handle her with the care you would want."

Jonathan didn't have much to say about that. Only because he was trying to be angry. Trying to take offense at the fact that the older man was questioning him. Trying to connect this conversation to what he knew to be true—everybody looked at him and saw someone who wasn't worthy. He certainly didn't deserve kindness from this man, not at all. Didn't deserve for him to sit here and try to forge some kind of connection.

Jonathan had taken advantage of Hayley. Regardless of her level of experience, she was his employee. Even if she had been with a hundred men, what he had done would be problematic. But, as far as he was concerned, the problem was compounded by the fact that Hayley had been innocent.

So he waited. He waited for that hammer to fall. For the accusations to fly.

But they didn't come. So he figured he might try to create a few.

"I'm sure there's a certain type of man you would prefer your daughter be with. But it's definitely not the guy with the bad reputation you'd want stumbling out of her apartment early in the morning."

John nodded slowly, and Jonathan thought—with a certain amount of triumph—that he saw anger flicker briefly in the older man's eyes.

"I told you already that I feel very protective of her," Pastor John said. "But I wonder if, by protecting her as much as I did, I shielded her too effectively from the reality of life. I don't want her to get hurt." He let out a long, slow breath. "But that is not within my control."

"Is this the part where you ask me about my intentions toward your daughter? Because I highly doubt we're ever going to sit around a dinner table and try to make small talk. This isn't that sort of thing." With those words, Jonathan effectively told Hayley's father that all he was doing was fooling around with her. And that wasn't strictly true. Also, he hated himself a little bit for pretending it was.

For saying that sort of thing to her father when he knew it would embarrass her.

But in a way, it would be a mercy. She cared what people in town thought about her. She cared about her father's opinion. And this conversation would make it so much easier for her to let Jonathan go when the time came.

She was always going to let you go. She has traveling to do, places to see. You were her dirty detour along the way. You're the one who needs distance. You're the one who needs to find a way to make it easier.

He ignored that voice, ignored the tightening in his chest.

"Why isn't it that sort of thing?" The question, issued from Hayley's father, his tone firm but steady, reached something deep inside Jonathan, twisted it, cracked it.

It couldn't be anything more than temporary. Because of him. Because of what he was. Who he was. That should be obvious. It would have been even more obvious if Pastor John had simply sat down and started hurling recriminations. About how Jonathan was beneath the man's pure, innocent daughter. About why a formerly impoverished man from the wrong side of the tracks could never be good enough for a woman like her.

It didn't matter that he had money now. He was the same person he had been born to be. The same boy who had been beaten by his father, abandoned by his mother. All that was still in him. And no custom home, no amount of money in his bank account, was ever going to fix it.

If John Thompson wouldn't look at him and see that, if he wouldn't shout it from across a crowded coffee shop so the whole town would hear, then Jonathan was going to have to make it clear.

"Because it's not something I do," he returned, his voice hard. "I'm in for temporary. That's all I've got."

"Well," John said, "that's a pretty neat lie you've been telling yourself, son. But the fact of the matter is, it's only the most you're willing to give, not the most you have the ability to give."

"And you're saying you want me to dig down deep and find it inside myself to be with your daughter forever? Something tells me that probably wouldn't be an ideal situation as far as you're concerned."

"That's between you and Hayley. I have my own personal feelings about it, to be sure. No father wants to believe that his daughter is being used. But if I believe that, then it means I don't see anything good in you, and that isn't true. Everybody knows how you took care of your sister. Whatever you think the people in this town believe about you, they do know that. I can't say you haven't been mistreated by the people here, and it grieves me to think about it."

He shook his head, and Jonathan was forced to believe the older man was being genuine. He didn't quite know what to do with that fact, but he saw the same honesty shining from John that he often saw in Hayley's eyes. An emotional honesty Jonathan had limited experience with.

The older man continued. "You think you don't have the capacity for love? When you've already mentioned your concern for Rebecca a couple of times in this conversation? When the past decade and a half of your life was devoted to caring for her? It's no secret how hard you've worked. I may never have formally met you until this moment, but I know about you, Jonathan Bear, and what I know isn't the reputation you seem to think you have."

"Well, regardless of my reputation, you should be concerned about Hayley's. When I came through that door this morning, it was unintentional. But it's important to Hayley that nobody realizes what's happening between us. So the longer I sit here talking to you, the more risk there is of exposing her to unnecessary chatter. And that's not what I want. So," he said, "out of respect for keeping it a secret, like Hayley wants—"

"That's not what I want."

Twelve

Hayley was shaking. She had been shaking from the moment she had walked into The Grind and seen Jonathan there, with her father in the background.

Somehow, she had known—just known—that everyone in the room was putting two and two together and coming up with sex.

And she also knew she had definitely made it worse by running away. If she had sauntered in and acted surprised to see Jonathan there, she might have made people think it really was coincidental that the two of them were both in the coffeehouse early in the morning, coming through the same private door. For reasons that had nothing to do with him spending the night upstairs with her.

But she had spent the past five minutes pacing around upstairs, waiting for her breath to normalize, waiting for her heart to stop beating so hard. Neither thing had happened.

Then she had cautiously crept back downstairs and come in to see her father sitting at the table with Jonathan. Fortunately, Jonathan hadn't looked like he'd been punched in the face. But the conversation had definitely seemed tense.

And standing there, looking at what had been her worst nightmare not so long ago, she realized that it just…wasn't. She'd never been ashamed of Jonathan. He was…the most determined, hardworking, wonderful man she had ever known. He had spent his life raising his sister. He had experienced a childhood where he had known nothing but abandonment and abuse, and he had turned around and given love to his sister, unconditionally and tirelessly.

And, yeah, maybe it wasn't ideal to announce her physical affair with him at the coffee shop, all things considered, but…whatever she had expected to feel… She didn't.

So, it had been the easiest thing in the world to walk over to their table and say that she really didn't need to keep their relationship a secret. Of course, now both Jonathan and her father were looking at her like she had grown a second head.

When she didn't get a response from either of them, she repeated, "That's not what I want."

"Hayley," Jonathan said, his tone firm. "You don't know what you're saying."

"Oh, please," she returned. "Jonathan, that tone wouldn't work on me in private, and it's not going to work on me here, either."

She took a deep breath, shifting her weight from foot to foot, gazing at her father, waiting for him to say something. He looked... Well, it was very difficult to say if John Thompson could ever really be surprised. In his line of work, he had seen it all, heard it all. While Protestants weren't much for confession, people often used him as a confessional, she knew.

Still, he looked a little surprised to be in this situation.

She searched his face for signs of disappointment. That was her deepest fear. That he would be disappointed in her. Because she had tried, she really had, to be the child Ace wasn't.

Except, as she stood there, she realized that was a steaming pile of bull-pucky. Her behavior wasn't about being what Ace hadn't been. It was all about desperately wanting to please people while at the same time wishing there was a way to please herself. And the fact of the matter was, she couldn't have both those things. Not always.

That contradiction was why she had been hell-bent on running away, less because she wanted to experience the wonders of the world and more because she wanted to go off and do what she wanted without disappointing anyone.

"Jonathan isn't just my boss," she said to her dad. "He's my… Well, I don't really know. But… you know." Her throat tightened, tears burning behind her eyes.

Yes, she wanted to admit to the relationship, and she wanted to live out in the open, but that didn't make the transition from good girl to her own woman any easier.

She wanted to beg her dad for his approval. He wasn't a judgmental man, her father, but he had certainly raised her in a specific fashion, and this was not it. So while he might not condemn her, she knew she wasn't going to get his wholesale approval.

And she would have to live with that.

Living without his approval was hard. Much harder than she had thought it might be. Especially given the fact that she thought she'd accepted it just a few moments ago. But being willing to experience disapproval and truly accepting it were apparently two different things.

"Why don't you have a seat, Hayley," her father said slowly.

"No, thank you," she replied. "I'm going to stand, because if I sit down… Well, I don't know. I have too much energy to sit down. But I—I care about him." She turned to Jonathan. "I care about you. I really do. I'm so sorry I made you feel like you were a dirty secret. Like I was ashamed of you. Because any woman would be proud to be involved with you." She took a deep breath and looked around the coffee shop. "I'm dating him," she said, pointing at Jonathan. "Just so you all know."

"Hayley," her father said, standing up, "come to dinner this week."

"With him?"

"If you want to. But please know that we want to know about your life. Even if it isn't what we would choose for you, we want to know." He didn't mean Jonathan specifically. He meant being in a physical relationship without the benefit of any kind of commitment, much less marriage.

But the way he looked at her, with nothing but love, made her ache all over. Made her throat feel so tight she could scarcely breathe.

She felt miserable. And she felt strong. She wasn't sure which emotion was more prominent. She had seen her father look at Ace like this countless times, had seen him talk about her brother with a similar expression on his face. Her father was loving, and he was as supportive as he could be, but he also had hard lines.

"I guess we'll see," she said.

"I suppose. I also imagine you need to have a talk with him," he said, tilting his head toward Jonathan, who was looking uncertain. She'd never seen Jonathan look uncertain before.

"Oh," she said, "I imagine I do."

"Come home if you need anything."

For some reason, she suddenly became aware of the tension in her father's expression. He was the pastor of Copper Ridge. And the entire town was watching him. So whether he wanted to or not, he couldn't haul off and punch Jonathan. He couldn't yell at her—though he never had yelled in all her life. And he was leaving her to sort out her own circumstances, when she could feel that he very much wanted to stay and sort them out for her.

Maybe Jonathan was right. Maybe she had never put a foot out of line because the rules were easier. There were no rules to what she was doing now, and no one was going to step in and tell her what to do. No one was going to pull her back if she went too far. Not even her father. Maybe that had been her real issue with taking this relationship public. Not so much the disappointment as the loss of a safety net.

Right now, Hayley felt like she was standing on the edge of an abyss. She had no idea how far she might fall, how bad it might hurt when she landed. If she would even survive it.

She was out here, living her potential mistakes, standing on the edge of a lot of potential pain.

Because with the barrier of following the rules removed, with no need to leave to experience things... Well, it was just her. Her heart and what she felt for Jonathan.

There was nothing in the way. No excuses. No false idea that this could never be anything, because she was leaving in the end.

As her father walked out of the coffeehouse, taking with him an entire truckload of her excuses, she realized exactly what she had been protecting herself from.

Falling in love. With Jonathan. With a man who might never love her back. Wanting more, wanting everything, with the man least likely to give it to her.

She had been hiding behind the secretary desk at the church, listening to everybody else's problems, without ever incurring any of her own. She had witnessed a whole lot of heartbreak, a whole lot of struggle, but she had always been removed from it.

She didn't want to protect herself from this. She didn't want to hide.

"Why did you do that?" Jonathan asked.

"Because you were mad at me yesterday. I hurt your feelings."

He laughed, a dark, humorless sound. "Hayley," he said, "I don't exactly have feelings to hurt."

"That's not true," she said. "I know you do."

"Honey, that stuff was beaten out of me by my father before I was five years old. And whatever was left… It pretty much dissolved when my mother walked away and left me with a wounded sister to care for. That stuff just kind of leaves you numb. All you can do is survive. Work on through life as hard as you can, worry about putting food on the table. Worry about trying to do right by a kid who's had every unfair thing come down on her. You think you being embarrassed to hold my hand in public is going to hurt my feelings after that?"

She hated when he did this. When he drew lines between their levels of experience and made her feel silly.

She closed the distance between them and put her fingertips on his shoulder. Then she leaned in and kissed him, in full view of everybody in the coffeehouse. He put his hand on her hip, and even though he didn't enthusiastically kiss her back, he made no move to end it, either.

"Why do I get the feeling you are a little embarrassed to be with *me*?" she asked, when she pulled away from him.

He arched his brow. "I'm not embarrassed to be with you."

Maybe he wasn't. But there was something bothering him. "You're upset because everyone knows. And now there will be consequences if you do something to hurt me."

"When," he said, his tone uncompromising. "*When* I do something. That's what everyone is thinking. Trust me, Hayley, they don't think for one second that this might end in some fairy-tale wedding bullshit."

Hayley jerked back, trying to fight the feeling

that she had just been slapped in the face. For whatever reason, he was trying to elicit exactly that response, and she really didn't want to give it to him. "Fine. Maybe that is what they think. But why does it matter? That's the question, isn't it? Why does what other people think matter more than what you or I might want?

"You were right about me. My choices were less about what other people might think, and more about what might happen to me if I found out I had never actually been reined in." She shook her head. "If I discovered that all along I could have done exactly what I wanted to, with no limit on it. Before now, I never took the chance to find out who I was. I was happy to be told. And I think I've been a little afraid of who I might be beneath all of these expectations."

"Why? Because you might harbor secret fantasies of shoplifting doilies out of the Trading Post?"

"No," Hayley said, "because I might go and get myself hurt. If I had continued working at the church, if I'd kept on gazing at the kind of men I met there from across the room, never making a move because waiting for them to do it was right, pushing down all of my desires because it was lust I shouldn't feel… I would have been safe. I wouldn't be sitting here in this coffee shop with you, shaking because I'm scared, because I'm a little bit turned on thinking about what we did last night."

"I understand the turned on part," he said, his

voice rough like gravel. He lifted his hand, dragging his thumb over her lower lip. "Why are you afraid?"

"I'm afraid because just like you said… There's a very low chance of this ending in some fairy-tale wedding…nonsense. And I want all of that." Her chest seized tight, her throat closing up to a painful degree. "With you. If you were wondering. And that is… That's so scary. Because I knew you would look at me like that if I told you."

His face was flat, his dark eyes blazing. He was… well, he was angry, rather than indifferent. Somehow, she had known he would be.

"You shouldn't be afraid of not getting your fairy tale with me. If anything, you should be relieved. Nobody wants to stay with me for the rest of their life, Hayley, trust me. You're supposed to go to Paris. And you're going to Paris."

"I don't want to go," she said, because she wanted to stay here, with him. Or take him with her. But she didn't want to be without him.

"Dammit," he said, his voice like ground-up glass. "Hayley, you're not going to change your plans because of me. That would last how long? Maybe a year? Maybe two if you're really dedicated. But I know exactly how that ends—with you deciding you would rather be anywhere but stuck in my house, stuck in this town."

"But I don't feel stuck. I never did. It was all… me being afraid. But the thing is, Jonathan, I never wanted anything more than I wanted my safety. Thinking I needed to escape was just a response to this missing piece inside of me that I couldn't put a name to. But I know what it is now."

"Don't," he bit out.

"It was you," she said. "All of this time it was you. Don't you see? I never wanted anyone or anything badly enough to take the chance. To take the risk. To expose myself, to step out of line. But you… I do want you that badly."

"Because you were forced to take the risk. You had to own it. Yesterday, you didn't have to, and so you didn't. You pulled away from me when we walked down the street, didn't want anyone to see."

"That wasn't about you. It was about me. It was about the fact that…basically, everybody in town knows I've never dated anybody. So in my case it's a little bit like announcing that I lost my virginity, and it's embarrassing."

Except now she was having this conversation with him in a coffeehouse, where people she knew were sitting only a few feet away, undoubtedly straining to hear her over the sound of the espresso machine. But whatever. She didn't care. For the first time in her life, she really, really didn't care. She cared about him. She cared about this relationship. About doing whatever she needed to do to make him see that everything she was saying was true.

"I'm over it," she added. "I just had to decide that

I was. Well, now I have. Because it doesn't get any more horrifying than having to admit that you were having your first affair to your father."

"You see," he said. "I wouldn't know. Nobody was all that invested in me when I lost my virginity, or why. I was fifteen, if you were curious. So forgive me if your concerns seem foreign to me. It's just that I know how this all plays out. People say they love you, then they punch you in the face. You take care of somebody all of their damn life, and then they take off with the one person you spent all that time protecting them from. Yeah, they say they love you, and then they leave. That's life."

Hayley's chest tightened, her heart squeezing painfully. "I didn't say I loved you."

He looked stricken by that. "Well, good. At least you didn't lie to me."

She did love him, though. But he had introduced the word. Love and its effects were clearly the things that scared him most about what was happening between them.

Love loomed large between them. Love was clearly on the table here. Even if he didn't want it to be, there it was. Even if he was going to deny it, there it was.

Already in his mind, in his heart, whether she said it or not.

She opened her mouth to say it, but it stuck in her throat.

Because he had already decided it would be a lie

if she spoke the words. He was so dedicated to that idea. To his story about who Jonathan Bear was, and who he had to be, and how people treated him. His behavior was so very close to what she had been doing for so long.

"Jonathan—"

He cut her off. "I don't love people," he said. "You know what I love? I love things. I love my house. I love my money. I love that company that I've spent so many hours investing in. I love the fact that I own a mountain, and can ride a horse from one end of my land to the other, and get a sense of everything that can never be taken from me. But I'll never love another person, not again." He stood up, gripping her chin with his thumb and forefinger. "Not even you. Because I will never love anything I can't buy right back, do you understand?"

She nodded, swallowing hard. "Yes," she said.

His pain was hemorrhaging from him, bleeding out of every pore, and there was nothing she could do to stop it. He was made of fury, of rage, and he was made of hurt, whether he would admit it or not.

"I think we're done then, Hayley."

He moved away from her, crossing the coffee-house and walking out the door. Every eye in the room was on her, everybody watching to see what she would do next. So she did the only thing she could.

She stood up and she ran after Jonathan Bear for the entire town to see.

* * *

Jonathan strode down the street. The heavy gray sky was starting to crack, raindrops falling onto his head. His shoulders. Good. That was just about perfect.

It took him a few more strides to realize he was headed away from his car, but he couldn't think clearly enough to really grasp where he was going. His head was pounding like horse hooves over the grass, and he couldn't grab hold of a thought to save his life.

"Jonathan!"

He turned, looking down the mostly empty street, to see Hayley running after him, her dark hair flying behind her, rain flying into her face. She was making a spectacle of herself, right here on Main, and she didn't seem to care at all. Something about that made him feel like he'd been turned to stone, rooted to the spot, his heart thundering heavily in his chest.

"Don't run from me," she said, coming to a stop in front of him, breathing hard. "Don't run from us."

"You're the one who's running, honey," he said, keeping his voice deliberately flat.

"We're not done," she said. "We're not going to be done just because you say so. You might be the boss at your house, but you're not the boss here." Her words were jumbled up, fierce and ferocious. "What about what I want?"

He gritted his teeth. "Well, the problem is you

made the mistake of assuming I might care what you want."

She sprang forward, pounding a closed fist on his shoulder. The gesture was so aggressive, so very unlike Hayley that it immobilized him. "You do care. You're not a mountain, you're just a man, and you do care. But you're awfully desperate to prove that you don't. You're awfully desperate to prove you have no worth. And I have to wonder why that is."

"I don't have to prove it. Everyone who's ever wandered through my life has proved it, Hayley. You're a little bit late to this party. You're hardly going to take thirty-five years of neglect and make me feel differently about it. Make me come to different conclusions than I've spent the past three decades drawing."

"Why not?" she asked. "That's kind of the point of knowing someone. Of being with them. They change you. You've certainly changed me. You made me...well, more me than I've ever been."

"I never said I needed to change."

"That's ridiculous. Of course you need to change. You live in that big house all by yourself, you're angry at your sister because she figured out how to let something go when you can't. And you're about ready to blow this up—to blow us up—to keep yourself safe." She shivered, the rain making dark spots on her top, drops rolling down her face.

"There's no reason any of this has to end, Hayley." He gritted his teeth, fighting against the slow, expanding feeling growing in his chest, fighting against the pain starting to push against the back of his eyes. "But you have to accept what I'm willing to give. And it may not be what you want, what you're looking for. If it's not, if that makes you leave, then you're no different from anyone else who's ever come through my life, and you won't be any surprise to me."

Hayley looked stricken by that, pale. And he could see her carefully considering her words. "Wow. That's a very smart way to build yourself an impenetrable fort there, Jonathan. How can anyone demand something of you, if you're determined to equate high expectations with the people who abandoned you? If you're determined to believe that someone asking anything of you is the same as not loving you at all?"

"You haven't said you loved me." His voice was deliberately hard. He didn't know why he was bringing that up again. Didn't know why he was suspended between the desire for her to tell him she didn't, and the need—the intense, soul-shattering need—to hear her say it, even if he could never accept it. Even if he could never return it.

"My mistake," she said, her voice thin. "What will you do if I tell you, Jonathan? Will you say it doesn't matter, that it isn't real? Because you know everything, don't you? Even my heart."

"I know more about the world than you do, little girl," he said, his throat feeling tight for some reason. "Whatever your intentions, I have a better idea of what the actual outcome might be."

She shocked him by taking two steps forward, eliminating the air between them, pressing her hand against his chest. His heart raged beneath her touch, and he had a feeling she could tell.

"I love you." She stared at him for a moment, then she stretched up on her toes and pressed a kiss to his lips. Her lips were slick and cold from the rain, and he wanted to consume her. Wanted to pretend that words didn't matter. That there was nothing but this kiss.

For a moment, a heartbeat, he pretended that was true.

"I love you," she said again, when they parted. "But that doesn't mean I won't expect something from you. In fact, that would be pretty sorry love if I expected to come into your life and change nothing, mean nothing. I want you to love me back, Jonathan. I want you to open yourself up. I want you to let me in. I want you to be brave."

He grabbed hold of her arms, held her against his chest. He didn't give a damn who might see them. "You're telling me to be brave? What have you ever faced down that scared you? Tell me, Hayley."

"You," she said breathlessly.

He released his hold on her and took a step back,

swearing violently. "All the more reason you should walk away, I expect."

"Do you know why you scare me, Jonathan? You make me want something I can't control. You make me want something I can't predict. There are no rules for this. There is no safety. Loving you… I have no guarantees. There is no neat map for how this might work out. It's not a math equation, where I can add doing the right things with saying the right things and make you change. You have to decide. You have to choose this. You have to choose us. The rewards for being afraid, or being good, aren't worth as much as the reward for being brave. So I'm going to be brave.

"I love you. And I want you to love me back. I want you to take a chance—on me."

She was gazing at him, her eyes blazing with light and intensity. How long would it take for that light to dim? How long would it take for him to kill it? How long would it take for her to decide—like everyone else in his life—that he wasn't worth the effort?

It was inevitable. That was how it always ended.

"No," he said, the word scraping his throat raw as it escaped.

"No?" The devastation in her voice cut him like a knife.

"No. But hey, one more for your list," he said, hating himself with every syllable.

"What?"

"You got your kiss in the rain. I did a lot for you, checked off a lot of your boxes. Go find some other man to fill in the rest."

Then he turned and left her standing in the street.

And in front of God and everybody, Jonathan Bear walked away from Hayley Thompson, and left whatever remained of his heart behind with her.

Thirteen

This was hell. Perhaps even literally. Hayley had wondered about hell a few times, growing up the daughter of a pastor. Now, she thought that if hell were simply living with a broken heart, with the rejection of the person you loved more than anything else echoing in your ears, it would be pretty effective eternal damnation.

She was lying on her couch, tears streaming down her face. She was miserable, and she didn't even want to do anything about it. She just wanted to sit in it.

Oh, she had been so cavalier about the pain that would come when Jonathan ended things. Back in the beginning, when she had been justifying losing her virginity to him, she had been free and easy about the possibility of heartbreak.

But she hadn't loved him then. So she really hadn't known.

Hadn't known that it would be like shards of glass digging into her chest every time she took a breath. Hadn't known that it was actual, physical pain. That her head would throb and her eyes would feel like sandpaper from all the crying.

That her body, and her soul, would feel like they had been twisted, wrung out and draped over a wire to dry in the brutal, unfeeling coastal air.

This was the experience he had talked about. The one that wasn't worth having.

She rolled onto her back, thinking over the past weeks with Jonathan. Going to his house, getting her first job away from the church. How nervous she had been. How fluttery she had felt around him.

Strangely, she felt her lips curve into a smile.

It was hard to reconcile the woman she was now with the girl who had first knocked on his door for that job interview.

She hadn't even realized what all that fluttering meant. What the tightening in her nipples, the pressure between her thighs had meant. She knew now. Desire. Need. Things she would associate with Jonathan for the rest of her life, no matter where she went, no matter who else she might be with.

He'd told her to find someone else.

Right now, the idea of being with another man made her cringe.

She wasn't ready to think about that. She was too raw. And she still wanted him. Only him.

Jonathan was more than an experience.

He had wrenched her open. Pulled her out of the safe space she'd spent so many years hiding in. He had shown her a love that was bigger than fear.

Unfortunately, because that love was so big, the desolation of it was crippling.

She sat up, scrubbing her arm over her eyes. She needed to figure out what she was going to do next.

Something had crystallized for her earlier today, during the encounter with Jonathan and her father. She didn't need to run away. She didn't need to leave town, or gain anonymity, in order to have what she wanted. To be who she wanted.

She didn't need to be the church secretary, didn't need to be perfect or hide what she was doing. She could still go to her father's church on Sunday, and go to dinner at her parents' house on Sunday evening.

She didn't have to abandon her home, her family, her faith. Sure, it might be uncomfortable to unite her family and her need to find herself, but if there was one thing loving Jonathan had taught her, it was that sometimes uncomfortable was worth it.

She wasn't going to let heartbreak stop her.

She thought back to how he had looked at her

earlier today, those black eyes impassive as he told her he wouldn't love her back.

Part of her wanted to believe she was right about him. That he was afraid. That he was protecting himself.

Another part of her felt that was a little too hopeful. Maybe that gorgeous, experienced man simply couldn't love his recently-a-virgin assistant.

Except…she had been so certain, during a few small moments, that she had given something to him, too. Just like he had given so much to her.

For some reason, he was dedicated to the idea that nobody stayed. That people looked at him and saw the worst. She couldn't understand why he would find that comforting, and yet a part of him must.

It made her ache. Her heart wasn't broken only for her, but for him, too. For all the love he wouldn't allow himself to accept.

She shook her head. Later. Later she would feel sorry for him. Right now, she was going to wallow in her own pain.

Because at the end of the day, Jonathan had made the choice to turn away from her, to turn away from love.

Right now, she would feel sorry for herself. Then maybe she would plan a trip to Paris.

"Do you want to invite me in?"

Jonathan looked at his sister, standing on the porch, looking deceptively calm.

"Do I have a choice?"

Rebecca shook her head, her long dark hair swinging behind her like a curtain. "Not really. I didn't drive all the way out here to have this conversation with moths buzzing around me."

It was dark out, and just as Rebecca had said, there were bugs fluttering around the porch light near her face.

"Come in, then," he said, moving aside.

She blinked when she stepped over the threshold, a soft smile touching her lips. The scar tissue on the left side of her mouth pulled slightly. Scar tissue that had been given to her by the man she was going to marry. Oh, it had been an accident, and Jonathan knew it. But with all the pain and suffering the accident had caused Rebecca, intent had never much mattered to him.

"This is beautiful, Jonathan," she said, her dark eyes flickering to him. "I haven't been here since it was finished."

He shrugged. "Well, that was your choice."

"You don't like my fiancé. And you haven't made much of an effort to change that. I don't know what you expect from me."

"Appreciation, maybe, for all the years I spent taking care of you?" He wanted to cut his own balls off for saying that. Basically, right about now he wanted to escape his own skin. He was a bastard. Even he thought so.

He was sitting in his misery now, existing fully in the knowledge of the pain he had caused Hayley.

He should never have had that much power over her. He never should have touched her. This misery was the only possible way it could have turned out. His only real defense was that he hadn't imagined a woman like Hayley would ever fall in love with a man like him.

"Right. Because we've never had that discussion."

His sister's tone was dry, and he could tell she was pretty unimpressed with him. Well, fair enough. He was unimpressed with himself.

"I still don't understand why you love him, Rebecca. I really don't."

"What is love to you, Jonathan?"

An image of Hayley's face swam before his mind's eye. "What the hell kind of question is that?"

"A relevant one," she said. "I think. Particularly when we get down to why exactly I'm here. Congratulations. After spending most of your life avoiding being part of the rumor mill, you're officially hot small-town gossip."

"Am I?" He wasn't very surprised to hear that.

"Something about kissing the pastor's daughter on Main Street in the rain. And having a fight with her."

"That's accurate."

"What's going on?"

"What it looks like. I was sleeping with her. We had a fight. Now we're not sleeping together."

Rebecca tilted her head to the side. "I feel like I'm missing some information."

"Hayley was working for me—I assume you knew that."

"Vaguely," she said, her eyes glittering with curiosity.

"And I'm an asshole. So when I found out my assistant was a virgin, I figured I would help her with that." It was a lie, but one he was comfortable with. He was comfortable painting himself as the villain. Everybody would, anyway. So why not add his own embellishment to the tale.

"Right," Rebecca said, sarcasm dripping from her voice. "Because you're a known seducer of innocent women."

Jonathan turned away, running his hand over his hair. "I'm not the nicest guy, Rebecca. We all know that."

"I know *you* think that," Rebecca said. "And I know we've had our differences. But when I needed you, you were there for me. Always. Even when Gage broke my heart, and you couldn't understand why it mattered, why I wanted to be with him, in the end, you supported me. Always. Every day of my life. I don't even remember my father. I remember you. You taught me how to ride a bike, how to ride a horse. You fought for me, tirelessly. Worked for me. You don't think I don't know how tired you were? How much you put into making our home...a home?

Bad men don't do that. Bad men hit their wives, hit their children. Abandon their daughters. Our fathers were bad men, Jonathan. But you never were."

Something about those words struck him square in the chest. Their fathers *were* bad men.

He had always known that.

But he had always believed somewhere deep down that he must be bad, too. Not because he thought being an abusive bastard was hereditary. But because if his father had beaten him, and his mother had left him, there must be something about him that was bad.

Something visible. Something that the whole town could see.

He thought back to all the kindness on Pastor John Thompson's face, kindness Jonathan certainly hadn't deserved from the old man when he was doing his absolute damnedest to start a fight in the middle of The Grind.

He had been so determined to have John confirm that Jonathan was bad. That he was wrong.

Because there was something freeing about the anger that belief created deep inside his soul.

It had been fuel. All his life that belief had been his fuel. Gave him something to fight against. Something to be angry about.

An excuse to never get close to anyone.

Because underneath all the anger was nothing but despair. Despair because his parents had left him, because they couldn't love him enough. Because he wasn't worth…anything.

His need for love had never gone away, but he'd shoved it down deep. Easier to do when you had convinced yourself you could never have it.

He looked at Rebecca and realized he had despaired over her, too. When she had chosen Gage. Jonathan had decided it was just one more person who loved him and didn't want to stay.

Yeah, it was much easier, much less painful to believe that he was bad. Because it let him keep his distance from the pain. Because it meant he didn't have to try.

"What do you think love is?" Rebecca asked again, more persistent this time.

He didn't have an answer. Not one with words. All he had were images, feelings. Watching Rebecca sleep after a particularly hard day. Praying child services wouldn't come by to check on her while he was at work, and find her alone and him negligent.

And Hayley. Her soft hands on his body, her sweet surrender. The trust it represented. The way she made him feel. Like he was on fire, burning up from the inside out. Like he could happily stay for the rest of his life in a one-room cabin, without any of the money or power he had acquired over the past few years, and be perfectly content.

The problem was, he couldn't make her stay with him.

This house, his company, those things were his. In a way that Hayley could never be. In a way that no one ever could be.

People were always able to leave.

He felt like a petulant child even having that thought. But he didn't know how the hell else he could feel secure. And he didn't think he could stand having another person walk away.

"I don't know," he said.

Rebecca shook her head, her expression sad. "That's a damn shame, Jonathan, because you show me love all the time. Whether you know what to call it or not, you've given it to me tirelessly over the years, and without you, without it, I don't know where I would be. You stayed with me when everybody else left."

"But who stayed with me?" he asked, feeling like an ass for even voicing that question. "You had to stay. I had to take care of you. But the minute you could go out on your own you did."

"Because that's what your love did for me, you idiot."

"Not very well. Because you were always worried I thought of you as a burden, weren't you? It almost ruined your relationship with Gage, if I recall correctly."

"Yes," she said, "but that wasn't about you. That was my baggage. And you did everything in your power to help me, even when you knew the result would be me going back to Gage. That's love, Jonathan." She shook her head. "I love you, too. I love you enough to want you to have your own life, one that doesn't revolve around taking care of me. That doesn't revolve around what happened to us in the past."

He looked around the room, at the house that meant so much to him. A symbol of security, of his ability to care for Rebecca, if her relationship went to hell. And he realized that creating this security for her somehow enabled him to deny his own weaknesses. His own fears.

This house had only ever been for him. A fortress to barricade himself in.

Wasn't that what Hayley had accused him of? Building himself a perfect fortress to hide in?

If everybody hated him, he didn't have to try. If there was something wrong with him, he never had to do what was right. If all he loved were things, he never had to risk loss.

They were lies. Lies he told himself because he was a coward.

And it had taken a virginal church secretary to uncover the truth.

She had stood in front of him and said she wanted love more than she wanted to be safe. And he had turned her down.

He was afraid. Had been all his life. But before this very moment, he would have rather cut out his own heart than admit it.

But now, standing with his sister looking at him

like he was the saddest damn thing she'd ever seen, a hole opened in his chest. A hole Hayley had filled.

"But doesn't it scare you?" he asked, his voice rough. "What if he leaves?"

She reached out, putting her hand on his. "It would break my heart. But I would be okay. I would have you. And I would...still be more whole than I was before I loved him. That's the thing about love. It doesn't make you weak, Jonathan, it makes you stronger. Opening yourself up, letting people in... that makes your life bigger. It makes your life richer. Maybe it's a cliché, but from where I'm standing you need to hear the cliché. You need to start believing it."

"I don't understand why she would want to be with me," Jonathan said. "She's...sweet. And she's never been hurt. I'm...well, I'm a mess. That's not what she deserves. She deserves to have a man who's in mint condition, like she is."

"But that's not how love works. If love made sense, if it was perfectly fair, then Gage West would not have been the man for me. He was the last man on earth I should have wanted, Jonathan. Nobody knows that more than me, and him. It took a miracle for me to let go of all my anger and love him. At the same time... I couldn't help myself.

"Love is strange that way. You fall into it whether you want to or not. Then the real fight is figuring out how to live it. How to become the person you need to be so you can hold on to that love. But I'm willing to bet you are the man she needs. Not some mint condition, new-in-the-box guy. But a strong man who has proved, time and time again, that no matter how hard life is, no matter how intensely the storm rages, he'll be there for you. And more than that, he'll throw his body over yours to protect you if it comes to that. That's what I see when I look at you, Jonathan. What's it going to take for you to see that in yourself?"

"I don't think I'm ever going to," he said slowly, imagining Hayley again, picturing her as she stared up at him on the street. Fury, hurt, love shining from her eyes. "But…if she sees it…"

"That's a start," Rebecca said. "As long as you don't let her get away. As long as you don't push her away."

"It's too late for that. She's probably not going to want to see me again. She's probably not going to want me back."

"Well, you won't know unless you ask." Rebecca took a deep breath. "The best thing about love is it has the capacity to forgive on a pretty incredible level. But if there's one thing you and I both know, it's that it's hard to forgive someone leaving. Don't make that the story. Go back. Ask for forgiveness. Change what needs to be changed. Mostly…love her. The rest kind of takes care of itself."

Fourteen

Hayley had just settled back onto her couch for more quality sitting and weeping when she heard a knock at her door.

She stood up, brushing potato chip crumbs off her pajamas and grimacing. Maybe it was Cassie, bringing up baked goods. The other woman had done that earlier; maybe now she was bringing more. Hayley could only hope.

She had a gaping wound in her chest that could be only temporarily soothed by butter.

Without bothering to fix her hair—which was on top of her head in a messy knot—she jerked the door open.

And there he was. Dark eyes glittering, gorgeous

mouth pressed into a thin line. His dark hair tied back low on his neck, the way she was accustomed to seeing him during the day.

Her heart lurched up into her throat, trying to make a break for it.

She hadn't been expecting him, but she imagined expecting him wouldn't have helped. Jonathan Bear wasn't someone you could anticipate.

"What are you doing here?"

He looked around. "I came here to talk to you. Were you…expecting someone else?"

"Yes. A French male prostitute." He lifted his brows. "Well, you told me to find another man to tick my boxes."

"I think you mean a gigolo."

"I don't know what they're called," she said, exasperated.

The corner of his mouth twitched. "Well, I promise to be quick. I won't interrupt your sex date."

She stepped to the side, ignoring the way her whole body hurt as she did. "I don't have a sex date." She cleared her throat. "Just so you know."

"Somehow, I didn't think you did."

"You don't know me," she grumbled, turning away from him, pressing her hand to her chest to see if her heart was beating as hard and fast as she felt like it was.

It was.

"I do, Hayley. I know you pretty damn well. Maybe

better than I know myself. And...I think you might know me better than I know myself, too." He sounded different. Sad. Tired.

She turned around to face him, and with his expression more fully illuminated by the light, she saw weariness written there. Exhaustion.

"For all the good it did me," she said, crossing her arms tightly in a bid to protect herself. Really, though, it was too late. There wasn't anything left to protect. He had shattered her irrevocably.

"Yeah, well. It did me a hell of a lot of good. At least, I hope it's going to. I hope I'm not too late."

"Too late for what? To stick the knife in again or...?"

"To tell you I love you," he said.

Everything froze inside her. Absolutely everything. The air in her lungs, her heart, the blood in her veins.

"You...you just said... Don't tease me, Jonathan. Don't play with me. I know I'm younger than you. I know that I'm innocent. But if you came back here to lie to me, to say what you think I need to hear so you can...keep having me in your bed, or whatever—"

Suddenly, she found herself being hauled forward into his arms, against his chest. "I do want you in my bed," he said, "make no mistake about that. But sex is just sex, Hayley, even when it's good. And what we have is good.

"But here's something you don't know, because

you don't have experience with it. Sex isn't love. And it doesn't feel like this. I feel…like everything in me is broken and stronger at the same time, and I don't know how in the hell that can be true. And when you told me you loved me… I knew I could either let go of everything in the past or hold on to it harder to protect myself." He shook his head. "I protected myself."

"Yeah, well. What about protecting me?"

"I thought maybe I was protecting you, too. But it's all tangled up in this big lie that I've been telling myself for years. I told you I didn't love people, that I love things. But I said that only because I've had way too much experience with people I love leaving. A house can't walk away, Hayley. A mountain can't up and abandon you. But you could.

"One day, you could wake up and regret that you tied your future to me. When you could have done better… When you could have had a man who wasn't so damn broken." He cupped her cheek, bent down and kissed her lips. "What did I do to earn the love of someone like you? Someone so beautiful…so soft. You're everything I'm not, Hayley Thompson, and all the reasons I love you make perfect sense to me. But why do you love me? That's what I can't quite figure out."

Hayley looked into his eyes, so full of pain, so deeply wounded. She would have never thought a man like him would need reassurance from anyone, least of all a woman like her.

"I know I don't have a lot of experience, Jonathan. Well, any experience apart from you. I know that I haven't seen the whole world. I haven't even seen the whole state. But I've seen your heart. The kind of man you are. The change that knowing you, loving you, created in me. And I know…perfect love casts out all fear.

"I can't say I haven't been afraid these past couple of days. Afraid I couldn't be with you. That things might not work out with us. But when I stood on Main Street… I knew fear couldn't be allowed to win. It was your love that brought me to that conclusion. Your love was bigger than the fear inside me. I don't need experience to understand that. I don't need to travel the world or date other men for the sake of experience. I need you. Because whether or not you're perfect, you're perfect for me."

"*You're* perfect," he said, his voice rough. "So damned perfect. I want…to take you to Canada."

She blinked. "Well. That's not exactly an offer to run off to Vegas."

"You want to use your passport. Why wait? Let's go now. Your boss will let you off. I'm sure of it."

Something giddy bubbled up in her chest. Something wonderful. "Right now? Really?"

"Right the hell now."

"Yes," she said. "Yes, let's go to Canada."

"It's not the Eiffel Tower," he said, "but I will take you there someday. I promise you that."

"The only thing I need is you," she said. "The rest is negotiable."

His lips crashed down on hers, his kiss desperate and intense, saying the deep, poetic things she doubted her stoic cowboy would ever say out loud. But that was okay. The kiss said plenty all on its own.

Epilogue

Jonathan hated wearing a suit. He'd never done it before, but he had come to a swift and decisive conclusion the moment he'd finished doing up his tie.

Hayley was standing in their bedroom, looking amused. The ring on her left hand glittered as bright as her eyes, and suddenly, it wasn't the tie that was strangling him. It was just her. The love on her beautiful face. The fact she loved him.

He still hadn't quite figured out why. Still wasn't sure he saw all the things in himself that Rebecca had spoken of that day, all the things Hayley talked about when she said she loved him.

But Hayley did love him. And that was a gift he cherished.

"You're not going to make me wear a suit when we do this, are you?" he asked.

"I might," she said. "You look really hot in a suit."

He wrapped his arm around her waist and pulled her to his chest. "You look hottest in nothing at all. Think we could compromise?"

"We've created enough scandal already without me showing up naked to my wedding. Anyway, I'm wearing white. I am a traditional girl, after all."

"Honey, you oughta wear red."

"Are you calling me a scarlet woman?"

He nodded. "Yes, and I think you proved your status earlier this morning."

She blushed. She still blushed, even after being with him for six months. Blushed in bed, when he whispered dirty things into her ear. He loved it.

He loved *her*.

He couldn't wait to be her husband, and that was something he hadn't imagined ever feeling. Looking forward to being a husband.

Of course, he was looking forward to the honeymoon even more. To staying in a little apartment in Paris with a view of the Eiffel Tower.

For him, trading in a view of the mountains for a view of the city didn't hold much appeal. But she wanted it. And the joy he got from giving Hayley what she wanted was the biggest thing in his world.

Waiting to surprise her with the trip was damn near killing him.

"You have to hurry," she said, pushing at his shoulder. "You're giving the bride away, after all."

Jonathan took a deep breath. Yeah, it was time. Time to give his sister to that Gage West, who would never deserve her, but who loved her, so Jonathan was willing to let it go. Willing to give them his blessing.

Actually, over the past few months he'd gotten kind of attached to the bastard who would be his brother-in-law. Something he'd thought would never be possible only a little while ago.

But love changed you. Rebecca had been right about that.

"All right," he said. "Let's go then."

Hayley kissed his cheek and took his hand, leading him out of the bedroom and down the stairs. The wedding guests were out on the back lawn, waiting for the event to start. When he and Hayley exited the house, they all turned to look.

He and Hayley still turned heads, and he had a feeling they always would.

Jonathan Bear had always been seen as a bad boy. In all the ways that phrase applied. The kind of boy no parent wanted their daughter to bring home to Sunday dinner. And yet the pastor's daughter had.

He'd definitely started out that way. But somehow, through some miracle, he'd earned the love of a good woman.

And because of her love, he was determined to be the best man he could possibly be.

* * * * *

LET'S TALK
Romance

For exclusive extracts, competitions
and special offers, find us online:

f facebook.com/millsandboon

🐦 @MillsandBoon

📷 @MillsandBoonUK

Get in touch on 01413 063232

For all the latest titles coming soon, visit
millsandboon.co.uk/nextmonth

MILLS & BOON

THE HEART OF ROMANCE

A ROMANCE FOR EVERY READER

MODERN

Prepare to be swept off your feet by sophisticated, sexy and seductive heroes, in some of the world's most glamourous and romantic locations, where power and passion collide.

HISTORICAL

Escape with historical heroes from time gone by. Whether your passion is for wicked Regency Rakes, muscled Vikings or rugged Highlanders, awaken the romance of the past.

MEDICAL

Set your pulse racing with dedicated, delectable doctors in the high-pressure world of medicine, where emotions run high and passion, comfort and love are the best medicine.

True Love

Celebrate true love with tender stories of heartfelt romance, from the rush of falling in love to the joy a new baby can bring, and a focus on the emotional heart of a relationship.

Desire

Indulge in secrets and scandal, intense drama and plenty of sizzling hot action with powerful and passionate heroes who have it all: wealth, status, good looks…everything but the right woman.

HEROES

Experience all the excitement of a gripping thriller, with an intense romance at its heart. Resourceful, true-to-life women and strong, fearless men face danger and desire - a killer combination!

To see which titles are coming soon, please visit

millsandboon.co.uk/nextmonth

JOIN US ON SOCIAL MEDIA!

Stay up to date with our latest releases, author news and gossip, special offers and discounts, and all the behind-the-scenes action from Mills & Boon...

 @millsandboon

 @millsandboonuk

 facebook.com/millsandboon

 @millsandboonuk

It might just be true love...

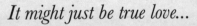